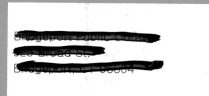

Stain

A. G. HOWARD

AMULET BOOKS · NEW YORK

Library of Congress Cataloging-in-Publication Data
Names: Howard, A. G. (Anita G.), author.
Title: Stain / A. G. Howard.
Description: New York, NY : Amulet Books, 2019. | Summary: Lyra, the silent princess of daylight, must find a way to make noise and pass a series of tests to stop a pretender from stealing her betrothed prince and crown.
Identifiers: LCCN 2018030085| ISBN 9781419731419 (hardback) | ISBN 9781683354079 (ebook)
Subjects: | CYAC: Fairy tales. | Princesses—Fiction. | Mutism—Fiction. | Identity—Fiction. | Magic—Fiction.
Classification: LCC PZ8.H828 St 2019 | DDC [Fic]—dc23

Printed and bound in U.S.A.
10 9 8 7 6 5 4 3 2 1

Amulet Books are available at special discounts when purchased in quantity for premiums and promotions as well as fundraising or educational use. Special editions can also be created to specification. For details, contact specialsales@abramsbooks.com or the address below.

Amulet Books® is a registered trademark of Harry N. Abrams, Inc.

ABRAMS The Art of Books
195 Broadway, New York, NY 10007
abramsbooks.com

I dedicate this fairy tale—fraught with grit and thorns—to those who delight in strange magic and dark sensibilities. May my creatures grace your slumber with moonlit-gilded nightmares, and may my characters give wing to aspirations as bright as the sun.

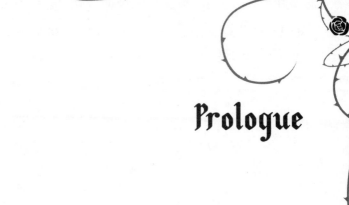

Prologue

There once was a humble land, surrounded by an ocean and afloat within its celestial sphere like an islet, where the sun and moon shared the sky. The stronger light shimmered upon the country-side each day, and the gentler provided a reprieve from darkness each night. Together, day and night were complete, like lovers united. But a magical war erupted between the two kingdoms. At battle's end, one kingdom dragged the night down into the belly of the earth, along with shadows and winter and ice, and those creatures drawn to darkness or cold. There, underground, the moon made its journey across a new firmament, travers-ing from west to east, and east to west, never to rest again. The other kingdom held tightly to the day above—hoarding the sun and its endless campaign across the skies, with the kinder seasons and all the variants of life making everything bright and colorful. An enchanted boundary fell into place between the two planes, allowing a flash of dawn in the night realm and a dusting of dusk in the day, a routine occurrence lasting only long enough to remind each kingdom of time's passage and what had been lost. Although the people appeared to thrive in their separation, without both day and night they were incomplete, and discontent brewed beneath the surface. For what they had forgotten, they would soon remember: disassociation breeds prejudice, bitterness, and apathy—emotions too monstrous for any one kingdom in any one land to contain, and too powerful to ever be defeated by magic alone.

Part 1

In Which the Thorn
Strangles the Rose

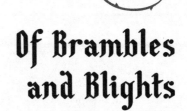

I

Of Brambles
and Blights

In one enchanted telling of old, a prince desperately seeks a princess to wed and rule by his side. But when his destiny arrives upon the castle steps, she fails to look the part of royalty, being drenched and forlorn after facing a cloudburst on her journey. To satisfy the prince's queenly mother, she must prove herself a real princess, with a constitution so delicate the slightest lump beneath a tower of eiderdown mattresses—a lump no bigger than a pea—bruises her flesh and hinders her sleep. Only a girl as tender as a budding rose may marry the royal son and become a queen in her own right.

However, that antiquated telling neglects one vital detail: roses need thorns, just as thorns need roses. If one looks closely at the partnership, they can see the balance a thorn provides—brutal enough to protect from predators, yet gentle enough to share the stem and never tear the fragile blossom. Only if that thorn should lose its rose does it become ugly, purposeless, vicious and vile, with ill intentions to expand its reach and dominate at the expense of all else.

This is the story of two very different princesses—one who lost her rose, and one who gained her thorns. Their journeys to prove their worth unwind within a fairy tale entangled amidst the briars.

It begins with "*Once Upon*," and a touch of morbid to set the tone . . .

❋ · I · ❋

Once upon a nightmare, a princess was born in the kingdom of perpetual daylight—a fine-boned babe who killed her queenly mother upon her entrance to the world.

Yet, that's not entirely true. Queen Arael had become ill seven months prior, after pricking her finger on a thorny rosebush yielding deep lavender blooms at the base of Mount Astra, the highest mountain in Eldoria.

The queen adored flowers, and this rose called to her with a seductive nuance of shadows and mystery her sun-bright, royally regimented days were lacking. She didn't stop to consider that its roots spread deep beneath the earth, far enough to feed off the alter-world of Nerezeth, land of eternal night. An impish, satiny voice whispered on the wind and tickled her ear. Convinced it was her own conscience inspiring her, she ignored any sense of impending doom and plucked the stem free. Some said the moment the thorn pierced the queen's skin her blood filled with a demon's curse . . . a darkness that crept into every facet of her being, intruding upon the babe she carried within. Her death while giving birth only validated the rumor for those foolish enough to believe such folly.

On that day of loss and life, a sorrowful hush fell over the sparkling ivory castle of Eldoria. The king's sister, the beautiful Lady Griselda—elegant as a statue carved of the ivory stones lining the garden ponds, with glossy hair both crimson and black—stepped forward to be the princess's governess.

Though Griselda put on a show of compassion for her brother, her heart waxed cold with envy, for she had three little daughters of her own who would never sit upon the throne now that an heir had been born to the king. Her embittered mind wasted no time concocting some means to amend this injustice.

Had the babe died with her gentle mother, her fate would have been kinder than what was in store . . .

King Kiran of the House of Eyvindur, so overcome with grief, had yet to look upon his new daughter. Weeping, he pressed his lips to the limp, cold hand of his lovely wife's corpse. The scent of soil and flowers still clung upon her olive skin from her time in the garden earlier that day. "If only Arael could've stayed long enough to see the babe but once."

"Better that her mother didn't see." Griselda's gaze, dark and hard as wrought iron, fixed upon her brother while she wrapped the wriggling bundle in an itchy lace blanket. "She's quite unusual. Her lashes . . . they're bone-white. And longer and more numerous than a centipede's legs." Griselda's own dark, thick lashes trembled as if in pity. "It is startling."

The newborn screeched out at her aunt's severe handling. The cry sliced through the silence and echoed through every hall and corridor. Each servant within the room—from those gathering up bloody sheets to the ones mopping the crimson smears off the white tiles—paused and held their breath. For the sound was anything but obtrusive. The child's wails formed a melody that wrapped around each particle of air, silver and resonate and pure—like a songbird's trill on a mild spring day. Other servants who had been occupied elsewhere congregated around the door to peer inside.

The king's tears slowed, and for the first time he turned to look at the babe, taking her gently from his sister's hands. "So lyrical. Her voice is music. I shall call her Lyra." He nodded, his white-gold crown glinting in the candlelight, since the curtains had been drawn to offer privacy while the queen struggled to give birth. "Arael would've liked that."

The baby snuggled into her father's gentle arms.

"Those eyes . . . that skin." Griselda observed the babe around her brother's sturdy shoulder; the tiny princess wriggled within her lace blanket, a faint, bluish-tinged creature that resembled a shadow on a saucer of curdled cream. "There's no denying she's been touched by moonlight. She'll have no shield from the sun. And she appears sickly; it must be the illness from the queen's blood. A contagion from the cursed land of eternal gloom and ice."

"She has a rare and melancholy beauty, it is true," her brother answered in that deep, wise tone that made him so beloved to his people, while his black beard nuzzled the babe's milky-soft head. "But you yourself can relate to tender skin, and how outward appearances rarely reflect inward strength. See how she grips my finger." Lyra's tiny pale hand curled halfway around his russet-colored thumb and squeezed. The king chuckled. "Such pith in one so small. Yes. I shall see her live to a ripe old age. She's blood of my blood and was born to gift our world with song. She will sit the throne and rule in grace and light just as her mother did." Even amidst the heartbreak over his loss, he loved this child more than his own breath, and the flavor of his tears forever imprinted upon Lyra's lips as the taste of purest comfort.

Over the years, as the princess grew, so did her differences. She looked nothing like her cousins—a trio of velvet-eyed beauties whose hair glistened auburn in the candlelight, whose ivory skin freckled from time spent outdoors. The elder two's figures were sure to be shapely and sensual like their mother's one day, but the cousin closest to her age, Lustacia, shared Lyra's willowy build.

However, no one shared her odd characteristics. Lyra had iridescent eyes—mother-of-pearl prisms that shifted from the rich amber of autumn leaves to a lilac so gentle and serene it was almost transparent; moonlit skin—the color of hydrangea petals faded to the lightest shade of blue—too spectral to hide the delicate network of veins beneath; and hair, eyebrows, and lashes so silvery-white and glistening, they rivaled the spiderwebs which draped the corners of the castle where even the candlelight couldn't quite reach. Over time, her lashes grew so long they stretched above her eyebrows and often tangled within her hair. Thus, any strands about her face were kept drawn into plaits, allowing her to blink freely.

To everyone but her doting father, she remained a creature of other-worldly strangeness. Her skin burned with excruciating pain when sliced by the slightest strand of sun. Her eyes had never shed a tear. They guided her through shaded corners and antechambers, glistening gold with the precision of a cat, yet shifted to purple-tinged and left her blind as a mole in daylight.

Outside of her brother's earshot, Griselda poisoned the servants against the child. "Her blood is contaminated. She walks in shadows like the gloom-dwellers. Already, we've lost the queen to her. Now her demon wiles have bewitched my kingly brother. And when it's her turn to reign, what then? What purpose can she serve to a kingdom where the sun shines eternally from our victory centuries ago? Will we all live locked up indoors, indentured to darkness for her comfort? Or will she split the earth so night can seep in once more to contuse our skies?"

On Lyra's fourth birthday, she toddled down the corridors, the floor cool and slick beneath her bare feet. Heavy drapes cloaked the windows; only candles were lit on the north side of the ivory castle in respect for her tender skin.

Three servants peered around the corner, dim light flickering across their faces. Upon seeing them, Lyra waved. They shook their heads.

"I miss the sun's warm glow," whined Brindle, the court jester. The bells on his hat jingled with each bob of his chin.

"Must we always live in hiding?" seethed Matilde, the head cook, her crossed arms cradling a soup ladle that dripped with a mouthwatering scent.

"Just for *her*?" snarled Mia from behind a basket piled with bed linens. She had served as Queen Arael's faithful lady's maid but was reluctant to do the same for the odd little princess.

Lyra didn't quite understand the septic bite of their words. All she knew was their murmurs tickled her ears like the tiny chattering mice in the storybooks her father read. She ran to greet them with a melodic giggle. All three servants' expressions changed . . . frowns becoming smiles, eyes once dim with mistrust brightening with optimism.

Matilde caught a breath and Brindle spun in place, his bells jingling merrily.

"Her voice . . . it be like sitting in the shade on a blanket of spring flowers, ain't it?" He laughed.

Mia set aside her basket. "What are we all standing about for? It's the princess's birthday, and as her lady's maid, I intend to see 'er pampered and spoiled."

The other two servants agreed. Matilde baked a honey-iced cake and tickled Lyra's feet with plucked goose feathers as she ate; Brindle crafted a chime of glittery, tinkling tin triangles to hang over her small bed; and Mia gave her a bubble bath scented with rich, woody magnolia and vanilla brandy. Lyra laughed as the bubbles perched weightless on her lashes and hands, thrilled by the candle glow captured inside. Nothing held more fascination for her than light.

From that point on, the cook, jester, and maid aimed to elicit the princess's laughter as often as possible. Hidden from sight, Griselda watched their loyalty grow and her grudge burned deeper and darker, branding her heart with an irreversible smudge.

Three more years tumbled by. Preoccupied with his daughter's needs, King Kiran was oblivious to his sister's darkening moods. He failed to notice how often Griselda stayed with her daughters on the east side of the castle, isolating her small family and half of the castle's servants where the curtains remained open to the never-changing sun.

One day, in the north wing, as Lyra stared sadly at the heavy drapes on the windows, the king stopped beside her to stroke her satiny hair. "Wishing for greener pastures, little lamb?"

She bowed her head low. Something was amiss with her tongue. She couldn't form words—only those lyrical sounds that seemed to make everyone either happy or confuddled. She'd given up trying to speak. Better to make no sound at all than be misunderstood. But she and her father had a special bond. He could read her gestures and expressions. No answer to his question was needed; she knew he understood better than anyone how she longed to go outside and feel the sun on her face, or the wind in her hair.

"Well," the king answered her silence with a cheerful note in his voice. "It just so happens I'm bringing the pasture to you. I've sent for the three royal mages. They're on their way from Mount Astra's peak to find a means for you to stand in the light."

So overcome with happiness, Lyra threw her arms around his leg and nuzzled the spiced scent of his royal robes.

The immortal triplet brothers arrived, walking barefoot and soundless through the castle halls like tethered spirits. Their feet and hands glittered, resembling pale beige sands that slipped through an hourglass. Descended from ancient seraphs, they were so bright and beautiful, no mortal could look upon their faces for fear of going blind. Thus, they wore shimmery, cowled robes and birdlike masks. Lyra studied them in reverent awe as they measured her head and neck. Renowned for combining their magic in clever ways, the mages designed a hood made of nightsky, a fabric woven at the hands of enchanted seamstresses—one part midnight shadows and one part stardust. Being customized for the princess only, it followed her every movement without touching, like a school of fish darting to-and-fro about her head.

With her hood in place, Lyra scampered to a window her father had opened. A floral-scented breeze wafted through the swirling fabric and she basked in its sweetness. She gestured toward a tree in the garden with a thick white trunk and twisty, twining branches adorned in feathery crimson leaves. It stood out like a flame in the center of the lush green backdrop, so bright she could see it even through the muted screen protecting her face.

King Kiran knelt beside her. "That is a sylph elm. Before your birth, the leaves turned red. Your mother told me the legend, that the leaves only bleed when an elm hides the severed wings of a sylph. If an air elemental brings an injustice upon someone pure of heart, they're cursed to be earthbound in their two shifting forms." He paused, and Lyra sensed him trying to keep his voice strong. She wondered if he was doing what she was: envisioning her mother in the garden right now. "But the sylph can be freed one day, once all the other leaves become richest gold—the color of your eyes cloaked in shade." He tweaked Lyra's nose. She giggled, knowing the chiming lilt would snuff out his sadness. His answering smile was her reward. "During that time—when only two red leaves remain among the gold—if the sylph performs a selfless deed out of the kindness of their heart, they can reclaim their wings and return to their true form."

As if prompted by his words, a red butterfly perched upon the window-sill. Forgetting the light's danger, Lyra reached farther than she should've with her bare hand. A strand of sun grazed her moonlit skin. Her fingers sizzled and charred. She howled in agony, her own cries mocking her with joyful lyricism.

Mortified, the king caught her up and watched somberly as the mages treated and bandaged her blisters. He commissioned an entire suit of night-sky. However, the hood had taken all of the materials preserved in jars from centuries before. The mages could find no current source of moon-born shadows or stars because Nerezeth had been hoarding the nights for hundreds and hundreds of years.

"Gather all of the shadows from the castle's corners and hearths! Dig them up from the dungeon if you must!" the king shouted.

"Your highness," the trio of mages said simultaneously in bass, baritone, and tenor voices—for they always spoke in unison. "Only the deepest twilight shadows will do, as they hold the night's turning point. And there is the lack of stars . . . without stardust to stabilize the shadows and weigh them down, they will simply escape."

For the next five years, Lyra had to be satisfied looking out from beneath her hood. Even with her body wrapped in heavy fabrics from neck to toe, the sun penetrated and burned. She could only see the beauty of her sparkling kingdom in muted shades from the safety of her home. Thus, her favorite time became that singular moment she could remove the hood to look out a clear window, unprotected, after the day's westward diurnal course. When that blink of dusk softened the light to a purple-blue haze, she was free for twenty full breaths before the sun brightened again to begin its eastern reversal across the sky for the cessation course.

Lyra loved the light with such fervor this was enough, until the tragic moment she saw herself within a mirror.

Avaricette, Griselda's daughter of fifteen, stood in the sunny kitchen with her two sisters. Twelve-year-old Lyra had followed, lured by the aroma of fresh-baked treats. Covered neck-to-toe-to-finger in heavy cloth, she placed teacups at the table in hopes her cousins might join her for a tea party.

"Lyra, perhaps we're too old to play such childish games." The most studious and brightest of Griselda's daughters, Lustacia, adjusted the glossy, auburn curls draping her shoulders and blinked her deep-blue, thick-lashed eyes. She had always been kinder than the others, being only a year older than Lyra, so her gentle scolding failed to discourage the princess. She continued to fold napkins and place them on saucers, her hood of shadows surging and swimming around her head.

"How could she know of anything that's normal?" Avaricette said before shoving a plum confectionery into her mouth. "She's too solitary." Avaricette narrowed her brown eyes and talked around the food squashed between her teeth. "She cannot even walk beside opened windows without wearing mittens and wrapping up like a mummy. Mother says she's a stain on our royal bloodline."

"Yes, a stain." Wrathalyne puckered her brow in disgust as she adjusted the satiny bows on her dress—the same rusty-brown as her freckles. "That explains why she can't speak. Stains don't have tongues. She *inveritably* belongs with the spiders and centipedes in the dungeon, amongst her own *sodiforous* kind." Wrathalyne considered herself very well-spoken for some-one of fourteen, often making up words in an effort to prove it.

Lyra stopped playing then. She backed into a corner and dropped a spoon with a clang beside her feet—ashamed, though not quite sure why.

"Hush." Matilde entered, her ruddy, wrinkled face glowering. She cov-ered Lyra's ears. Those work-roughened fingers were sweet and soothing compared to the sharp-toothed words her cousins had spoken. As if sens-ing Lyra's affection for the cook, the nightsky fabric enveloped the elderly woman's hands, allowing the contact, then closed again over Lyra's head as she pulled free. Matilde lifted a wooden spoon and shook it in Avaricette's direction. "I ever hear you speak such ugliness about the princess again, I'll lose the recipe for your favorite honeyed confits. Could be I'll forget how to make desserts altogether."

Wrathalyne narrowed her licorice-dark eyes, prepared to unleash a retort from her "corpulent vocabulary," but Avaricette took both her sisters' hands and dragged them from the room. Having an abundance of sweets at the ready was of utmost importance to her.

In their absence, insecurity swarmed in Lyra's head: Was she a stain? As hideous as the hairy spiders rumored to live in the dungeon?

She'd never looked upon her image . . . had only seen painted portraits of herself, her complexion altered to some normalcy by the artists. Blurred reflections in copper pans and bathwater weren't enough. Her father kept the mirrors in the castle put away for fear the glass might catch a ray of light and magnify it upon her skin.

Determined to know, Lyra climbed to one of the highest towers where her mother's childhood items were stored. There in the dimness, she found an antique mirror gilded with coppery accents. She perched on a pile of books, nose tingling from dust, and slipped off her hood, slippers, and bindings so only her chemise and bloomers remained. After wiping a powdery haze off the glass, she saw her ghostly reflection. Her eyes glowed amber in the darkness and illuminated fanlike lashes. They resembled the silvery metallic strands of tinsel people strung upon lampposts and gates to honor Eldoria's victory over ice and snow during the sun solstice (a three-month-long celebration that took place in what once served as the winter season centuries earlier).

Lyra stared. How startling her differences were: such a far cry from the portraits of her mother, her father, cousins, or aunt. Even the castle's servants and citizens of Eldoria—varying shades of ivory, rose, gold, copper and ebony—didn't match her anemic pallor.

Other than her lips which were shaped like her mother's, "bee-stung" her father often teased, she looked like no one and nothing she'd ever seen, except the sugary cookie dough Matilde tinged with one drop of blue cornflower syrup before baking. If only she could bake to golden perfection so she might stand in the sun, barefaced and sturdy, and at last embrace the light she loved. If only she were a cookie.

Stain, she repeated in her mind, though didn't dare try to speak it aloud. Wishing she could somehow trap her grotesque image within the glass, Lyra stretched her hood over the mirror's frame. She yanked at the seams, pulling so hard the mirror toppled off balance. The glass broke, renting the astral fabric in half. As shadows are prone to do when loosed, they escaped into the farthest corners of the room, leaving nothing but a pile of golden stardust on the floor.

Lyra regretted the mishap immediately. Warm trickles wet her face and she peered at the broken mirror. Tears of inky violet trailed her cheeks. She had seen other people cry—streams clear as water.

Even her tears were stained.

It was too much. Sobbing, she sprang barefoot into the dust and glass. The shards jabbed into her tender skin, and small footprints smeared with blood trailed her as she ran down winding stairs through the castle.

"Lyra!" As she rounded a corner, the king caught her in his strong embrace. He held her, bleeding and weeping. The dark purple of her tears seemed more unsettling and terrible to him than the cuts on her feet, and she wondered if a bruise was seeping from her soul. He carried her to the kitchen, where even her favorite sugar cookies failed to console her.

❋·I·❋

Had King Kiran's precious child not been heartbroken, and had the nightsky hood not been ruined, perhaps he wouldn't have started another war. But as often happens in fairy tales—as in life itself—the ripple of one small tragedy can be far and widespread.

The king sent his best horses and men to uproot the thorny vines at Mount Astra's base which marked the iron stairway to the dark kingdom of Nerezeth, the selfsame rosebush that had tainted the queen's health and caused her to die. He intended to take back the nights by force—along with their midnight shadows and stars—so he could at last secure his daughter's happiness and welfare.

The night-folk defended their borders with a vigorous determination that matched the king's desperation. There appeared to be no victor in sight. Griselda saw her opportunity and took it.

"You must go to the battlefields yourself," she said to her brother while he paced the floor after speaking to his field marshal one day. "Call for a temporary truce so you might descend Nerezeth's iron stairway. King Orion has been ill, but you can negotiate with his queen. Make her understand your daughter's plight. Their son is only a few years older than Lyra; Prince Vesper . . . the evening star, they call the him. It's rumored he has caused some sort of upheaval himself. Perhaps that commonality can breed compassion, if not an alliance." She laughed in her black heart, knowing that peace would not be so easily won. Her brother's life would be in danger, and if by some dire chance he died, Griselda would be regent to the kingdom until Lyra was of age. All she would have to do was rid herself of her niece, and one day her daughters would reign.

The king hesitated, fearing something might go wrong and his little Lyra be left an orphan.

Griselda would not relent. "Do you watch our princess? Each day she cries her dusky tears. Each day she retreats a little deeper into the corners of the house, becoming one with the darkness. Arael would be grief-struck were she here. Your queen would insist we staunch Lyra's hopelessness before she loses her love of light altogether."

In less than a fortnight, the king left for the battlefields with three of the kingdom's most faithful guards in tow, handpicked by Griselda herself. He carried three gifts for Queen Nova as proof of his daughter's soul sickness: a thick, braided plait of Lyra's silvery-white hair, a vial filled with her violet tears, and an echo of her birdsong voice captured within an ensorcelled seashell upon a silver stand.

On a rainy autumn morning, a fortnight later, news came of a treaty, but only the king knew of the details, for it had been a private meeting between him and the queen. He was said to be behind the messenger so Lyra waited by the window, wrapped in the heavy drapes, imagining her father's red steed trotting up the path.

In the king's absence, the servants had been appointed various tasks by Griselda, keeping them busy so they had little time for Lyra. Not once had she fallen asleep to the gentle stroke of a tender hand, or heard a kind voice practicing writing or reading with her. She'd been lonely. One kiss upon her head by her father, and everything would be right again.

The door rattled open on a rain-drenched gust, and it was all the princess could do to stand back so the sun filtering through clouds wouldn't catch her. But King Kiran did not step inside. His limp body was carried in by two of his three guards. Their armor was dented and their heads wounded and bleeding, just like the king's.

The minute the door shut, Lyra stumbled toward them, touching her father's unblinking eyes which looked past her in a faraway stare. Emotionless. Lifeless. A piercing sensation tweaked her heart, as if a thorn burst through the organ's walls. Her fingers tangled in his hair, chilled by his scalp. She stifled the shouts of anguish growing inside her until she feared she'd bleed musical notes from her eyes and ears. She couldn't let even one escape, for her song was far too jubilant for this monstrous day.

Explanations abounded: Night Ravagers, the pale, skull-faced mercenaries of the under realm, attacked them. The guards tried to save the king but were outnumbered; the third one lost his life in the struggle.

The war would never end now. Neither would Lyra's sadness.

At her father's interment ceremony two days later, she said farewell to his body, which would be buried beneath the ground where moonbeams, absorbed into the soil from the night realm, would cushion his eternal cessation.

He was gone forever. Just like her mother . . . just like the nightsky hood.

They held the service in the castle's great hall with all the drapes closed. The scent of candle wax that had once comforted Lyra hung in her throat, and the smoke stung her eyes.

The two guards who had fought to save the king were knighted by Griselda for their bravery. They stood at the head and foot of the coffin, bedecked in glistening gold medals and gems.

Lyra looked upon her father's body one last time, sunken inside the red satin lining, remembering how safe she felt within his strong arms. How cherished she was, in spite of her differences.

Dried lavender rose petals drifted across him, sprinkled by his royal subjects to honor his lost queen who loved the plant so much it killed her. The very same plant that had poisoned Lyra's life from the beginning. Inspired by the floral cascade, dark tears fell to her feet, a violet rain spattering the white marble.

Griselda stood in the deepest shadows of the room wherein only Lyra could see. Her aunt's lips curled upward—revealing teeth as unnerving as bleached-out bones at the bottom of a creek. Within that smile, the princess saw the deadly slant of her future, and for the first time in her life, she knew fear.

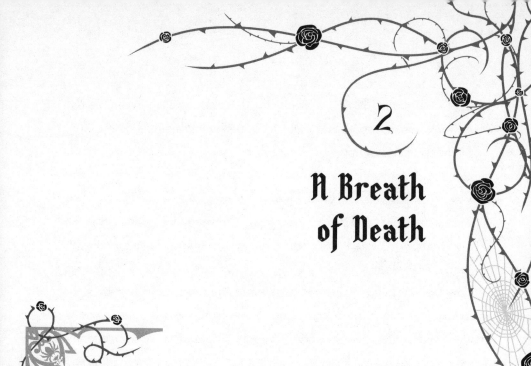

2

A Breath
of Death

Every land has a place where evil congregates. Like a gaping wound, it reeks of spiritual rot, a stench that calls to those of similar faithlessness and disorder.

In Eldoria, this place was the Ashen Ravine.

The deep rift in terrain had been caused centuries earlier, when Nerezeth retreated underground with night and all its occupants in tow. The land sutured, but it didn't fully heal. So, nature and magic came together, forming a mystical forest to cover the wound.

Large, brambly trees grew almost overnight—their thorn-tipped branches and roots warped and knotted, as if they couldn't decide which direction to grow, for they fed off both the night from below, and the day from above. The trunks, black as pitch, stooped like withered old men yet had the illusion of eternal youth with leaves that never faded or changed when spring surrendered to summer, and summer to fall.

Like lions' manes, the foliage thickened over time to riotous lengths until the dreary gray-green velvet blocked the sunlight. Beneath the conjoined canopy, any wrongdoer could find sanctuary. Thus, it became a metropolis for smugglers, murderers, degenerates and outcasts. The leaves worked as a sponge to absorb the sins of the ravine's occupants, and they grew thicker and denser each day until at last the trees could no longer bear all of their weight.

The wickedness began to slink down the trunks in mossy trails—furred and pulsating—a living, breathing umbrage. It overtook the ground, carrying the stink of decomposition, and made smoldering mounds of whatever goodness and beauty—blooms of columbine, bleeding heart and larkspur—had managed to adapt to the sunless terrain. Soon a gray carpet of shifting, rustling ash dusted the base and slinked from tree to tree, resulting in the ravine's title.

This was the in-between, a great crack in the earth stretching for hundreds of leagues. Beginning at the northern base of Mount Astra, it carved a distant scar on the other side of the Crystal Lake and the lush hilly valley where the ivory castle and its township nestled, fecund and plentiful with farms, cottages, gardens and shops. The crack then continued off to the west into the lapping waves of the endless ocean.

Even with its stooped trunks, the ravine's woodland stood tall. So steep was this pit, that to look down from the castle's highest turret, the treetops appeared level with the ground, and the crack resembled a living thing that slithered along in the sun with leafy scales shifting from gray to green. To venture within was to risk a fatal fall, unless one followed the steep, winding path without straying—no easy task with the forest's dangers lying in wait to distract the wayfaring wanderer.

The day after King Kiran's burial, Crony emerged from this powdery, poisonous terrain that she called home.

She was the only one of her kind: a harrower witch. She had existed long before the great magical battle rent the earth and separated night from day centuries earlier. Long before the citizens of both kingdoms were altered by magic to adapt in their new worlds and terrains. Those in Nerezeth became tall and willowy and learned to speak mind-to-mind so they might tread nimbly and quietly on snowdrifts; in the same instant, they absorbed the moonlight and starlight—a silvering that started in their hair and skin then gave amber illumination to their eyes. Eldorians, in contrast, retained their sturdy builds and varied complexions, growing more durable, able to face the sun's radiance with no pain. Crony had lived long enough she could feel the changes affecting her own comfort.

She had many reasons for wanting the sky as it once was—a courteous turn from light to dark—and some were tangled with regret. No one would believe a witch could feel any such emotion, so she never spoke of it.

Clasping the neck of her cloak in place, Crony clambered along the path leading out of the ravine, toward the entrance where the leaves thinned to let in dapples of grayish-yellow light.

She paused upon hearing a blood-curdling screech and turned to her right where a gurgling puddle skimmed through the ash—scattering powder on either side—in pursuit of a brown squirrel. There was rarely a bug, bird, rodent, or scavenging animal here, being little vegetation or rotting flesh for them to feed upon. The Shroud Collective in the lowlands left only the bones of their prey which most often fell to wayfaring quag-puddles—swallowed whole and digested—leaving no remains to claim: the very fate to befall this pitiful rodent that had dared to venture in.

Crony hobbled down off the path, knowing it was already too late. When she reached the squirrel, only its tail could be seen amid the stinky, gurgling spume, flapping like a bushy flag. Shaking her head, Crony used her staff to fish it free. The puddle burped a growl in her direction then turned and fled, being averse to the taste of wood. The rodent's skeleton had dissolved, leaving nothing but the furry appendage—the thickest end slimy with sludge. Crony tucked the tail behind her, into the rope belted around her waist, thinking to use it for trade in the black market.

She resumed her trek to the entrance. On the ravine's side of the vine-cloaked opening, a dripping, jellylike trail of sunlight coated the trunks. Sun-smugglers from the night realm came often to gather the sticky, hot substance into jars for light and warmth. The warped magic of this place not only made light a commodity that could be gleaned, but also affected time and distance across the forest. The expanse should've taken weeks to traverse, but somehow the shifting ash acted as momentum—the clustering tree branches as propulsion—and a person could wander one end to the next in mere days while moving at a normal pace.

The witch drew her oversized hood tighter around her multiple gray braids in anticipation of the wide-open's glare. Her form was human enough—discounting the obsidian horns, similar to a ram's, spiraling out from either side of her head—but the likeness stopped there.

She had no irises, just pupils the color of swirling mud that spanned the entirety of her eyes. They offered a panoramic view and insights into the depths of a soul, but poor protection from brightness. And her translucent eyelids aided little in that respect. Of course, for an immortal creature who hadn't a physical need for sleep, there was no real reason to begrudge her lack of traditional eyelids. It was the memory attached to losing them that caused her woe.

Serpentine briars slithered around her bare ankles and feet, gnawing at them with fang-like thorns in an effort to drag her off the path. She kicked them away, untouched. Her hide resembled an acorn's cap—brown and rough with scales—and was near impenetrable.

Some said the same was true of her heart. *Impenetrable.*

She rumbled a laugh to distract from the ever-present twinge in her chest. If only the fools were right.

Using the skull impaled upon her staff to knock away the snapping briars that curtained the entrance, she plunged through, out of the ravine's cloying stench and into the fresh air. Her hood shaded her eyes as she adjusted to the sunshine. Lifting the hem of her cloak, she made for the hilly outskirts of Eldoria's township.

The castle's highest ivory tower rose in the midst of a clearing, draped in soft white clouds. The usual golden banners that flapped atop each turret, emblazoned with a red-and-orange sun and an orange soaring bird, had been replaced with solid navy flags—mourning the great king's death, honoring his noble life. Sentries, wearing long capes in the same navy fabric, were posted on regal blood-bay stallions at the gate and around the great white wall surrounding the castle. Traditionally, black might have been a more appropriate color, but Eldoria refused to use anything that would pay tribute to Nerezeth's own black-and-silver banners.

Out of sight in the distance, soldiers practiced maneuvers—archery, hand-to-hand combat, and sword play—in preparation to return to the base of Mount Astra, where Nerezeth's iron stairway descended into the earth. When all the roses' roots had been ripped up under King Kiran's command, the ground beneath became unstable. Now, with all the rain from the past several days, a muddy avalanche had sealed off the stairway and trapped the Nerezethites in their icy domain.

This unexpected event bought Eldoria time enough to reinforce the battlements, and shore-up the walls of the outer bailey. But it was only a temporary reprieve; Eldoria's infantry planned to tunnel their way in. The distant scuff of hooves in the dirt, the clang of swords and shouting men, crackled on the air and drowned out the chirping birdsongs in the trees as proof. Retaliation for King Kiran's murder had been ordered by Lady Griselda. A king's blood for a king's blood.

Orion, the king of Nerezeth, already laid abed dying. What good did it do to hasten the inevitable? Crony, of all creatures, knew the benefit of patience in these things.

She was troubled by how the war had been stirred anew. How King Kiran's soldiers hauled away the lavender blooms. How they uprooted the one symbol of peace between the two kingdoms without considering the consequences.

Crony and her ilk would need to be wary now; they could ill afford to be captured with Lady Griselda as regent. The king's sister bade no tolerance for anyone magically inclined who didn't serve the castle. And, as Crony

26

had learned lifetimes ago, there were sacrifices to be made when under the employ of any one kingdom. Thus, she dared not pledge fealty to any but herself. In the absence of King Kiran's fair trials for all prisoners, such a refusal could warrant death. Or, in an immortal's case, unrelenting torture.

The danger was an acidic burn on the back of her tongue.

A flash of vivid color caught Crony's eye as she rounded a hill. She ducked beneath an outcropping of shrubbery, cringing when bits of glass in the bag at her waist chinked together. Parting the branches, she peered at the red-and-silver fox a few feet ahead, seated on his haunches and licking his paw. A flock of swans took to the sky, soaring on their daily sojourn to the Crystal Lake. The fox snapped to attention and watched them. One might think him hungry for flesh, but his craving was for flights of solitude—the wind streaming beneath hollow bones and fringed wings.

He called himself Elusion; Crony called him Luce. In their true ethereal form, sylphs were air elementals imperceptible to the naked eye. They stirred up trouble, enjoying the fruits of their mischief from an aerial view. Luce, however, was cursed aground, and could only take his bestial and human forms now. When Crony met him over twelve years ago, he'd been shunned by his own kind for losing his wings to the sylph elm in the royal gardens.

She befriended him because he made her smile—a courageous feat, considering her smiles could wilt flowers. And his otherworldly nature meant he assisted her dark occupation without complaint. They had a kinship, as his sins were as grim as her own.

Or so she let him believe . . .

No one in this sun-smote land knew of her gravest misstep; but there was one who had shared the experience and held that secret close, living beneath her feet in Nerezeth.

The fox's unnatural scent—a mix of animal dander, man, and flying creatures—wafted toward Crony on the warm breeze, tickling her flat, slitted nose. Sensing her, he looked up—his orange eyes lit to embers of intelligence. His long muzzle parted on a grin that could double as a sharp-toothed snarl.

Crony slipped out from her hiding spot. "Good diurnal to ye."

"Huh. Took you long enough," the fox answered. No matter which form he chose to wear, the same baritone, silken voice always greeted her. "There's only so much time can be spent preening parasites from one's own tail." He gave said 'tail' a swoosh and stood, shaking grass and dirt from his fur until he shined like a polished summer apple.

"Aye." Crony stepped around her four-legged companion, her staff playfully batting the pendant around his neck—a talisman of protection formed of her own hair. "But we both know yer a fair bit too calloused for any parasite to latch upon."

His silvery whiskers wriggled. "If that were true, you'd never have burrowed your way beneath my skin."

Crony smiled, and the shin-high grass feathering her steps withered at the sight. She'd been the cohort of death for so long, there was a residue on her.

The fox sauntered soundlessly to catch up at her ankles. "I see you finally grew a tail of your own. Always knew you envied mine." The direction of his amused gaze indicated the squirrel's remains in her belt.

She snorted. "If ye can't save the critter, ye salvage the remains."

"Nicely done. Winkle should be interested in a trade." That said, the fox's triangular ears perked and he sniffed the air. Having a nose for gore and death made him a harrower witch's ideal partner. "Our prey is just over the other side of the ridge there. Fresh meat, but ripening fast in this swelter."

Crony nodded. The sun beat down, hot and unforgiving to those who spent most days in ash and shade. Yet even shade couldn't offer an inkling of the peace they once had. Over seven hundred years gone by, and still she could remember the cool brush of moonlit air scented with jasmine and carrying the chirrups of crickets. Night had been her sanctuary—night and all its creatures.

Now Eldoria had only the day. The second twelve hours were no different from the first, save that singular softening of the sun after its east-to-west diurnal course, before it reversed its trajectory across the sky.

Eldoria's citizens liked to boast that they were superior in their winnings. For surely Nerezeth grew cold in their eternal winter; surely they thirsted and starved without the promise of bountiful harvests, cascading waterfalls, and burgeoning spring foliage. What could possibly be sown, harvested, or admired in that icy, shadowy terrain? Did that not explain why there were smugglers carrying sunlight to Nerezeth, yet no one here ventured into that dark land to steal their moonbeams?

Yes, how little Eldoria needed the night.

Crony's jaw ground against her cheek. How easily Eldoria had forgotten those early years, when so many fell to madness from lack of sleep and sought out shade in the Ashen Ravine, giving their spirits to the cursed forest and becoming shrouds—half-life silhouettes that craved the flesh they once had. How easily Eldoria had forgotten that this was why King Kiran's royal ancestors initiated the cessation course: a nine-hour curfew set upon the entire kingdom, requiring by law that after the daily flash of dusk people were to retreat indoors, where heavy drapes blotted out the light, so they might rest and slumber. How easily Eldoria had forgotten the moon's calming breath and the nightingale's restorative song.

Until now. With the birth of the child princess and her peculiarities, Eldoria had been forced to remember. And everything had been upended.

"This way," the fox said, his long, pink tongue lolling from the heat.

Together, Crony and her companion trudged a steep, rocky path dividing a field of fragrant purple heather. She followed as he vanished through a weeping willow's fringe, then caught sight of his tail, the tip glistening like a plume of silver smoke.

There, at the fox's front paws, a knight lay dying, half-hidden within a thicket of elderberry trees. Mud-smeared greaves stretched across his shins, their metallic surface catching glints of light. Crony trailed the heavily plated legs deeper into the brush to where his helmet and breastplate, embossed with Eldoria's sun-sigil, were cast aside. The rest of his armor lay bent and crumpled on the grass—as useless to him now as the lavish white gold from which they were forged. Splatters of dried blood marred the bright metal and formed a crust across his ebony skin. Crony swatted at some gnats grazing upon his wounds.

"Curious." The fox panted. "The three guards who accompanied the king were accounted for. Two knighted for their bravery." He licked away some drool dripping from his muzzle. "One laid to rest in the royal cemetery."

"May-let someone miscounted." Crony knelt close enough the salty-sour stench of infection overpowered the perfume of greenery surrounding them. "Or, may-let this man had his own set of orders, apart from the others."

The fox's ears perked higher. "So, either he's a traitor, or an unsung hero. I'm guessing the latter. I remember him from my time at the castle. He's the king's first knight. An honorable man, even in his youth."

A large, jagged hole in the knight's chest spewed out fresh blood with each cough of his heart. His skull had caved with some blunt trauma and squashed his eyelids permanently shut.

Crony's own eyelids grew heavy. She found herself wishing for the thousandth time that upon closing, hers could offer sanctuary—an oblivion of blackness. Instead, the filmy flaps merely softened her view. It was her curse, to never stop seeing the world: its hatred, its bitterness, its mistakes.

Her companion circled the body, a graceful skim of red and silver, then licked the dying man's right ear, the only part of his head which remained as perfect as a babe's.

The fox's gaze turned up to Crony, keen and challenging. "Won't you chase away this one's death, should he prove a hero? Isn't that worth another chance at life?"

Crony knew the fox wasn't asking out of altruism. His heart was not pure enough, elsewise he'd be soaring in the air where he belonged.

Luce wished for entertainment, to see Crony perform the one talent he knew she possessed that she'd never used. It didn't matter how often she claimed none had proved worthy of the miracle of resurrection, Luce insisted one day someone would.

He didn't know what it would cost her when that day should come, and why she held fast for the proper time.

Crony moved the breastplate away to kneel next the knight. "This man lived his life full out." She nudged her fox companion aside, setting down her staff and drawing back her hood. Her braids fell across her shoulders. "Ye'll not be seeing the trick today, cur."

Luce barked a laugh. "Me, a mongrel? I'm wounded."

Red glitter and silver smoke enveloped his form. His ears and muzzle shrank, his vulpine features blurred then cleared to sharp cheekbones and a masculine countenance; the burst of magic wound about him, transforming his fur to coverings that stretched to accompany the shift of ribs, forelegs, and hinds to a man's torso, arms, and legs. He stood, shaking out his mop of red hair.

A sly spark ignited in his orange gaze. Along with his pointy white teeth, his eyes and ears were the only part retaining any canine qualities. Otherwise, he was inhumanly human in the way of all air elementals: youthful, fine-boned as a bird, tall and slender, with luminous skin and delicate hands. The only things missing were his feathery wings and the ability to walk the line between spiritual and corporeal—the very trait that had contributed to his exile in the first place.

Luce smoothed wrinkles from the fuzzy white shirt, red jacket, and breeches that had earlier served as his hide, kept intact by a trick of glamour. He bowed at the waist, the braided talisman swinging from his neck. "Fair Lady Cronatia. May I present my gentlemanly side, here to serve?"

Cronatia. No one had used her given name for centuries; the sound of it made her nostalgic. The fact that Luce had guessed without her ever sharing it made her shake her head in an effort not to smile. There was death enough already in this thicket without withering the plants. "Dapper or no, ye still smell of dog."

"Ah, but now I have opposable thumbs." He wriggled his long, elegant fingers.

"D'ye remember how to use 'em?" Crony arched a brow and smoothed a cloth across the dying man's chest, so as not to be distracted by his exposed pulse.

Luce's thin, pretty lips lifted to a sharp-toothed smirk as he gathered up the rest of the fallen armor and shoved it into a space between a large rock and some tall weeds. It was his job to take anything of value off their corpses-in-waiting, so the treasures could be carried to the ravine once Crony finished her task. Today's was the best haul they'd managed in years. The white gold could be melted into bars or coins, and used for currency on the dark market.

Stirred awake by the preparations, the knight whimpered.

Crony touched two pruned fingers to the man's lips, his salt-and-pepper whiskers tickling her skin. "Ye be two gasps from the grave," she said with a gritty voice that was made to rasp a dying soul like a cat's tongue—a chafing comfort. "I'd ask ye don't waste them." He tried again to speak so she pressed her palm across his mouth and nose, subduing him with her scent of myrrh and decayed flowers. Just as she worked in death, she smelled of it also. "Anything ye need be sayin' can be shared with the skellies in the boneyard. I've important things to do. Shushta now, and save yer breaths."

Crony untied the bag at her waist and laid it on the ground. She withdrew a paper-thin triangular plane of glass to hold over the knight's mouth. "It be time to remember. Let the most important moments of yer life pass afore yer eyes." He exhaled, his breath fogging the clear surface. Crony blew a breath of her own across it then trapped them together by placing another glass triangle atop the first. It sealed with a white snap of magic. She did the same for the man's last breath and wrapped the trinket, tucking it into her bag. As for the first memory she'd preserved, she held it close while whispering an invocation over the knight's dying form to release his spirit.

A sullen mood overcame Luce as he waited for the man's life to fully slip away. Then, without preamble, he shoved his hand into the knight's chest and tugged at his heart. The organ released with a grisly, sucking pop. Blood drizzled from the dangling valves and veins—red and sticky on Luce's human hands. He licked it off hungrily, his gaze averted from Crony's. She turned her back to give the sylph privacy, knowing how he despised the predator he'd become—a beast that craved the nourishment of raw organs and blood and flesh.

Air elementals supped upon sunlight and moonlight and became drunk upon rain and wind. In his invisible ethereal form, Luce had once whispered into the ears of earthbound beings, tricked them into thinking he was their conscience, coaxed them into losing their inhibitions and doing things—not against their nature—but against their better judgment. He hated being tied to the earth and its rules now, no longer capable of such chicaneries. Even more, he hated having lost his immunity to time's passage. Sylphs were not immortal, but their airborne lifestyles kept them young. Without flight, he could only outrun age by feeding upon death.

Crony ignored the squishing and gobbling and walked toward an opening in the branches where strands of sunlight filtered in. She held up the knight's first captured breath in its glass frame, waiting for an image to reveal itself.

Luce sighed deeply from behind—more a sound of disdain than content. She peered across her shoulder. He wiped his face clean with a sleeve then scattered leaves and soil atop the empty hole in the knight's chest, as eager to cover up his gluttony as he was the corpse.

"So, what do you have then?" Luce stood, all levity gone from his expression.

Crony turned back to her trinket. The sylph's height allowed him to look over her head and around her horns.

"A glimpse of a cherished childhood?" he asked, close enough his warm, blood-scented breath brushed her temple. "The love of a beautiful woman?"

Within the sandwiched planes, a multitude of monotoned shapes danced in slow motion. Crony brought the glass closer. "Patience, me doggish dandy. The image still be forming."

In this raw state, a captured memory could only be seen by her eyes and heard by her ears. Even after she gave life to the tableau so anyone could watch it unfold across the glass, only her magic could bridge the moment to another's mind and imprint it there, making it their own. At least in *this* kingdom. There was one other with magic enough to manage a memory animation or weave. But Crony hadn't had contact with them in centuries.

Brushing off the melancholy thoughts, Crony concentrated on her prize. She hoped Luce's guesses were correct about their dying man's last memories. Happiness was the most lucrative. The patrons who came seeking her wares were covetous souls, always yearning for the satisfaction they'd never had.

However, violent and disturbing memories had their place, too. Those she saved for weapons to unleash upon enemies—a tactic that had won her a feared and revered status among even the deadliest miscreants occupying the ravine.

At last the jumbled scene unfolded with clarity and the sound reached her ears in sync with the images. The king, along with the dead knight lying behind her, spoke in hushed tones. The memory came to an end as the king and his confidante were attacked by the same three Eldorian guards who had escorted King Kiran to the battlefield and back.

Crony hissed. *"Traitors."*

"Who?" Luce asked. "Tell me what you see . . ."

So shocked by the man's memory, Crony didn't notice the approaching footsteps. Luce's vulpine senses kicked in before the four Eldorian soldiers stepped through the foliage surrounding them. He transformed into the fox and snatched Crony's bag of glass with his teeth, escaping into the underbrush.

"What have we here?" One of the soldiers—hot and sweaty from military drills—caught Crony around the neck from behind. Her glass trinket fell to the ground and cracked. The trapped breath released on a wisp of shimmery flakes. Crony inhaled it before it could blow away and be a memory lost forever. Held safe within her, she'd have the means to imprint it upon someone still, should the time come.

"Appears to be a witch of the wilds," a female soldier answered as she lifted the skeletal staff. The woman wrinkled her dirt-smeared nose upon seeing the squirrel's tail tucked at Crony's waist. "She reeks of dead things."

"And thievery to boot," a third soldier added, finding the knight's armor tucked into the rock's edge.

Crony lunged to escape but was helpless against her captor's vise.

None had discovered the knight's corpse until the fourth soldier nearly tripped over it. He knelt to rake the leaves and dirt away. His face paled. *"Sir Nicolet."*

The other three soldiers gasped in unison.

"Lady Griselda has been searching for him," said the man holding Crony. He tightened his grip when she tensed. "Murderer!"

Crony struggled against the rough hands wrestling her to the ground, but spoke not a word in defense as a dark bag came down over her head, blocking out all light. Why complain? At least she had her oblivion.

The Splendor of Velvet and Vermin

ollowing King Kiran's death, darkness blighted Eldoria's spirits—a mockery in a land where the sun never waned.

Only one day after the burial, and war loomed once more. Soon, the infantry would go by foot to Nerezeth's iron staircase with orders to dig their way through to the gates. There was rumor the bedridden King Orion had been bonded somehow to the lavender-colored roses that were uprooted over a month ago, and by now, his fight to live would have dwindled and he would be easy to quash. Griselda wanted to ensure death would be at Eldoria's hands. No one in court believed Nerezeth's claim of being innocent of King Kiran's blood, and there was a statement to be made.

Within the castle, a statement was being made as well. Along with her daughters, Griselda was moving to the north wing. "I should stay close to my niece," she said. "I must keep her safe."

Lyra *had* felt safe on this side of the grand ivory fortress, where the curtains stayed drawn and shadows slipped in and out, playing hide-and-seek with the candle flames. Here, she could escape her burden of heavy trappings and run about the winding halls and stairways half-dressed, unmasked, bare-footed, and free to be herself. All her life, it had been only her and her father's advisors—along with his most trusted knight, Sir Tristan Nicolet—occupying the northern tower, chambers, and corridors. This place had served as her playground in the waking hours, and a haven when time to rest. But when Sir Nicolet didn't attend the king's funeral or return to the castle, rumors abounded that he had also fallen prey to the Night Ravagers. Now, with both him and her father gone, a chilling change was on the air that smelled dank and moldering, like loneliness—despite all the people milling about.

Lyra crept in and out of dark corners as servants she barely recognized marched back and forth with trunks and baskets. To cross their paths won her fearful glances and curious glares, more biting than the sun's rays had ever been. Her aunt's servants had lived with her on the east side, leaving them as much strangers to Lyra as she was strange to them.

Finding a safe spot beneath a stairwell, she spied on a blond chambermaid walking alongside another with dark hair and a limping gait, both carrying baskets of linens and dried flowers that smelled musky and sweet.

"'Ave you 'eard?" the blonde asked the brunette, oblivious to Lyra's presence. "Brindle and Matilde 'ave been exiled to the servants' quarters. They're only to come out for meal preparations. Regent Griselda says they been forgettin' their places, wiling away work hours playing with the princess."

"That sounds right enough," the other answered. "A cook belongs in the kitchen preparing food, and a jester in the dining hall delivering jokes to aid with digestion. Don't know why anyone would choose to be here in the darkness with that feral little beast anyway. So unearthly silent . . . and those eyes, the way they glint? It's enough to give ya nightmares for weeks."

Lyra backed herself deeper under the stairwell, lowering her gaze to keep it hidden.

The blonde stalled and looked around to be sure no one overheard. "Well, 'tween you and me, I'm relieved I didn't get assigned to attend 'er. There's rumor those lashes be made of metal shavings. That's why they're so jagged and silver-white. Can you imagine getting sliced by all them?"

Lyra touched her lashes, their softness belying the maids' accusations. She wished to tell them how wrong they were. But how could they listen when she had no words? She could write them a note, but not everyone in the castle could read.

The brunette shivered. "Who's to tend her then? I thought the regent had a falling-out with Mia."

"Put 'er foot down, is all. Told Mia she'd still be permitted to be the princess's personal maid, but only at the beginnin' and endin' of the cessation course. To 'elp bathe and prepare for bed, and in the mornings to dress for the day. But the regent said she'd keep a close eye on things, so Mia mightn't come between Lyra and 'er true family."

Lyra teetered on a tightrope of emotions—itching to jump out and defend Mia, but at the same time tempted to slink away like an unwanted ragdoll. As they passed, she compromised and slipped from her hiding spot to follow silently.

Their small procession stopped at her mother's room. Her aunt had insisted the queen's chambers should be her own, "until the princess comes of age enough to appreciate its splendors."

Lyra ducked in behind the chambermaids, unseen, looking on as her aunt made a show of it: shaking the dust from the heavy drapes until several servants sneezed; folding back the brocade bedspread to line the sheets with musky-scented pillow-soaps of black amber and jasmine—Griselda's signature fragrance; and opening the wardrobe to chase away the moths so she could air out the late queen's beaded and bejeweled gowns of damasks, velvets, and silks.

Griselda's hands already sparkled with ruby rings and white gold bracelets—pilfered from the royal jewelry box—as she lifted a gown free and held it against herself. Although unsettled by the image, Lyra couldn't escape how her aunt seemed to belong in this room. How her confidence and poise favored her queenly mother in portraits more than Lyra ever would. How much more regal her aunt's ivory complexion appeared in those warm, lush colors, compared to Lyra's ghostly pallor.

Yet, in the back of the wardrobe, there remained a few pastel gowns of pale citrine, periwinkle, and seafoam that Lyra aspired to wear one day.

She looked down at her own unadorned gown of sage chiffon. Carnation-pink lace gilded the sleeves where they kissed her elbows, and a hem of the same skimmed the floor at her ankles—long enough her bare feet could only be seen in snippets when she walked.

In one cherished memory of her father, Lyra had followed him to the seamstress's chamber and listened as he requested special gowns for her. "It's of utmost importance that she's comfortable. Airy fabrics free of embellishments. Nothing to weigh her down. Already she bears enough, wrapped in cloaks just so she can frequent other parts of the castle. And none of those deep colors that are fashionable in court. Something soft and delicate. Pastels, perhaps. They'll flatter her coloring and be gentle on her eyes."

Though his heart had been in the right place, her special wardrobe had the undesired effect of magnifying her differences, making Lyra stand out like a faded lily in a field of brilliant poppies and wildflowers.

"From this point on, we'll visit our subjects daily in the commons, accompanied by the royal guards." Griselda's statement recaptured Lyra's attention as the two chambermaids helped her into a black damask gown. Once the lacings on the corset back were tightened to fit her curves, she spun so the exquisite fabric rustled and whirled around her. When the dress came to a stop, a seamstress adjusted the diamond pin tucks across the bodice. "It's time to refurbish our wardrobes. Our late Queen Arael wouldn't have wished for her things to go unused . . . gathering dust." Griselda raised her arms theatrically, delivering the speech as if to a great audience, although it was only Lyra, her cousins, and a handful of servants remaining. Griselda leveled a glance at her daughters who were seated on the bed. "We'll deconstruct some of her less fashionable gowns and have the seamstresses reprise their embellishments and gemstones, so you will also have new accoutrements for our constitutionals. And this mattress . . ." Griselda snatched the seamstress's scissors and scored a slit in Queen Arael's bed, revealing the goose-down stuffing within. "Have the chamberlain bring us lamb's wool to replace this filling," she directed the blond chambermaid. "I won't suffer sleeping upon feathers."

At the thought of those same scissors ripping apart her mother's beautiful things, Lyra stepped out of hiding and shouted, "No, please!" The room went completely silent. As always, her words held no shape. Even to her own ears, the sound rebounded in musical notes, and the only emotion the songs portrayed was joy . . . a bird's trill despite that her heart cried in plaintive desperation.

Everyone in the room stalled their activities to stare at her. The moths that had been hiding since being chased from the wardrobe came out to hover along the ceiling—drawn by the enchanting sound.

Defeated, Lyra slumped against the cushioned headboard.

Griselda's razor-sharp focus sliced into her. She dragged out her glossy crimson-and-black side braid to hang along the bodice of Arael's gown. "Perhaps our princess would wipe the pout off her lips." Lyra's lowered her lashes, hiding from the attention beneath fans of snowy fringe. "Although you can't accompany us on our diurnal processions, I am sure you can be satisfied to wait here for our return. We are each making sacrifices, dearest one. Ours is the most substantial, living here on the dark side of the castle. But I am willing to do that, for just as our kingdom needs to see that their royal line is still thriving and strong, my niece needs to be assured that I'm not only regent over Eldoria, but over her as well. *I am your mother now.*"

Lyra's rapid heartbeats denied the lie even as her cousins chattered in agreement.

Wrathalyne sorted through Queen Arael's books piled on the bed. "Mums, since we're to have an extra sister now, we should move into Sir Nicolet's chamber. It's the biggest on the floor other than the king's. It can be a wallowship of royal sisters!"

"*Fellowship*, Wrath," Avaricette corrected around a mouthful of confections while shoving a lexicon off the top of the book pile toward her sister. "And may I suggest you start with this book and read it from front to back?"

While her cousins bickered, fresh sadness surged through Lyra at the reminder of Sir Nicolet's absence. He, her father, and her aunt had grown up together, which made him the closest thing to an uncle Lyra ever had. She adored how his skin and eyes were a rich ebony, a comforting depth that reminded her of safe places, but how he also beamed like strands of sunlight each time he'd reveal his white-toothed smile. The day her father was to travel to Nerezeth to bargain with Queen Nova, Lyra secretly hid beneath the bed in the king's chambers to stay close to him until he left. Sir Nicolet had visited to speak privately with the king as he sat his desk, gluing the pieces of her mother's broken mirror back together. "You will stay behind and watch over Lyra," her father insisted. "When you hear of my returning, wait at our secret meeting place where I'll give you an update."

Lyra had kept the clandestine conference to herself, and hoped against all hope that Sir Nicolet was still waiting in that secret place and would come out soon.

Griselda *tsk*'d at her daughters. "There will be no moving into Sir Nicolet's chamber. He's an experienced knight. We must have faith he'll return unharmed. Now, come choose your favorite embellishments."

Avaricette dropped the plate of cherry-jams she'd been munching upon, sending them rolling around on the floor; Wrathalyne set aside one of Queen Arael's gardening books she accused of being "*mundanian* and pedantic"; and Lustacia stood from sorting through rubies, emeralds, sapphires and diamonds. Her eyes met Lyra's and glistened with something akin to compassion before she joined her sisters. Candlelight bounced off their expertly coiffed locks as they stepped together to the wardrobe, finding favorite gowns to be used as scrap materials for their own ensembles.

Lyra hedged into a corner where the moths had gathered—where the shadows swirled thick as a black cape.

The moths, spiders, and occasional rat occupying the castle were the only night creatures left behind after Eldoria's victory over Nerezeth. Since then, most of their slimy, spindly-legged, and fuzzy-winged kin had migrated to the starlit realm. Lyra was grateful some chose to stay. They were outcasts like her, and she shared their desire to stay hidden.

Her father had always told her, "Beware the light." Over her lifetime, she'd come to understand the true meaning: *Beware the light, for those who love it hate you.*

Just as that thought occurred to her, the beating of the moths' wings blended to a murmur: "*Be-be-be-ware-ware-ware, be-be-be-ware-ware-ware.*"

Lyra looked up at them, stunned. Her cousin Lustacia stirred from admiring a plum underskirt embroidered with gold-beaded ivy, as if also hearing the airy mantra. Her gaze locked on Lyra for all of three blinks, then she furrowed her brow and looked down, as though convinced she'd imagined it.

But it wasn't imaginary. Lyra's chin trembled. The moths' wings had echoed what was in her mind, as if they were the mouthpieces for her defective tongue. For the first time in her life, her unspoken words had reached someone's ears.

A sense of belonging welled within, filling spaces that had been empty ever since her birth. She decided she loved moths . . . and they loved her, even more than her family did.

Griselda stood beside her mother's torn mattress, ripping out goose down and tossing it in the air. Dancing beneath the feathers, her cousins raided every corner of Queen Arael's room. Jewels, gowns, and tapestries littered the marble floor—a lush and glittering rainbow of violation and gluttony.

Wrathalyne and Avaricette knocked over knickknacks and gimcracks that had once been important to Lyra's mother for some sentimental reason she would never know.

Her cousins' antics moved ever closer to a potted lavender rose upon the dresser—that tempting bloom Queen Arael had brought back after being pricked by its thorn. It was the one remaining piece of the rosebushes King Kiran had kept alive, albeit hidden away. In his queen's superstitious mind, she believed its magical reach was not limited to death, but to life as well, much like the sylph elm within their garden. And such things should always be protected. So the king had honored her dying wish to let it live, keeping it harbored within her room and opening the curtains to give it sun.

Lyra couldn't trust her aunt to continue the tradition. Under her keep, the rose would die of neglect. So, before the flowerpot could topple, Lyra lunged forward into the candlelight, sweeping it up.

No one noticed. The servants had left, and her aunt and cousins were kicking the spilled cherry-jams atop the pile of pastel gowns from the queen's collection that Griselda had proclaimed unflattering and out of style; soon, all the candies were trampled to a gooey mess, and red footprints smeared across the fabrics in the wake of Lyra's dancing cousins.

Lyra's eyes stung. Griselda had scolded her harshly yesterday for staining the great hall's pristine marble with her discolored tears at her father's interment. To save her mother's floor, Lyra slunk along the wall, arms hugging the potted plant tightly. Only when she was two steps from the doorway did she notice that the shadows had clustered around her, camouflaging her movements. She'd felt a fondness for them ever since first wearing the nightsky hood, but until today, didn't know they felt the same.

A half smile lifted Lyra's lips as she stepped outside the chamber and into the empty corridor with the moths and shadows at her side. She chanted in her mind: *Quiet-quiet, hush-hush. Be the feral beast they say you are . . .*

Quiet-quiet, hush-hush. The bugs' flapping wings echoed the command. Hearing her words upon the rustles made her smile flourish.

Tiptoeing, she nuzzled the fragrant rose, careful to avoid the thorns climbing the stem. The petals smelled crisp, like fresh-fallen snow. She shouldn't know such a detail. Perhaps her shadowy, winged companions imparted a wisdom they shared with all other night creatures. Or perhaps the flower told her itself—like the tempting whisper that had drawn her mother to touch it in the first place.

The scent of coolness frosted Lyra's heart, so no fear could penetrate. She braved taking a turn toward a part of the castle her father had forbidden her to explore. It was the one safe place for the moth and shadows trailing her . . . the one safe place for her to cry her violet tears . . . the one place her cousins had said she belonged, and the only haven she had left in this fortress that had once been her home.

When the winding staircase appeared below, she didn't hesitate. Together, Lyra and her new friends braved the cool descent into the yawning depths of the dungeon.

❈·I·❈

None of the torches were lit, but Lyra's eyes penetrated the darkness, and she easily found her way down without tripping or falling.

There were no prisoners, which meant no guards. She had all forty cells to herself. The closest was left ajar due to a busted lock. Unsure where they kept the keys, Lyra settled for the broken room. She pushed the door and the rusted hinges wailed and leaked a red, powdery dust, welcoming her like an old acquaintance weeping blissful tears.

Following her tiny escort of wings and furry antennas, Lyra stepped in.

The stench of stale urine and old sweat fell away to the memory of the fresh breeze once shared with her beloved father while standing by a window and speaking of sylph elms. She had cried for him all through her sleep. Now she wanted to remember their happier times.

Lyra set aside her mother's rose, confident that Mia could help find a sunny spot for it somewhere. The dusty grit on the floor slickened the bottom of her feet, and she skated from one wall to another, the same way the children crossed the ice in the stories Father used to read. The shadows joined in and formed a trail at her toes; Lyra chased them, as if following the silhouettes of shimmery goldfish beneath a frozen pond—something she'd seen in a painting upon the library wall.

She pretended the gray moths swirling about her head were jeweled butterflies, like the ones Sir Nicolet used to collect for her in shadow boxes— sapphire, topaz, and emerald—their colors so vivid they tickled her eyes and made her laugh, jubilant and breathless. But these weren't pinned to a backing, or muted by a nightsky hood. These were flying free in the open air, as was she . . .

While dancing, her heel kicked a tin cup. A spider scurried from beneath. A wave of babies followed. Their legs would soon be spindly and lengthy like their mother's . . . like Lyra's lashes. Their graceful surge filled the wall—like raindrops drizzling a windowpane in reverse.

Lifting the tin cup, Lyra gathered her rose and carried them both to where an empty wooden crate sat beside a cot. She flipped the box over to serve as a table, not even pausing when a vicious splinter tore into her thumb and made her bleed. She willed the pain away, determined to have a tea party like the ones she used to have with Mia, Matilde, and Brindle.

Her cousins thought themselves too old for games of pretend. Yet her father had encouraged her imagination. He believed, without the blank slate of a night sky to open up their minds to the possibilities of other realms and cultures, Eldorians could no longer imagine anywhere or anyone other than their simplest selves in their own set places. Stardust lit the footsteps of the heroes and heroines of old: those who conquered dragons and basilisks; those who befriended immortals, sorcerers and mages; those who built the two magical kingdoms with a balance of both logic and vision. In comparison, the sun's harsh yellow beams inspired the sensible side of a mind.

Aunt Griselda blamed Lyra's inability to face the sun for leaving her sensible side malnourished. Lyra lifted her chin, taking pride in it. This was a part of herself her father loved.

Surrounded by gray walls and grime, she spun her games within the splendor of solitude. Her new friends didn't mind when her lacy hem and feet became tinged with grime, or when the blood from her thumb smeared across the bodice of her dress. In darkness, she forgot the troubles of the world outside, until she heard a clamor coming down the stairway that chased the shadows, spiders, and moths to their hiding places.

Lyra's chest tightened. She didn't recognize the men's voices, but Griselda's burned her ears and melted the icy tendrils she'd wound around her heart, leaving her exposed.

Huddled atop the cot with her mother's rose and the tin cup, Lyra strained to listen.

"So, we brought the prisoner here. As we knew you'd wish to question her."

"And you've told no one else of her capture or your findings?" Griselda's inquiry echoed down the corridor alongside swishes of light.

"As you instructed, Your Grace. You made it very clear any news on Sir Nicolet should come straight to you."

Lyra swallowed a delighted gasp. Sir Nicolet was on his way back! She would go to him about her mother's things. He would help her rescue all that was left.

Lyra scooted to the cot's edge. Since her cell's lock was broken, she assumed the soldiers would choose one of the other rooms for the prisoner. When the footsteps scuffled closer, she shoved the potted rose beneath the cot and sought a better hiding place for herself. She'd just managed to fold her body under the box when they entered with lanterns. There was a knothole in the slats wide enough for her to spy through. The soldiers lit the torches on each wall, chasing the shadows even farther into the corners.

Lyra muffled a gasp as the men peeled a bag away from the prisoner's head. A set of black horns jutted from a grimy, reptilian face, followed by sharp teeth and eyes devoid of any white—their color murky like dirty dishwater. The prisoner hissed at the guards as they wrestled it into wrist and ankle manacles secured to the wall.

Griselda paced the dirty stone floor, out of reach of the chains. "You saw her do it?" Her voice cracked slightly upon the last word of the question.

"Well," the taller soldier answered. "Truthfully, Sir Nicolet was dead before we got there. His heart was ripped clean away."

Lyra gnawed on her cheek to stifle a sob. The tears she had earlier kept at bay rushed down her cheeks, joining the blood that already stained her dress.

"The witch must've ate it or some such." The stumpy soldier standing by the door added.

"I hear they're the most powerful organs for rituals." The first soldier chimed in again.

Griselda held up a hand for silence, then looked directly at the prisoner. "Did you talk to the knight before you stole his heart, witch?"

"Aye, I be a grand listener." The prisoner's answer rattled like sand scattered across a windowpane, sending a chill through Lyra's spine.

"Are you, now?" Griselda's profile offered a glimpse of her scowl, although her usual arrogance held a tremulous air. "And what did he say?"

"Me ears be attuned to a dyin' soul's breath, not their words." The witch scowled in return, her fanged teeth biting into her lip and drawing blood. Her forked tongue sloughed away the black, oozing liquid, leaving her lips slimy like earthworms.

Lyra barely managed to look at Sir Nicolet's murderer. With her scales and split tongue, the prisoner was a horrifying sight. Her snaky features and skin brought to mind drawings of legendary drasilisks in the kingdom's history scrolls—hybrid gargantuan creatures that had the head, wings, and front legs of a dragon and the long, coiling serpentine body and venomous fangs of a basilisk.

"Filth and foul." Griselda glared at the soldiers. "Do you not know anything? This harrower witch is an immortal . . . descended from gargoyles. She has an impervious hide and is immune to poison. She doesn't age and she can't be killed. How are we to force her to admit to anything?"

"We could try torture, Your Grace. Her tongue is vulnerable enough. The choke pear might prove helpful." Lyra watched the soldier take down a silver tool hung upon the wall. Four metal blades, curved inward to meet at the center, separated like razor-sharp petals as he turned a screw at the top. "Not exactly sure how to use it. We could send for the dungeon master and have him bring new torches, too. The broom sedge in these is stale and damp. The light won't last much longer."

"Bah. We've time aplenty." The other soldier plucked the torture tool from his companion's hand. "Any simpleton can use it. We shove this end down her throat, turn the screw, and gore the truth out."

Lyra shuddered at the gruesome thought, tightening her arms around her cramped legs to silence the rustles of her dress.

"No!" Griselda's dark eyes reflected the torches' flames. She grabbed the choke pear. "One twist too far, and you could cripple her tongue and render her speechless. Don't I already have enough of such nonsense in my life? Go fetch fresh torches and the royal mages. It takes magic to break magic."

"May-let it's *ye* at risk of breaking, yer grace." The witch's threat caused the soldiers to halt at the door. "May-let ye should strike a bargain to save yer perfect self."

Griselda barked a throaty laugh—a sound that raised the hairs on Lyra's neck. "You have no authority to demand bargains. You are not under the employ of this kingdom, so your magic is unsanctioned, and you're accused of murdering King Kiran's First Knight!"

"I follow death, but ne'er bring it. If ye wish for witness to me character, ye can question the fox who ate yer good Sir Nicolet's heart."

Passing a smug smile over her shoulder to the soldiers, Griselda rotated the screw on the choke pear, forcing the silver petals apart. "How inconvenient for you. Your pet is your only witness? Some simple beast of the field can't articulate his thoughts any better than my niece."

Lyra's eyes stung hotter at her words.

The witch blinked her own cloudy brown eyes—a filmy flash of skin both unsettling and mesmerizing. "Ah, but this fox be no one's pet. And I be given to understand ye've already spake with him at length, many a time, afore yer elm's leaves turned red in the garden. May-let he ne'er showed you his four-legged side. He didn't have much use for it—what when he could fly. But now it serves 'im well enough."

Griselda paled and she cast another glance over her shoulder at the soldiers. "Didn't I command the mages be brought? Why are you both still here?"

"Are you sure you should be alone with her, Your Grace?" the tallest one asked. "She's speaking in riddles. And we don't know what spells she's capable of."

Griselda turned back to face the prisoner. "Her magic is limited to those already dying. More a parlor trick than anything. She obviously can't use her words to vanish into thin air or break her chains. Otherwise you'd never have managed to drag her here."

The two men exchanged glances then bowed to Griselda. "At your command." They left the cell, pulling the door half-closed.

"And bring the dungeon master, too!" Griselda shouted after them.

"Ye won't be needing any mages or masters." The witch's husky voice scraped along the stone walls as the men's footsteps faded up the stairs. "I be glad to tell ye what I know."

Griselda tapped her palm with the choke pear, simpering. "Of course. The promise of torture can bend any creature's will. But, just so you understand, once you confess, you'll still be our guest. The dungeon master needs a new plaything. And I want to hear more about this . . . fox."

The witch huffed. "Nay. I won't be stayin' on for yer hospitality. Ye'll set me free afore yer soldiers return."

"And why would I do that? I've no fear of the nightmares you wield."

"Me weapon be reality. Yer dyin' knight was alive enough to share his final moments with yer kingly brother. I heared the details of the treaty—afore the two be attacked. Should *ye* want to hear who killed 'em, or better yet, keep what we both be knowin' between me and ye, I bid we bargain now."

Lyra crinkled her nose at the witch's cryptic taunts. It hurt to hear the mention of her father, but it felt important she listen.

Griselda stiffened, her hand fisted so tight around the choke pear her knuckles bulged. "I think instead I'll gouge out your tongue so you will never speak again."

"I needn't have a tongue to imprint a memory. And this memory will win accolades to them who holds it, be sure. The king's final words to his knight will salvage yer kingdom from another war neither ye nor the night realm can e'er win."

A tense pause stretched between Griselda and the prisoner. Lyra's arms and legs twitched from their awkward positions beneath the box and the dust threatened her nostrils with a sneeze, but she forced herself to stay rigid.

"All right, give over the memory to me, and I will free you. With the understanding that should I ever need your services, you'll return and pay your debt." Though Griselda's words were a command, Lyra had never heard her voice so unsure.

"Nay, the debt I owe not be yers. It belong to King Kiran's royal seed. And I don't be seein' his child here. Unlessen . . ." The witch tilted her head in Lyra's direction. "Unlessen that's *her* breaths be mufflin' beneath the box."

Lyra slapped her palm across her lips. The moths darted from their hiding places and fluttered around Griselda as she stormed toward Lyra's corner.

She scattered them with the choke pear, then tossed it down with a clank. Lyra didn't have a chance to protest before her hiding place was lifted off.

"You wretched little ferret! Always the perfect princess. Tender-skinned and docile. Never heard, only seen—" Griselda stopped short at the sight of Lyra's dirty hands, grungy bare feet, and ruined clothes. "Why, just look at you!" She caught Lyra's hair and tugged it hard enough she had to stand on tiptoes. Lyra yelped at the throbbing in her scalp, but the beautiful sound only fed Griselda's rage. "Playing in the dungeon like the filth you are. You're no proper princess at all. You're a stain on our kingdom's name! I'll put you on display for all to see . . . strap you up like a dirty sheet and let everyone beat you clean."

Lyra covered her face. There was no escape without ripping out her hair by the roots. The prisoner's chains jangled and caught both their attention.

"Best ye let her go." The witch's mud-filled eyes appeared to swirl in the dimming torchlight—hypnotic. Her slimy lips opened on a sharp-toothed grin so terrifying to gaze upon, Lyra felt her knees weaken. Griselda's legs actually buckled, yet she managed to maintain balance by using Lyra for a prop. "Without that child, yer kingdom be doomed." Contrary to her grisly smile, the witch's voice was solemn and low, like a warning. "King Kiran made a blood pact with Queen Nova . . . that be the peace treaty: his daughter to marry her son when the princess be of age. There be a prophecy, revealed by the dark world's grand sorceress." The witch winced at this, then continued on. "Balance, held within the joined hands of a prince and princess who ne'er belonged to their own, but equal to one another in every way. Alone, they're to conquer one another's worlds. Once united, each will be complete and embrace their oddities to bring the sun and moon together again. A raven-eyed star-boy forged of sunlight, and a silver-haired songbird girl who commands the shadows. No question who that last one be." She gestured with her manacled hands, the chains rattling in midair. "The night creatures already deem yer niece worth their fealty."

Lyra had no time to process the witch's proclamation of a prophecy or an arranged betrothal, for her mind was on the shadows peeling free from the walls.

Griselda whimpered, dropping Lyra's hair as the shapeless silhouettes hovered in place, awaiting instruction. Lyra hesitated only long enough to rub her tender scalp, then she nodded. The shadows curled around the dying torches and snuffed out each quivering flame one by one until they all stood in pitch blackness.

The prisoner's chains jingled and clanged to the floor. Lyra's eyes lit up, casting amber glares along the walls—tiny searchlights passing over the now-empty manacles and the shadows siphoning out of the keyholes like black smoke. Her gaze stopped at the open door where the prisoner stood free. The witch tipped her head, her obsidian horns reflecting Lyra's glowing eyes as she pulled her hood into place.

"Thank ye, wee princess." Her jagged grin stretched to appalling lengths, teeth shimmering yellow. She redirected her attention to Griselda, who'd fallen to her knees upon seeing her smile. "As this child be yer only light in this very dark place, I'd stay on her good side, were I ye."

With that, the witch leapt from the cell and Lyra closed her eyes, welcoming the darkness once more.

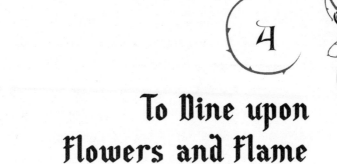

4

To Dine upon Flowers and Flame

While in Eldoria a king's death was being mourned, in the land of ice, star-filled skies, and midnight, another king struggled to pass from this life and his young son struggled not to hate.

Prince Vesper, son of Orion Astraeus and heir to the throne, leaned forward in his saddle. The scent of musk radiated off Lanthe's purplish-tinged mane. Vesper held the reins loose, guiding his mount with his knees on their climb up a hill. He'd been the one to break the colt, a gift from his kingly father on Vesper's thirteenth name day, using gentle measures to gain the animal's trust from the moment it was foaled. Now, two years later, Lanthe responded to Vesper with even the slightest nudge. As they reached the top, Vesper coaxed the reins around and spun them, taking a moment to admire the view below.

"The perfect venue for blood sport, wouldn't you say, Lanthe?" he asked, and the stallion whickered in answer.

Neverdark—Nerezeth's arboretum—had always been a beacon in their world of midnight. Other than the lead-glass window in the top that allowed a view of the outer night sky and the blink of dawn occurring once each day, the domed enclosure was forged of solid iron and filled with daylight. Or at least a reasonable facsimile. Thousands upon thousands of fireflies—fed with a special mix of pollen and liquid sunshine smuggled in from the day realm—drifted like infinitesimal stars along the shrine's curved roof and everywhere the gardens and meadows flourished. Their glimmering strands were comparable to the real sun, though weaker, much like rays peering out from heavy clouds. The homogenized violet-gold light lacked the brilliance to blind tender eyes or irritate moonlit complexions—frailties only Vesper was exempt from—but offered enough fluorescence to nurture herbs and other plants.

These grounds spanned hundreds of acres and, in spite of the emotional weight bearing down on Vesper's shoulders and chest, he still warmed at the sight of the rolling hills lit up like an overcast spring day. Fragrant meadows with fruit-bearing trees and shrubs stood out in lush shades of lilac and lavender. On the east end, alongside horse pastures and stables, ran gardens of fruits, vegetables, and edible flowers that bloomed all year round, irrigated by melted snow. From where Vesper sat, the saltwater lakes—channeled in from far below where the oceans surrounded the underside of the world—shimmered turquoise and thrived with aquatic creatures that skimmed the surface like luminescent wraiths. When captured and roasted, the glowing fish offered another level of nutrients to the Nerezethite diet. Since there was endless snow to heat for drinking water and bathing, the lakes were never drawn from, and never ran dry.

Joyful birdsongs and the occasional nicker, bellow, or bleat of an animal added to the illusion of life—robust and flourishing. Vesper swallowed back the bitter irony, for this haven that had once nurtured his people was now killing some. The arboretum had been the brainchild of the royal sorceress, Madame Dyadia—along with a handful of Nerezeth's finest horticulturists centuries earlier—as a means to provide the night realm inhabitants a reprieve from their bleak terrain while offering a frost-free landscape more conducive to harvesting vegetation, training messenger jackdaws, and pasturing livestock.

However, the same manufactured irradiation that tinted the flora shades of purple had begun to have the same effect on hair belonging to animals or humans. The royal horses' glossy cremello coats were now forever tinted periwinkle from centuries of breeding within the enclosed pastures. On the tail of that discovery, certain citizens began to show an intolerance to the vegetation grown within the homogenized light—a lung malaise that ultimately caused death.

The panacea roses of Eldoria's terrain—a flower that grew only aboveground in wild, pure, undomesticated sunlight—were key in countering the effects. A medicinal tea, brewed from the roots, had been keeping King Orion and others alive. Now the roses were extinct. All of them uprooted and dead at King Kiran's hand. Thanks to the war, a month had passed since the roses were laid waste, unprotected in bundles that withered in Eldoria's harsh sunlight. The roots—rotten and unsalvageable—could no longer be planted to grow a new supply.

A hot rush of rage seared Vesper's flesh beneath his royal riding vestments. He forced his gaze to the latticework edifice in the distance: the shrine wherein laid his lord father's inert form. Surrounding the gazebo-styled structure, an assemblage of guards and citizens, laden with furs, waited to escort the royal family back to the castle through the tundra outside once they'd said their good-byes to the king. Some in the group sang haunting hymns to the stars.

Vesper sought his best friend among the crowd of silvery hair and moonlit complexions. Cyprian's black-and-silver surcoat was easy to spot, being new and crisp, as he'd only recently made the guard. Their gazes met across the distance and Cyprian sent a mental query that Vesper refused to acknowledge. Instead, the prince willed the entire captive audience to look his way. He wanted their attention for this grand gesture, since the next one would be performed in solitude. No one ever expected their strange prince, nightblind, dark-haired, copper-skinned and bedeviled, to do what was right. Many had expected the worst of him since his birth, and he'd done his best not to let them down. He would give them one final impulsive act before proving them wrong.

In a clearing at the bottom of the hill waited a figure—draped in a makeshift king's robe of Eldoria's colors with a rope cinched about its neck just beneath its bulbous head. Vesper had no lance; didn't need one. The warriors of his world used their bodies as weapons against the monsters that threatened their livelihood. Focused on the object of his scorn, he pictured King Kiran. Vesper had seen him at a distance when the man came to propose a treaty to his queenly mother. He remembered every angle of his sun-burnished face, every tumble of dark hair, every flash of white teeth. He remembered it as vividly as the wheezing suction of his own lord father's dying gasps.

Someone had taken the Eldorian king's life before Vesper could. Contrary to rumor, no Night Ravagers had been involved. They were only sent aboveground in search of Nerezethite criminals. They never involved themselves in war.

None of it mattered. For despite that the sun-king received his due reward, Vesper still ached for justice.

"Are you ready to fly, Lanthe?" he asked. The stallion's ears twitched eagerly.

Shifting in the saddle, the prince raised a gloved fist and shouted, "For King Orion! Long live the moon and stars!" He squeezed his knees and an enthusiastic nicker burst from Lanthe's throat as together they took the plunge.

Down the hill they raced, Vesper's fury spiking his pulse to a thundering roar that matched his mount's hoofbeats. Clumps of grass, torn from the ground, flung upward and pelted them. Lanthe's harsh rhythm jarred Vesper's bones, a pain that fed his resolve. He narrowed his eyes against the updraft of wind whipping through his shoulder-length hair.

The singing had stopped in the distance, and several shouts went up in alarm. They feared Nerezeth's heir would break his neck; but it wasn't his neck in the noose.

Vesper wrapped one gloved hand in Lanthe's mane and slid sideways, holding on with his legs. They came upon the captive figure in a rush of wind. Shouting, Vesper caught the rope around its neck with his free hand and tugged as they passed. The head ripped free and plopped to the ground—bursting open with a splatter of seeds and stringy pumpkin pulp.

Vesper spun his horse and dismounted. "A proper beheading," he grumbled, "ends with a gutting."

Taking his rapier, he split the jousting dummy's decapitated body from neck to groin, gouging out the stuffing, sans any grace of form, until all that remained was a limp casing of gold, orange, and white cloth upon a stake's drunken slant. The prince stood there and panted—sweat beading on his forehead where strands as purple-black as a winter plum hung across his eyes. Overpowered by the scent of raw pumpkin, he felt vicious and unfulfilled.

A hand caught his shoulder from behind, and only then did he realize that the people stood silent while startled birdcalls filled the air.

"Quite a spectacle, Your Grace."

Vesper stiffened at the stern voice of Sir Andrian Nocturn, his father's Captain of the Guard. The prince turned to the serene, delicate features that reminded him more of Cyprian's each day. "I feel no shame."

"That's what concerns me."

Vesper's ears flushed with heat; he wasn't being entirely honest. He knew his display had been callow and reckless. But there was a purpose to it. "My people need to know that I will always avenge them."

There was movement in the crowd as Cyprian stepped out from the line of guards to make his way over.

"A true leader inspires harmony and provides anchorage for his people," Sir Andrian said. "There is a time for vengeance, yes. But it isn't now. This is the time for you to *lead*." Awkward silence ensued as they awaited Cyprian.

Upon arrival, Vesper's friend offered him a sympathetic smile. Sir Andrian released Vesper and patted Cyprian's back in greeting. No doubt the captain considered himself blessed by the night to have a son so calm and reasonable. So unlike their prince.

Vesper ground his teeth.

"The queen requests your presence in the shrine," Cyprian said to Vesper, compassion darkening his purplish eyes. "Your father's passage is at hand."

The prince squashed a pumpkin rind under one heel as he fought the sting burning his heart and blurring his vision. "I should see to Lanthe first." He stroked his stallion's purplish-hued flank. The horse nibbled some grass, seeming no worse for wear despite their harried run. "He needs a rubdown."

"That's for the grooms to do." Sir Andrian picked up Lanthe's reins. "I'll take him to the stables. Go now, be the man your family . . . your kingdom . . . needs you to be."

Vesper didn't respond, though he intended to do exactly that. Taking up stride with Cyprian, they followed the path that led to the shrine.

"Take heart. My father doesn't appreciate the art of pantomime." Cyprian eased the tension with his usual good humor. "I, however, am an enthusiast, and I say it was a fine portrayal of Eldoria's fallen sovereign."

A half-hearted grin tugged Vesper's lips. How long had it been since he'd smiled?

Cyprian clapped his back. "Shall I clean up his remains for you?"

"Leave it to the birds," Vesper answered. He glanced over his shoulder at the black crows and grayish-purple jackdaws flocked upon the ground, pecking at seeds and gathering stuffing that blew softly on the breeze. "His innards came from my eiderdown mattress. Let them nest in royal luxury."

Upon their arrival at the latticework structure, Cyprian returned to the line of guards. Vesper made a point not to look at any faces, then ducked through the tall, arched opening in the framework. He paused inside, careful of the royal pets. The glossy white-and-black crickets scrambled about, their chirping songs the one comfort in this place of sorrow. His sister, Princess Selena, knelt with their lady mother at the king's deathbed: a dais formed of woven moonflowers and twigs soaked in cinnamon oil. A canopy of crystallized cobwebs hung over his ailing body.

Being younger than Vesper by two years, and doted on by their lord father, Selena was taking this tragedy harder than anyone. She laid a bouquet of moonflowers on the pillow beside the king's iron crown and kissed a face resembling Vesper's own. During Vesper's younger years, vicious rumors abounded that he was a bastard child . . . that his queenly mother had been unfaithful. King Orion never believed a word of it and was rewarded for his faith, for as Vesper grew into manhood, none could argue their relation. Other than the differences in his coloring, the prince was the mirror image of his father: virile and aristocratic with the same high cheekbones, long, straight nose, and angular jawline. Though now, with muscles atrophied and skin tight and sunken, the great king appeared gaunt. The tracery of veins running beneath his diaphanous skin from neck and ears to cheeks and eyelids seemed to writhe as his choked inhalations gave way to a rattling cough.

"Lord Father!" Selena wailed at his unconscious struggle to catch another breath. She'd been spending so much time here and in the gardens, her long, pale curls shimmered periwinkle in the dimness, a few shades lighter than her violet tears.

Queen Nova helped her daughter stand and nodded to the three guards in black-enameled armor behind Vesper. One stepped around to aid the queen but teetered in an effort to miss a cricket. Vesper instinctively reached out to steady him. The guard's eyes widened beneath his great helm—his expression caught somewhere between fear and revulsion.

"Thank you, my young lord," he mumbled while quickly withdrawing from the prince's grasp. The strain in his voice didn't match the gratitude of the words. He tried to hide the act of rubbing his arm with a gloved hand. Even through the leather, he considered the prince's touch tainted.

Vesper suppressed a growl. He hadn't asked to be born so useless his people had to alter their way of life. For lampposts to be erected where none used to be. For more trees to be hewn down so they might have torches at every turn—a staple for the only Nerezethite prince who'd been born night-blind in centuries.

Frowning, Vesper moved aside so the guard could lead his weeping sister out. The prince grasped Selena's hand as she passed. They exchanged meaningful glances, then she squeezed his gloved fingers before releasing him. He took his place beside their lady mother while the other two guards resumed their positions at the shrine's entrance.

The smoldering incense and therapeutic herbs around the deathbed stung Vesper's nose. The twinge offered a less shameful explanation for his tears. He wiped away the clear streams from his cheeks.

"It is time to release our king unto his eternal rest, my son," Queen Nova said with a catch in her throat. "He cannot light his star in the dark firmament until we've all said our good-byes." Her fingertips gently cupped Vesper's hand where he clenched the scabbard beneath his sable cape.

Compared to the king's blue sodalite–encrusted broadsword, hanging as heavy as a bag of apples from a hook on the canopy's frame, Vesper's rapier was a customized blade of steel—slight enough for graceful parries and thrusts—with a narrow grip for younger palms and fingers. Moments before, he'd used it to enact his rage upon a cloth dummy. His lord father's weapon now belonged to him, and he had plans for breaking it in, too. Just as his lady mother knew nothing of his jousting performance yet, he didn't want her to bear witness to the second act he had to play, either.

Queen Nova squeezed his hand. He couldn't miss the starkness of her bluish-white flesh against his black glove. Uncovered, the contrast between their skin was equally startling. Vesper released his scabbard and laced their fingers together.

Assure him we won't let his passage be for naught—his lady mother's thoughts tapped his mind privately, lips pressed tight and tongue held motionless—*that you'll honor his legacy and bring the sun back to Nerezeth; elsewise, more of our people will die from the illness that struck him down.*

Two years ago, Vesper's head had already aligned with the queen's. Tonight, he was almost as tall as his lord father had been and had to look down to see into her eyes. The calm resignation there was as different from the disquiet that filled his soul as her pale heather irises were from his own—such a deep brown they were almost black. She'd always said his gaze was unnerving, fierce and unflinching as a raven's. He used that to his advantage now, to underscore a refusal to respond.

Her hand stiffened in his. *For years, Eldoria has turned away as we siphon day from their skies. Now we must turn away from their offenses.*

No, Lady Mother. He focused on her, so only she could hear his answer. *They did not turn away. They are afraid to seek out our smugglers in the Ashen Ravine. Eldorians are cowards, fearful of the flesh-eating shrouds created by their own inherit insanity. Cowards so malicious they uprooted an entire crop of roses whose only crime was pricking a lady's flesh. Their queen should have had sense enough to wear gloves.*

The uprooting was done in ignorance, not maliciousness. Vesper could feel the vibration in his lady mother's answer within his own brain. *It is the duty of a noble king to set aside his pride. He must think of his kingdom, make compromises for the greater good, hone relations to ensure a peaceful future.*

Vesper pulled free of her touch. The thick, silvery hair that matched the gleaming crystal of her crown fell past her shoulders and hid the disappointment on her face. He was glad for that, as it might have swayed him to tenderness. But why give in to such a weak emotion? Anger was much more productive.

Before his murder, King Kiran vowed to Queen Nova that one of the precious panacea roses still existed—alive and intact—within the castle's walls. The blood pact between their kingdoms hinged on it.

Vesper grimaced and resumed his mental conversation with his lady mother. *A treaty should never have been enacted concerning my future reign without my counsel or consent. A prophecy carved by shadows upon the walls of the mystic ice caverns should not be the road map for the rest of my life. Perhaps I don't wish to marry once I'm crowned. Perhaps I don't wish to marry at all. Why should my becoming king hinge in any way upon marital status?*

Queen Nova clamped her lips. *You're being entirely unreasonable.*

Why should I be otherwise? You won't even tell me the details of the prophecy. What were the exact words?

Set aside your cynicism and I will tell you. Until then, it will only make you angrier.

The prince couldn't refute her point. After having gone to Madame Dyadia seven years earlier, and begging her to make him like everyone else . . . after having her refuse to help, insisting that he'd been born as he was for some monumental reason yet unseen, he'd lost all faith in the forces of witchcraft, soothsaying, and the like. Practitioners—be they mages, witches, necromancers, or conjurers—were fickle, choosing only the projects that furthered their personal gain. Elsewise, why couldn't they use their talents to save a noble king, or to soften a people's hearts toward their prince's differences?

His queenly mother stroked the moonflower bouquet's stems, her finger straying to caress a strand of the king's hair lovingly. *Your father would've agreed with the council's logic, with my decision. Eldoria will replant the one remaining panacea rose in the soil above Nerezeth's stairway. After a hearty crop has grown, we will supply all the midnight shadows and stardust Eldoria needs to keep their princess clad in nightsky. In return, their three royal mages will supply us with liquid sunlight, so there will be no more smuggling it. Other than that, we keep to ourselves until you're both of age to marry. This joining will be of mutual benefit—an opening for our kingdom to accept you, and also to amend relations with Eldoria. Their princess is said to need shadows as much we need the light.*

Vesper huffed. *She's obviously too pampered. All of Nerezeth's citizens are sensitive to the sun, but it isn't anything a slathering of obsidian balsam and layered clothes can't solve. It's not as if the sun-smugglers singe to ash each time they traverse into the Ashen Ravine to gather strands of daylight. At least the girl can hide from the sun inside her pristine castle walls. We* require *parcels of sun to grow food and medicines, so her "need" for comfort doesn't even compare.*

What has become of your benevolent spirit? Do you forget where you're standing? his mother scolded.

He shifted uneasily in his boots. This shrine was hollowed—a tribute to meditation, thankfulness, mourning and communion. When Vesper was smaller, Neverdark itself, alive with magical topiaries and animated leaves that danced on their branches to stir a natural breeze, had been the one place that made him feel hopeful. Even the footbridges—built from enchanted rocks that heated the water and warmed the fragrant air—represented a path to growth, a means to carry his feet to another side where he could cease being the aberrant blemish upon this kingdom, and become the heir and son his parents had wished to have . . . the prince his people needed.

How can you harbor such resentment, the queen's voice interrupted his musings, *when all around us are symbols of peace?*

He had no answer. Even the drifting insects and their serene wash of light felt different in this moment, feeding his rage . . . promising power over a powerless situation. Vesper's attention settled at the head of the deathbed. Soldered to an ornamental holder that came to his sternum, a large globe of hollow copper—pierced with starry shapes—imprinted a galaxy across the king's face. The luminary was strictly ceremonial, and emanated radiant golden beams, though not from a flame. The same special mix of pollen and sunshine that was fed to the fireflies filled the luminary and powered its light, symbolizing their world's starry sky to which their dead would return after being burned to ash.

That dazzling mixture called Vesper closer. He leaned over the heat source and a new line of sweat dampened his hairline. He swept some strands behind his ear then raked a thumb across his lord father's silver-white locks splayed out on the black pillow beneath his head. Their lack of color was not a sign of age or illness, but rather another inherent quality that set Vesper apart from every member of his family . . . from his entire kingdom.

What would you have had me do? His lady mother's thoughts nudged him again, an obvious attempt to shake him from his silent brooding. *How else would you propose to bring genuine sunlight to our world, in the expanding amounts we need for our growing populace?*

Vesper kept the exchange between their two minds so the guards wouldn't hear: *I would order the princess to deliver the last panacea rose herself, then bind her within the cadaver brambles.* The wicked suggestion caused his lips to twitch. The savage, frosty-white thorn creatures that slithered like viperous skeletons across their land could bleed the sun in fiery red stripes from her veins. *Let her pierced tender flesh provide our natural light.*

Seeing the shock on his lady mother's face only strengthened his resolve, and he added aloud so all could hear, "I would rather rule alone than with a day-walker by my side. How would she survive the wilds?"

The queen's eyes met his. "The wilds of your land, or of your heart?"

He considered her question. The one likeness he shared with the citizens of Nerezeth was their lithesome builds, tall and more faerie-kind than human—characteristics mistaken for weakness. Their spines, however, were steel, and their spirits glaciers—men and women alike. It took courage to brave the mystic ice caverns and the dark, frigid landscapes . . . to withstand the frosty sting of a rime scorpion, to survive a bone-spider's bite rendered from fangs the size of a clouded leopard's, or to hazard an encounter with tinder-bats, whose dung could set fire to stone if ignited by a torch. The milder winters were opulent and scenic. But the prim and proper citizens of Eldoria weren't stalwart enough to face the night tides, where the snow crashed like tidal waves. In places, the drifts stood as high as any castle and caved beneath clumsy feet like the hungriest quicksand. And then there was the dead air, everything muffled by loosely piled snow, and avalanches waiting to tumble, lest one move graceful as a cat and relay their thoughts without sound to preserve the silence.

Vesper had his answer. "Ours is a land for the daring . . . and only the brutal of heart can survive."

He smoothed the silken banner where it draped the lower half of the king's prone form. He admired Nerezeth's sigil: a black background behind a silver crescent moon standing tall and majestic beside a nine-pronged silver star, celestial bodies representative of the king and queen; three small obsidian stars—the same contrasting shade as the dark background—shadowed the middle of the moon, dark reflections of their silver brother. These stars stood for the three generations that first shaped Nerezeth, those who reigned during the earlier, treacherous years . . . those whose wisdom and courage transformed the land into something tenable.

"Those of the sunlit skies have flapping mouths and weighty bones," Vesper elaborated. "They're weak, soft, and spoiled. Smooth complexions, with no scars or frostbite burns. I've heard the royal house themselves are as rigid and flawless as bronze and ivory statues untouched by the elements."

And the truth of your hatred looks us both in the face, his lady mother answered silently.

Vesper clasped his lord father's larger hand. He wouldn't admit she was right. That seeing King Kiran had been like staring into a mirror. A mirror Vesper would've once busted into a thousand pieces, to roll within the shards until they ground him down, until his flesh thinned and his veins rose to the surface. Anything to pass as one of midnight's children—skin forged from moonlight so finespun the paths of their heartbeats were showcased like maps for all to see, and eyes of glittering stardust that could pierce any darkness.

He himself had looked upon the silvery plait of hair and the vial of violet tears King Kiran had brought as proof of his daughter's tragic predicament. The sun-king had called it a sickness. Vesper snarled. *Sickness* . . . there was a time he would've traded his future crown to contract such a malady; to finally be accepted and embraced without fear, suspicion, or wonder.

Now, standing next to his lord father's prone form, the defiance Vesper had so long wrapped within to stay warm frayed to threads. He needed to provide anchorage for his people, as Sir Andrian said. He would earn the respect that came with the crown by warranting his kingdom's devotion and love, like the king who had ruled before him.

And his differences would play a bigger role than anyone had imagined.

Only Vesper could equip Nerezeth with the sunshine it required. But a blood pact with their rival kingdom wasn't the way to accomplish this.

Vision blurring, the prince lifted his father's limp hand and placed it atop his head. Three months ago, on the celebration of his fifteenth name day, this very palm had ruffled his hair when Vesper defeated a sparring partner, and applauded when the prince and Lanthe moved as one and hit all the targets dead-center during the equestrian archery contest.

Making his father smile, winning his laudatory touch . . . such moments had been few and far between. Tonight was the last opportunity. Although the king had slipped into the great sleep and lost the ability to connect, vocally or telepathically, perhaps he could still sense his surroundings.

Sniffling, Vesper returned the king's hand to his sunken chest and moved closer to the luminary, basking in its radiance, drawing strength from its sovereign potential—something he'd always felt unworthy of but was ready to claim as his own.

"I would be alone to meditate. You may lead the processional." He glanced at the guards, to ensure his lady mother took them as well. Both of the men's gazes turned down the moment they were met by his.

"You won't accompany us?" the queen asked, one silvery eyebrow raised.

"Leave a lantern and my fur. My place is by my king's side, until his final breath."

Queen Nova's lips formed a whistling-chirping sound—calling the white-and-black crickets to her. They hopped onto her silk skirts, forming alternate tiers with the molted nightingale feathers and spider's lace already in place. The combination of fabric and nature glistened and rustled as she strode to the door.

Vesper rested his hand on his scabbard again.

"Make your father—your *king*—proud," his lady mother murmured, somewhere between a thought and a word. "Let him leave this world on a bed of tranquility, knowing you've accepted your differences as the blessings they are, and have embraced your obligation to our kingdom."

"That's exactly what I intend to do, fair Lady Mother."

She gave him one last look, as if measuring his sincerity, then said, "I'll have Cyprian wait by the iron door to accompany you back to the castle." She stepped out with the guards at her heels. The kingdom's assembly of mourners followed in their wake.

Vesper waited long enough that they would be out of earshot. Casting aside his gloves, he opened his palms—scarred from battles with cadaver brambles and frostbite—then stared at the backs of his hands and wrists. Beneath his clothes, the rest of him reflected the same reddish-brown depth, as if he spent every moment outside in the day realm . . . despite that he lived in a moonstruck land and had never faced the sun's true light. This contradiction no longer dampened his spirits. Instead, it gave him courage.

He dragged his lord father's broadsword from the hook. It took both hands to lift, and every budding muscle to swing. He strained against the weight and hammered the luminary. Harsh clangs reverberated through his arms and spine. With three solid hits, he broke the brass's seal. The large gold bubble within held its form. Using the sword's tip, he pierced the membrane and the incandescent liquid began to seep like molten jelly.

Vesper dropped the blade. If anyone had heard his clanging, there was no time to spare. He knelt and cupped his hands to capture the sticky flow. It wasn't unbearably hot, only warm enough to singe. As he held it up to his lips, he smelled the pollen—nectarous and raw with a roasted edge—and his mouth watered to taste it.

If a tiny insect could sup upon the mixture and channel its radiance, why couldn't he?

His eyes focused on Nerezeth's banner again, on the large silver star seated next to the moon, on the background and smaller stars—as eternally black as their sky. For fifteen years he'd questioned his existence . . . why he looked so different. Why he was the only one in his kingdom who couldn't find his way in the dark. All along he should've questioned why he was the only one never ill-affected by the light.

At last he understood what Madame Dyadia had meant, what his "monumental" calling was to be. He wasn't born to be Nerezeth's evening star. He was born to be their *sun*. Pure and unfiltered. And after tonight, they would never need to rely on Eldoria for anything again.

He tipped his head back and poured the essence of daylight and flowers into his mouth, gulping it down until his body went to flame and his mind to ash.

❋·I·❋

He awoke to blinding flashes of light. Shouts of horror echoed in his ears, Cyprian's voice blending with the guards, before he succumbed to darkness again. A nightmare folded around him like ink smearing in water, brilliant red and gloomy gray in turns—a summer sky chasing the winter. Fire embroiled his veins and he writhed in agony. A full body shiver followed, bones and skin ablaze with frostbite. The stench of roasted flesh, scorched hair, and burning blood singed his nose.

When the pain became so excruciating he would die, he heard someone chanting—an ancient discerning voice. The sound elevated him, and his eyes opened to find he floated above his body, a tethered spirit. Magic was at work here: a veil of gray mist as substantial as glass stood between his consciousness and the happenings below. Two outlines stood over his naked form where it lay atop an altar beside a background of glistening ice. He'd been brought to the mystic caverns.

"Did you tell him the details of the prophecy?" It was the voice that had been chanting, and it belonged to Madame Dyadia, the royal sorceress.

"He was being too stubborn to listen." The second voice—frantic and remorseful—was his queenly mother's. "If only I had! It would have prevented this."

"The result would have been the same. A prophecy will be fulfilled, taking whichever detour it must. Our prince unknowingly aided in his effort to prove worthy of his kingdom. Though he chose the deadliest path for himself."

The sorceress's silhouette skimmed her hands across his body. Radiant, reddish-orange flares leapt beneath his skin, lighting up his veins and all the organs laboring to keep him alive. His spirit stayed safely above—a witness to his own undoing where no pain could reach him as puffs of black smoke rose from his nostrils. Flames crackled in his ears and molten gold seeped from the soles of his feet then spread from his toes to his ankles, coating them with a metallic sheen.

The queen sobbed, falling to her knees beside the altar. "Please, can you save him?"

"The damage is not without, but within." The sorceress withdrew a blade and made an incision in his skin above the metallic coating. The sensation was distant, more of a throb in a dream. His skin returned to its natural state as the gold leaked out from the slit, becoming liquid sunshine to be collected in a vial. "This is just the beginning." Madame Dyadia cut off several strands of Vesper's dark hair and wound them about a spool where they multiplied into a coarse thread. Using a fine needle, she sewed the opening closed; the moment she knotted off the thread, the stitches disappeared and a fully healed scar stood in their place. "The sun will try to overtake his humanness in increments. He must be strong enough to withstand the thrashes of gold. He'll have to bleed it from his flesh, like a snake's venom, to purify his blood. Though we cannot prevent it, the incisions can slow it. And there is a way I might tender the agony of the intrusion."

"Yes. Please . . . stop his suffering."

The sorceress placed a hand on the queen's shoulder. "I understand your determination to save him, in a way few others could. But if I do this, there will be repercussions. The burning flame has adhered to his wildness, pride, and rebellion—emotional fires feeding celestial ones. That part of him must be cast out."

"What? No!" Queen Nova's wail carried through the cavern's icy depths, loud enough to shake the icicles. "I love him as he is. I can't have him altered forever!"

"Not forever, Your Grace. Merely long enough." Madame Dyadia attempted to comfort. "The princess is younger than he. Five years stand between now and her coronation. Should we leave him intact, his rage could grow into something even more monstrous than it already is."

His lady mother reached for his hand, yelped at the contact, and jerked back. She rubbed her fingertips. "If I allow this, what will become of him? How will he live as only half of who he was?"

"He will not remember his time in this cavern, or know of his missing piece. He'll awaken to feel incomplete, and convinced the princess will make him whole again. Thus, he'll be focused upon one goal: to honor his betrothal to a girl he's never met, to win her hand at all costs. With his rebelliousness cast aside, he'll accept her. Which he must, to be cured, for only her moonlit touch can tame the sun in his blood. We are not killing any part of him, simply giving one half a sharper resolve and purpose, and the other a new vessel—as protection from the sun's searing burn."

"Can he one day be whole again?"

"Even should I exile his rebellion and rage, he will be drawn to it, wherever it might be. The princess will play a role in giving him focus, but he alone will have to face and conquer his true self. Only then will he be complete once more."

"Too many secrets; too much risk. Perhaps if we leave him as he is—"

"He will die."

There was a pause.

"Then we do it and bear the consequences," Queen Nova answered, though her voice trembled with doubt. "Nerezeth has lost their king. Should we also lose our prince and all that's promised through him, our kingdom will fall."

The sorceress chanted, more ancient words Vesper's ears had never heard, followed by five he understood: "Be gone from this place!"

A rippling sensation guttered through his chest as one part of his spirit ricocheted back into his body, torn away from the other. He watched through eyes half-closed as the liberated part—fluttering darkness and flickering light—hovered along the cave's roof, dipping and swaying, at war with itself until it found a shape. The prince's mind attempted to put a name to it, but the object swooped out into the winter wilds too quickly.

The absence in his core burned deeper than the flames. Tears seeped from the outer corners of his eyes, hot as smelted metal. The shimmery curl of a seashell appeared within his peripheral where the sorceress stood over him. She released a song trapped within: a songbird's trill so fluid, joyful, and pure it quenched the loneliness in his heart and made him forget his missing half, imprinting upon his soul a longing for the music instead.

"You will know her by her voice," the sorceress whispered in his ear.

Overcome with exhaustion, he vowed to find the source of that beautiful song one day. It was the only way to be cured, to be complete. An image of Princess Lyra's silvery hair and violet tears danced upon the back of his eyelids; then, cradled by the icy surroundings, he slept.

5

R Lady, Both Grisly and Glittering

At Eldoria's castle, there was to be no rest for Lady Griselda, trapped as she was in the pitch-black dungeon.

Upon the harrower witch's escape from the cell, Griselda's princess niece closed her eyes and cast them both in darkness. Griselda groped blindly about, trying to catch Lyra's hair to use as a lead rope, but the girl whisked by without making a sound. In the farthest corner came the scrape of something being dragged from beneath the cot, then the sensation of Lyra moving through the cell again.

"Lyra . . . I'm your mother now. You must obey me. Help me find my way back."

The princess stalled at the cell's entrance and opened her centipede lashes, illuminating Queen Arael's potted rose cradled against her chest. Griselda smiled smugly, convinced she had tightened the noose of compliance around the girl's neck, until Lyra opened her lips with an indecipherable song. Griselda shuddered as shadows dispersed at Lyra's command, flapping across clothes and skin, before whisking out the doorway.

Lyra's footsteps scraped confidently up the stairs, taking her light-giving eyes with her. Griselda's jaw went slack. The recalcitrant child had abandoned her.

In the darkness, Griselda froze at the stir of moths and spiders brushing over her feet and head. She held her breath until they, too, slipped from the room, drawn to their songstress.

Alone in a gloom so complete it mattered little whether her eyes remained opened or closed, Griselda sat upon the cot and drew her feet up, winding her arms about her legs. She burrowed her nose in the fabric at her knees to ward off the scent of urine absorbed by the rock walls. Panic swelled hot within her chest upon each inhalation.

One who cannot love themselves, cannot be loved.

The voice—from a lifetime ago—hissed within Griselda's ears as if the monster sat beside her. Griselda swallowed a yelp, stiffening at the thought. She intimately knew the danger that lurked in dark places. Shadows, spiders, centipedes, scorpions, salamanders . . . things that belonged to dankness and night, and were silent while being filthy, clammy, skittering and scuttling . . . made her skin crawl. If those same abominable creatures were to obey her niece's songs like faithful pets, her reign over the wretched child was ended. Perhaps her past had come to call . . . perhaps she hadn't escaped after all.

A bubble of helplessness and hate rose from her chest and burst to an animalistic wail in her throat. She clapped a hand over her mouth upon the echo.

The harrower witch had triggered these memories, and alone and anxious, Griselda couldn't stop from falling into that time long ago when she first acquainted creatures of darkness.

Griselda was christened *Glistenda* upon her birth. A tribute to Eldoria's glittering hills and glistening valleys each day in that moment when the flash of dusk left in its wake a wave of dew, and the sun reclaimed its radiance.

As she grew, everyone in the kingdom agreed that Glistenda was the most dazzling princess ever to grace the castle halls with her flaxen hair as yellow as sunshine and a flawless ivory complexion, both inherited from her royal mother. Her loveliness was so absolute, she could bruise simply by laying upon a feather mattress—the barbs and shafts being too prickly to withstand.

Glistenda's kingly father doted on his delicate princess, so long as she was blushing, docile, and soft-spoken. Her queenly mother taught her that to be seen, not heard, was a lady's most honorable calling. But during her sixteenth year, the emptiness of vanity as an aspiration hit Glistenda full force, after she witnessed the king falling from his steed during a jousting event. After, all he could do was lie abed, be propped on his throne, or be carried in a litter about the vicinage. Kiran was always at his side—there to learn the ways of a kingdom fallen upon his youthful shoulders earlier than anyone anticipated.

Glistenda was rarely allowed to visit the king. Kiran's time with him was too important, too pressing. Everyone said Kiran was the spitting image of his father's own russet hardiness—also possessing his wisdom, patient temperament, and military acumen.

Glistenda was to be available for family appearances, but would never have a say in politics, legislative counsel, or the kingdom's economics. Her royal parents, along with every adult in the castle, became too busy preening her younger brother to think about her. Had she been born a son, she would've been the heir, and every heart and mind hers to consume and command.

Instead, she had no voice; no say in anything. She was left to her own devices—reduced to glean attention through games played with the young men of the court. She used her wiles to get the obedience and devotion she craved.

The only exception was the one boy she desired above all others: Tristan Nicolet—beautiful ebony skin wrapped around a stalwart frame. Her brother's best friend, and son of their father's most trusted knight, Tristan often stood between her and her suiters. He stepped into the shoes of a brother who was too busy becoming king to defend his sister's honor. Yet no matter how she tried to tempt Tristan into her skirts, he denied her. The very code of honor that made her love him became the thorn in her side.

Determined to tarnish his shining resolve, she concocted the perfect plan.

She chose a morning Tristan was assigned to relieve his father's post at the tallest lookout tower. She left a note there for him, equal parts drama and poetry, wrapped in a scented scarf. She swore he was the only boy she loved, and if he wouldn't douse the fire in her heart, she would quench it with madness and shade in the Ashen Ravine.

Wearing a page boy's uniform over her clothes, she borrowed a pony from the royal stables and eluded the guards at the main gate. She and her mount trotted onto the trail that twisted about the Crystal Lake and ended at the ravine. From his tower, Tristan would be her singular witness. Halfway there, she discarded the page boy's clothes, revealing a diaphanous pink chemise with matching slippers. Placing a circlet of braided white yarrow atop her blond hair, she continued until the ravine's entrance appeared.

She slid from the saddle, surprised when the dark maw of the haunted forest opened to her, having heard rumors of how difficult it was to get within. A chill breeze raked her skin like phantom fingernails, carrying whispered warnings—breathy, hissing inhuman things—and a rotten stench, somewhere between decomposed vegetation and rancid meat.

She almost turned away, but then Tristan called her from behind. She glanced over her shoulder as he rounded the lake on his blood-bay colt. Smugness replaced fear. His lesson would be best learned should she actually step within the looming darkness. Make him face the rumored dangers. Make him earn her affections the way she'd had to earn his.

She left her pony and had no sooner taken one step toward the ravine when a barbed, black vine snapped at her ankle and flopped her to her rump. The thorns dug into her tender flesh, staining her chemise's hem with blood. Scenting the danger, her pony reared and galloped away. Glistenda struggled to breathe as the resulting cloud of dust descended.

She sobbed in unison with Tristan's panicked shout when two more vines struck out, snatching her wrists. Her body went numb as the thorns pumped venom into her veins, rendering her unable to move or scream. The snaky plants dragged her into the ravine.

Her gaze slanted back as the briars formed a curtain over the opening. All that could be seen of the warm sun was a jellylike substance glazing the tree trunks. The light overhead grew hazy, leaving her in a dim, grayish world. The pounding of hooves and Tristan's voice were muffled as he arrived. A loud metallic hammering proved his determination to break through the barrier with his sword. Glistenda wrestled a momentary regret for coming up with such a petty farce.

Her body rolled off the steep, winding path, an unresponsive deadweight as something new dragged her through a shifting carpet of ash. Bits of her hair clung to twigs and tree roots, tangling and ripping from her scalp. Farther and farther grew Tristan's urgent shouts, until she no longer heard him at all.

Glistenda came to a stop in a dark clearing with an impenetrable canopy of leaves overhead. Smoky, black silhouettes slipped in and out of the tree trunks, shifting from humanlike to shapeless blobs. The one constant was their glowing, white eyes. A sob of terror clogged her throat.

"So, a soft, unbroken child has graced us with a visit." A silhouette glided forward, shapelessness resolving to a woman's torso. This one shifted from the color of midnight to a cloudy white as she leaned across Glistenda's paralyzed form. Onyx bones protruded from her face in the form of a beak and horns. "I am Mistress Umbra, mother of the Shroud Collective. We are your ancestors. Those who lost their minds to the promise of darkness and rest centuries ago. You have two choices: become one of us and strengthen our cerebral framework, or offer your flesh for us to consume. Should you not choose, we choose for you." A multitude of phantasmal hands raked across Glistenda's frayed and sullied gown, taking the shape of jagged branches and twigs that ripped the gauzy fabric down the center from neck to waist.

Exposed, Glistenda watched her pulse kick so hard in her chest she thought it would shatter through her sternum. She couldn't speak, couldn't even whimper. Growing impatient, Mistress Umbra clasped her victim's wrist. The pressure made bruises on Glistenda's delicate skin that spread alongside her veins in jagged strands.

The inky lines resembled spiders and scorpions that scuttled beneath her flesh on their way to her chest. She ached to writhe, to escape the creeping plague, but couldn't move.

She was becoming vaporous, her mind slipping in and out of consciousness.

"Enough." A voice of masculine silk broke through her torment. "You've had your jollies. I want her now." A man appeared out of nowhere, his form lithe and ethereal, yet more substantial than the smoky shrouds around her.

"For her *beauty*?" Mistress Umbra asked. "You're so predictable."

His countenance glowed bright beneath a wild blood-red mane and pointed ears. "There's much more to this one. There is great potential for wickedness within that pretty frame."

"Ah, yesss," she hissed his direction. "It's all about entertainment for your kind. Want to see what chaos the girl can wreak?"

A feral smile graced his mouth, showcasing sharp white teeth. "Ours is not to question why. Ours is but to lust, laugh, and lie."

"Always so clever." The multi-handed grasp on Glistenda's wrists and arms grew tighter and the spidery infestation beneath her skin hummed within her rib cage, feeding off her erratic heartbeats. Mistress Umbra chortled, as if she shared the sensation and it tickled her. "You're too late. We captured this gem on our own. She tastes of royalty, and we are keeping her."

The formless silhouettes peering out from behind the trees multiplied, eyes alight and piercing. Glistenda's windpipe tightened with a wail that couldn't break free.

The man opened two giant red feathery wings, stretching them until he loomed tall and threatening over Mistress Umbra's ghoulish subjects. "Do you forget our bargain? I can request mercy for anyone, in return for all the sinful souls I lure into these depths. For all the times my tempting whispers feed your ravenous appetites. Refuse me, and we no longer have a covenant between us."

"But this one is tender-skinned, and so young . . ." the mother shroud half-whimpered, half-snarled. "She can make us remember what it's like to be flesh, before infirmity or death."

"Take only part of her then. Take her conscience. Her capacity for remorse is a small fraction . . . she rarely listens to it. Cage it; gorge yourselves on the sins she commits, so you might indulge in feeling human again. But let the girl go. As you said, she's a princess, but with grand and vile ambitions. That is a rare thing. I'd like to see how it plays out."

Mistress Umbra's beakish mouth drooped. "You know it isn't so easy as that. A choice must be made on her part. Between flesh and death."

"And *you* know that she can choose a third option," the celestial man said. "To forfeit an integral part of her soul, in place of her flesh."

"Ugh. Very well!" Mistress Umbra glared at Glistenda, her eyes beady and prying. "Would you offer it to me, child? Your conscience for your freedom? Should you agree, you will never know true love. One can't love themselves without a conscience by which to measure their own worth. And one who cannot love themselves, cannot be loved."

Glistenda couldn't answer, but she felt Mistress Umbra's gaze drilling into her chest, prying the truth out of her very heart: *Yes. I'll give up anything to live. Love has made my insides as weak as my outsides, something I never want to be again.*

"Very well. Let it be so." The mother shroud rushed her twiggy hands across her once more.

Glistenda's skin returned to corporeal. She gulped a relieved breath. The darkness beneath her flesh rushed from her fingertips like spilled ink. Her arms and legs twitched with feeling. She tensed against a ripping sensation as a flock of emerald shadows burst free from her chest. They screeched and transformed into teal-feathered starlings.

She sat up, at last able to move.

"Know this, little princesss," Mistress Umbra hissed. "We saw your fate unwinding within your veins. You will become powerful and see your grandest hope to fruition. Your role will be essential in returning the heavens to their glorious splendor. But no accomplishment will countervail the love you betrayed." The creature's jagged fingers held out a strand of Glistenda's hair, and it became as black as the shroud's themselves, tinting all the other strands to match. "We have marked you as ours, for you will come again seeking company with us in this forest, seeking a place where you can hide your sins that twist and twine like the branches of a tree. And we will show you the same mercy you practiced throughout your life. No more . . . no lesss."

Seeing the change in her hair, Glistenda worried what her insides must look like. She almost called the birds back—to reclaim that part of her she'd given away. But she didn't want to appear weak.

She waited too long and the formless shrouds—hidden behind the trees— swooped in to capture the starlings in cages of spindly, vaporous hands and fingers. They sank into the ground, becoming one with the ash.

Glistenda took a last look at the man, *the unearthly being*, who'd saved her, then lost consciousness.

When she awoke in her bedchamber, she thought she'd dreamed it all, if not for her ebony hair, lashes, and eyebrows. Even her family couldn't refute those changes. A week later when she was strong enough to go out into the palace garden alone, she saw the winged man again, waiting in a copse of honeysuckle. This time he became flesh, extending his hand to help her sit beside him. A breeze blew his hair around, uncovering the tip of an ear. It was furred and pointed like a fox's.

She learned he was a sylph named Elusion. He had carried her body to the ravine's opening and convinced the briars to open from the inside then hid so Tristan could find her.

She told him that Tristan was the boy she had been trying to win.

"You did all of this to capture someone's heart?" her sylphin companion asked, his orange eyes lit to wildfires as he handed her a flower. "Was it worth it?"

Sniffing the honeysuckle petals, Glistenda shook her head. For although Tristan had wrapped her limp, bruised body in his cape and carried her to the castle on his horse, although he stood vigil with her family as the physician and royal mages cleansed her blood with leeches, then roused her with a magic elixir—he still couldn't offer his love. To him, she was nothing but a prize to be protected and placed upon a shelf.

"I will cut him down one day," Glistenda vowed, shocked and pleased to feel no remorse for the violent thought. "Does he expect me to be nothing but a silent, customary princess forever?"

Elusion smiled—a turn of lips so tempting and beautiful it took her breath. "You are more than customary, and far too remarkable to waste time seeking affections from a man-child."

"It doesn't matter," Glistenda answered, twirling a strand of dark hair around her finger. "I can no longer be loved." She felt a twinge when admitting this, but it was tempered with freedom. Confidence that she would never have to suffer heartbreak or be weak again.

"You didn't crave love to begin with," Elusion answered. "It was power you sought. And as a woman, yours is already immeasurable." He leaned in and cupped her temples to kiss her. His warm, soft mouth tasted of wind, rain, and sunlight, elements that had structured the world since the beginning of time. "Hearts are cursory things. The flame of love fades with age." He whispered this against her neck, nuzzling her. "If you want lasting fire—an ascendancy you can pass down to your offspring—aim for the jugular." He nipped at her throat, a pinch of sharp teeth that titillated. It would leave a bruise. "Choose your men wisely. Wealthy, with marked positions in parliament. Those who will give you leverage in politics and law. Be subtle and decisive. Convince them you're the piece of meat they wish to gorge themselves upon. Then be the gristle that chokes them instead."

She followed Elusion's advice to the letter, changing her name to reflect her *insides* as opposed to her outsides. She dyed several strands of her black hair to bloodred, in honor of her sylph coconspirator. At first her royal parents refused to acknowledge her new identity, but she would only answer to Griselda. Soon they could do nothing but accommodate, attributing her bizarre behavior as a means to cope with whatever horrors she'd encountered in those deep wilds—an experience they had caused with their own negligence. Their penance and guilt were absolute, and they watched helplessly as her heart became as grisly, hostile, and brier-filled as the Ashen Ravine itself, and her mind as cunning as a fox.

Or a sylph . . .

She invited Elusion to her bedchamber where he spent every cessation course for two years, sating his lusts and hers. It was him who led her into the dungeons where he'd found a hidden doorway. Upon sharing the secret to opening it, he coaxed her into a tunnel harboring a small dirt room.

"Some grand enchantress once occupied this place," Elusion told her, motioning to shelves filled with strange and mystical ingredients. He picked up a book entitled *Plebeian's Grimoire*. "There are recipes for potions, spellchants and poisons which combine mystical and natural ingredients that can be used even if one has no inborn magical abilities."

Griselda took the book from his hands, her dark mind concocting all the advantages such a tool could give her.

"I knew you'd be pleased." He smiled. "I have one request. Don't use these things unless I'm here to aid you. There will be hidden curses on the pages, and I wouldn't wish to see you entrap yourself."

Griselda didn't like being told she needed anyone. She used a love potion to capture the Chief Justice of Common Pleas—fifteen years her senior—to increase her standing in the court and secure heirs for the throne, for her brother and his young bride appeared unable to produce one of their own. Elusion left her to her married life until the day her husband died, just after the birth of their youngest daughter.

When Elusion returned, having missed Griselda's bed, she boasted of how she'd used the grimoire without his help.

Those were her golden days. The kingdom fawned over her princesses— only the youngest suffered her easily bruising affliction, and all three were aptly named to be fearsome and formidable, not precious and predictable. Her brother relied upon her, seeking counsel for governing domestic and private affairs.

However, a few months into this blissful new life, Lyra was conceived, shocking and delighting everyone in the kingdom but Griselda. The child's birth would cost her everything she'd murdered, lied, and strategized to gain. Elusion offered to help, but later disappeared when the sylph elm's leaves bled to a brilliant crimson in the garden.

Over the last twelve years, Griselda had wondered upon the synchronicity of the two events. And today, the witch had given confirmation. He was tied to the ground now, paying the price for luring innocent Queen Arael to prick her finger upon the tainted roses . . . for being the seductive voice whispering on the wind in her ear.

Ironic that Arael lived long enough thereafter to give birth to the king's heir: a proper little princess, seen but never speaking, who would soon sit the throne without any effort on her part other than being born—*despite that she was a girl.* All the rules had changed when Kiran spawned a daughter.

That thought shook Griselda from her reverie. She rose from the dungeon cot, refusing to be nostalgic. Elusion chose his path. She didn't force his hand any more than he forced her to commit mariticide. Now she had his wings upon the sylph elm in the garden. She could play that card if necessary, but for the time being, there was work to be done.

She felt her way out of the cell—hands skimming across sticky walls. A powdery grit caked between her fingers and under her nails, and her hem tore from snagging upon the chains in the floor. She gagged to think she would be filthier than Lyra by the time she managed to find the stairs.

After taking the first step, she ascended in a dizzying spiral, her grimy hands leading the way along stones bulging from the retaining wall. Her malicious little niece had snuffed the torches. Every unidentifiable sound reverberated in her pitch-black trek and crept up her spine like icy fingertips plucking an out-of-tune harp.

She'd had the perfect strategy to win the crown for her daughters: dig up Nerezeth's stairway, kill King Orion; then a few days later, stage a counterstrike by supposed "Night Ravagers" on Eldoria's castle in which Lyra would be assassinated. But the witch's confession rendered it impossible.

A peace treaty, signed in blood by both Kiran and Queen Nova, would be undeniable proof that Nerezeth did not order her brother's death. As much as the gloom-dwellers needed sunlight, they wouldn't dare endanger such a beneficial alliance.

Griselda narrowed her eyes, nails scraping the stones until her manicure was in shreds and blood seeped from beneath the broken white tips. She'd managed at last to punish Tristan Nicolet for not loving her. But once again, her brother had fouled her chance for the crown.

Or had he?

Griselda had slipped a precise mixture of wolfsbane, castor plant, and snakeroot into her husband's hunting flask so many years ago. While he was out with his retinue, he became convinced he'd swallowed a hive of bees that broke loose inside his gut, stinging from the inside. Crazed and delirious, he threw himself into a wild stag, bathing its antlers in his blood and entrails. Only Griselda knew that he wasn't crazed; he had been desperate to staunch the intestinal and mental agony she'd thrust upon him with the help of the grimoire.

Within the same book, there was another more elegant recipe with traces of baneberry; the effects made one drowsy and stopped their breath within a matter of hours once they slept. As frail and odd a creature as her niece was, no one would question the grief-stricken Lyra slipping away while she slumbered.

Griselda took the final dark flight of stairs as if floating on air. She arrived at the top where the stairwell opened to a quiet corridor. The drapes had been drawn on every window; blue globes covered the sconces on the walls, softening the candlelight. The cessation course had begun and everyone in the castle was abed.

Her niece's reign of shadows and vermin would end this very day.

She paused to wipe her hands on her skirts upon hearing a scramble of footsteps. Sir Erwan and Sir Bartley appeared from around a corner, breathing heavily. Their expressions tightened upon seeing her.

"We heard there was a prisoner," Erwan, said, straightening from a deep bow. Black hair swung across his wide, tawny forehead. He nudged the strands aside, revealing panic in his deep-set, sharply angled gray eyes.

"And that she had information on King Kiran's final moments," Bartley added, his auburn hair, pink flush, and freckled snub nose reminding Griselda of her late husband.

"The witch escaped and is no longer a concern." She held out her hand so they might both kiss the queen's ring on her finger.

Bartley pressed his mouth to the ruby, then drew back with his brow raised—as if there were more.

"What? Has she been recaptured?" Griselda asked, hoping against hope she hadn't.

Both men shook their heads but exchanged worried glances, their ears blushing to match the crimson sun embroidered upon their white surcoats.

Griselda waved her hand to dismiss their worries. "Yes, she has Sir Nicolet's final memory intact within her. But all she wanted was to return to her home in the ravine. As long as we leave her be, she'll not set foot here again. She has nothing to gain by it. She can do no damage lest she imprints the memory upon someone living in Eldoria."

"Your Grace." Erwan chewed on his puffed-out lower lip. "She already did."

Griselda almost lost her footing. Each knight grabbed a hand and dragged her to the wall to prevent her toppling into the dark stairwell behind.

"A page boy saw a stooped female figure in a hooded cloak corner the constable by the stables," Bartley explained. "She touched either side of his face, as if to kiss him. When the figure left, the page boy swore he spotted horns simmering with white sparks beneath her hood. The constable's face was aglow, as if he'd been struck by lightning. The boy followed him as he found a town crier. The news is traversing from home to home. Soon all of Eldoria will know."

Griselda's blood turned cold. "Will know of our *conspirings*?"

"No." Erwan grasped her elbow gently in comfort. It was far too familiar a gesture to be showcased in public, regardless that the corridor was abandoned. Bristling, Griselda jerked free. His focus shifted to his polished boots. "They know of your niece's role in the kingdom's future, Your Grace. The crier is forecasting the prophecy. Nothing more, but it is enough."

Bartley nodded. "The fear we've instilled by framing the Night Ravagers has been effective indeed, for the commoners were terrorized by thoughts of the battle moving into the village and castle gates. Now people are rising up, insisting the princess is the kingdom's most precious commodity. Lyra is to be protected and revered as such until her coronation, when she comes of age to marry."

Griselda tasted smoke on her tongue as the embers of her newest plan snuffed out. Her niece would be under constant supervision. For *five years*.

Should anything happen to her, accidental or no, Griselda would be held responsible as the kingdom's regent. The prophecy specified Lyra by its very description. And as superstitious as this kingdom was, no one else could fulfill the requirements. Only a silver-haired princess with violet tears . . . with a song in her throat her only sound.

As was the way of such matters, within the week, Nerezeth would use their alternate path into the day realm through the ravine, sending a delegate to publicly address the court's council and assure the pact would be upheld.

"We must call off the attack on Nerezeth," Griselda said. "The soldiers who found Nicolet's body today can attest that the witch was responsible for the murder of Kiran's first knight, and logic will dictate she slayed the king as well. We'll keep close watch on the ravine's borders. Should the witch set one foul foot toward our kingdom, we'll capture and hold her imprisoned in hiding, so she can wreak no more havoc."

Griselda was surprised the prisoner had chosen not to share all that the memory had contained. She suspected the witch had some ulterior motive for harboring the details of her brother's and Sir Nicolet's deaths, but couldn't dwell on it. There were enough things to fret about.

"Then what should we do, Your Grace?"

"We sleep," she answered through gritted teeth, glancing down the empty hall. The stress of the climb from the dungeon and her confrontation with the witch had resulted in memories that weighed heavy on her bones. "On the morrow, I will think of a new plan."

The knights escorted Griselda to the queen's chamber three flights up. She secured the door, shutting out their worried faces. Other than fresh water in the pitcher, the room was just as she'd left it when the two soldiers sent for her earlier: heavy drapes drawn shut; wardrobe door hung askew; jewels, gowns, and goose feathers scattered across the marble floor; broken knickknacks and gimcracks; and most beautifully of all, the scarlet footprints of her daughters where they'd tromped across Lyra's royal heritage.

Griselda took off her jewelry, scrubbed and rinsed the dungeon filth from her skin, changed into her nightclothes, and brushed her hair. Breathing in the scent of jasmine and lavender, she studied the room in the soft blue glow cast by the wall sconces. She'd barred the servants from cleaning while she was away. She had wished to look upon her spoils again.

However, the small red footprints looked more like harbingers of the king's blood Griselda had spilled, the same blood that pulsed through Lyra's veins . . . the one thing standing between Griselda and her greatest victory. Sighing, she pulled back the covers to attempt sleep, curious if the mattress had been stuffed with lamb's wool as she'd commanded. She would have the chamberlain's head if it hadn't.

Then she saw them: tiny, eight-legged, creeping things set loose in her bed. *Infestation.*

A scream burned inside her. She stumbled backward, almost bumping into the wardrobe. The hanging door flung open from within, and moths swooped out. Griselda ducked left and right, wracked with revulsion.

There in the wardrobe, in the moths' wake, stood Lyra, commanding it all. With one arm, the princess hugged the potted rose. With the other, she pointed to the chamber door, a demand for Griselda to leave.

She was claiming Queen Arael's room and possessions as her own.

Griselda moaned and moved toward the entrance, dodging the flying and scrabbling bugs. She opened the door and tottered backward from the room. She stalled in the empty hallway, staring at the whirlwind of moths and shadows. Their gusts and wings formed a strange rustling whisper, unmistakable in its message: *Not . . . my . . . mother.*

Lyra's hair rippled in the downdraft like a cascading silvery waterfall, and her plump, frosty lips pressed to a scowl. Her eyes flashed amber-bright in triumph as her obedient shadows rushed to slam the door in Griselda's face.

Loose tendrils of Griselda's own hair flapped about her temples and cheeks. She trembled, leaning against the door to trace the ruby knob, even as her frown lifted to a sneer.

The little princess had grown a spine. Griselda was almost impressed, but—even more—pitied the irony. For a spine served small purpose to a corpse.

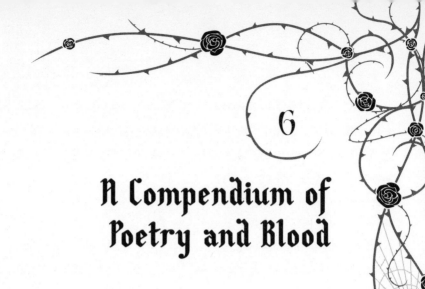

6

A Compendium of
Poetry and Blood

Over the next week, Lyra's subjects abandoned superstition and welcomed her with open arms. It was a feeling she'd never experienced, and one that at times overwhelmed. All of the castle's servants, even those who had once been strangers, rallied around her, devoted to her comfort. Not a curtain anywhere was left open. Even the east, west, and south sides lingered in perpetual darkness, brightened only by the harmless glow of candlelight. New glass panels were crafted for the tower windows, tinted with blue dye. When a cloudy sky presented itself, drapes were opened so Lyra could look out safely upon her muted kingdom.

Joyful shouts arose as Lyra peered from behind the curtains of the dormer window in the southern tower's turret, high enough to be seen by the commoners. She looked down at the sea of waving hands, caught a breath, and jerked back into hiding. In her childhood, the one time she reached a finger toward a window, she'd been scalded by the sun. Those who stood in the light had always been separate from her. That had changed with her betrothal to the night prince, Nerezeth's evening star.

Lyra tried to picture Prince Vesper with only the prophecy to go by: a starboy forged of sunlight. It was breathtaking to imagine—golden rays gleaming from his eyes . . . his flesh and hair as dazzling-bright as the sun glinting off water like in the paintings that decked the castle's halls and corridors.

She would barely even be able to look upon him, much less touch him. Despite how she might long to, for in her most secret heart, she had never stopped loving the sun, even though it hated her.

A few weeks into this new life, Mia arrived one morning to awaken the princess. The maid removed the blue globes from the candles to brighten the room, then prodded Lyra's feet gently, as was her ritual, in memory of how Matilde used to tickle her toes with goose feathers. Lyra awoke with a smile that flitted away as quickly as the moths darted toward the rising flames on the wicks. Mia had settled at the wardrobe to pull out Queen Arael's dresses.

Lyra threw off her covers to stand, her feet chilly on the marble floor. Mia glanced across her shoulder as she folded a velvet gown. The princess shrugged—an unspoken query.

"Something astonishing 'as happened." Mia's face beamed with happiness. "The townspeople . . . they're changing. Oh, how 'is majesty your father would've loved to see it." Her round, full cheeks flushed. "The children of the kingdom are pretending to be made of moonlight. The girls are coating their hair with the silt that oozes beneath the silvery pebbles along the banks of the Crystal Lake . . . slopping their brows and lips with cream made of crushed periwinkle pearls. Some are even using 'oney to glue molted goose feathers upon their eyelids as lashes. And they're playing games with their brothers in the root cellars, commanding shadows by waving candles in the air and casting silhouettes along the walls." She chortled deep in her chest. "Wouldn't be surprised if they trade their pet cats and dogs for sparrows. They're all imitating birdsongs, in 'opes to sound like you—though none could ever capture the purity of your voice." Mia winked.

Lyra's cheerful friend pulled out a damask gown. The princess's eyebrows drew tight in question again as she pointed to the folded clothes piling up next to Mia's feet, still confused about what this had to do with her mother's things.

"Oh, this." Mia sighed—a relieved sound. "I will only take out a few and store them safely away. But I must make room. You're about to receive a new wardrobe. We all are! The clothiers are scrambling to meet demands for tunics, gowns, chemises, and corsets in lightweight fabrics like yours. The deeper hues are being cast out for shades of blush and pastel. They say it better pays 'omage to the blooms of spring and summer."

Lyra fashioned part of her hair into a hasty side braid—the symbol for her aunt Griselda that she'd been using for years with her father and Mia.

Mia laughed again. "Ah, well, 'ere was the grand regent's reaction . . ." She stuck her nose in the air and flapped about the room, holding an outdated gown in front of her. "*Tsk.* I simply cannot understand why it took everyone so long." Mia parodied Griselda's commanding voice and snooty mannerisms to perfection. "I've always said Lyra's ensembles are breezier than the weighty velvets and brocades of the past. This kingdom would run so much smoother if everyone listened to meeeeee!"

Lyra slapped a hand across her mouth, but not fast enough to stifle a bubble of musical laughter. Mia placed one of Arael's ruby rings to hang loosely on Lyra's thumb. "You see, my little delight, you've given the kingdom a reason to be curious. A reason to wonder upon what we've been missing all these centuries. You're paving the way for your night prince to bring back the moon to our skies. Come five more years, and they'll be laying out white-gold bricks for his feet to trod upon when he comes to claim your hand."

Lyra winced. She returned her mother's ring to its satin-lined box, her fingers yet too small for such precious gems. She knew little about marriage. Both her father and aunt had lost their spouses early. But she'd read enough romantic poems to know that courting involved the touching of lips and hands and fingertips. Skin pressed to skin. To be bound to a man as bright as the sun would mean a life of excruciating pain.

Should it come to that, she would choose to suffer the agony of his sunlit touch. She'd had enough of loneliness in her past to know she didn't want it in her future.

Mia released the princess's hand and began folding clothes again. Lyra reached over to help her smooth out the wrinkles in the heavy fabrics, though she couldn't straighten the crimp in her forehead.

"I know what you fear," Mia said, her intuitive, dark eyes tender in the candle glow. "But perhaps the prophecy isn't literal on the prince's end. Though your part is, undeniably."

Lyra hadn't tried to hide her new friendship with the night creatures. The curtains always being drawn enabled her shadow attendants to accompany her everywhere, even during court sessions, meals, and the occasional formal banquet or ball. People accepted the strange sight—for this was the prophecy. However, Lyra didn't miss the uneasy side glances when her shadows rose tall and spindly from the corners, so she kept them shrunken small; she wanted her human subjects to be comfortable with her, too.

She also kept her creeper bugs well hidden. Since they feared getting trampled, following Lyra's new daily routines with people frightened them. Also, Griselda turned into a mass of quivering bones at the sight of any night creatures, so having them guarding the queen's chamber was the best way to keep her mother's things safe.

Lyra had yet to show anyone else, even Mia, how her pets could be used as a mouthpiece when in the room with her. It was something she kept secret between herself and Griselda, to shock and command attention once more should the day ever prove necessary. After all, Lyra wanted to honor her father by being a great ruler—like him and her mother. She needed power for that, and her odd attendants offered this. But there was more to being a majesty than power; she needed to learn how to make day-to-day decisions for the kingdom and was invited into council by Prime Minister Albous to learn.

"Sit here, little majesty." The minster directed her to a long oval table in the library late one afternoon. Only a few scholarly types occupied the room, and they were busy looking at books of their own. None of the council attended this meeting.

Lyra pointed to the empty seats at the candlelit table, indicating their missing council members.

"Today it will be just the two of us. I aim to teach you to speak, and don't want you feeling pressured by an audience." The minister's ebony complexion reminded her of Sir Nicolet. The biggest difference between them were their eyes. Albous's were a glittering green that sparkled when he was teaching Lyra, as though he gleaned as much enjoyment from giving lessons as Lyra did in the taking.

Lyra sat and her shadows mimicked her movements before settling around her. Several of the scholars in the room balked, but Prime Minister Albous didn't even flinch. She appreciated his effort. It made her feel less different. But she *was* different, undeniably, and she pointed to her throat to remind her teacher of that.

A bright smile lit his face. "I'm aware of your voice. It's a miracle, and a lovely one at that. No need to think of it as a hindrance. You're going to speak with a part of yourself you'd already been using with your father." As if catching the sadness that flashed across her face, the prime minister took one of her hands in his. He shaped three of her pale fingers into a curve, then showed her how to sweep her hand upward in a gesture that ended with her pinky held high. "King Kiran. That's how you say his name. He had me seeking a way for you to communicate visually, with your hands, for some years now. A special language I could teach everyone on the council to understand." Lyra's jaw dropped as he unrolled several ancient scrolls. Each had hand signals sketched upon them, with words or singular letters written out underneath. "I found these a week before he left for Nerezeth. You were to learn them together upon his return. Will you let me teach you now? The council can join our lessons, once you're comfortable in the speaking."

Lyra's face flushed warm, as hope overflowed within her. With this, she could communicate, truly have conversations . . . speak her mind! She nodded enthusiastically.

"Just the relish for learning I like to see, little majesty." The prime minister's smile widened, and together, they began.

Lyra practiced every day. During cessation courses, if she had trouble sleeping, she'd pull out a poetry tome and use her signals to spell out the verses. It was lovely, as though her hands and fingers were waltzing with the beautiful words. She caught on quickly, and with the prime minister's help, her vocabulary and understanding of politics also grew. One day she would take Griselda's place, presiding over the domestic life and squabbles of the people within her keep, using sign language and the written word to arbitrate.

Lyra wondered if this caused her aunt any jealousy. If so, Griselda hid it well, never once calling herself Lyra's mother again . . . ever treating her as an equal. Yet Lyra dared not lower her guard. Her scalp still remembered the hair-wrenching tugs in the dungeon, just as the cryptic conversation between the witch and her aunt still haunted her.

Lyra couldn't quite tie the pieces together, but she suspected Griselda knew more about her father's and Sir Nicolet's deaths than she let on. Lyra wasn't convinced the witch was wholly responsible, despite what the soldiers insisted.

However, her skepticism about the witch's guilt shattered when murder once again darkened the candlelit halls of the castle, a few months after her father's own.

It had become routine for Lyra and her three cousins to sit together in the solar at teatime. Curtains drawn tight, they practiced embroidery and beading, surrounded by the scent of melting candle wax, the steam of tea and fruit pies, and the songs of chickadees caged in the corner.

In Eldoria, it was tradition for the royal bridesmaids—any girls related to the bride—to sew the veil, gloves, and headdress for their queen's wedding. Griselda had already been teaching her daughters the skill, and now she insisted on Lyra sitting in to supervise.

In the past, Eldoria's royal brides wore crimson velvet trimmed in gold ruffles, but in keeping with the new style, Griselda substituted a blush-pink organza with cream lace to flatter Lyra's complexion and small frame. The girls were learning to sew on scraps of the thin, slippery fabric before tackling the real project. Each afternoon, once they were settled, her aunt occupied herself elsewhere; all four girls would await Griselda's exit, needle and thread in hand, impatient to share newly learned tidbits of kingdom gossip. That afternoon was no different.

"You'll wish to hear this, Lyra . . ." Avaricette paused to guide her threaded needle through one of the creamy pearls that filled the porcelain bowl on the table between them. "It concerns your betrothed." She looked up and her brown eyes sparkled with something akin to malice.

Lyra's skin bristled. Sensing her unease, the shadows crept closer. Mentally, Lyra commanded them back to the corners. She coaxed a pearl onto her own needle and tacked it in place on a swatch of organza, for she refused to simply supervise. She wanted to be a part of her own wedding preparations, not a bystander. Gritting her teeth, she waited for her eldest cousin to continue.

Avaricette smiled sweetly, though her gaze flitted to her middle sister. Judging by the smirk on Wrathalyne's face, she already knew what Avaricette had to share. "I overhead Sir Bartley speaking to Mother. He saw Prince Vesper with his own eyes, months ago, when he accompanied King Kiran to Nerezeth. You've been wishing to know what he looks like?"

Lyra nodded again, her fascination with the prince a welcome distraction from the slash of agony that gored her chest at the mention of her father.

"Sir Bartley said he's all that a prince should be. Striking and regal. Tall and bronzed, with hair the color of a raven's wings. He looks more like your parents than you, which means the kingdom should have no trouble accepting him." The insinuation of Lyra's hard-won reception among her own people hung in the air between them. "And I'm sure everyone will be relieved that the royal portraits can once again have some tincture." Avaricette's lips twitched on a sneer.

Wrathalyne snorted. "Why, if the painter uses a background of duck-egg blue, Lyra will blend in and everyone else in the portraits will be positively *kaleidomatic!*" Completely unaware that mixing up kaleidoscopic and prismatic made her sound like a buffoon, Wrathalyne beamed.

Avaricette barked out an unladylike guffaw and Wrathalyne joined in—oblivious that the joke was partly on her. Their combined laughter shook the bowl until the pearls rattled.

Lyra's cheeks warmed. She didn't like to blush. Each time she did, the veins behind her diaphanous skin grew darker, more prominent—making her look even closer to an apparition. She had just learned that her betrothed wasn't literally made of the sun, which meant she had nothing to fear physically from him. This would have offered relief had she not been left to question if her kingdom would flock to him as their leader and leave her an outcast once more.

Her two hysterical cousins flopped on the floor. Lyra allowed the shadows to stretch along the walls, closing in. The chickadees fluttered nervously in their cage. Lyra would've tried to settle them, but only night creatures seemed to understand her . . . to respond to her. She focused instead on her laughing cousins.

Prime Minister Albous often spoke of how her father chose mercy over wrath unless the kingdom or a loved one was in danger. That was why he never went to battle with Nerezeth until he feared for Lyra's welfare. Just as Lyra had only confronted Griselda when her aunt endangered her mother's memory.

Wrathalyne and Avaricette were already endangering themselves by writhing so precariously close to the wheeled tea cart. After so many years of taunting, Lyra debated: why resist acting when all it would take was a wayfaring shadowy gust to overturn the steaming brew onto their heads?

Placing her sewing on the table, Lyra started to rise. A hand on her elbow stalled her. Lustacia had left her own seat and knelt by her chair. She was the only cousin not laughing. Lately, it was Lustacia who walked with Lyra in the dim corridors instead of going into the sunlit gardens or aviary where the princess couldn't follow; it was Lustacia who patiently attended as Lyra practiced her gestures with the prime minister, although she didn't quite understand the sign language.

"Lyra, wait, please." Lustacia's eyes, shaded a deeper blue by her thick lashes, squeezed Lyra's arm.

The physical contact stunned her. None of her cousins had ever touched her, as if they feared she might be contagious. It struck her as so unnatural, she almost jerked free, but the promise of camaraderie melted her back into her chair. With just a thought, she sent her shadows sinking into their corners.

Lustacia patted Lyra's elbow and released her. "That's better. Don't let these ninnies bait you. They're blinded by jealousy. Neither one will ever marry a prince. Truthfully, they're both so vapid, why would any man want them?" Lustacia's older sisters silenced and glared at her between gasps for air, faces flushed from laughter. "Ava has eaten so many sweets her personality is rotting along with her teeth. And Wrath, well, if she would only read that lexicon of words from your mother's room, she'd save herself a lifetime's worth of tantrums because she wouldn't look so *idiosensical* all the time."

Both girls sputtered, as if unable to make their mouths work.

"If you two are so bored you can think of nothing to do but be nasty," Lustacia said, standing, "I can offer an option." Not missing a beat, she dumped the bowl of pearls atop their perfectly coiffed hair.

"How dare you!" Avaricette screeched, shaking her head so the beads fell from her curls and tapped the floor like petrified raindrops.

"I'll tell Mother!" shouted Wrathalyne, spitting out three pearls that had dropped into her mouth—opened wide on a gasp during the dumping.

"Oh, *will* you?" Lustacia asked, leaning across the table. "Or will I tell Mother how you offended our future queen? We're all that's left of the royal family. We're to be kind and support one another now." She then pointed to the pearls careening across the room, some vanishing beneath the chaise lounge and others behind the harp and a collection of instruments propped against the walls. "Pick up the mess."

Avaricette and Wrathalyne snarled as they knelt, cushioned by the multiple ruffles on their silky dresses, and gathered the beads, returning them to the bowl with tiny *clacks*. Lustacia scooted her chair closer to Lyra's, putting her sisters out of earshot on the other side of the solar, where they were united in their efforts to gather pearls from beneath the chaise lounge.

Lyra smiled a thank-you.

"You're welcome," her cousin answered, as if she'd been deciphering Lyra's expressions all her life. "There's actually been some lovely news. I heard it from Mother myself."

Lyra cocked her head, half-curious, half-wary. She often rode this pendulum, swinging between trusting people and her own cautious nature.

"The midnight shadows and stardust have arrived from Nerezeth." Lustacia picked up her organza swatch and resumed her vine embroidery. She was careful to use a thimble today, having bruised her thumb the week prior while pushing a needle through the fabric. "The enchanted seamstresses will begin construction of the nightsky fabric in a few days. There's enough to make an entire suit, so you'll soon accompany us outside the castle!" She paused and her lashes lowered. "And . . . the prince sent a note for you." She dipped her fingers into the lacy cuff at her wrist and dragged out a black vellum cylinder.

"Mother intended to save it for when you're older, but I slipped it away while she wasn't looking. I'll need it back, so she won't know."

Lyra nodded and took the soft, pliable cylinder; it appeared they used calfskin vellum like the scrolls from which Prime Minister Albous taught her the ancient sign language. Though theirs was dyed black. As she unrolled it to read, she smelled a leathery scent and something cool and crisp, like the taste of winter she used to experience each time she held her mother's panacea rose. Nostalgia tickled her nose. She glanced up to ensure her other two cousins were still preoccupied, then spread it open on her lap with the table's edge covering it for protection.

The gold ink stood bright against the dark vellum and called to her. She traced the slanting, elegant script—her fingertip held just above it. The ink moved. It seemed drawn to her, drifting upward across her skin in tiny glittery particles like dust motes swirling in dim light, as if rays of tender sunshine lived in each line. Lyra swallowed a surprised gasp and looked up at Lustacia, but her cousin was watching her sisters with a keen eye, motioning them farther across the room for some beads they'd missed when they moved too close.

The sparkles stung Lyra's fingers with heat—not uncomfortable but intrusive—as if wanting to fill her up. Disoriented by the sensation, she withdrew her hand and the ink fell back into place on the vellum in a dusting of gold, then blended again into words.

Shaking her head, Lyra caught a breath. She kept her hands at her side this time and concentrated only on the message.

Dear Princess Lyra,

> *Minutes ago, I watched our night sky flash with that
> fleeting glimpse of dawn. For one instant, I was in your*

world beside you. The colors swirled in a riot of violet, lilac, and silver, much like your hair and tears. I've yet to see your face, but I know your song. It lights my imaginings with the same wonder each flash of daybreak brings. I've heard what your kingdom thinks of mine, but do not let them make you fear our future. I will keep you safe. And know this: there is beauty here, too. True, we have no trilling mockingbirds, blue jays, swallows, or thrushes. What would they celebrate, without the sun for inspiration? Yet we have symphonies of our own. Crickets, nightingales, owls, and wolves who laud the glory of our snow-swept moon. Even the tinder-bats rejoice with a melody unique to the night. Upon your seventeenth year, I will bring you to Nerezeth to share all of this. Until then, I will keep you ensconced in shadows and stardust chosen by my own hand, so you might know the splendor and comfort of your daylight world within the safety of darkness, and so you might trust the scope of my devotion. Think of me each time you see the dusting of dusk, as I will think of you at each blink of dawn.

Yours in both night and day,

Prince Vesper

Lyra's pulse sped to a dizzying staccato, her skin flushing warm, but this time it had nothing to do with intrusive sparkles of ink. She'd never read such pretty words given so openly from the heart—at least not directed to her. Her hands covered her cheeks to hide the veins that must be glaring through her sheer skin. She wanted to answer the letter with one of her own, but Griselda would never allow it.

Lustacia retrieved the vellum and rolled it closed without making a sound. As she did, Lyra noticed the ink didn't respond to her cousin as it had with her. She raked a palm across the blank side to test it once more. The script lit up, showing through backward from the front. For an instant, the tips of Lyra's fingers glowed gold in response, as if the light she'd absorbed earlier remembered its source.

"I hope you don't mind, but I looked over Mother's shoulder as she read the missive earlier." Lustacia held her attention firmly on Lyra's face as she tucked the cylinder away in her cuff. "Isn't it wonderful? He's overseeing all your supplies!"

Lyra opened her palm, too preoccupied with her skin's odd reaction to the ink to care that her aunt and cousin had read her note before her. The glowing at her fingertips had vanished and Lustacia seemed unaware it was ever there. Could Lyra have imagined it? Perhaps she had been swept away to a world of make-believe and wishes upon reading the prince's poetic sentiments.

"I see you're as enchanted as I am," Lustacia said under her breath, a dreamy smile softening her features. "The prince's own hands gathered and wrapped the pieces that will form your shield from the sun. Only fifteen, and already he's making romantic gestures. Can you imagine what he'll be like as a grown man . . . as a husband? As your king?"

Romantic. Lyra had no real concept of such a thing. But kindness? That she knew. She had yearned for so long to step outside one day . . . to breathe the summer air and look up at the swans as they blended into the clouds with their matching feathers; to watch frogs and fish flop in and out of the Crystal Lake and catch a spray of cool water upon her face through her hood; to gather the silvery pebbles that littered the banks and nestle them within satin-lined boxes, for those were worth more than all the jewels and gems within the kingdom's treasury. Now, at last, this could be a reality—at the prince's very hands.

Hope of such a day was the reason her father had insisted on the supply of materials for nightsky fabric in the peace treaty. Even with him gone he was taking care of her—helping her belong—and it appeared the prince shared her father's compassion.

The resulting happy swell in her chest reminded her of Eldoria's end of the bargain, and how Nerezeth needed the panacea roses for medicines. She'd given up her mother's keepsake to be planted atop their iron stairway. She needed to know it had been worth the sacrifice.

Lyra gathered her organza scrap into spiraling folds to mimic petals and held it out to her cousin, a question in her raised brow.

Lustacia knotted off her thread and snipped it free of her embroidery. She studied Lyra's upheld hand, then her eyes widened. "Oh, yes, the roses. They are doing well. There are enough buds that I could bring you back a clipping of your own to fill your mother's pot again. Should I?"

Lyra nodded enthusiastically, then frowned, worried for her cousin's welfare. She took her needle and demonstrated being pricked in the finger.

"Oh, don't worry for the thorns. I'll wear my heaviest gloves."

Lyra considered that, then gestured to the doorway where a guard was stationed in the hall. It was forbidden for Eldorians to clip any of the buds. Only Nerezeth was approved to harvest the bounty.

Lustacia bowed her head close, her whisper scented of pears and cinnamon from the tea. "One small stalk won't be missed. I can be as quiet as your shadows, you'll see. I'll wrap my hair and disguise myself as a page boy. During the cessation course, the guards play dice and drink ale while everyone sleeps. They hardly pay attention to anything but the steins and money trading hands." She tossed a sidelong glance at her sisters who were on their way back to the table. "We'll keep it secret, between us."

Wrathalyne and Avaricette arrived thereafter, bowl of beads in hand, and took their seats. Soon, talk fell to courtly gossip once more.

The rest of the day passed without event, but during the cessation course, thoughts of Lustacia's promise kept Lyra awake. She twisted in bed until the moths abandoned their perches and fluttered around her face and ears, their shushing wings lulling her to sleep.

In her dreamscape, she visited the night realm where shadows lifted her into the air to meet her betrothed—the faceless Prince Vesper; a liquid song sluiced through her vocal cords in greeting, and glistening gold ink bled from his fingertips. Inspired by her melody, he wrote out every note, scripting a musical composition in strands of sunlight across the black sky. And the sun and the moon danced in harmony.

Lyra shot up out of her slumber, awakened by screams and loud sobs. She crept into the bluish glow of the corridor in nothing but her nightgown. Griselda's two knights, several guards, and a handful of servants gathered around a sobbing heap on the floor. Wrathalyne and Avaricette were there, too, drowsy-faced and on their knees, trying to console their mother who curled, fetal position, around a scarf that belonged to Lustacia—now ripped to shreds and stained with blood. Griselda convulsed and vomited. The resulting sour-acid stench overpowered the melting wax from the candelabra by Lyra's doorway.

The servants whispered, questioning why Lustacia would've wandered so far from the castle gates; why a panacea rose was found alongside a page boy's bloodied cap and her scarf by the entrance to the Ashen Ravine, yet all the page boys of the castle were accounted for, asleep in their quarters.

"There must have been a conjurin' of some dark force. Seduced the girl through her dreams," said one.

"Lured her to sneak out in costume and pick flowers? What's to become of us, if our minds are prey to such bewitchments? The ravine might still be hungry. We could all be dragged into the serpentine briars by morning," answered another.

None of the guards had witnessed anything, and Lustacia's remains and clothes had not been found, other than a clump of her lustrous auburn hair—matted and muddy—alongside the harrower witch's skeletal staff.

Lyra's eyes burned. She wanted to step forward and help comfort, but she didn't belong . . . and worse, she was to blame. Not only had she freed the witch from the dungeon months ago, but Lustacia had left on a favor for her.

Backing into her room on shaky legs, Lyra shut the door and crawled into the wardrobe. She sealed herself in, letting the darkness cradle her. Her chest constricted as she envisioned her cousin's softly freckled skin, contused with bite marks and thorns, torn to shreds like the bloodied scarf they'd found. Lyra's sobs escalated to wails—a birdsong muffled by one of her mother's remaining gowns wrapped around her head and stuffed in her mouth.

After her tongue grew dry against the fabric and she was all sung out, she hunched in quiet despair—chest and lungs sore and hollow.

Mia opened the wardrobe some time later.

"Oh, Princess!" The lady's maid loosened Lyra from her tangle of velvet. "You gave us such a start! We couldn't find you, and after what happened to Lustacia . . ." She bit her lip, as if unsure how much Lyra knew.

Lyra's violet-stained cheeks must have given her away, for Mia opened her arms so the princess could fall against her ample bosom—a comforting cushion scented of talcum and clean cotton.

"There, there, child." Mia stroked Lyra's frazzled hair. "You're going to be safe. Regent Griselda will see to that. If any good could've come of this tragedy, it's that your aunt's eyes 'ave been opened to how precious you are to us all. Let's pack your things. You're moving to the dungeon."

7

Milk, Toast, and Unfortunate Ghosts

To most princesses, dungeons were cold, formidable places. Lyra, however, had already found solace and succor amid the shadows and vermin there. Still, with her heart aching over the recent loss of her father, Sir Nicolet, and now her cousin, she felt more alone than ever. The anticipation of being shut away felt like punishment instead of protection.

Lyra hadn't told anyone why Lustacia left the castle, but did Griselda somehow know? Was this her aunt's vengeance . . . to lock up her niece and ensure she'd be forgotten by everyone in her kingdom?

The morning following Lustacia's bloody disappearance, Lady Griselda gathered Wrathalyne, Avaricette, and Lyra on the dais in the grand hall. They were each adorned in solemn navy-and-mulberry gowns to signify their grief—Lyra's borrowed from her dead cousin's wardrobe, for she had no such styles herself. The council, a crowd of subjects, and all of the servants filed in to listen.

"This was not the random act of some magical beast wandering out of the ravine and past the vicinage's borders," Griselda began, swishing the long train of her silk gown as she scanned those in the room. "The creature who lured my daughter away was the wild witch we'd held imprisoned. We have proof." She held up the skeletal staff and half the audience exclaimed in fright.

Lyra swallowed the knot in her throat. Surely Griselda would blame her for the witch's escape, here and now. The weight of everyone's stares doubled her guilt and she kept her gaze averted to the white marble at her feet where her faithful shadows waited, mirroring her movements.

Her aunt continued without turning her direction. "The witch has a proven vendetta against Eldoria's royalty. She killed my lord brother, our king, then ate the heart of his dearest friend and most loyal knight, Sir Nicolet. Now she's taken my precious Lusta—" Griselda's voice caught and she dropped the staff with a *clack* that echoed through the halls. She wavered.

Worried her aunt might be sick again, Lyra instinctively stepped forward, but retreated upon remembering how Griselda always bristled at her touch. One of the knights, Sir Erwan, moved forward to offer his elbow as a brace. Griselda took it, tears streaming her pale cheeks in the candle's glow.

Lyra watched, sharing in her sorrow . . . seeing her aunt in a new light. Griselda could have pointed out to everyone that Lyra set the witch loose. Yet she didn't.

Griselda took a trembling breath and continued. "As some of you know, the nightsky materials have gone missing as well."

Several gasps bounced around the dim room, Lyra's included. This was the first she'd heard of thievery. The fact that the articles Prince Vesper took such care in sending were now gone affected her over anyone else, an obvious strike against her personally.

Positioned behind her aunt's skirts and beside her two sniffling cousins, Lyra shut her eyes so her tears would not stain the white lace collar on the borrowed dress. Knowing Lustacia would never again wear it put things in perspective—how foolish to be sad for lost materials. At least she still had her life.

"It's obvious that the witch is not working alone," Griselda continued, though her voice wavered. "A dark spy haunts these halls. We must hide our future queen." With this, she reached behind to guide Lyra forward and gently placed a hand on her head—so different from the last time she had touched her hair. "To assure she lives to the age of coronation, and that she fulfills the prophecy and treaty as the bride of Nerezeth's prince, she must be secreted away to the dungeon out of the sun's reach and protected from unseen enemies. No one can be trusted to abide with her other than family." She motioned to her daughters and herself. "The two knights who were guarding my bedchamber when Lustacia disappeared are the only subjects with an alibi I can corroborate. With this in mind, Sir Erwan and Sir Bartley will exclusively guard our door. They alone will deliver our meals, see to any personal requests or needs, and transport our laundry to and from the washerwomen. Once Nerezeth sends more materials for a nightsky suit, our knights will accompany us around the walled garden for daily constitutionals."

Prime Minister Albous stepped forward, his green eyes narrowed in a way that spoke of deep introspection. "The princess must continue her training with me and the council. She's become quite proficient in the art of signing, but there's so much more to politics and carrying a kingdom than simple communication. How's she to learn diplomacy and the administration of justice, locked away with only her family?"

Griselda's body tensed, but to Lyra's shock, she responded with an even tone. "Princess Lyra and I will correspond with both parliament and council via letters, so we might carry out our judicial and royal duties. She will still have her hand in politics and learn diplomacy, deciding the proper action upon facts presented. I'll brook no argument. Her safety is of upmost importance. The livelihood of our kingdom, the very balance of our skies, depends on it. Thus, the four of us will remain in sanctuary until the witch and her spy are captured and imprisoned. Even if it takes the next five years."

Among a burst of murmured concerns, Griselda clasped Lyra's fingers without even cringing, surprising her for a third time. With her free hand, Griselda guided Wrathalyne, who clung to Avaricette. United, they descended the dais and headed to the door with their appointed knights flanking them. The silent pilgrimage of Lyra's bugs followed, too, hidden behind the walls.

Her shadows swept alongside her feet, stretching and shrinking as passing candles dictated. She cast a final look at the council members and servants—familiar as they had become—stopping on the prime minister. Her heart ached already with the loss of their time together, and even more to see that he'd been left as speechless as she had ever been.

The rest of the morning, amidst a whirlwind of preparations, Lyra watched items being carried to the largest cell in the farthest corner of the dungeon: family portraits, tapestries, books, writing and sewing appurtenances, furniture, a large trunk stuffed with clothing (including Queen Arael's remaining gowns), bed linens, dried spices, and potpourri soaps. There was also a hip bath, chamber pot, and a wrought-iron box fireplace, for their hygiene and comfort.

Two hours before the kingdom retired for the cessation course, she descended the twining stairs alongside her family to enter their new abode for the first time.

Bright tapestries—scented with spices—draped the walls from top to bottom, deftly arranged to conceal cold stones while masking the stench. A long golden cord hung from the ceiling, connecting them. Griselda's knights had been in charge of this arrangement before the cell was furnished. They explained if the cord was pulled, the tapestries would peel free to simplify cleaning.

Two oversized canopied beds with wool-stuffed mattresses sat against one wall, their white lace curtains so ethereal and gauzy they could have been fragments of clouds held open with red ribbon ties. The trunk, brimming with linens and supplies, sat at the foot of the largest bed. At the foot of the smallest was a long, pine box with a latched lid to be used for any soiled clothes and bedsheets the knights would need to carry out for washing.

A small dining table with four padded chairs and the fireplace—complete with a shiny copper chimney that connected to a freshly drilled damper for filtering smoke from the room—replaced the cot and torture devices which had once been the only furnishings. Soft candlelight flickered in lanterns secured on tall stands. The flames reflected off a long mirror—strung up to spin from the ceiling's center—creating a luminary effect across the walls, a safe alternative to windows.

Then came the final changes that transformed the cell to something like a cottage in a fairy tale. Freshly cut honeysuckle vines, to be replaced each day, spilled out of large vases. Standing birdcages housed chickadees, mocking-birds, and swallows. The nectarous scent and lyrical chirps filled the room with the illusion of the outdoors.

Against the surreal sensations tapping her spine, Lyra stepped within. Her slippers trounced lightly upon brightly woven rugs and bearskin throws, in direct opposition to the weighted hesitation in her heart. As opulent as everything was, it was still only one room to be shared with the aunt and two cousins who were once so cruel. Was this truly where they would live for the next five years if the witch and her spy weren't captured? At the end of it all, would Lyra's kingdom even need her anymore?

Exhausted from weeping all day, Wrathalyne and Avaricette tottered over to a bed and belly flopped atop fluffy quilts.

A few servants remained, rearranging and straightening until Griselda commanded they leave. Mia strayed over to a corner where the royal family portraits had been set in a pile. Lyra's aunt insisted they be carried down, every last likeness of Lyra and of her parents, so she mightn't forget them over time. Griselda had even insisted on bringing Queen Arael's broken mirror, so painstakingly glued back together by Lyra's father before he left for Nerezeth.

"Could I 'ang these, or find a spot for the mirror, Lady Griselda?" Mia asked.

"No. We'll need something to do to pass the hours," Griselda answered while wrestling the dustrag from the maid's hand. "Time you go."

Mia tried once more to plead her fealty. "I've served the little princess all 'er life. Might I come once a day at least? In the evenings, for baths, or to read stories and poetry. I made a lifelong commitment to serve Eldoria's monarchy, your ladyship."

Griselda's expression transformed from weary to shrewd. "If you wish to continue to serve, you may be our food taster. You're obviously very practiced." She squeezed Mia's plump forearm and led her to the door. There, the knights waited on the edge of the threshold, having already sent the other servants through the long stone corridor and up the winding stairs back to the castle.

"In a time like this," Griselda added, "meals are perilous undertakings. We are defenseless to the cook and kitchen hands. Prove yourself courageous and loyal by sampling our food, and in time I'll trust you enough to allow your service within our sanctuary." She gave Mia a push, breaking the eye contact the lady's maid had been keeping with Lyra.

The door slammed shut with a thunderous echo of latches and bolts. The metallic cacophony vibrated through the floor, then up Lyra's legs and all the way to her chest. It stopped there and snapped into place, as if the cage of her ribs locked around her heart.

With the knights stationed outside, utter silence fell over the room; even the birds hushed, leaving only the flutter of their feathers, the pop of the lanterns, and the soft whimpers of Lyra's grieving cousins.

Griselda and Lyra watched one another, reflections of candleflame spinning around them in a dizzying sequence. Her aunt's lip curled up, revealing teeth clenched in a wretched smile. It was that same expression that clutched at Lyra's heart on the day of her father's interment.

Her aunt had not forgiven her for releasing the witch who killed her daughter. Not at all.

Lyra wavered, then looked around. Being in a dimly lit dungeon allowed endless perches for her shadows. They hovered in the wall corners and under furniture, giving her courage. She had her own faithful guards, just as Griselda did. That in mind, Lyra signaled her bugs mentally, calling them from her mother's room in the northern wing of the castle, bidding them to make haste to the dungeon, on the chance she might need reinforcements.

Griselda broke her stare and arranged the refreshments the servants had left on a tray beside the table. She poured steaming milk from the porcelain pitcher into teacups and coaxed her girls to her. "It has been a harrowing day. We will not await the cessation course to seek our rest. Let's have milk and toast, then off to bed. Lyra, you, too, please. I've something to speak to you about before we sleep."

Cautiously, Lyra followed her cousins, sitting where her aunt directed. There were just enough place settings and chairs for each of them. The absence of a fifth that would've accommodated Lustacia tugged at everyone's emotions. It reflected vividly in Lyra's cousins' red, swollen eyes and puckered lips as they nibbled the iced raisin bread on their plates. Lyra sipped milk to ease her stomach, unable to bring herself to eat. The creamy warmth seeped into her bones, though she still couldn't relax.

Griselda touched her daughters' heads in a comforting gesture. "We'll have no more tears today. They are for those who are weak and hopeless. But *we . . .* we are powerful, and we have hope." She left the table. Her gown's train dragged across the rugs on her trek toward the birdcages. "What say we have some music?"

"Is that why you brought our pet birds from the aviary?" asked Avaricette while licking white icing from her crust. "Are they to sing our sadness away?"

"I brought them to keep our home vermin-free. You know how I abhor infestation." Griselda's dark gaze circled around to meet Lyra's. "They haven't eaten since yesterday. It makes them better hunters, keeping them on the edge of hunger."

Lyra polished off the last of her milk in a painful gulp as Griselda opened each cage. The birds fluttered in chaos until they found places to settle: on the bed canopies, on the copper chimney plugged into the one slip of wall not covered with a tapestry, on the mirror strung from the ceiling.

Taken aback by her aunt's ingenuity, Lyra blotted the milk from her lips with her sleeve. Her mind called to the moths and spiders that now scurried behind the stone walls, forbidding their entrance. She couldn't risk them coming out just to be eaten. They were too dear to her.

After aiming a smile upward at the chirping birds, Griselda turned to the trunk at the foot of the largest bed.

"Aren't you to sit and take refreshment with us, Mother?" Wrathalyne's chin quivered as she blotted her face with a napkin.

"No, my darling." Griselda traced the carvings of Eldoria's sun on the trunk's lid. "That place setting does not belong to me. It is for your sister."

Lyra's pulse scrambled. She wriggled in her chair, holding her shadows at bay though they pressed to come forward. Surely her aunt had lost her mind to grief, and all of this pomp and pageantry would disintegrate in a fit of weeping and wailing.

"Y-you mean . . . we're saving a place for Lustacia's *ghost*?" Avaricette questioned, grasping Wrathalyne's hand atop the table. The girls' knuckles whitened as they watched the birds preen their feathers and coo quietly.

"Do not look so anxious, my darlings. I had to keep it secret from you. You're both too excitable." She waggled her forefinger. "Couldn't risk your tongues running ahead of your rationale. And your grief had to be genuine. But rest assured, your sister is no more a ghost than I am *defeated*." Fisting her hand, Griselda knocked on the trunk's lid three times. Three knocks answered back from within.

Lyra and her cousins gasped simultaneously.

Griselda laughed upon opening the lid. The hinges creaked at their stop-ping point. Something wormed from beneath the folded bed linens, seeking a way out. The sheets avalanched from the trunk and slid to the floor. Lyra almost lurched up her milk as a headful of long silvery hair—identical to her own—emerged from the trunk's depths. The face, wearing a rueful frown, belonged to the very alive Lustacia. Though holding a wilted bouquet of panacea roses, she hadn't a scratch upon her.

Griselda helped her daughter climb out—a feat made easier due to her ensemble: the torn page boy's trousers and tunic that they'd been unable to find at the bloody scene of her vanishing.

Lyra's mind spun. Why would Griselda put everyone through Lustacia's death, why fake being heartbroken to the point of soul-sickness herself? And why was Lustacia's hair so like Lyra's own?

Upon the final question, a dark perception prickled inside Lyra's chest, as if she'd inhaled shards of glass. The answer took shape—an explanation so vile and cunning her lungs withered on an unsung cry.

Wrathalyne and Avaricette leapt from their seats and ran to hug their younger sister, unconcerned for the logic of it, merely ecstatic to have her back again.

Trembling, Lyra stood from her chair. *You . . . are me.* She mimed the accusation to Lustacia, underscoring it through their joined gazes. If only her moths weren't hidden away, they could help her relay the words aloud. But Lustacia's attention dropped to the roses in her hand, proving she needn't hear Lyra to feel remorse for all the lies she'd told.

Griselda stepped into Lyra's line of sight, blocking her view of her daughters. "A shame you couldn't accompany us on all those sunny walks throughout the kingdom. Constitutionals have such an invigorating effect on one's thought process. Why, just weeks ago I stumbled upon a group of com-mon urchins playing at the Crystal Lake, imitating their princess's ghoulish coloring, her metallic hair. And I had a glorious epiphany. I said to myself,

'Why Griselda, just think. Given time enough, any one of these street urchins could look the part of the princess in the prophecy. She'd simply need to share her slender bone structure.'"

Lyra looked down at the flocked navy-and-mulberry gown fitted so nicely to her shape. She backed toward the table again, numb. They had been planning this for weeks, perhaps months. Griselda, she expected . . . but Lustacia? She thought they were becoming friends. Family.

Agony gored her heart and singed her eyes.

She'd been a fool. She had no family. Not anymore. Not ever again.

Wrathalyne and Avaricette scooted atop the smaller bed. Their faces brightened in malevolent delight, mesmerized by their mother's confession.

"This was a simple dusting of silver sand." Griselda continued. Lustacia drooped as her mother stroked her lustrous pale hair, the misery in her down-turned features deepening. "Imagine what I can do with a bit of alchemist trickery. And a person's features often change as they mature. Especially if they're out of sight for some years, never seen except for walks in the garden, hidden beneath a suit of nightsky. It wouldn't be so difficult, to manage a replacement. Other than some moonlit alterations to her coloring, all a girl would need to win Eldoria's and the prince's hearts is a songbird's voice." Griselda reached into the trunk, pulling out a seashell secured upon a silver stand. "Look at that. It would seem the midnight shadows and stardust weren't the only articles to go missing from the mages' keep yesterday."

Lyra dropped into her chair, taken back to one of the last moments she had with her father before he left for Nerezeth. They spent a day in the library together. For the hundredth time he had shared the silly story of how he met her mother, and the instant Lyra released a musical strain of laughter, he trapped the sound in an enchanted seashell.

"It's just a bit of magic," he explained when she held out her hand, asking to hold the pearly treasure. "Our mages take seashells and lure out the ocean's song with incantations, leaving them longing to be filled again. Today, you've given this one

a treasure more rare and invaluable than the sea's very breath. I will share it with Queen Nova. She'll fall in love with you upon hearing it, and refuse us nothing."

Griselda clucked her tongue, recouping Lyra's attention. "When your father took an echo of your laugh, did he tell you that if a shell is filled to the brim and sealed with a cork of bespelled willow wood coated in sea salt, one can either listen to the trapped sound by loosening the stopper in increments until it's all used up . . . or one can grind the shell, cork, and salt to powder, combine it with a simple transference potion, and swallow the sound whole, making it their own?"

Lyra's chin sagged. From within this insulated dungeon, no one would ever hear her musical wails. She sent a desperate glance to the royal family paintings no longer decking the castle walls, fixating on those of her father and herself. Griselda couldn't make everyone forget their true princess existed, but she could make them forget Lyra's face.

A chilling shiver started inside her head and traversed to her feet, leaving her drained and weak. She swayed in her chair.

Griselda unlocked the pine box at the end of the smaller bed and laid the shell within. "Are you feeling out of sorts, dear? A bit drowsy? I've the perfect place for you to sleep."

Only then did Lyra notice how much the box looked like a coffin.

"I must admit, you impressed me for a moment." Griselda tapped the open edge with her ring finger, whereupon sat Queen Arael's ruby band. She must have pilfered it from Lyra's room as they were packing. "However, your mind is no match for mine. Age does have its boons. A lifetime of hard-won wisdom is worth more than all the gloom-dwelling magic in your frail body."

The room swam and Lyra caught the table's edge for balance, causing the teacups to rattle. Something was wrong inside her head. Everything felt . . . blurry. Out of sorts and out of reach.

She called upon her bugs, unable to remember any reason not to. As the birds swooped down upon the intrusion of moths and spiders, the crunch of exoskeletons and snapping wings brought tragic clarity to Lyra's thoughts. She called upon her shadows, feeding them with the rage of betrayal.

Dazed, she watched the slow and cautious eclipse—melding together from every corner and furniture edge like storm clouds gathering capacity. Rising from underneath the beds, their gusts whipped tangles through Lustacia's dusty hair and ripped at Wrathalyne and Avaricette's clothes. The three girls dove under the quilts, screaming. Unfazed, Griselda rushed to the middle of the room and tugged on the golden cord that joined the tapestries. Simultaneously, they peeled from the walls to reveal copper panels, stretched ceiling to floor. The light in the room reflected from them—onto the mirror and back again, magnified tenfold, and rent Lyra's shadows to pieces.

She fell to her knees, unable to open her eyes for the sizzling pain. The hairs on the back of her neck raised as she sensed Griselda bending to whisper in her ear.

"That trick you pulled last time won't work here. Those torches were dying already. These lanterns are fueled by a blend of paraffin and liquid sunshine. Their brilliance will burn for months. The prophecy is flawed, you see. For a princess whose most devoted subjects are the shifting shadows that can't reach beyond deep corners and dark stairways, has no hope of building an army in a *world of eternal light*."

The door opened and closed, the knights' heavy footsteps tromped closer . . .

Warding off the room's brightness behind sealed lashes, Lyra was lifted, carried somewhere by strong arms wrapped in metal. Wrathalyne's and Avaricette's footsteps shuffled alongside and the girls scolded her for tearing their clothes with her shadows. As for Lustacia, only her sniffles indicated her presence.

The scent of pine surrounded Lyra upon being laid inside the hard and splintery box.

"Drop them in with her, along with the roses," came Griselda's command at a distance. Her voice shook with revulsion.

The potent rose scent tickled Lyra's nose, then something writhing and bristly fell atop her chest, stinging as it curled around her wrists, arms, ankles and legs—like ropes made of thorns. Then another sensation—thumping across her body and spreading out while releasing a wave of flaming pinpricks that pierced through her clothes.

Unable to open her eyes and face her attackers, Lyra screamed—her anguish reduced to lovely melodies. In response, Wrathalyne and Avaricette burst into a rash of nervous giggles.

"Mother!" Lustacia's outburst broke through. "Your plan was to send her away . . . using the secret tunnel beneath the dungeon—"

"And I will."

"But you weren't to harm her!"

"What did you think was to happen? The only chance you have to *become* Lyra is for Lyra to stop existing. Our knights will use the tunnel to take her body to the mouth of the Ashen Ravine. It will be a gift to the Shroud Collective for letting me live all those years ago. Thus, should anyone ever breech the ravine in search of your remains, they'll find nothing but a pile of bones."

"I've changed my mind!" Lustacia's cries clawed at Lyra's hot, stinging ears.

"Then *I* will be Lyra," Avaricette said.

"No, me!" Wrathalyne intoned.

"Hush now. All three of you have a queen's beauty, but your sister was born with the delicate skin of a princess, and the acumen of a diplomat. The shrouds once predicted my part in reuniting the heavens. I came to realize that role was to train Lustacia. She's already adept at forging Lyra's handwriting, and is learning the hand signals our prime minister has taught her." Behind Lyra's eyelids, Griselda's voice drifted near and far—in and out of focus. "Your sister's destiny is inevitable and set in motion by Lyra's death. One can't *un-poison* someone, after all."

Lyra's throat clenched.

"You didn't tell me you were to poison her!" Lustacia's cry sounded hoarse. "You didn't say you'd expose her to those . . . those horrible things—" Her statement ended in a sob.

"Those horrible *things* are cadaver brambles and rime scorpions, indigenous to the realm of your betrothed. My knights paid a hefty price to have them smuggled in. How else am I to secure the princess's song for you, unless she screams herself dry?"

"It's too much, Mother."

"Oh, please. Lyra's most at home with night creatures. She delights in threatening me with them. I would think having them surrounding her as life slips away would be a comfort. Do you need to see the note again? The prince's words to his future bride? You read it one time and lost your heart. You were willing to go along with any plan, if the result was his hand. Will you give him up to her now? Do you love her more than yourself?"

The absence of Lustacia's answer stretched out interminably as Lyra struggled against the fog in her brain, the fever beneath her skin, and the fissures spreading through her chest.

"Lustacia," Griselda's tone softened. "Think of it. One queen ruling both kingdoms. I gave away the best years of my life to win my blood right to this throne. And now, I will get twofold for you. Herein, everything is put to rights, for I am the firstborn. I have suffered and sacrificed in ways my spoiled brother never did. I gave away my very conscience, and power has been easier gained without it. I would suggest you do the same, but since you wish to love and be loved, you must have it intact. So, give me the dirty labors, and I will see that your heart is granted its greatest desire as mine never was."

Lustacia's sobs escalated to wails.

Griselda sighed. "Sir Erwan, guard the staircase to the dungeon. Sir Bartley, take Lustacia and her sisters to another cell until it is finished."

"But we wish to watch, Mother," Avaricette whined.

"Do it now."

An assemblage of footsteps stirred all around, then grew distant. The door slammed and locks clacked into place.

The piercing light dimmed as the box's lid closed, sealing Lyra in. She opened her eyes to the darkness—always her friend and comfort—and watched the glowing scorpion and bramble attackers with horrified fascination. Despite the pain of jutting blue stingers and white thorny binds, they belonged to the night, like her.

Through her tears, she saw her fingers illuminate for an instant, casting a golden glow. It taunted her, triggering the memory of magical ink staining her fingertips and the kind words written at the hand of a prince: *I will keep you safe.*

She would never know him, and he would never know he was being fooled.

Lyra suppressed an outraged cry, her attention turned to the seashell nestled beside her head.

"Surrender to the pain. You'll feel better if you scream." Griselda taunted from the other side of the lid. "How about I get you started, with a song of my own?" She cleared her throat. "See the shell beside your head . . . fill it up until you're dead. Your father took but one musical cry, but I won't stop until you're bled dry."

Struggling to breathe, Lyra ground her teeth and refused to open her lips.

"Just do it!" Griselda attacked the lid with her fists. The pounding echoed through Lyra's bones, rattling them. "Ghastly, ghost-faced girl." Her aunt paused, regaining her calm. "I always knew you were but a smudge staining the walls of this castle. And that one day, I would scrub you out, and you would haunt us no more. I suppose I should thank you. By freeing the witch while we still had her staff, you made this entire setup possible. So I'll return the favor and tell you how it all ends, since you won't be here to see for yourself. After you give up your voice, you'll become drowsy and your breath will slow. You won't be able to stay awake. And once asleep, you will slip away. Give no thought to your faithful subjects. Any who become too curious or concerned will be cut down one by one. Mia will be first. Someone will attempt to poison our fare and she'll die a hero, proving her loyalty to Eldoria once and for all. As for the kingdom, Lustacia and I have it well in hand. You can slumber in eternal peace knowing this, little perfect *princess*. That is my gift to you."

Hot tears raced down Lyra's cheeks. She writhed beneath the fire lancing her skin, tormented by dear Mia's fate. She had to save her. She had to be here for her kingdom, to be the queen her father always hoped for her to be. Emotional turmoil boiled over to feed the flames already searing her veins. A thousand puncture wounds filled with blazing venom bled into her mind and melted her thoughts into a red slag. The harder she tried to hold her pain in, the hotter her fever grew. Screams built behind her chest and throat until eruption became her last hope for relief.

Stretching her jaw wide, she turned her head and retched up bile, venom, and tainted milk. Then came the deeper purge . . . the musical screaming and screaming and screaming that scraped her hollow until no more sound would come.

The empty ache in her throat and the stench of sickness grew distant as her shadows returned to her in the darkness. They broke her binds, tamed the scorpions, and numbed her wounded skin with airy caresses. Her eyes grew heavy as her shadows carried her to a place of rest—with no interruption of nightmares, with no fear as to what fresh horrors tomorrow might bring. She took the hand Death offered, and fell asleep.

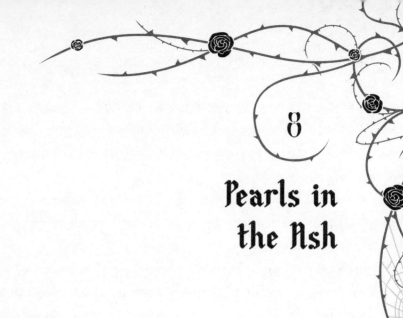

8

Pearls in the Ash

I n the selfsame hour Griselda sent away her niece's dying body and reveled in her most cruel and profound triumph, Crony and her sylphin companion wandered the Ashen Ravine in search of fresh stock. The witch's supplies of herbs and memories were dwindling as she hadn't set foot outside the ravine in months for fear she'd be captured by Eldoria's royal regent again.

"Ye be sure these rumors are true?" Crony laid it out as more of a threat than a question. If Luce was leading her through these cursed terrains on a wild corpse-chase when she should be peddling her wares in her shop, she would have his pelt.

The fox slipped in and out of the creeping ash ahead of her, stirring up gray clouds. "I coaxed out the details myself." His power of persuasion was most effective when he preyed upon a desire held secret within the victim. Which meant the informant must be someone who liked to gossip.

Crony frowned. "Yer source not be Dregs, do it? That dullard goblin always be tellin' tall tales to compensate for his teensy stature. He sweared he saw a fire-breathin' horse with wings burn two o' his goblin acquaintances to ash. As if all the Pegasus didn't be eaten up centuries ago by the drasilisks."

"We've both seen hoofprints of late."

Crony snorted, wrestling her cloak's hem from a tangle of irascible vines. The bag of glass at her waist clinked with the effort. "The Nerezethites trek this forest. We always be seeing their mounts' hoofprints."

Luce flattened his body to squeeze through a tunnel of dead roots. When he popped up at the other end, the red of his belly and muzzle were coated in ash, taking on a dusty white. "But there's the peace treaty. They no longer smuggle sunlight. So they've not been coming around."

Crony rolled her eyes. As if she weren't aware of that fact. The sun-smugglers used to visit her stall on their bimonthly excursions. They would purchase her wares for protection against the forest's shrouds. The ravenous creatures always kept watch over the liquid sunshine inside the entrance. Memories were the one thing a person could bargain with to keep their flesh intact, since the shrouds couldn't resist a glimpse of what they once were. Crony had missed the extra funds.

"But ye be overlookin' the crimp in Dregs's tale . . ." She resumed her and Luce's conversation upon catching up with him. "Since when do a horse with wings leave *hoofprints*?"

"We're getting off subject, as always."

"Ah, but I thought yer kind liked chasin' rabbits."

He sneezed in derision before resuming his trek. "A boy lies dying in the ravine, his coffin dragged in and snapped open by the serpentine briars. He appears to have been flogged with barbs. His skin is worse off than the shreds of his clothes. More than one eye saw it."

"Multiple eyes. So, it weren't the word of a cyclops then. Be good, that. They have tunnel vision 'bout most things."

"Ha." Luce leapt over a quag-puddle. The living murk spread in an effort to trap him. He sailed to the other side at the last minute, scrambling to his left on nimble paws. The puddle burbled in frustration, releasing a putrid stench. The fox barked a laugh, his silver-tipped tail high and proud.

Crony chose a longer route to escape the puddle and had to duck to miss low-hanging branches as black and ungiving as onyx. Her left horn hooked around one and jerked her back. Head throbbing, she freed herself before skidding behind her companion along the sharply declining path to the lowlands. Even using her staff for balance, she could barely keep up with Luce's four legs. "Ye know we not be welcome in this part of the forest. They despise me for not sharin' me pilfered memories. And ye—"

"And I talked them out of a kill years ago by suggesting they could feed off her conscience. Is it my fault they misplaced it? The shrouds are about to strip the boy of his flesh. What's left of it. I assumed you'd want to claim his dying thoughts and maybe his bones. You've been needing a skull for your new staff, yes? We can strike a bargain with one of his final memories."

"Hmmm. Judging from the one and only bargain ye ever striked with them, I venture they not be so receptive. Stay in yer doggy form and I do the quibbling."

"Once again, you underestimate my charm." Luce's retort muffled beneath a rush of inhuman whispers and hisses. He rounded a bend, his pointed ears perked.

Dropping to her knees, Crony crouched with him behind a fallen stump. She clutched the gnarled wood, her brown leathery hands blending in. Her staff rested atop the ash that slithered about their feet.

Up ahead, the shrouds drifted in a dusty clearing—an uneven circle devoid of trunks and shrubbery that still managed to be claustrophobic, cloaked in darkness by the thick, low-hanging canopy stretching from the trees around it. A coffin was toppled open, its small occupant slung over the edge with arms splayed across the ground, unmoving. The vaporous collective had yet to notice their two visitors. A shroud's wit tended to be as thin as its smoky silhouette, making it easy to elude when preoccupied with the promise of a feeding. But this situation was different, and only one look told Crony why.

Each time Mistress Umbra skimmed forward to attack the dying child, a merging of shadows and luminous-blue rime scorpions rose to defend the supine form. The Shroud Collective cowered behind trees surrounding the clearing, eyes glimmering white. They had no means to pass through, either as unsubstantial shapeless creatures or shifted to their humanlike forms. On one hand, their barrier was as vaporous as they, and on the other, venomous stingers waited to attack. It was a standoff between a cursed darkness and an appointed army. A standoff that could go on for hours.

Judging by the putrid scent of infection and toxins in the air, the victim didn't have that kind of time. And loathe as Crony was to admit it, said victim was no boy. Even with the child shaved bald . . . even in a page boy's shredded tunic and pants, with her exposed pearlized skin marred by ash, mud, and hundreds of seeping puncture marks . . . Crony would know Eldoria's sovereign heir anywhere by the fealty of her night creatures.

Turning to her canine companion, Crony whispered, "That be no page boy. That be the royal princess, what that freed me from Eldoria's dungeon."

Luce bowed his head and long muzzle. He hadn't been happy leaving Crony that day to be captured by soldiers; but the two had a code: should one of them ever be captured, the other did their best to escape so they could help from the outside. Luce had been trying to come up with a plan when Crony found her way home to the ravine.

However, it was more than the guilt of that day weighing on him now.

His wet, black nose wriggled. "I know who did this child ill. I can spot that woman's handiwork anywhere. And I'm guessing she used some poison to aid her crime."

His orange eyes blazed. He rarely spoke of his past, yet there were a few details he had divulged. He once flew above the world with a bird's-eye view of the humans, leaving him detached enough to take advantage of Queen Arael's pure heart under the advisement of his lover. Even before that, he was indirectly responsible for a human death, first, by suggesting Griselda do away with her conscience, weak as it was, and second, by giving her a spell-book, which she used to rid herself of her husband.

Now that he was grounded, making him a part of the order of things, he had to face the consequences of his actions daily, as any human would.

Crony turned again to the ethereal standoff, her slitted nose sniffing the scent of panacea roses. The princess's limp arms cradled the dark purple bouquet. Crony recounted seeing the child holding a flower pot during her stint in the dungeon. Regent Griselda had degraded and man-handled the princess that day—calling her a stain. She must be cackling her harpy heart out in that plush castle, convinced she'd rid herself of her niece forever.

May-let this could be Luce's chance to find redemption for his part and win back his wings. May-let Crony could repay her own debt to King Kiran's bloodline, to the sun and the moon—a debt known only by she and one other. Crony had made a sacred vow not to intervene directly with king-dom goings-on, which is why she hadn't shared who'd killed King Kiran. She'd only given away the prophecy half of the memory to the constable, information that would've come out on its own via missives or talks between kingdoms. Crony had hoped it might keep the girl safe until she reached a marriable age, yet here she was in a worse state than before.

Retrieving her spirit from the dead without interfering would take some doing. There would have to be a compromise. To save the princess's life, Crony would have to make the girl anonymous, inconsequential—even to herself. Then Lyra would have to rediscover her true identity without Crony ever telling her.

It could put things right in both kingdoms. Allow the shattered pieces of the prophecy to find their *own* way back to completion—however messy that reconstruction might be.

Crony whispered again to Luce: "I don't know 'bout ye, but I be feelin' a new thirst in me roots of late. Shall we bargain with the fleshless devils and save the girl? Turn over our old ne'er-do-well leaves for a chance at atonement?" Casting him a sidelong glance, she waited.

His long pink tongue lolled out in a half grin. "Are you saying what I think? You're to perform the trick that outshines all tricks? Recall her from the other side of death?"

Crony suppressed a tremor of panic along her spine, wishing she could share his eagerness. What Luce didn't realize was that summoning a mortal back from the dead came at a heavy price—her own immortality. Her hide would soften with age; all the years she'd outrun would catch up. And her innards would no longer be impervious to sickness or toxins.

This information she would take to her grave. Were he to know, her sylphin companion would try to talk her out of it, and she needed all the courage she could muster. If anyone was worthy of a second chance at life, it was this broken child, and truth be told, Crony had been anticipating . . . and fearing . . . this moment for centuries. "If ye wish to see me greatest trick, first ye must perform a grand gesture yerself."

Luce tilted his head in a purely canine manner, curiosity clear in his puppy-eyed expression.

"I can't be takin' on such responsibility alone," Crony explained. "Will ye help me? Stand by the princess in thick and thin? Be there, if for some reason I can't."

"Why wouldn't you be there? You will outlive us all."

She squeezed her staff for comfort. "I've been known to take a trip or two for leisure. Ev'ry lady needs her private moments for reflection."

"Ha! Of course. You're the essence of 'every lady.'" He twitched his whiskers.

"As for yer help, will ye do it? Give me a tail wag for yay, or a bark for nay."

Glaring at her, Luce flicked an ear in annoyance. "You're aware I can talk."

Crony smiled freely. Here in the ravine, everything was either as good as dead, or the cohort of death already, so there were no flowers or grasses to wilt. "Aye, but we be making a contract. I need yer pledge, me courtly mongrel, that in either form, yer whole body be willin' to see this through to the very end. The very end bein' yer fat, fluffy tail."

Growling softly, Luce gave said tail two shakes, but no more. She was happy to accept it. Let him keep what remained of his dignity.

As for herself, Crony shuddered at the thought of relinquishing her armor; but she would hang her courage on one hope: to live long enough to watch the girl win her prince, claim her throne, and bring the nights back. It would be worth it all, so long as Crony could hear a symphony of crickets in the darkness one last time before taking her final breath.

Her lot decided, Crony stood, staff in hand. Fur bristling, Luce snarled a warning, and together they stepped from behind the stump and into the midst of the collective.

⋇ · I · ⋇

The wee princess died the instant her unlikely saviors finished bargaining for her remains, though the witch managed to capture the tail end of her final breath and the memory tied to it. That's all Crony needed to bid a spirit from beyond, and to split a past wide open so she could carve out the identity hidden in the nooks and crannies of a person's mind.

To Crony's relief, the shadows and scorpion army receded once the flesh-mongering shrouds withdrew, seeming to understand their charge was now in healing hands. Crony and Luce left the pine box and roses behind. By the time Luce shifted to his human form to carry the princess out of the low-lands, the girl's breathing had resumed and her lashes, having been trimmed down to stubs, grew long before their very eyes. Luce studied her shaved head, her troubled, sleeping face cradled in the crook of his arm. Her breath ruffled the red hair draped across his shoulder.

Crony had never seen the capricious sylph look more somber. He would see this through to the end, in spite of his selfish past. Or may-let because of it.

Once home, with the princess unconscious, the witch began her task. Using the captured memory to lure others out, Crony sandwiched them between paper-thin glass triangles and sealed them after blowing her own breath across. She continued the process, joining one contained memory to another with magical threads that streamed like lightning from her horns, similar to a spider using its spinnerets. Crony labored, withdrawing the next and the next and the next—hundreds upon hundreds—over two cessation courses and into a third day while Luce managed her booth in the market and restocked herb supplies.

Upon finishing, Crony stood back and viewed the stack of memories, folded together with glowing thread down their spines. It resembled a fat, miniature book made of stained glass. Were she to animate it, at the turning of each page a new scene of the princess's life would play out. She'd taken care to leave the princess's memories of language, communication, the written word, and knowledge of the natural world intact, so as not to risk a blank mind and stunted acumen. It was this intricate mental probing that made a memory-cleanse such a challenging venture.

Crony drizzled a healing potable between her ward's drowsing lips, as she had done over the past two days to keep her alive. The witch sipped some for herself, feeling a sudden weariness, due to her own exchange—immortal advantage for mortal limitations. For the first time in all her years, she ached deep within her bones. Once Luce left for market, Crony hid her eyes behind a blindfold, curled upon her mattress, and slept.

In the next room, the girl continued to sleep as well, having nothing left to dream of but the residue of memories in blurred colors and fuzzy stimuli: the salty flavor of tears; a velvety rain of lavender rose petals; a red-leafed tree standing vigil in a courtyard so stark white it singed the eye; gauzy dresses in soft pastels, minty green, buttery yellow, and sugared blue; fuzzy gray moths and biting brambles; and golden ink catching fire to black paper and curious fingertips.

The scent of decomposing leaves, combined with something medicinal, seeped into the girl's consciousness. She awoke to the sensation of her hands burning.

No, not just her hands—every facet of her skin . . . itching and blistering. She attempted to move, her bones sluggish. Her teeth ground together and she would've groaned, but her vocal cords quivered—as inefficient as a lute with no strings. She tugged at bandages wrapped around her limbs, neck, and torso, beneath an ankle-length gown and a threadbare blanket, trying to remember where . . . how. And most essentially, *who*.

She couldn't remember a name, or even her own face. The unknowing sat upon her chest, weighing her down and stealing her breath. She moved her hand up to her throat where a necklace rested atop her collarbone. Lifting the circular charm, she studied it in the soft light. It appeared to be a braid of white hair wound upon itself. Was it important to her? Sentimental?

A distant, piercing roar—feral and inhuman, like a horse bugling in fury—sent her scrambling to sit up, rebelling against reluctant muscles and throbbing flesh. She could see her surroundings clearly, despite the thick, leafy canopy stretched overhead that stifled the light. It was as if she'd awakened within the belly of a skeleton. There were no walls here, nor doors, nor windows. Only a framework of wood. Yet there was no breeze either, no moving air or birdsongs, no sounds of nature other than a rustle beneath and around her mattress—as if the ground itself moved.

A soft snore, from a blindfolded figure, curled up and sleeping a few feet away, gave her pause. She didn't recognize the hideous reptilian face, or the black, curving horns, or the gaping, muddy lips.

Dread chilled the blood in her veins as she looked upon her bandages.

Something terrible had happened. This creature had captured her. Tortured her.

The bugling cry sounded again, but this time, the girl heard a shout woven within—a raspy, male voice underlining the horse's helpless indignation, as if they spoke in unison. She caught a breath, stretching lungs that ached as if carved hollow. Her captor slept on, so firm in its sleep not even a third roaring neigh woke it.

The girl backed away, pushing through warm, powdery ash across a stone floor, avoiding dilapidated furniture and wooden planks until she'd crossed the threshold into a yard. Spinning around, she stumbled along a path, out of the small grove and into the thickening trees. With each step, her body acclimated to her injuries, her movements awkward but gaining strength.

She followed the horse's brays tangled with the husky male shouts. The duo songs of agony, anger, and loss were emotions she could relate to; they felt familiar.

Yet her enchanted surroundings felt foreign—claustrophobic and dark. The airtight canopy overhead stretched on as far as the eye could see. Sunrays pierced through intermittently, warming the sooty ground cover that sifted across her feet like a low tide. She skirted the areas of light as she tromped onward, discovering that even through her bandages they seared her skin. Strange, vicious puddles appeared out of nowhere and followed until she outran them. She made a note to anticipate them by their stench.

Closer now to the duel cries, she rounded a bend. A new smell assaulted her nose as she tripped into a thicket of briar vines where the canopy hung low. Unless one was a small woodland creature that could weave in and out of the prickly maze, there appeared to be no clear pathway. Thorns snagged the girl's bandages and gown, piercing already tender skin. She yelped soundlessly, thinking to back out, but stopped in her tracks.

Just ahead, a black stallion struggled to get free from a gurgling bog in the midst of the thicket. A silvery light glowed from within the sludgy liquid, seeming to rise from the bottom. The domed thicket absorbed the light, making the surroundings brighter than the journey here.

The horse's front hooves, coated in muck, pawed for purchase on the bank. A giant bracken had sprouted from the depths, wrapping around his neck. The fernlike leaves worked with the mire to drown their prey—like a frog's tongue might capture a fly.

Already, the ooze had claimed his tail and flanks . . . the rest would soon follow, as with every movement he sank more. The horse might manage to climb out if she could free his neck.

Stop moving, please. She couldn't say the words, could only think them. But the horse stilled in response.

His graceful neck craned. Across the short distance, a fire ignited within his eyes' dark depths, orange and flickering behind the whites of rage and fear that rimmed them. A reflection of the same orange sparks flickered within his mane. The girl stared, gaping, as cinders stirred at his withers where something unfurled.

Magnificent wings, gilded with orange-and-gold embers, opened and flapped wide. This was no common horse. He was something rarer than a black pearl . . . he was a Pegasus.

This detail revived her determination. She wrinkled her nose, strategizing. Though the briar's vines hung too low for him to fly, his wings could aid his escape; with their thrust, he could drag himself out of the bog if she untangled the binds around his neck.

She made her way forward, pressing through the thorns that ripped her gown and bandages until the cloth hung in shreds. Fresh blood slicked her feet and skin. She winced instead of whimpered, and plunged through to find herself face-to-face with the Pegasus, a few steps from the swampy pit. His hot breath overpowered the bog's stench with a fusion of musk, charred grass, and sweet clover.

An indignant nicker greeted her and again she heard the voice, gruff and masculine: *Danger. Kill. Fly.* But it wasn't aloud. It was inside her head. She could hear his thoughts . . . as he could hear hers.

His wings labored with loud thuds—a futile attempt to escape the monstrous bracken clutching his neck—and sent gusts of wind across her scalp. She rubbed her nape with a bandaged hand. The baldness felt peculiar and out of place. She didn't have time to consider why because the Pegasus's efforts to escape had sucked him deeper.

Stop moving. It's pulling you under. Holding out five bloody fingertips, she tried to calm him. *Do you have a name?*

He snorted, curls of sooty smoke rising from his nostrils. *I require no name. I am destruction. I am flame. Step back.*

I only wish to help you. She exhaled a shaky breath.

I need no help. I will save myself. Step back or I will scorch you to scars.

His wild beauty fascinated her, and his arrogant pride made her forget the blood dribbling from her fingertips, the agonized throb of her flesh. *Then I have nothing to fear, for I am already one big scar.* She suddenly remembered how to smile. *I will call you Scorch. And once I rescue you, you'll belong to me.* The possibility gave her hope, to have a companion she could ride upon—to fly above all this desolation. To leave the confusion behind.

His head reared up, flinging goopy sludge across her face. *I belong to no one but the sky.*

The goop leaked into her mouth and she spat out the taste of rot and dying things. She braved grasping a thorny vine in her hand. Unsung wails clumped in her barren throat as she wound the length around her waist to form an anchor line.

Scorch grew still once more, watching her. *Witless mite. You're much too small to rescue anyone.*

Ignoring his disparagements, she huffed. *Well, your beastly brawn seems to be more a detriment than a help. Small could be the advantage here. Why are you in this mess to begin with?* She wasn't trying to distract him as much as herself as she slipped into the cold, slimy liquid and the spikes at her waist punctured her flesh like angry talons. The anchor allowed movement without being sucked under, holding her secure as bones floated around her within the luminescent sludge. She shivered.

This place is called the moon-bog. When the Pegasus answered this time, there was something gentler about his inner voice, as if he sensed her pain and terror. *It's said to be a window to the night realm. I wished to look for myself. I live for adventure.*

Well, you might very well die for it today. The girl managed the retort even as the thorns gouged deeper into her waist. Strangely, no tears would come despite how her eyes stung. Grinding her teeth, she towed herself toward the Pegasus. Upon reaching him, she tugged on the leafy tangles at his neck with mangled hands.

Scorch ground his front hooves deeper into the bank, but held his wings folded to heaving sides, waiting. She sensed his impatience in the twitches of muscle, his distrust in the huffs of hot breath. The heat radiating from his sweat-slathered coat and his immense size frightened her, but she didn't shy away.

At last, she broke the bracken's hold. He flapped his great wings, accidentally pounding her head. She capsized and her body plunged beneath the surface.

The Pegasus climbed free and the murk rose, buoying her to the surface. She choked for air. The thorns embedded deeper in her waist as something tugged on the vine, dragging her up.

She clutched at her anchor, letting the barbs grip her palms for added leverage. Once she emerged, she slumped on the bank next to prancing hooves. She laid there panting on her belly, clammy clothes stuck to her weeping flesh, one side of her face buried in ash.

You are fierce, tiny trifling thing. Scorch's muzzle, bleeding from the briar vine he used to drag her out, nudged the odd necklace that draped the back of her neck. He snuffled upward to her head—gentle against her baldness. *But I still belong only to the sky.*

Just as she rolled over to argue, he reared, his hooves missing her skull by inches. Instinctively, her arms flew up for protection. Her fingers lit to a golden glow, startling both herself and the horse. Flame leapt from his nose, burning the skin in the spaces between her bandages. The tang of roasted flesh and singed blood filled the air. She coughed a silent scream. A flash of crimson darted in her peripheral where a fox wove through the briars toward them, snarling. Scorch whinnied and crashed out of the thicket—tail held high and wings trailed by glittering cinders. He offered one last nicker in the distance, this one rife with fury and elation.

The fox became an elegant man dressed in red fineries, though his ears remained furry and pointed. Upon seeing her state, his orange, bestial gaze narrowed. He dropped to his knees at her side, smelling of dog, feathers, and wind.

She was too weak to struggle as he cut the binds at her waist with a knife, then scooped her up and stood. Her eyes fluttered closed, her blood draining away in rhythmic drips at his feet.

"No. Look at me." His voice wasn't in her head. It was persuasive and silky—an irresistible command that echoed across the glowing moon-bog. She forced her heavy eyelids open, squinting at his unearthly perfection, at his sharp-edged teeth. "You will not die twice on my watch. I won't have you costing me my wings again. Stay awake now, little Stain. The fates have grand plans for you."

Part II

In Which the Forest
Swallows the Rose

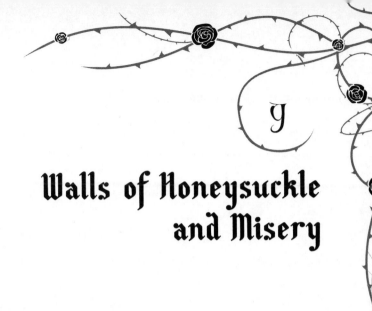

Walls of Honeysuckle and Misery

Deep within the Ashen Ravine, in a clearing isolated from prying eyes, hidden inside a house without walls, the girl with no identity drifted in and out of consciousness. Time passed immeasurably. The gray, hazy light that filtered through the leafy canopy overhead never seemed to wane and fever racked her body with shivering shudders.

At one point upon waking, she tried to peer out from heavy eyelids, but it was like looking through hedges of white thistledown. She realized the fringe grew from her own skin . . . that it was her lashes blinding her. Reaching up, she plucked several free. An excruciating pain reached all the way into the pit of her stomach, as if the hairs were rooted to the very core of her being and scored her insides on their way out. She dropped the long hairs and doubled over on her pallet in agony. On the blankets beside her, the discarded lashes became liquid, forming a pool of moonlight. Just as the gutting pain began to ease, a fresh crop of lashes sprang from her eyelids.

She slapped a hand over her mouth. Not only did she not know where or who she was . . . she didn't know *what* she was.

Too exhausted and confused for an escape attempt, she trembled in silence as the witch with a mud-pie gaze opened the patchwork curtains around her pallet to tip her horned head inside. Stain—as Luce the beautiful sylph had dubbed her—choked on silent yelps when the witch plied a diluted minty soup of meadowsweet down her throat, put comfrey ointment on her skin, or wrapped bandages over her throbbing wounds. Stain kept waking again and again to find herself trapped in this unsettling reality that both consoled and mortified in the same breath.

On some level, she considered that her warden, who introduced herself as Crony, must be trying to help, for why else would she feed and minister to her? Unless they needed her alive for some ill purpose. Or were those of magic-kind capable of kindness? Speaking of "kinds," did Stain belong to this place, among these otherworldly creatures? Why couldn't she remember?

Unfortunately, it was just as impossible for her to ask these questions as it was to communicate pain and fear. Without working vocal cords, all of her bottled emotions compressed tight within . . . a swelling, hot pressure that threatened to explode.

Until at last, that's precisely what it did.

Stain awoke in semidarkness. Her wardens . . . or captors . . . spoke in hushed tones on the other side of the drapes that muted her surroundings.

"The Pegasus has been sniffing about again." The sylph man's voice drizzled sweet like satiny honey despite the underlying acidity of the words. "There are char marks on the trunks surrounding the house."

"May-let we should let him see her." Crony's voice was the opposite of Luce's, like bowed, barren branches scritchity-scratching together in the wind. "May-let he'd be the medicine she need."

"How's that to work?"

"A creature that breathes fire and outlived the extinction of its own be a worthy guardian, wouldn't ye think?"

"He almost killed her in the moon-bog. I saw him aim to strike her skull with my own eyes. He's feral. Unpredictable. Extend the wards beyond the house's frame. The trees that surround us . . . plant your nightmares there to keep him at bay."

Scorch was only warning me. Stain wanted to shout his defense. Her muscles tensed atop her thin, lumpy pallet at the mention of nightmare wards. She wasn't sure what such things were, but they sounded horrific. She thought back on the moment the Pegasus's hooves came down inches from her head. She'd sensed his unspoken message: that he owed her nothing, for he had saved her from the bog just as she had saved him. He was showing her he didn't belong to her, that he wasn't to be tamed.

But she didn't wish to tame him. She wished to be heard . . . to be understood. The Pegasus was the one beast that seemed to have that ability. That made him the only prospect of a friend in this place she couldn't remember. She wouldn't allow anything to happen to him.

Stain forced out a screech that erupted as little more than a gusty breath—unheard by any ear. Clenching her useless throat, she noticed the strange necklace again . . . a pendant of braided hair at her collarbone. A witch's trinket. That must be what was silencing her. They'd rendered her unable to speak to keep her helpless and at their mercy.

A nicker shook the leaves in the distance, and she realized her silent screech had been heard after all. Luce cursed from the other side of the drapes. "Our house is but a tinderbox, woman. With only a sneeze he could set us to flame. Cast your spell!"

Before Crony could respond, Stain mustered all her strength to rip off the necklace and tuck it under her pallet. She plunged out from her sanctuary. Her vision blurred with feverish sights. The house loomed like a skeleton, a dizzying disarray of boards, nails, and discarded, unwanted things.

Gooseflesh prickled along her body—beneath a tunic two sizes too big that hung to her knees—as she teetered between chills and feverish flashes. She scrabbled over the stony floor through a layer of ash, pushing beyond the torment of torn flesh to thrust her torso over the threshold before Crony and Luce could catch up.

Something jolted through her the moment she crossed and hit the powdery terrain outside. A startling hiss filled her ears, though it didn't come from either of her captors. It was locked within her head. Her vision faded; her body curled to fetal position and spasmed as her entire being funneled down into a malevolent darkness that scraped her hollow with claws and teeth. She sensed rather than saw the ground soften and swallow her whole. Underneath, in a suffocating earthen tunnel, formless creatures reached for her . . . things made of bone and shade that craved human flesh. She raised her hands to protect herself. Her fingertips lit to a brilliant gold—a light that scalded her skin and eyes.

"She's locked in a nightmare." Luce's panicked remark carried across a great distance, through the soil and ash spanning between them. "What is happening with her fingers? They're lit up like lanterns! Stop thrashing, Stain. You'll only tear your skin more!"

"Where be her talisman?" Crony asked, sounding as far away as Luce. "Find it while I bind her to reality."

Stain burrowed through the dirt, subterranean like a worm, to escape the creatures she sensed gaining on her from behind. If she didn't dig her way out, it would be her death. The light radiating from her fingers illuminated dormant seedlings cradled in pockets of soil that screamed to be renewed. Instinctively, her fingers burned brighter, hotter, as if all the fever in her body gathered at their tips. The seeds sprouted in answer, roots spreading and blossoms blooming, pushing upward toward the surface. Stain grabbed on and held tight—a flower's roots wrapped around each wrist—springing out from the dirt and choking for breath against a heavy cloud of smoke and heat. Her eyes refused to open.

"Stay back, rabid donkey." Luce's harsh warning broke through in the same moment Stain felt a string drop into place around her neck.

Her eyes opened then, and the nightmare faded away to a scene of fire and flowers in the witch's front yard. Stain had never been underground. It had all been in her mind. Scorch whinnied, prancing through the small clearing, nibbling on petals and leaving sparks in his wake.

"There now, wee one, ye be back with us." Crony caressed her fuzzy head. "No more crossin' the threshold without yer necklace, aye? That be yer protection again' the wards."

"How did you do that?" Luce asked Stain, barely allowing the witch to finish her instructions. "How did you call up the flowers?"

She had no answer. Only then did she notice her hands were embedded in the soil, and with each painful pulse of her fingertips, the ground lit up and other blossoms sprouted: reds, oranges, golds, and purples. A rainbow giving life to the ash alongside Scorch's trail of embers.

"Let's get you back to bed," Luce said. He helped Stain stand and led her aching body over the threshold. Crony was already inside the cadaverous framework, tidying the mess Stain had left in the wake of escape.

Stain stalled at the door, wavering on weak legs, catching Scorch's fiery gaze. *You came to find me.*

His gruff voice tapped her thoughts: *I came to torment the fox-man.*

She grinned. *You will return. We need each other.*

What use is a pesky little child to a steed of wings and flame? He stood on a path close to the doorway—yet too far to touch or be touched.

Luce snarled for the Pegasus to leave but Crony intervened. "Let the wee one see the sky . . . it be twilight's blink."

They all looked up together where a small opening in the leaves showcased a glimpse of blue. For one enchanted instant, the sun's blistering brightness dimmed. Stain was able to view the endless heavens without her eyes burning. She saw new colors—purple, blue, and red—and imagined flying with wings of her own. During that flash of darkness, she looked back at the

Pegasus and saw her eyes reflected off the dark mirrors of his gaze, amber and glinting like coins.

He shook the sparks in his mane. *You are not of this place. Your lashes are slivers of the moon, and your eyes pierce the darkness with starlight.* He turned and trotted into the thicketed surroundings without another word.

Stain backed into the house and plopped onto her pallet. Emaciated and flawed as it was, Scorch had given her her first glimpse of self.

Crony handed Stain a teacup while Luce grumbled something about the yard. He carried out a pitcher of water and doused the tiny fires burning her flowers. The care he took in saving each one impressed her, and she began to trust him, yet remained wary of the witch.

Crony withdrew the bandage on Stain's waist and some scabs ripped free, reopening wounds. Stain choked on a soundless cry, wriggling to escape.

Crony gripped her shoulder. "No need to hold back, wee one. Start makin' some noise. It'll help ye feel better. Grunts and growls be just as fine as speakin' to one such as me. So don't be afeared to try."

It was obvious then that neither of her keepers realized how broken she was. She suspected they knew no more of her than she knew of herself. Had they stumbled upon her . . . found her somewhere half-dead?

She touched her throat, her eyes stinging with that bewildering hot dryness that should've preceded tears.

Crony's swampy gaze narrowed. "Ye have no voice?" She reeled back, as though the thought almost knocked her over. She turned to Luce, who stepped across the threshold with a bouquet of flowers in hand. "She has no *voice*."

Luce's features—so lovely amid all the ugliness—fell. He shook his head and turned away with a low growl.

In spite of Crony's attempt to comfort, Stain feared her for all the wrong reasons: her reptilian face, the gruffness of her mannerisms, the horns that caught the hazy daylight, accentuating sharp, curved tips. The witch seemed wounded when Stain pushed her away. But there were walls erected between them that Stain had no means to break down—no way to communicate or common ground to stand upon.

Crony moved aside and allowed Luce to redress Stain's wounds. He managed to be gentle until he tied off a bandage too tight around her knee. At last, Stain's bottled-up frustration overflowed, and instinct overtook. Her arms lifted and her fingers moved in symbols and letters that both surprised and empowered her. She yelled at him with her hands.

He jerked back, bewildered. "What is she doing?"

Crony moved closer, her soupy eyes wide with wonder. "Speakin'. She be tellin' ye that ye tied up her leg like a tourniquet. Loosen it."

Luce did as he was asked. Thrilled to be understood outside of her mind, Stain signed a thank-you to Crony. Then told her everything she could remember: the truth about the Pegasus, how she awoke without any recollection and was frightened by Crony's slumbering form, how the strands of sunlight that peered through the leaves burned her skin.

Crony responded patiently. The witch confirmed that they'd found Stain dying close to the entrance of the ravine, and that anything of her past was a mystery. But Stain pushed aside the loss she felt, for now she had made another connection. Her trust burgeoned like the flowers she could call with her fingertips. She realized Crony had a kind soul and wasn't the monster she'd mistaken her to be.

Two weeks passed and Stain used the time to heal, though Scorch didn't visit again. While Luce and Crony went to market, she was permitted to explore, but only if dressed as a boy. Crony insisted this disguise was necessary to keep word from getting out that a girl was living in the forest, to protect her from whoever had left her for dead. Her guardians delayed her introduction to the inhabitants, so Stain could practice a boy's mannerisms and appearance. This she did in solitude each day while hidden in the maze of trees and brambles close to their home.

During her solitary wandering, she dropped slices of dried apple on the path she walked. At last, one day, he clomped behind her. She turned, holding the remainder of the apple in her hand: brushed with honey and rolled in oats—an irresistible treat to any horse. But he wasn't just a horse. He was feather, flame, and shadow, a mythic creature fueled by pride.

The Pegasus looked up from eating the last slice on the ground.

She stretched out her palm, the oaten-apple balanced atop her scars.

His nostrils flared, proving he smelled the treat. He nickered. *Toss it here.*

You must eat it from my hand, Scorch.

He pawed, his hoof stirring up ash. *I am not a trained pony, witless mite. And I can find my own apples.*

Not like this one. She took several steps forward, though her feet shook within her boots. She'd forgotten how lofty and intimidating he was when not half-sunken in a bog. *I made it special for you. To bring you happiness.*

He snorted and smoke escaped his nostrils. *Trampling humans. Burning them to cinders and crunching their bones to powder beneath my hooves. That's what makes me whicker with happiness.*

She noticed three arrow shafts sticking out from his flanks. He must've recently enjoyed such a tirade. *Why do you hate humans?*

They are beneath me, yet they wish to tame me.

Her fingers curled around the apple to feel the rough, sticky coating, then opened again. *I don't seek to tame you. I seek a partnership. I'll take nothing you're not willing to give. No arrows, no ropes, whips . . . no reins or saddles. Meet me halfway. Compromise tastes sweetest when offered by a friend's hand.*

His eyes sparked with a gentle flame. *What does a Pegasus need with a friend?*

A friend is loyal—a second defense against danger. I'll be your eyes on the ground when you're flying. I'll be your ears when you're too high to listen. And I'll be your hands should you ever be trapped again.

He lifted his smoldering wings to their impressive span and took three steps until he loomed over her. *You are no bigger than a speck of dust. Too small to be of any use.*

Her whole body trembled now. She stiffened her bones to hide it. *I've already proved my fierceness is a match for yours.*

If you are so brave, then walk the final step toward me.

She stretched her arm out as far as it would go, forcing her hand not to shake. *Sometimes it takes more courage to stay in place than to move. I'm standing my ground.*

Her fingers lit up to that burning sensation that was almost unbearable.

Grunting, Scorch clopped forward, his smoky breath bridging the small space between them. His inscrutable gaze met hers. He arched his neck and nuzzled her fingertips until the agonized light faded, calmed by the contact.

Thank you. Cautiously, Stain lifted her free hand to scratch the soft place behind his right ear. His tail swished in contentment as his lips moved to nibble the sticky bits of apple on her palm.

She leaned closer, pressing forehead to forelock. Her long lashes caught on the wisps of mane that flopped down between his ears. *It is as I told you, Scorch.* Her thoughts were but a whisper. *Friendship has many rewards. I can help with the arrows . . .*

He broke loose and jerked his neck before galloping off into the trees. Stain smiled. Though her past still eluded her, her present no longer did. She had a friend and a family; she wouldn't be alone in this journey.

※·Ⅰ·※

Five years came and went, much slower than a wink of twilight in the day realm, or a blink of dawn in the night. Both Nerezeth and Eldoria kept to themselves, other than the exchange of imports and exports necessary for the welfare of their people and princess, respectively. Such trades were conducted at the base of Mount Astra, where a tunnel channeled through the burgeoning harvest of panacea roses and led down to Nerezeth's iron gate.

Within the first year, Eldoria's efforts to capture the slippery spy associated with the witch responsible for Lustacia's, Sir Nicolet's, and King Kiran's murders ended abruptly when a scourge of dementia infected the castle's occupants.

Mere weeks after Griselda first holed up in sanctuary with her two daughters and the kingdom's princess (her grand deception having gone off without a hitch), Mia sampled a pigeon pie to be delivered to the royal family. She suffered stomach cramps so piercing, she imagined the birds pecking her from the inside. The maid tried to cut them out, and her dying screams could be heard throughout all wings of the castle. Wrathalyne and Avaricette assured their mother that this must be the only drawback to living in the dungeon, insulated from all sound, since they would have delighted in hearing the poisoned fruits of Griselda's labor firsthand. Lustacia, undergoing a steady transformation to Princess Lyra, sat out of the conversation entirely. Other violent self-induced deaths followed over the next twelve months, including Matilde the cook's and Brindle the jester's, to name but a few. Griselda stopped short of Prime Minister Albous, allowing him to live for two reasons: one, he was respected for his wisdom in diplomatic strategies and the upkeep of the kingdom, even by Griselda herself; and two, because the death of a member of government would've been cause for closer scrutiny. By focusing her vengeance on a handful of servants, it was easy enough to blame the witch, yet again.

Griselda conferred with Eldoria's royal mages, convincing them that the hag not only placed a spy in their midst, but a curse upon the castle as well. Each person who lived within the walls had been exposed to the mental malaise, which meant the royal army must remain on the grounds at all times on the chance a hysterical mob might erupt. This put an end to the military expeditions to the Ashen Ravine in search of the witch, whom Griselda secretly preferred never be caught and questioned. The change in orders mattered little to the army, since up to that point the forest had been impossible to breach, due to the thorny briars that closed off the entrance upon the arrival of any soldier. Most everyone moved out of the castle for fear of going mad, leaving behind less than thirty occupants. Only the extended royal household remained, including three council members and their families along with the most necessary servants—all under Griselda's close supervision.

With the harrower witch still at large, the shimmery triplets decided protection for Eldoria was of utmost importance. From their home upon Mount Astra, the mages sent out incantations simultaneously in their bass, baritone, and tenor voices. However, though they spoke in unison, each had his own idea of what they should evoke. The first called forth an impenetrable camouflage that would feed off the sun; the second conjured a scented curtain to soothe the senses and counteract the witch's curse of mania; and the third beckoned a palisade with bite enough to ward off outside dangers.

A living sheath of honeysuckle vines rose in answer, creeping up to cloak every cottage, thoroughfare, and fence in the land, then enveloping every wall and tower of the castle. All but the windows and doors disappeared within the blossoming pink-and-green armor. However, as often happens when too many wands stir a pot, the magical entree ripened to something unruly and unexpected. A coating of burrs—as large as a babe's fist and as pointy and vicious as the bronze needles used by the castle's seamstresses—coated each leaf and stem. The fragrant, blushing blooms attracted swarms of stinging bees. Traversing to farm or market proved difficult; one had to wear thick clothes, boots, gloves, hoods, and masks to protect skin and hair, along with carrying torches—treated with fire repellent to release heavy smoke in lieu of flame—that could clear a path through the bees. These preparations made going outdoors hot and uncomfortable. Children could no longer play outside for risk of their tender flesh.

Spurred by the people's unrest, the mages attempted to reverse what they had wrought, but no amount of magic had any effect on the flowering vines, which daily grew thicker and stronger due to the never-waning sun. The burrs themselves prevented pruning or tearing away the roots. Fire only seemed to make them grow bigger. The only thing that shrank the stickers so the greenery could be stripped down was to douse them with the self-same midnight shadows sent by Nerezeth for the princess's nightsky fabric. Sadly, there would never be enough to sprinkle upon the entire kingdom. Only a powerful wash of moonlight cast down from the heavens could counteract the regenerative power of the sun and provide time for the plants to be uprooted. Since there was no night to counter the day, there was no hope. The mages considered conjuring up a plague of spiders to capture the bees, but knowing many Eldorian citizens shared the regent's disdain for creatures of darkness, it would be trading one problem for another.

So, things were left as they were, and a people who had once spent every waking moment outside stayed ensconced within their homes except when absolutely necessary to venture out. The bustling land of perpetual light became a lonely and quiet place, with its occupants peering at the radiant sky and lush landscapes from windows and doorways, rarely feeling the sun on their faces. For the next several years the Eldorians stayed tucked away, sad and miserable, awaiting Nerezeth's prince to come claim his bride, relying on the prophecy of "night and day united" to offer a reprieve from their enchanted prison.

For Griselda's part, she rejoiced. Though in the beginning Wrathalyne and Avaricette grumbled about giving up their freedom for their sister's happiness, Griselda was able to staunch their jealousies by assuring them that being sisters to the queen had its advantages . . . handsome knights from both kingdoms at their beck and call, for one. After that, she and her daughters adjusted to life in their luxurious, paraffin-sunlit dungeon cell. What did it hurt for the villagers and subjects to have to hide away as well? Despair and suffering would lead to loyalty and gratitude.

Griselda knew that one day, they would all thank her. Just as the shrouds had predicted, she was bringing the prophecy about by making her daughter fit the princess's mold. Soon Lustacia would meet every detail word for word.

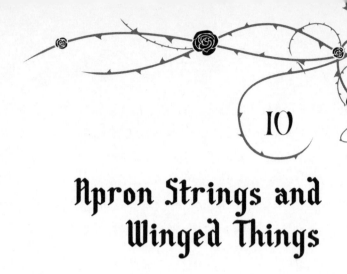

10

Apron Strings and Winged Things

nbeknownst to Eldoria's smug regent, within the dark metropolis of the Ashen Ravine, the real princess lived on, as did the harrower witch who knew Griselda was preening an imposter. And Crony had a different outlook on prophecies.

In the witch's centuries of experience, a foretelling would see itself fulfilled in absolution no matter who tried to interfere. This gave her comfort, considering the child she once saved no longer had a birdsong voice, nor lustrous silver hair, nor was she even a girl, at least to the goblins, murderers, degenerates, and outcasts living there. To the ravine's occupants, she was known simply as Stain, the wraith-like boy—origins unknown—who had wandered into the forest five years earlier and been taken in by the witch and her cohort for a set of extra hands. Even the shrouds themselves still believed her to be a boy, for the shadows and scorpions had never let them close enough to learn otherwise.

Yet there were two things the princess possessed that could never be compromised or taken away: her father's noble spirit and his royal blood. Crony hoped those would be enough to lead her back to her identity and the throne—and soon—for now that the princess was seventeen, Prince Vesper's arrival in Eldoria was imminent.

Crony stepped into her yard, feeling the press of time more than usual. The cessation course had ended an hour ago, and she needed to be rid of her two tenants for the day. She didn't want an audience for the dark task she must undertake. She didn't want Luce to know why she moved slower of late . . . that her bones had begun to brittle . . . that her blood ran sluggish and her heart puttered with a lackadaisical beat.

The old witch knelt, knees creaking, to study the flowers on either side of the rock pathway leading to her door. She leaned close enough their delicate perfume tickled her nostrils. They looked like brushstrokes of red, fuchsia, blue, and apricot floating atop the shifting ash.

Many of the ravine's occupants carved out homes within the massive tree trunks, or some perched up high in canvas tents balanced on the branches. Others braved sleeping out in the open in the lowlands where the ash was thinner, though to do so risked being swallowed by a wandering quag-puddle or dragged by vines into the domain of the shrouds.

As for Crony, she'd claimed a secluded, airless grove. Her home was a scaffold with no walls, set atop a floor of wide, flat rocks to keep out quag-puddles. The wooden frame—fashioned of willow, the most receptive wood to magic—was propped between a circle of black trunks and nailed slipshod into place, forming three bedrooms, a kitchen, and a doorway around her dusty furniture. The discarded furnishings from Eldoria's citizens partnered ideally with her cadaver abode: chairs purging their cushioning from ripped-out seams, torn mattresses restuffed with straw and rotted leaves, ottomans made of upended boxes, a fire pit hedged in with broken bricks, one splintering cedar chest, and several busted casks that smiled like snarl-toothed jesters.

The windows were empty frames as well, each crafted of four pieces of wood nailed together and hanging midway in the air, supported by wires secured to the intertwined tree limbs overhead.

Luce liked to tease her about the absurdity of windows in a home devoid of walls, but Crony insisted even an old, grubby witch needed some semblance of refinement. Upon each sill sat a fractured vase or chipped teacup packed with bird feathers or fresh flowers. Silk and velvet patchwork valances lined the top of the window frames, stitched from clothes Crony had peeled off the best-dressed corpses she'd pillaged. Similar patchwork curtains stretched overhead from the branches to the floor to hide the princess's room—an addition she'd made for the girl's privacy. Any leftover fabric covered Crony's supplies: potions, potables, and food stores, all tucked within stairstep branches and knotholes serving as shelves and cupboards in the kitchen. She'd lost her spell-recipes centuries earlier but knew the important ones by memory.

Some might think hers a primitive way to live, but there was no need for windowpanes or sturdy walls in an enclosed wood where the rains never penetrated and the winds never wailed. In the civilized world, walls, roof, and glass kept the wilds out. But being of the wilds herself, Crony welcomed such things—moldering moss, ash, and grime alike.

In this wasteland, the mortal occupants were the vermin. To stave them off, Crony had infused her house's framework with horrific visions—an attack by phantasmal, skull-faced figures in dark robes; a growing quagmire enveloping the surroundings; falling face-first into a pit of vipers—memories of the dying so vivid the prowler would believe them to be their own.

In the earlier years, Crony had often returned home from the market or hunting to find a would-be attacker or thief rolled up in fetal position beside the door's frame. Today, her reputation preceded her, making it a rare occurrence for anyone to enter even her yard.

Thoughts of said yard drew Crony's attention back to the rainbow at her knees—the only flowers in the whole ravine, other than the ones decorating her shop. She barely heard Luce's footsteps shuffling over until two feet stopped at her side, encased in dusty black boots. He wore his human form today and looked ostentatious and completely out of place here in his red fineries.

"They're withering." A canine growl punctuated his observation as he nudged a cluster of larkspur with his boot's toe. "She's been neglecting them to spend time with the jackass."

Crony hesitated to respond, half-amused by Luce's annoyance, but also saddened. Before the princess had come, Crony's and Luce's lives had been limited to shades of black and gray, like everyone else's in this accursed place. Nothing but ash and brambles met the eye. In so many ways, the princess had brought color to their world. Crony wondered how long the flowers would last once she and Luce lived alone again. Though in truth, she didn't expect to be alive long enough to know.

Jaw clenched, Crony shoved a hand beneath the sooty ground cover and found it hot to the touch. "May-let it has more to do with the heat than any negligence. It be blistering in Eldoria. Though me bones decry a storm on the horizon." The ravine was always cooler than Eldoria; but the ash writhing about their ankles carried hints of the kingdom's weather, being warmed by patches of sunlight that seeped through thinner spots in the canopy.

Luce bent down to pluck a stalk of columbine. The periwinkle petals and maroon foliage stood out vivid against his luminous flesh. "You're just looking for excuses. She's growing irresponsible. Goes off with her fancy donkey until all hours. Exploring every inch of this ravine. She's lucky the shrouds haven't eaten them both."

"Ye bein' a bit hard on her. Seein' as she helps us in the market each day."

"But her heart's rarely there. She's always wishing to be with him, caught up in frivolities that can't possibly lead her to the throne. You're the one who says she needs to practice her gifts and 'political' skills, however difficult and boring."

"Aye, since we can't be touting who she is."

"Exactly so. We can't even share her age. Her responsibilities are the only way she'll rediscover her identity. It's time she starts taking them seriously.

And to that end, I aim to see she rectifies the garden today, before we head out."

Crony glanced up, stifling the smile that wanted to break free. She couldn't risk withering the flowers further.

"What?" he asked, his dazzling face scowling down on her.

"Just ne'er thought a doggish dandy would fit the parental mold so ably. Those apron strings will need to be loosed one day soon."

His pointy teeth glinted on a mocking laugh that reverberated through the trees. "Apron strings, bah. We stuck out our necks for her. I won't let the last five years of sacrifice be for nothing." He shifted two large leather pouches strung from his shoulder by straps. "Stain owes me a set of wings, and owes you . . . well, whatever it is you expect to gain. Redemption, was it? Come to think, you've yet to share the details of your misdeeds and why we're bound by this vow of noninterference." He tapped his lower lip with the plucked columbine, his gaze pointedly narrow.

Crony redirected the conversation. He'd learn of her secrets soon enough. "D'ye forget? Yer wings hinge on a *selfless* sacrifice. Ye best be taking yer wants and needs out of the equation to meet that criterium. Aye?"

Before he could answer, they heard movement in the house as Stain stepped from behind her curtain. Her flesh blended into the dimness— permanently tinted a dingy gray by the enchanted sun-solvent clay Crony insisted she wear, both for protection from strands of daylight and to hide her true identity. Her loose muslin tunic, burlap vest, and canvas breeches served the latter purpose, too, as did her shorn scalp. For some inexplicable reason, the girl's long silver locks had never grown back after Luce and Crony rescued her—not past a fine fuzz. One of several oddities, for her lashes couldn't be pulled or clipped without causing the child immense internal pain, as if they were a living part of her, formed of nerves and purest moonlight. Crony had surmised that was why they grew so long and curled upward, reaching for the sky where the moon once hung. Since they couldn't change her eyes, they'd concentrated on making the silver sheen upon her scalp more ordinary, dying the stubble with blackberry juice and maintaining it thus to this very day.

As a result of these changes and the abuse her body had endured, the girl was nothing special to look upon. Her only attributes were lashes and lips a mite too pretty. Those didn't seem to matter, as people couldn't see past her grimy, scarred, and stick-slender shell. Crony worried the transformation had been too complete. For what grand prince would find the girl marriable in such a ruffian state?

Stain paused where the kitchen window was strung over a sink made of a discarded wine cask. She glanced up—framed by the four slats of wood— and waved to her keepers. Her sparkling lilac eyes and smiling lips lit up the dim house.

Crony had to avert her gaze or risk responding in kind. That smile, and the depth of kindness and wisdom in those eyes, shone so bright against the girl's plainness it was contagious.

As if proving Crony's point, Luce offered an answering wave and grin. Crony raised a brow and gave him a knowing look. He caught himself and cursed, tucking his hand into his pocket.

"Let's get a move on," he barked to cover up his momentary weakness, gesturing toward the forest. Within the maze of trees and brambles, a wind- ing onyx trail led to the market some quarter-league away. "Crony wants us to open shop today and carry over stock. We're already late, and the garden still needs your attention."

Furrowing her eyebrows, almost transparent against her discolored skin, Stain nodded. She dunked her entire head into the sink's water—reserves from the Crystal Lake that Luce kept filled for her. She jerked up and gasped at the chill. Shimmery streams slicked her furred scalp then ran into her face. Glistening droplets clung to her extensive lashes. Drying off with her sleeve, she left a blotch of gray from yesterday's clay upon the muslin. After smear- ing on more sun protectant, she wriggled into some gloves and grabbed a handful of breakfast, opting for the dried, leathery bites of quail and shriveled apple from a cracked bowl.

Popping some food into her mouth, Stain hastened across the threshold. An eager whinny lanced the thick air and the girl's stunning smile returned, even brighter, as the Pegasus cantered out from the trees and into the yard.

Ears back, the beast snorted at Luce and Crony while he sauntered over to Stain, stirring clouds of ash beneath his hooves. He halted, towering above the girl, wings folded to his sides . . . waiting. He scolded her with his eyes and she chuffed a soundless laugh before offering a few pieces of apple.

Scorch nuzzled the snack and twitched his tail contentedly as she reached up to scrub behind his right ear with gloved knuckles. The embers in his mane cast light along her ashen complexion and his black coat, resembling stars against stormy skies. A fitting analogy, as they often seemed to be two constellations having a conversation imperceptible to those tied to earth.

A grumpy frown clouded Luce's features. "Well, so much for her not getting distracted. What . . . does he sleep in the trees now?' He looked up at the branches. "Surely there's a horse-sized nest up there somewhere."

"If so, we be in good fortune. Poached Pegasus eggs be a delicacy."

Luce rolled his eyes.

Crony laughed within herself. She couldn't decide if the sylph's dislike of the winged horse stemmed from having to share the attentions of their ward, or if he envied Scorch's wings. She imagined a bit of both. Either way, Luce's discomfort provided her hours of endless amusement.

Many in the ravine had tried to capture the stallion, but he always broke free, leaving behind a trail of fire-crisped corpses. In deference to their lives, the denizens had finally learned to let him be. Only Stain could get near him. She'd told Crony that deep within Scorch's coal-black heart thrived a gentle diamond, precious and rare, and she would one day mine it.

Pulling away from Scorch, Stain made a sign for the sun aimed in Luce and Crony's direction.

Luce nodded. Crony had taught him the language—how to read the letters and signals Stain formed with her hands. Crony knew it from centuries before, when Nerezeth and Eldoria had been allies. It was a lost language, once universal to both kingdoms—a way of communicating silently across short distances. Back then, drasilisks consumed the night skies. The nocturnal creatures were half-blind and like bats, and relied upon keen hearing and echolocation to find their human prey. The two kingdoms had combined their infantries and used hand communications for strategizing and at last defeated the winged, serpentine plague by working together.

Few knew how to cipher the signals now, just as few remembered a time when Eldoria and Nerezeth coexisted in harmony. But Crony remembered—as only those who were dead or immortal would.

Someone in Eldoria had thought to teach the princess the old language, and Crony was grateful. It was the only way she'd managed to gain the girl's trust.

After making another sign for water, Stain knelt at the horse's ember-fringed fetlocks and ran her gloves across the drooping flowers as the Pegasus stretched his neck to nibble the wetness from her scalp.

Luce crouched down. Swatting at the swish of ash stirred by Scorch's pawing front hoof, he took the waterskin from his waist and held it next to a limp sprig of larkspur.

Stain wrinkled her nose, preparing herself. Removing a glove, she dug her fingers—tips lit to a golden glow—into the ashes. Then she called up the dormant seeds of columbine, larkspur, and bleeding heart left over from centuries before.

Scorch shook his mane, graceful legs and silver hooves dancing as the sooty groundcover blinked with a flash of light. Luce added water from the canteen and four new blooms burst from the ground while the existing flowers grew bigger and brighter.

"Well done, child." Crony patted Stain's tense shoulder.

The girl snapped her head in acknowledgment, too intent on riding out the pain to meet the witch's gaze.

The princess's ability to rouse life from seeds buried far beneath the earth, so far below they should've been dead long ago, was inexplicable in the beginning. Crony couldn't understand how someone, formed and revered by the night, could harbor sunlight in her hands. But after watching the girl's memory of when she opened a very special letter written in gold on black parchment, the witch had a hypothesis that involved the prince himself. And if she was right, there was a connection between the two already in place.

Taking a measured breath, Stain gathered a bouquet of the fullest blooms and held them up to Crony. *Fresh, for the vases*, she signed with her shimmery-gilded hand.

Crony cupped the girl's chin. "Thank ye, wee one. Always nice to have some frippery for me windows." She took the flowers and limped toward the doorway, then turned. "Ye both should be on yer way."

Stain stood and dusted off her palm, allowing Scorch to nuzzle it. The glow faded from her fingertips, as if he absorbed it. Crony had never asked, but it was clear. Somehow the horse was able to ease her pain.

Luce offered Stain a leather pouch for market. Not to be forgotten, Scorch nudged between them, wings spread high—each feather's barbs studded with orange cinders.

Luce grumbled something under his breath that made Stain shake her head affectionately, then the three started toward the thickening trees bordering Crony's plot.

Stain absently tugged at the talisman around her neck. It was the girl's ritual, to touch it each time she ventured away. May-let she sought security, reassurance that the key to her skeletal home wouldn't vanish like the past and family she couldn't remember.

Stain believed her amnesia was a result of the abuse someone had dealt her when they left her for dead inside the ravine. Crony nurtured the lie, though oft wondered if the princess would forgive them if she ever learned the truth of her guardians' contributions to the ills that had befallen her family—of the roles they had played in her personal tragedies. Then Crony would ask herself when it was she had started to care.

Stain waved good-bye before stepping with Luce along the glittering trail of embers left within Scorch's trotting wake, into the brambles and trees, leather pouches dangling from their hands.

Crony buried her serpentine nose in the flower bouquet, inhaling. Soon, she would be seeing the girl leave for the last time, if she could find a means to get her to the castle. The true princess must be there to greet the prince so all could fall into place for the prophecy. But Crony couldn't convince Stain to go, nor could she have Luce do the same. It had to be Stain's own decision some way. Yet she feared it was dangerous for the girl to make the journey and face Griselda alone without her memories. The Eldorians believed they already had their princess, and Stain no longer fit the description. The impossibility of the riddle vexed Crony's ancient mind.

She stepped into her bedroom and bent over the cedar chest at the base of a black elm's trunk, where she and Luce kept their stolen weapons and enchanted items. Opening the lid, she searched for a small, scaly box with black hinges. She'd chosen to craft it of drasilisk hide due to its indestructible quality. The words *princess - resolution* were scribbled across one particularly large and pale scale in black ink. As she searched, a needle, partly embedded in a dead man's tunic still needing hemmed, pierced Crony's thumb. A driblet of dark blood welled at the site.

The witch cursed. There was a time her hide would've bent something so benign as a needle in half. Upon blotting the wound to steep the flow, she found the box she sought, but a drop of blood had fallen upon the "s" in the word *resolution* and smeared it to resemble *revolution*.

She decided it didn't matter. Luce would know what the box was for when the time came. She lifted the lid and drew out the princess's glass book of memories. Crony knew every aspect of her childhood now, and Luce knew all that the witch had chosen to share.

She opened a page to watch the fragmented pieces of a scene play across in muted shades of whites, grays, and blacks: Stain's memory of standing upon her kingly father's shoes and learning to waltz. As Crony had yet to enliven the images, they could be viewed only by her eyes.

It was time to lock up the precious moments, until the princess's future aligned itself. Returning the book to the box, Crony whispered an incantation over the lid. The magical sealant would glue the box closed until the moment the princess regained her crown and earned the fealty of both kingdoms.

Setting the box in the trunk, Crony dug deeper, drawing out the note she'd started shortly after she and Luce first saved Eldoria's heir. She had procrastinated finishing it far too often. The words forced her to admit her mortality, something she didn't like to think upon. However, with the prince coming, final arrangements must be made.

She unfolded the note to reread what she had scripted thus far:

Luce,

If ye be reading this, I be gone. May-let yer angry how I left. Ye must understand, had ye known, it would have lent unwelcome complications. But I still aim to help ye, as ye have always aided me. I have the means for ye to claim yer true form again. But first, I ask one last grand gesture. That ye deliver the princess's box to Madame Dyadia, the royal sorceress of Nerezeth. It be locked shut, unable to surrender its contents until our girl wears the crown that once sat upon her queenly mother's head. After that, Dyadia can return the memories to their rightful owner. I shared the knowledge when our kingdoms stood as allies, long afore the division of the skies. Dyadia will tell ye all me secrets then, if ye still wish to know. The box marked for Griselda, it be yers. Therein lie the regent's many sins. May-let it can be a tool to free ye and our ward from Griselda's poisonous hold, may-let her contrition will be yer claim to those wings ye been missing so long.

Crony dipped a quill in ink to complete the note, but paused, attention drifting back to the chest where a red box, the shape and size of a domed birdcage, was buried beneath cloth and other sundries. If she concentrated, she could hear the pieces of Griselda's conscience flapping inside.

Luce didn't know Crony kept it hid here, or that she'd stolen it years ago while the shrouds lost themselves to a feeding frenzy. It had been meant as a gift for her sylphin companion, a means for him to get revenge. But when the princess fell into their keep, it became leverage.

No one could have more power over Griselda than the one who held her conscience . . . the one who harbored the acrid flavor of the sins she committed while charmed enough not to choke on them herself. Should the full essence be unleashed upon the regent in one fell swoop, it would bring her to her knees.

However, Crony didn't have the magic to reunite Griselda's conscience with her body and mind. Only Mistress Umbra did. It would be up to Luce to find a way to lure his past love back to the ravine . . . to throw her at the mercy of the mother shroud.

Frowning, Crony pressed the quill to the note to commence writing, but stopped cold when the caw of a crow echoed in the distance—a distinctive wail that ended on a howl, closer to banshee than bird.

Crony's breath caught . . .

It had been so long, but she would know that bleak sound anywhere. She dropped the note and inkwell in her haste to stand, a paste of ash and ink staining her cloak's hem as she spun to look upward.

The crow soared along the underside of the canopy: large as a vulture, one pink eye centered above its white beak, feathers as pure and pale as fresh cream. It slowed, then perched on a branch high out of reach, watching Crony intently.

"*Thana.*" The crow's name fell from the witch's lips, a word she hadn't spoken in centuries. It felt like music on her forked tongue, and she would've smiled at the nostalgia. But logic belayed any such reaction. If Dyadia had conjured her albino bird to scout with its portending eye here in this forest, it could mean only one thing: The prince had opted to journey through the ravine on his way to the castle. He was in this place already, or close at hand.

Elation wrestled with dread inside of her. Uniting Stain with her prince would no longer be an issue. But what would happen upon their meeting, seeing as Stain looked more boy than girl and had no voice?

Crony hurriedly scrawled her name along the bottom of the note. She dropped the note next to the box containing the glass memory book already within the chest.

Upon closing the lid, she rushed across the threshold toward market, staff in hand. She couldn't interfere, but nothing would stop her from watching.

The crow lifted from its perch and followed at a distance, the thud of its powerful wings raising the hair along Crony's nape. Thana following her didn't bode well—though there was no point brooding over it.

The moment had arrived for Stain to claim her fate, and all of Crony's mistakes were coming home to roost.

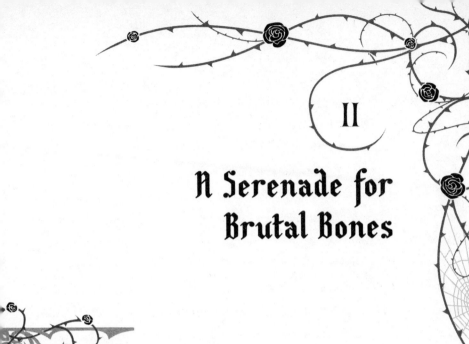

II

A Serenade for Brutal Bones

ithin the Rigamort, Nerezeth's most beautiful mystic ice cavern, there was a passage guarded by the most majestic of the night realm's creatures: the brumal stags—enchanted to be loyal to each successive king and protect the land's hidden border.

For centuries, the tunnel they guarded had been used by hoarfrost goblins who sold things on the black market, royally appointed sun-smugglers, and the occasional Night Ravager who had a secret mission, as it led directly up into the Ashen Ravine. That haunted wasteland provided the ideal camouflage for those stealing the sun or who wished to stay hidden from prying Eldorian eyes. However, none could enter Nerezeth from this same passageway, unless they belonged to the night. Brumal stags could sense their own kind, and anyone of the day realm, creature or man alike, foolish enough to attempt entry, fell prey to deadly antlers.

It was this very tunnel Prince Vesper planned to take for his trip into Eldoria. He knew, from notes he'd exchanged with his betrothed via jackdaws, that the princess and her family had been locked inside a dungeon in Eldoria since the peace treaty—all due to their fear of a murderous witch. Not only did the imprisonment affect Lady Lyra, but every cottage, wall, and tower within her land was swallowed by barbed vines that had been meant to protect them from the same vengeful conjurer. He'd promised long ago to keep her safe and intended to see it done. It was the least he could do, for without her song and her touch, his curse would harden him to a statue of gold and burst his stony bones into a thousand pinholes of light. But *with* her, together, they would reunite the sun and the moon and heal both lands.

Within the hour, he and his entourage would begin the journey to the day realm. Since there was only night here, his people took to their beds after that hazy glimpse of dawn in the sky, much like the Eldorians' cessation courses began at the blink of twilight. However, the prince had commanded everyone in his entourage to retire early, so they would be rested enough to leave once the sky flashed pink.

Too unsettled to take his own advice, Vesper stopped at the castle's infirmary. Wet coughs and labored breaths preempted the smells of sickness, panacea tea, and incense as he stepped into what was once the great obsidian ballroom. Cots lined the black walls and littered the open floor. Small pathways opened between them, allowing a mazelike passage. This place housed only the castle's affected occupants. Other temporary infirmaries had been assembled inside cottages throughout the province, for both nobles and commoners. Illness harbored no prejudice; it affected the young and old and rich and poor alike. Mortality and its frailties were the most humbling equalizers.

Humbling even for royalty, for here in this room, Vesper wasn't the king-in-waiting, or even the dark prince. Here he was the carrier of hope. A hope that was waning. Only one thing would save his sick people: pure daylight. Not only eating plants grown with it, but to stand beneath sunrays and absorb them, even if in small doses through windows or open doorways. With his sunlit blood, he could give them some of what they needed, but not enough.

Hardly even a head raised as he passed through the walkways, as most of the occupants were so ill, they struggled for breath and coughed without waking.

A small hand reached out from under a blanket and gripped Vesper's thumb, stalling him. Though the moonlit complexion was stark against the prince's deep coloring, like a layer of ice upon a hemlock, the child's touch was as hot as fire.

Vesper's heart pricked as he knelt beside the cot. "Good diurnal, Nyx." He affectionately mussed the silvery bush of hair upon the seven-year-old's head, noting the smear of gold peeking out from the boy's nightshirt upon his chest. "How do you fare today?"

"I'd be better, were Elsa to shut her teeth about the princess."

On the cot across from Nyx came his younger sister's voice, hoarse from coughing yet lilting with innocence. "I haven't been opening my teeth 'bout it. You're more chatty than me!"

"Liar! I only care about the witch." Nyx's eyes, dull and purple, blinked up in the dimness. "You're to lop off her head as a gift for your bride, aren't you, Majesty?"

Vesper bit back a grin, seeing his younger self in the lad's bloodthirst and boldness. "Not the head, no. I don't have the proper wrapping for horns. And a princess's gift must be immaculately presented. Don't you think it so, Elsa?"

A giggle erupted from the tiny girl's bluish lips. "Yes, Majesty! Especially for a princess of moonlight and music!"

"So, you're not to kill the witch at all?" Disappointment peppered Nyx's response. "Isn't that why you're going into the haunted forest. *Isn't it?*"

Their mother, the head cook, who had been busy preparing menus for the upcoming feasts, had apparently heard the rumors of Vesper traversing the Ashen Ravine and passed it on to her children. She was a firm believer that gossip provided better sustenance than food itself.

"I intend to capture the witch, yes," Vesper answered. "It will be for the princess to decide her fate. But I'm also going that way to check on the royal gatekeepers. Now, shouldn't you two be resting, so you can be well enough to attend the wedding?"

"I don't wish to rest! I want to help. I'm aged enough to be a page, you know!" Nyx turned his head into his pillow to muffle a hacking cough.

Wincing, Vesper patted the boy's rattling chest. "Of course you are, and when you're better, we'll see what we can do about that. First, you have to be hale and hearty enough to train. Even a knight needs to sleep."

"Tell us the tale of the brumal stags and the little prince, *please* . . ." Elsa's tiny lips scrunched into a pout impossible to resist. "We'll fall asleep then, Majesty. Promise."

"Fair enough," Vesper conceded. "But you must both lay down upon your pillows and close your eyes. It's far better to envision their beauty on a blank slate."

Elsa grinned. Both children shut their stubby white lashes, and took rattling breaths as Vesper sat upon the cold floor between their cots. He propped his elbows on his knees.

"The prince was but a child when he first saw them." He began the tale he'd told the castle's children many times before . . . the tale that hinged upon his personal memory. "He took the journey to the Rigamort with his kingly father for the ritual of binding that every young prince before him had experienced. He was nervous of the interaction, for most Nerezethites never see the creatures. Only those who use the Rigamort, who keep secrets locked tight within themselves."

"Was he scairt to smoke the pipe?" mumbled Nyx, halfway to sleeping already.

"Perhaps a little. But more, he was afraid the stags wouldn't recognize his royal station . . . wouldn't accept him, as this prince was different than all those before him."

"He couldn't see in the dark," Elsa interrupted. "And his hair was black as soot and his skin shimmered like a copper bell." Her own skin blushed, showcasing the blue veins beneath, and she squeezed her eyes tight to keep them closed.

Nyx's own sleepy eyes snapped open. "Elsa, stop hornin' in! And plus, swooning is for milksops."

She harrumphed at that.

Vesper smiled, waiting for Nyx's eyelids to flutter down. "The prince and his father descended deep within the cavern, past the frozen blue waterfalls and beyond the sparkling stalactites—and there in the depths were the gatekeepers. At first glance they looked frail: white, sleek, and deer-sized with moonlit-fringed fetlocks and long tufted tails resembling a lion's. But the silver-glowing scales that curved from their spines to their chests were as impenetrable as iron shields. And their claws rivaled any panther's, just as their razor-pronged antlers could shred a man to pieces—"

"With one duck of the head," Elsa added, beating her brother to his favorite detail.

Nyx's answering grumble evolved to a yawn.

Vesper paused reverently for the end of the telling. "Without any fear, the king took the prince's hand and stepped forward. He knelt beside his strange son, showing the stags his acceptance so they would accept him, too. And they did, nuzzling his little head with muzzles as soft as eiderdown. The king lit up the ceremonial pipe, and both he and the prince inhaled the incense—filled with enchantments, smoke, and starlight—and breathed a shared breath into each of the stag's nostrils."

Elsa yawned, as if triggered by her brother. "It bound them to you. In their minds." She rolled to her side and drew her blankets over her ears, her breaths growing even and slow.

"Yes. Exactly that." Vesper was glad the children slumbered, for he would never share the rest. It made him feel powerless, that from the moment he drank the sunlight, he'd lost his mental ties with the stags, just as he'd lost it with his people. Ever since, he had visited the gatekeepers in person, but an abundance of night tides had prevented the journey over the last several months. When the royal sorceress, Madame Dyadia, reached out to them with her spiritual portents, she reported the creatures had grown less responsive. The sorceress assumed it a natural evolution—since sun-smuggling and assassinating had become a thing of the past and those under royal employ no longer sought usage of the tunnel, the enchanted beings had little to report. But Vesper was concerned enough to take the backward route into Eldoria, so he might confirm the brumal stags' welfare with his own eyes.

Pulling the covers up to Nyx's chin, the prince reached across to squeeze Elsa's blanketed ankle and stood.

A physician spotted him and motioned him to a small table filled with medicinal herbs and waxy cones that could be melted down to ease breathing.

"Do you need a supply?" Vesper asked, eyeing the two remaining vials of golden liquid they'd drained from an incision a week earlier. "I'll be gone for several days."

The physician shook his pale head. "We want you strong and able-bodied for the journey, Majesty. We'll make do until your return."

Only recently they had discovered that Vesper's sunlit blood had healing qualities. It could be painted directly onto the ribs and chest of the sick. Though it initially caused a burning sensation, it helped clear the lungs.

When he'd first devoured the arboretum's daylit concoction, he had been unbearable for any of his people to touch. However, within a week they discovered that once the sunlight's poison entered his veins, it became less potent—to anyone but him. By pressing droplets of the drained golden mixture to vellum, others could handle it in small increments and lose sensitivity to his fiery skin. It was a matter of desensitizing with exposure. This anomaly had prompted Vesper to send letters written in his golden blood to Princess Lyra. He hoped to acclimate her to the sunlight so she wouldn't suffer when he touched her, so she wouldn't have to fear him when the time came for them to be together as husband and wife. By now, Lady Lyra should have absorbed enough that they would be able to share a dance in Eldoria's ballroom before leaving for Nerezeth, hand in hand.

Vesper left the infirmary and strode along corridors of obsidian stone, the ceilings and corners strung with glowing white spiders that lit the darkness like stars. The squeaks of fuzzy mice, so black they blended with the stones, followed behind as he arrived at the winding stairs leading down to the dungeon's cells.

Only a few were occupied with prisoners, none more dangerous than thieves or drunken vagabonds. Following the glass-encased torches along the walls—each lit strictly for him and fueled by tinder-bat dung—he entered an empty chamber at the end where he could no longer hear guards talking or prisoners snoring.

He dragged out the princess's latest note from his pocket, then laid down upon a bed of nails to read it. Every cell in the dungeon had beds like this one. Each had hinged lids, also lined with iron spikes. An indention was made for the face, the pointed tips filed down to protect the eyes. Thus, the lid could be pulled into place atop a supine body—to torment the flesh on both sides.

Lying there, with the points pressed against his nape, spine, shoulders, torso and limbs, he considered closing the lid. In Eldoria, the nailbed would be a torture device. Yet, in his kingdom it provided training for young men and women alike who wished to serve in the royal infantry, not for self-flagellation, but to toughen their skin. Wearing metal armor outside the castle walls proved more detrimental than helpful, due to sleet storms that immediately froze to ice. Within minutes, the weight of a suit of chainmail could double or triple and harden beyond all movement, rendering its wearer as good as paralyzed. Instead, they crafted their armor out of rainbow-scaled fish skins insulated with leather, naturally water-resistant, lightweight and flexible—attributes that unfortunately also made them permeable by the creatures of their terrain. Thus, their skin had to serve as a third layer of protection.

After years of training, Vesper understood the pressure points and how to position one's body to reap the least damage. The iron stabs kept him grounded . . . reminded him of his youth when his kingly father accompanied him to the wilds, where he learned to battle both cadaver brambles and rime scorpions. Day after day, Vesper endured searing stings and punctures—for longer stretches each time—until at last he could withstand the pain and had built up an immunity to both kinds of venom, much like his blood desensitizing people to the sunlight's burn.

The prince now had scars enough that it no longer hurt to be pricked by thorns or nails. In fact, he had more scars than most, after uncountable incisions to drain the resurgence of toxic sun in his veins—each sewn shut with magical thread that left him healed, but flawed. Surprisingly, he could hardly feel the fiery infestation internally; there was minimal pain other than his dismal dance with the blade.

His hand clenched the knife sheathed at his waist. Even his face had suffered a cleansing gash, leaving a scar along his left cheek that could be partially masked beneath a beard. But pain and vanity were the least of his worries. Of late, the golden tinge in his blood grew thicker, more difficult to leech away. One day, it would stop flowing, and his heart would cease beating.

Other than the welfare of his people, this was his greatest concern. And that was why the princess was his only hope. His *kingdom's* only hope.

"You should be sleeping." The statement was followed by a wave of pearly crickets swishing across the floor.

Vesper tilted his head. His queenly mother's silhouette stood in the doorway, draped in shadows cast by the torch. Her pets settled into the corners to chirp merrily. The queen held a small bundle in her arms. In the dimness, her eyes glinted amber—a contrast to the icy silver of her crown and hair.

"As our cricket subjects are zealously proclaiming, Lady Mother, this is a time for celebrating, not sleeping." He rolled to his side and winced as a nail pierced his skin, just beneath his lowest rib. So, there were still a few tender places left on him. He rather liked the proof of humanity, knowing he wasn't yet a man of metal and stone.

His grimace gentled as he refolded Lyra's unread letter and pressed his boots on the floor to stand. "What do you have there? Is it the midnight shadows and spiders? I thought Cyprian was to gather those." Vesper and his troop were taking an abundance of both, to intimidate the bees and shrink the thistles so they could break through Eldoria's honeysuckle-imprisoned stronghold and claim his bride.

"Your first knight has no part in this. These are personal gifts for the princess from myself and her late father . . ." Her explanation fell short as her eyes narrowed. She laid the bundle atop a small stone table. "You're bleeding."

Her familiar scent of snow and crisp cranberry wine drifted around him as she raked a fingertip across a swirl of glittery gold mixed with bright red seeping into his white tunic along his rib cage. She gasped when she grazed his abdomen—as ungiving as a plate of armor—where the ripples of his muscles had been captured in a metallic sheet of gold that was slowly petrifying toward his chest.

It wasn't the first of such a patch. He had a golden left forearm, and a golden right shin. He couldn't bend his wrist, but considered himself fortunate it hadn't affected his sword arm . . . and though he walked with a slight limp, he could still sit a horse better than any man or woman in his kingdom. This newest golden infestation, causing no obvious mobility issues, had been easier to hide.

He tried to delay the horror creeping across his lady mother's face. "We should take any open wounds as a good omen, yes? The day I stop bleeding—"

"Dare not say it." Queen Nova's voice trembled. "This one . . . it's so close to your heart." Her silver hair hung free, the long strands serving as a curtain to the orange, flickering light. Within that slant of purple shade, her expression resembled a bruise.

Vesper lifted her chin. "I wonder, what are you to do with your time, once you no longer have to fuss over me? When my blood runs pure red, and I'm strong and whole once more? Have you a hobby in mind? Perhaps calligraphy. As crowned king, I'll have leverage to arrange a spot for you on the chancery." He winked and wiped the gold-tinged blood from her hand onto the back of Lyra's letter. It left a smear of pinkish, flaxen glitter against the cream-colored parchment.

Queen Nova managed a reluctant smile. "I'd rather be a chronicler. Recording history would be more stimulating than scripting charters and writs upon sheepskin hour after hour. Though I hope never again to see another vial of golden ink." She pressed the princess's letter to his chest and patted his cheek. "You need a shave, if you and your first knight are still masquerading as Ravagers on this journey." Having said that, she withdrew to the table where she began to open the bundle.

Vesper tucked the note into his pocket and absently rubbed a knuckle over the dark whiskers hiding his scarred cheek. Cyprian would have an easier time preparing. The only places hair grew on other Nerezethites were their heads, eyebrows, and lashes, leaving Vesper as the singular man in his kingdom who could grow a beard.

It was Cyprian who had proposed they wear disguises for their trek through the ravine. The two of them, swathed in fitted black eel-skin uniforms and skintight hoods that covered their hair, would present an imposing sight. An assassin's party would inspire fear in the hearts of the depraved populace there, instead of tempting thievery or hostility. The others in the group, including Vesper's sister, Selena, would be dressed as foot soldiers.

Vesper crossed to the queen while assuring his stiff leg didn't crush any crickets. "How did you know where to find me?

"I asked Cyprian of your whereabouts. He told me you were to meet here with Madame Dyadia." She glanced about the room for the sorceress.

The prince took over where his mother had left off, working free the purple wool knotted around the gifts. "Our sorceress sent Thana on an errand. I'm awaiting the bird's report before we leave."

"A report about the *witch*?" His queenly mother's lip curled on the final word.

Vesper pushed aside some hair that had slipped from the rest of the shoulder-length strands bound with a tie at his nape. He looked down to meet her gaze—a soft heather in the torchlight.

"Yes. I still plan to find her." He resisted the urge to use the imperialistic tone reserved for political and militaristic councils, loathe to pull rank with her.

For three years, he'd been serving as king. Although he would not officially wear the crown or title—or even sit the throne—until his coronation, what he said was law, and everyone respected that. Even those who still thought him unusual, who looked upon him as foredoomed. Yet this dear lady who'd birthed him couldn't see past the toddler she once held in her lap when he'd scuffed a knee or couldn't sleep.

"Time is not a luxury for you, my son." She stalled his attempt to reveal the items inside the woolen wrapping—her hands glaring bright against his own. The crickets' chirping escalated to a bothersome pitch. "Taking the ravine's passage . . . it could add weeks to your trip."

"Quite the opposite. By taking the Rigamort into the Ashen Ravine, we'll save at least three days. The ravine's magical effect on distances will result in a two-day journey from there to Eldoria, as opposed to five were we to go north and take the iron stairway." Though the stairs were shallow and wide enough for horses to maneuver with ease, they had to be dismounted and led. It was a long climb, and the journey around Mt. Astra to reach Eldoria's palace was equally long.

"What if you're caught in a night tide in the badlands?"

"Madame Dyadia's spiritual wards have predicted clear, starry skies," Vesper interrupted. "The horses have been shod with steel spikes, so managing the ice and tundra will prove no issue. We should arrive at the Rigamort within eight hours after we leave the castle."

"And the dangers?"

He huffed. "I've battled snow leopards, cadaver brambles, and bone spiders since I was seven. Thirteen years is enough to consider myself well-seasoned."

She shook her head. "You know I speak of the ravine. There are things in that haunted forest you've no experience facing. Quagmires that move, flesh-eating shrouds . . . the murderers, degenerates and thieves."

"Thieves." He quirked a brow. "Precisely the reason it's the perfect route. And I'm taking two of our best sun-smugglers, who know the ravine's secrets within and without. Now, may I please have a look?" He gave her a tender smile, then nudged her hands aside to reveal the royal gifts. His thumb tracked the elegant lines of a glossy, pearlized hairbrush. His breath caught in appreciation of the craftsmanship.

"The bristles are constructed of the princess's very own braid," his queenly mother explained. "Madame Dyadia's artisans used the sample that King Kiran brought those five years ago, and strengthened the strands with enchantments and fire and wax."

"Beautiful," Vesper murmured as he ran his palm across the brittle, silvery fibers. He remembered that braid, how soft it was to the touch. Many a time, he'd imagined how it would feel to caress his bride's true hair on their wedding night, to follow the long, sleek strands down her naked body where they flared at her waist and framed her spectral flesh.

"And this." The queen held up a crescent-moon hairpin with three starry, purple jewels in the middle. "We fashioned it in honor of our sigil. These gems are forged of the princess's own tears, spellbound to stay crystalized until she releases them herself."

Vesper took the metal pin and turned it in his hand. So delicate and perfect. Just as he imagined her to be.

He grew somber, thinking upon the princess's latest note. He almost dreaded reading it. Her exchanges about the happenings in her kingdom had always been filled with an underlying sadness. Regret, even. Though her words came across as rehearsed and guarded, she didn't feel worthy of the crown; that was obvious even without her saying it. He'd battled the same insecurities. According to the prophecy, these differences would make them strong when united. Just as Eldoria would embrace him for his likenesses to them, here in his homeland, Lady Lyra would be revered for those things her people once marked as odd and disquieting.

He was eager to experience that alongside her—for neither of them to ever feel inadequate again.

"What do you think?" His mother broke through his musings.

He laid the pin next to the hairbrush atop the wool. "They're resplendent. I'll give them to her when I give her the panacea ring." Vesper had never forgotten how King Kiran had kept one alive, and how Eldoria's princess had sacrificed it for his people. After that rose had birthed a bountiful harvest, he took a deep lavender blossom and requested Madame Dyadia use her craft to shrink and preserve it, thus retaining its unique scent. The bloom now sat secured atop a band woven of tarnished copper—a wedding ring to resemble the barren beauty of his world in contrast to the lushness of her own.

"So, now that you have these gifts," the queen pressed, "will you abandon the witch hunt?"

"These gifts won't give Lady Lyra what she's been missing all these years. The harrower witch must be captured for sending her family into captivity in the dungeon, for killing her father and cousin. There is penance to be made, and a spell of madness to be lifted off the castle."

"Penance. Feels more like vengeance." Queen Nova folded up the items once more, her silvery eyebrows furrowed.

"*Noble* vengeance." Vesper mirrored her expression, a more imposing gesture with his thick, dark brows.

"I've seen the snares you're taking. Incendiary and body-gripping devices do not imply nobility."

"This harrower witch is immortal. Madame Dyadia assured me she can't be wounded or killed." Vesper frowned. "You must know I would never consider using fireballs or pit snares on a typical old woman. But it takes harsher means to entrap someone who's invincible."

"It is this invincibility that concerns me. You . . . are the furthest thing from it."

"She's one, against me and nine of my most trusted confidantes. She must be contained. How else will my betrothed and her regent aunt feel safe enough to leave their kingdom in her council's care and ride with us back to Nerezeth for our joint coronation and marriage, lest their persecutor be captured and dealt with? I am honor bound to give the princess back her power. She's been too long without it."

"You are honor bound to be her *helpmate*. Take the iron gate's safe passage to Eldoria. You may be a few days later, but you're guaranteed to arrive in one piece. Send your troop to capture the witch—after you're cured, after you're wed."

Vesper's chin clenched. He could sense his mother's frustration at not being able to connect to him mentally. He shared it.

Queen Nova shook her head. "I saw the cloak you're taking for the princess. Your sister is attending the journey to serve as chaperone, yet you've given her no such exaggerated wardrobe."

Vesper had commissioned a hooded lacewing cloak sewn of silk and nightsky, lined with fish scales, and embellished with molted nightingale feathers, fur, and spider's lace to wrap his princess within on their journey back. Though the moon would be a comfort to her, she hadn't had a lifetime of puncture wounds in preparation for the harsh terrain. He knew from letters how fearful she was of thorns and nettles and bees. He only hoped her trepidation wouldn't hinder her acceptance of the royal pets in his castle.

"Selena is accustomed to this land," Vesper countered. "But Lady Lyra . . . you've heard the stories. She can't even wave an arm out a window without her flesh searing in the light. I can only imagine what brambles will do."

"The prophecy says that as your shadow-bride, she will be capable of embracing this world and you as you are. I believe those words. Perhaps she simply needs a chance to show her resilience. No better place than Nerezeth to test her mettle. 'Ours is a land for the daring, and only the brutal of heart can survive.' Those were your words. You wished to wrap her in brambles yourself before you lost—" She bit her explanation short.

"Before I lost what, Lady Mother?" He growled when she averted her gaze. "For five years you have tiptoed around the subject of that night, of how I've felt incomplete since the moment I awoke in my chamber after swallowing the sunlight. You and Dyadia were standing over my bed, here in this castle, yet I felt as if I'd been floating elsewhere for hours. Then there was the sense that some piece of me was missing. Something monumental. It was true, for I could no longer connect to you, my sister, or any of our people mentally . . . no longer have silent conversations between us. You assured me that what I was missing was the princess—that she can put me back to rights. There must be more. I tumble every night into sweat-drenched dreams, with the taste of steam on my tongue and the scent of kindling in my nose; I awaken out of sorts, out of breath, as if I've been running and running, somewhere both dark and light. Yet when my eyes open, here I am, tangled within my bedsheets. What don't I remember? What are you keeping from me?"

The queen rubbed her temple until her knuckles bulged pale under the moonlit flesh that bound them. "Nothing. Once your princess quells the sun's blaze within you, your nightmares will end." Her long gown swished as she turned back to the table. "Lady Lyra is as capable as you. Have faith in it. She is your equal already—today. She needs *you* standing on the steps of her castle, not the witch."

"It would be ill thought, to leave the witch at large." Madame Dyadia's voice rippled like a purr in the stony cell, silencing the crickets. "The wedding itself is in harm's way, as long as she's free."

Vesper scanned their surroundings. The sorceress had slipped in without notice. Squinting, he at last saw her form, leaned against the wall beside the spiked bed, her flesh blending into the gray stone. Madame Dyadia had the ability to move without walking, to float like a night mist, and being descended from primordial chimeras—chameleon-catlike creatures—could match her surroundings at will. Her signature ivory robes trimmed in ebony lace were also ensorcelled to reflect her environs.

"What do you mean?" Queen Nova faced the sorceress after knotting the woolen binds around the princess's gifts.

"Thana has Cronatia in her sights, as you commanded, Majesty." The sorceress bowed to Vesper, acknowledging his rule. Synchronized with the movement, her flesh resumed its natural coloring: a mix of black and white stripes that along with her feline features and two-toned upswept hair had always reminded Vesper of a white tiger. "I spied through the bird's eye, a box lined with drasilisk flesh within the witch's keep. Written upon the lid were the words: 'princess - revolution.'"

Vesper cursed, pounding the table with his left hand. His golden forearm scraped the edge and loosened a chunk of stone, sending it to the floor. He glared at it, jaw twitching. "She's raising a rebellion against my bride. As if she hasn't already done enough."

"It would seem the witch has havoc yet to wreak. So very like Cronatia, to interfere no matter the consequences." Madame Dyadia's brow furrowed. In the midst of her striped forehead sat a pink, empty socket that usually housed a third eye unless she plucked and conjured it alongside a handful of white feathers into a scrying crow. The sorceress could even place her mind within the gruesome creature and use it as her mouthpiece.

"I understand it's a difficult and painful process, but couldn't you converse with the witch yourself, through the bird?" The queen offered up the suggestion in synch with Vesper's thoughts. "It would give us a better idea of how to broach her."

"I haven't will enough to attempt a dialogue, knowing she wouldn't answer truthfully. She's a consummate liar." Dyadia frowned and the raw, meaty divot on her forehead puckered and swelled, as if breathing. "Cronatia's explanations are owed to Eldoria's royalty, not me; those are the wrongs she must answer for now. Thus, she must be taken to the palace."

Vesper crushed the broken rock beneath his boot's heel with a gritty pop and wondered again at Dyadia's strained familiarity with the witch. He'd questioned her about it more than once, but the sorceress skirted answers, insisting things that happened centuries ago belonged in the past, for they couldn't change the future. He disagreed. Learning from yesterday's mistakes is what made for a better tomorrow.

"I spied also a note," Dyadia continued. "Wrinkled within the witch's grasp. Too difficult to cipher. The contents might prove telling. Thana's sightings suggest Eldoria's princess is yet in danger. The bird's precognitions have never proven false."

Queen Nova shifted her feet and the sorceress turned to her, pressing her thin black lips to a line as their gazes locked.

Sensing a silent conversation taking place, Vesper stepped between them, breaking the connection. "You will address me directly and not speak behind my mind while in my presence. *Both of you.*"

His lady mother bowed her head humbly and Dyadia knelt before him, gaze turned to the floor. "Majesty, I was telling our queen that you must take the ravine despite her reservations. If for no other reason than the brumal stags."

"Why? What have you learned?" Vesper asked.

The sorceress looked up then, torchlight gilding her complexion and slitted pupils to disturbing proportions—a wildcat set afire. "During Thana's flight in the Rigamort, I spied through the bird's eye: antlers piled upon the ground in bloody silver-blue stacks. Some within the herd appearing sick and weak. We must determine what has happened, on the chance it could infect our world with ills no princess can cure."

12

Of Monsters and Men

erezeth, set deep beneath the earth, had a claustrophobic terrain. The magical, moonlit sky arched upward from massive, icy dunes, leaving an extensive valley that ran as long and wide as the Ashen Ravine—located thousands of leagues above. Having only two tunnels leading up to the day realm, it gave one the sense of being trapped within a snow globe. Though, unlike a child's toy, there was nothing safe or frivolous in this harsh land.

The obsidian castle's back wall rested flush against an embankment of earth and ice. The north, south, and east sides of the palace, along with Nerezeth's colonized territory, were surrounded by the Grim—a thorny woodland that formed an imposing fortress around the obsidian castle, stony cottages, and Neverdark's iron arboretum.

Before venturing through, Prince Vesper and his troop trussed the horses in barding made of the same toughened fish skin as the royal armor to protect their tender horseflesh from static and barbed obtrusions.

Once past the Grim, they removed the barding to journey southwest through the glacial badlands and reach the Rigamort. Tonight the scent of snow prickled the air; the skies extended clear and star-filled above the barbed, leafless trees lining the path, and the wind held a bitter bite that kept even the snow leopards in their lairs. When at last the rime-rimmed branches thinned to reveal a wide span of untouched snow dunes where the cavern's entrance rose like a spire of dark ice, a concerted sigh of relief washed over the troop.

Prince Vesper cinched his fur-hooded cape around the white skull and black sockets painted across his face. He narrowed his lashes against gusts of air so brutally cold they burned the eye. Including himself, his cavalcade consisted of ten: Lieutenant Cyprian Nocturn; Princess Selena; two sun-smugglers, Alger and Dolyn; a husband-and-wife tracker team, Leo and Luna; and three of his best foot soldiers—Tybalt, Uric, and Thea—who also manned the three jackdaw cages they'd brought on the chance sending missives became necessary.

Vesper would have preferred to head the procession, and in the day realm he would; but since he didn't have the night vision, he had given his first knight that privilege here.

Selena rode behind Cyprian with Nysa, her rye-colored tracker spaniel, snuggled belly-down between her mount's withers and the saddle horn. Third in line, Vesper kept a close watch on the shadows cast by fir thickets and deciduous thistly trees. Glistening powder stirred by spiked hooves hindered visibility, but he utilized snatches of moonlight through the branches, searching for unusual movements beneath the drifts.

His world's terrain, spawned of the same broken magic that supplied the day realm's Ashen Ravine with flesh-eating shrouds, had given Nerezeth its own inherit monsters made of the bones of any humanoid who died out in the open alone. Skeletons would shed their flesh and blood and limbs—like a snake changing skins—and take root in frozen soil, rocky topography, or ice. They sprouted forth as white carnivorous predators that resembled human spines, varying from viper-sized to the length of giant moray eels.

Cadaver brambles hid deep within the drifts, attuned to vibrations like a spider relying on the tingling signal of a web. If there was more than one in the same vicinity, they hunted in packs. They were patient, lying in the darkness, ready for any man, woman, or beast to cross their territory so they could feed upon the marrow that once gave them life. Having no scent for the horses to detect, a bramble could propel upward and topple them, claiming both mount and rider with little warning.

Vesper's glove stroked his stallion's neck—a shimmer of sleek periwinkle beneath the moon's creamy haze. He leaned forward to whisper: "It's all right, Lanthe. We've nothing to fear of the cadavers this night. Pass the word up to Dusklight, would you?" Vesper gestured toward his sister's silvery-purple mare. Lanthe nickered and jerked his head, playing coy. "Come on now, everyone knows you're sweet on her." Lanthe's ear pivoted backward to capture his master's fogged breath.

In preparation for this journey, Vesper had updated the census and found that none of their populace had died or gone missing in the tundra. As an extra precaution, he'd commanded their route be cleansed by utilizing special tools with five long, curved blades like scythes attached to broom-length handles. Digging deep through the snow, the movements lured the hungry creatures to attack so they could be sawed down and the roots destroyed. None had been found.

Still, Vesper allowed his shoulders to relax only after Cyprian led the procession into the clearing that sat like a white valley between snowy banks, where the moonlight was bright and plentiful. Cyprian stalled his horse and signaled to the prince in sign language: *Safe to dismount?*

Vesper nodded. Since the horses were laden with gear and baggage, the rest of the journey would be taken afoot, leading them to the entrance and through the steep cavern until they reached the tunnel. Vesper pointed two fingers to his eyes then turned his hand outward to encompass the surroundings: *Keep a lookout.*

Five years earlier, when Vesper lost the ability to connect mentally, he'd determined to find another way to communicate in silence, so he might still traverse the snowy drifts and powdery banks without causing avalanches. In one of his and Lady Lyra's exchanges, she mentioned her prime minister was teaching her sign language shared between their kingdoms centuries earlier. Vesper appointed his royal litterateur to find records, so he might master it himself. Although the princess admitted since then that she hadn't much patience for the learning, Vesper continued to study the scrolls of the ancient language and assured everyone in Nerezeth's high court and military forces knew it as well.

My flask is leaking, Selena signed to Vesper while still atop her mount. She bent over to search through her saddlebag where water stains darkened the leather. Her long braid swung across Dusklight's flank, the colors so close they blended together beneath the moon's glow.

Vesper caught Cyprian watching his sister beneath his white lashes. The skull painted upon his friend's face had little hope of hiding the tender, love-lorn expression behind it. Yet somehow, Selena was blind to it. The prince wondered if his friend would ever be brave enough to tell her.

Preparing to dismount, Vesper hesitated as something shifted the powder beside Dusklight's left hoof. Nysa's floppy brown ears perked and she barked, spurring the jackdaws to screech in their cages. The spaniel wriggled from her perch before Selena could catch her.

A pale, bony tentacle hurled out from the snow, scattering tufts of white mist into the air. Nysa leapt at it. Selena guided Dusklight's hooves to safety while whistling for her dog. The spine-like plant uncoiled to the size of a boa constrictor, then snapped its barbed tip out to catch Nysa's long, furry tail. The dog yelped, disappearing into a snow drift—leaving only drag marks. All ten horses squealed and shimmied, ears back, scattering as their riders attempted to calm them.

Vesper threw off his fur cape and dove from Lanthe's saddle to tackle the retreating end of the bramble. He hit the ground with a metallic thud that echoed through his abdomen. Selena attempted to dismount but Dusklight released a panicked neigh and reared. Selena leaned into her knees to stay balanced. Vesper spun through the snow and plunged an arm into the drift where Nysa's yelping form had vanished. Knees straddled around the bramble, Vesper dragged out the sneezing, gasping ball of fur. The spaniel nipped at her tail, trying to free it from the vine. Vesper struggled to help her while the rest of his troop slid from their mounts. Amidst the muffled chaos, Vesper sensed instead of heard the mental shouts taking place between Cyprian and the others.

The prince pounded the bramble, the spiny points eating through his gloved fists. His brisk movements captured the predator's attention. It released the dog, threw Vesper off balance, then lashed out at him instead. Vesper snapped up his left arm to block his face and the bramble twisted around it. Spiky stingers shoved through his eel-skin uniform but were unable to breach his gold-plated forearm. Scrambling to his knees, he pulled up fast to stretch the bramble taut, using his stiffened limb like a pry bar.

The sun-smugglers contained the bucking horses as Cyprian and the foot soldiers gathered around Vesper with handheld shovels. Boring through the snow, they found the vine's entry point in the frozen ground. Selena hacked away with an axe until the bramble split apart, releasing the prince. The tentacle continued to thrash, seeking a new victim. It could live for weeks without its roots, so long as it had marrow to feed upon. But this one was chopped to bits by Selena's blade and the others' shovels. The pieces shriveled and turned gray then scattered on the wind. Vesper plugged the exposed root socket—a hollow white tube—with a cloth doused in mineral acid. It curled upon itself, withered and dead.

Panting, Vesper accepted Cyprian's help to stand. His muscles ached, his left elbow drizzled golden blood, and the skull paint on his face blurred his eyes as wet and cold droplets ran down his forehead from sweat and snow. He shivered, but there was warmth, too. Back before he was infected by sunlight—before it altered him internally—battling the elements used to fire his rage, feed his determination to prove he belonged. Sometimes, he missed that rage. However, tonight, he'd managed to use his golden affliction as an advantage. At least some good had come of his mutating form.

After scooping up Nysa, Selena rushed over and hugged him. Vesper held her—cheek pressed to her head. It wasn't often they were open with their affections; Selena kept a respectful distance and abided the rules of obeisance when in the presence of court and council. But here, among friends, Vesper welcomed it. Having once known what it was like to avoid contact for fear of searing his loved ones' flesh, he refused to take such moments for granted.

Nysa shoved her muzzle against his ear to lick it, leaving behind a wash of slobber and dog scent. Vesper grinned and rubbed the scruff of her neck. "Glad you're all right, little spitfire," he said on a quiet breath.

"Thank you for saving her," Selena whispered.

He nodded, knowing she would've done the same for Lanthe. He and his sister shared a deep compassion for animals, and each had their favorites. His was an affinity for the equestrian lot. They understood and accepted him in a way few people did.

"You're hurt," Selena said, preoccupied with the rip in his left sleeve and the flaxen-red smear of blood.

"It's just a few shallow cuts. Not worth stitching up." He was spared her fussing when Cyprian offered her Dusklight's reins and then turned to Vesper with Lanthe's.

"What do you think it was?" Cyprian asked.

"It was smaller than a man's leavings," Vesper answered as he ran his hands across his stallion's legs—checking the joints and bones—then lifted each hoof to ensure the spiked shoes remained secure and free of debris. Lanthe stood patiently for the examination, his tail swishing from side to side. "Had to have been a hoarfrost goblin's corpse. Must've sprouted over the last week for the scythe-cleansing to have missed it."

Cyprian nodded. "These treks would be easier by far would they concede to living among us, or at least take part in our censuses."

Vesper shrugged back into his fur cape. "Until they trust us enough to abide our laws or respect our ruling class, there's not much chance of that."

For centuries Vesper's kingdom had tried to make peace with the small anthropoids, but it was forfeit. Goblins were envious—coveting the height, power, and humanness of the Nerezethites. They wanted places of prestige on the council, yet their jealous and shifty ways made it difficult to trust them. Over time, they'd become reclusive, their stick-thin bodies and rough-textured skin blending into the gray-glazed trees they now called home. Since they weren't an official populace of the kingdom, it was impossible to keep track of their deaths out in the wilds.

Vesper gripped the bridle and coaxed his stallion's large head close. He pressed his cheek against Lanthe's curled forelock. Although every person in the troop was desensitized to cadaver-bramble venom, horses couldn't build up such an immunity, making it risky for them outside of the province. Thus, they were ridden out only for trips into Eldoria.

"Sorry, old boy. My promise for a safe trek was a bit premature. Hope you didn't lose any footing with your lady love." Lanthe nudged him. Vesper grinned. His stallion had the best sense of humor of any horse he'd ever met.

Cyprian and the others fell into line once more for the walk to the cavern's entrance. The horses' unsettled snorts took up again as Vesper felt a thundering in the soles of his boots. He glanced over his shoulder at a wall of snow tumbling down and swelling toward them like a wave—triggered by the earlier uproar.

"Avalanche!" Vesper and Cyprian shouted simultaneously. Everyone vaulted atop their mounts and galloped for the Rigamort's entrance, leaping within only seconds before the flurried rush enveloped the trail and the trees they'd wound through just minutes before.

Vesper was all but blind in the sudden darkness. The sound of metallic-spiked hooves scraped the ice and the dank of cold stone stung his nose. Nine pairs of eyes lit to amber glows around him. He dismounted and drew his sword. Selena slid from her saddle and flipped her dagger from its scabbard with all the skill and dexterity of any foot soldier.

After what they'd just encountered, he couldn't help but hope his mother was right about his delicate princess being sturdier than their missives had indicated. How could any lady rule by his side if she feared his world as much as she feared her own? How would she be strong enough to take on his curse if she had no tolerance for pain and discomfort?

The skin at the edge of his sternum prickled, and he swallowed a groan along with the taste of metal. Such sensations accompanied the golden spread along his flesh. He was dying more every day. He didn't have the luxury to wonder upon the logic of magic and prophecies, or to seek a princess who was perfectly matched for him and his brutal world.

He had to have faith: *You will know her by her voice.*

Attaching spikes with leather straps to their boot soles, his troop took the slow and treacherous decline along a winding outcrop of rock barely wide enough for man and horse side by side. The heavy press of darkness was softened only by the long, glossy stalactites catching flashes of amber eyes. Far, far below a bluish glow winked and wavered, like ripples in water. Smaller lights, the size of lightning bugs from these heights, hovered around it.

Other than the rustle of clothes, the gripping crunch of hooves and boots, and the occasional flapping of a tinder-bat, silence reigned until halfway down. Then the scrabbling foot-pricks of bone spiders set everyone on full alert. One passed through Vesper's peripheral view—a shadow the size of Nysa. It scuttled up a slick, frozen waterfall using an anchor line of web as thick as a man's arm. The creatures had white, brittle bodies the shape of winter squash, with six hinged legs and two pincer claws. They moved like crabs, but had long, snapping jaws with fangs opening side to side like scissors. Horses were their mortal enemy, prone to stomp through their delicate shells when spooked, so the spiders kept their distance.

The others had to stop and wait for Vesper to recover balance once or twice, his limp proving a cumbrance on the icy ledge. This cavernous journey always brought his flaws to surface: his blindness, his gimp leg, his inability to partake in silent conversations. But this time, the moment he stepped into the cave's lowest plateau—heard the coughs and wails of dying stags, saw their once graceful, majestic forms fallen to decay and abuse—he forgot his imperfections as a man and remembered he was king.

A shimmering blue tunnel gilded the icy chamber with an incandescent glaze. Some of the stags flocked around the flickering passage that led upward into the ravine, others lapped hungrily at rock formations so long they reached to the ground, drawing nutrients from the mineral-rich stalactites and ice that encrusted every crevice of the caverns. These were still healthy and turned toward Vesper and his companions—pronged heads held high. The thick scales upon their backs and chests exuded such a bright gleam that Vesper had to squint. He was always surprised anew when seeing them up close, considering they appeared as small as fireflies from above.

The stags that laid beside decomposing corpses and hollow skeletons were sick, easy to spot as their scales were dulled to a dim gray. Vesper didn't see a pile of antlers as Dyadia's eye had; he did, however, see empty sockets upon two corpses' heads and black blood, speckled with lambent glitters—reserves of the magic that filled their prongs. Their wounds tainted the air with a sour tang.

His stomach clenched and he moaned, sheathing his sword.

One of the stronger stags approached, head low, antlers gleaming and pointed toward them. Vesper stepped forward, putting himself between the creature and his troop.

"Brother." Selena reached to pull him back. Her voice echoed in the cave, carrying notes of fear and awe. Even Nysa, on her rope, remained at his sister's ankles, quietly observant as if she sensed the stags were dying.

"Selena, I've been here before. They know me."

"Yes, but . . . they appear not to recognize anyone." Remembering her place, she dropped her hand but finished her thought. "Perhaps Alger and Dolyn might take the lead."

She had a point. Having used the glowing blue tunnel in their sun-smuggling days made them the logical choice to approach the stags. They'd passed this way many more times than he had.

But this wasn't a typical passing through. There was a ritual: The creatures would form opposing lines and lift their heads, touching prongs, tip to tip, like the saber arch tradition for military weddings in his kingdom. Just as a bride and groom would stroll beneath the swords, the hopeful traveler would walk under and through the antler arch. It was the stags' way of absorbing the impressions of those using the tunnel, to trigger a remembrance upon their return—a foolproof method to ensure anyone entering Nerezeth from this point belonged in the night realm. However, the creatures weren't moving into any formation this time. They seemed disparate, unorganized.

They were vulnerable, and they'd lost their purpose.

Vesper glanced at the nine concerned faces behind him. "These are my gatekeepers, that I imprinted upon as a child. And they need me." He dropped Lanthe's reins. The others did the same with their horses and made to follow, but halted when Vesper raised a hand, forestalling them. "This is mine alone." Though he'd lost his mental connection, he had to have faith that if magic could unite him with his other half, a girl he'd never met, it could bind these wild creatures' loyalties to him for life, as it had every other night-king before him.

He took a second step.

The brumal stag charged backward, its panther-like claws scraping the icy floor. It lowered its head again in warning, releasing a threatening sound—part snort, part growl. The antlers caught a flash of light from the tunnel and sparkled—mesmerizing, yet deadly. The soft keening cries of the ill and dying in the background gave Vesper the courage to move forward two more steps, to take off his glove and open his palm, holding it low.

"I'm here to help, Beauty. I won't harm you. I know my voice hasn't been in your mind of late." He lifted his brows, imploring. "But I'm still the prince . . . your king. Come closer. One sniff, and you'll remember."

The creature whipped its long tail, slender and white like a snake, with a bushy tip as iridescent as a pearl. It snorted, antlers raised and nostrils flared on a deep, misty breath. Its white eyes widened, then it bobbed its head, like a horse catching scent of something familiar, something beloved. It pranced forward and nuzzled Vesper's hand. Vesper smiled and glanced over his shoulder where his companions looked on with astonished expressions.

When he scratched the stag's pointed ears, he was rewarded with a blissful whinny. The horses whickered in response, as did the other healthy stags. Then one by one, each guardian pushed forward and insisted Vesper pet them, snuffling his bared palm as if it were coated with sugar and honey.

Moments later, Vesper made his way past the two corpses with severed antlers, hissing at the sight of them and the skeletons. He would see it all buried beneath rocks before he and his crew took the tunnel into the ravine.

Approaching the sick, he knelt, his heavy heart pulling him down. Selena's hand squeezed his shoulder from behind as others of the troop befriended the healthy stags somewhere to the left of the cave.

"I feel so helpless," he told her quietly.

She reached down to stroke the neck of the closest one. It bleated pitifully and its eyelids twitched, straining to open.

Cyprian knelt beside Vesper. He pulled off his skintight hood, leaving his shoulder length white hair mussed. The paint upon his face reflected the flickering lights of the tunnel—adding a gruesome and ironic element to the skull mask. He looked like death itself. It reminded Vesper of his own painted face. No wonder the stag had shied away from him at first.

"What has happened to their antlers?" his first knight asked.

"How are they being gored off to begin with?" Selena added. "As defensive as they are?"

Vesper clenched his jaw. "Not all of them are defensive. The sick ones have no fight left. If someone were to distract the stronger and lure them to other side of the cave, the weaker would be defenseless."

"So, what is weakening them in the first place?" Selena asked. The ripples of light from the tunnel enhanced her pale skin—making it bluer than usual—and her hair and eyes reflected the phosphorescent glow. She looked like an angel. He wished she was, so she could heal his gatekeepers.

"I can't imagine," Vesper finally answered. "For centuries they've been all but invincible."

The moment he said this, the stag his sister had been petting dragged its head toward Vesper's bleeding arm. It brayed, its tongue flitting out. Puzzled, Vesper lowered his arm. With a strangely human sigh, the creature snuggled against his wound. In moments, its eyes opened and the scales upon its back brightened. It was gaining strength.

Vesper and Selena exchanged stunned glances.

"The sunlight in your blood." Selena was the first to say it aloud, though they were both thinking it. "All these centuries, the sun-smugglers came back through, transporting sunlight. Is it possible the stags also need exposure to it, however small?"

"And these past five years, we've been depriving them," Cyprian took over. "We made them weak. *We* made them susceptible."

Vesper winced, horrified. The importance of the sun's touch upon Nerezeth grew more apparent each day. "I will send Alger or Dolyn back through with a supply after we capture the witch. Enough of a supply to last until my union with Lady Lyra heals our worlds." He turned back to the bleeding corpses. "Such cruel butchery *demands* vengeance. When I find the criminals responsible, I will slay them where they stand."

❋ · I · ❋

Inside Eldoria's dungeon cell, tucked within the plush fabrication of her own making, Griselda stood beside the small dining table where she and her daughters had taken meals for the past five years.

There, she unwrapped a fresh delivery: two sets of brumal stag antlers, still oozing brackish, magical blood that sparkled like the starlit sky in portraits of old. Griselda barred herself against that strange stinging—as if something ached under her scalp above her temples. It always accompanied these transactions. Had she a conscience, she'd suspect it was sympathy pains.

She laughed inwardly at the impossibility; once all of this was behind her, she'd have the castle's physician see to the strange pains. Considering Lustacia had also been complaining of headaches—the one daughter who had inherited Griselda's tender skin and physicality—most likely it was a nutritive dearth from lack of sunlight and fresh air.

"Is the quota met, Your Grace?" Sir Erwan asked, observing from beside her while Sir Bartley stood guard outside the door.

"Yes."

Erwan raised a dark eyebrow as something shuffled behind him.

"I trust the exports have gone unnoticed?" Griselda asked the hoarfrost goblin that sidled out from behind the safety of the knight's red breeches and white surcoat. The top of the creature's head came to Griselda's knees. It was fitting he called himself Slush, as he looked every bit as muddy and trampled as Griselda imagined mucky snow to be.

"Thus to date, Magistrate," he answered, his voice rustling and airy, like the shift of ash from Griselda's wretched memories of the ravine.

She winced, annoyed with the rhyming, childlike dialect. All of his kind spoke thusly, so she'd had to be tolerant. That would end today. "It's *Majesty*. And you will reserve that title for the princess. *She* will be your queen."

Slush sneered, his spiked teeth slick and grimy. The hair atop his head was wiry and thick—the color of mud streaked with milk. Crystalized growths caught the light and shimmered from his chin like a beard of icicles. Similar jagged tapers, smaller in number and length, dripped from long, pointed ears that resembled those of a donkey.

His gray, glassy eyes, protruding like oversized marbles in that small, rough face, turned toward said "princess" with an odd mix of idiocy and inquisitiveness. There, at Griselda's daughters' feet, hunkered Slush's crew of four—slobber dribbling from their lips onto apparel made of tree bark. There had been six at one time, but two had been lost to a fiery death in the ravine several years back. All said, this smaller crew had served well enough.

The girls, dressed in lace and velvet, sat upon cushioned stools. Wrathalyne and Avaricette talked around their sister—Lustacia, now so adept at being Lyra, maintained silence around anyone other than family—while stitching the final touches on her wedding trousseau. They attached pearls on the veil, gloves, and headdress, along with creamy lace across the low-cut neckline of the pink organza gown.

Beside them, the birds cooed and tweeted in their cages, adding to the odd serenity of the scene. Even with her wretched niece dead and gone, Griselda had opted to keep the chickadees, mockingbirds, and swallows close at hand. One never knew when an infestation might occur.

She supposed on some level, this was an infestation: a half circle of gruesome goblins with long, pointy noses that sagged almost to cover their mouths, surrounding three lovely girls. However, none of her daughters minded. Being down in the dungeon all these years without social interaction, they had come to think of the goblins rather as servants. A logical evolution, considering the five bandits had been delivering parcels from

Nerezeth ever since Griselda first needed scorpions and cadaver brambles to torture her niece.

If anything, her daughters were bored by their guests' presence. On the other hand, the goblins were fascinated. Everything about humanness and stateliness intrigued them . . . they coveted such characteristics more than Eldoria's white gold. An insatiable greed that Griselda had latched upon and exploited from the very beginning.

"And we'll rule at her side, tall as men full of pride. Aye, yer Graciousness of all spaciousness?" Slush's question grounded Griselda's thoughts.

She rubbed the infernal niggle along her scalp, frowning when she noticed two small bumps. Those were new. "That's *Your Grace*," she corrected the goblin, preoccupied with his insolence.

"*I* am the Grace? But I haven't the face . . ." He smooshed the end of his long nose with a thin, crooked finger, as if he could push it into his skull and make it smaller.

"You are to call *me* Your Gra— Oh, never mind." Stupid as he was, he had a keen sense for what got under her skin. But she would have the last laugh. "I promised you'd be the mirror image of men, didn't I? A lady always keeps her word."

Having answered—a stark truth he would soon comprehend with horror—Griselda smoothed her hair into place. She'd consider the knots later, when there was time to look in a mirror. For now, she had no desire to see herself in her brown day dress. Working with magical ingredients in unstable conditions had proven messy in the past, and she'd ruined enough fineries to learn that plain could be better, in rare instances.

She stalked across the chamber and hung the antlers from hooks beside the fireplace, situating them so the black glistening blood could drain into a porcelain bowl. It took two pairs to fill one jar. She had two such jars already lining the shelves, hidden behind bottles of peach wine, reserves of paraffin and liquid sunshine, and bags of dried meats and cheeses. Today her blood supply would at last be of use.

Smirking, she dropped another set of antlers from four months earlier—seeped of all life essence—into a granite mortar and pestle the size of a large cooking pot. Grinding the prongs to sparkling powder so the wintering-frost magic could be released always took some labor. But Griselda enjoyed the process. Pulverizing them was therapeutic, knowing the harvest it would reap, though her hands were permanently bruised and stained a shimmery bluish-white.

What were a lady's finest satin gloves for, if not to hide her ambition?

She made her way to the shelf and pushed aside everyday items, taking down the two jars of blood. The contents sloshed and coated the glass, leaving oily streaks that glittered like liquid obsidian diamonds in the lantern light—rich with the promise of alchemy and ambiguity. This was the last ingredient for the final step in Lustacia's transformation.

Sir Bartley had brought the news earlier—a missive sent from Queen Nova via jackdaw—announcing her son's arrival within a few days. She'd also mentioned a spy had seen the harrower witch in the ravine, that she possessed a box marked "princess - revolution." If the old hag set foot within their gates, Griselda would have her arrested again. The only thing that mattered today was that Prince Vesper was at last coming to claim his bride. Her daughter, not Kiran's.

A silver-haired songbird girl who commands the shadows.

Griselda's checklist was all but complete, short of one thing. And once done, not a body anywhere could deny Lustacia was the true princess of the prophecy.

Placing the jars in a small basket, Griselda looked about the room. The table was scuffed from the time the girls had used it in a game of pitching quoits. The metal horseshoe they'd been tossing over a clay spike dented the wood irreparably. The mirrors magnifying the lanterns were blackened in spots from all the times the girls had polished them; the rugs were worn from waltzing during imaginary balls; and the spice-scented tapestries and fresh flowers were more powerful nostalgic triggers than anything else—harkening back to hours the girls spent in front of the fireplace, giggling about snippets of town gossip delivered by Erwan and Bartley.

Somewhere deep within, Griselda understood she had robbed her daughters of their youth by isolating them, especially the eldest two. As much as she searched for regret, she felt only an empty yawning, devoid of any sentiment other than her desire to be free of this claustrophobic cell forever.

Dropping the basket into an iron pot, Griselda motioned to Erwan. He rounded up the goblins and led them out the door, heading toward the secret tunnel. There, the hidden room awaited with dirt walls and mossy floors, where Lustacia's royal destiny would be finalized.

As Slush stepped across the threshold behind his four compatriots, his bulbous eyes turned to her.

"Today was your final delivery," Griselda answered, waving him on. "As such, your payment is due. Sir Erwan is taking you all to our most private quarters. I'll be there shortly to make restitution."

That seemed to satisfy him, for his shoulders lifted, as if he already felt taller. The door pounded shut behind him.

Lustacia stood, even before Griselda motioned her over. Wrathalyne and Avaricette followed her lead, stashing away the sewing. Their eyes held less trepidation than their sister's, both obviously eager for a brush with the black arts. They were to be disappointed today.

"Are we going to the special room, Mumsy? Where you hide the old family portraits and the prince's letters and roses?" Wrathalyne asked the question, and Lustacia's features collapsed in dread.

Upon seeing her youngest daughter's expression, Griselda frowned. Ignoring Wrathalyne's query, she turned her attention to Lustacia as she placed the grimoire into the iron pot alongside the basket. The remaining ingredients waited in the dirt room upon some shelves. "Do not worry, my princess daughter. I've piled the keepsakes in the darkest corner alongside Queen Arael's reconstructed mirror and covered everything with her moth-eaten gowns. We'll have to fill your royal chamber with them, once you've married the prince. Lyra was fiercely nostalgic. However, with the alterations in your appearance, you favor the ghostly child in the portraits enough that none would question your heritage."

"Fine." Lustacia's answer came in a singsong voice, out of synch with her weary expression. "Let's have done with the magic spell."

"Truly? No pleading for the goblins' lives? No bleeding heart?" Griselda asked, pleased and surprised by her daughter's boldness.

"My prince is coming. *He* has my heart." Lustacia's gaze was heavy with remorse, as it often was, a failing brought on by her sensitive conscience. She withdrew Prince Vesper's latest letter from a small box along with its part-nered panacea rose—stripped of thorns and deep lavender petals just starting to curl with age. Every so often, the prince sent a rose with his monthly note in honor of the one she'd given up as a child, though in truth, it had been her cousin's sacrifice.

Lustacia cradled the two items as if they were babes. She always read each missive and answered as a princess should, alluding to her delicate constitution . . . her fear of the giant nettles and angry bees that held her castle hostage. Hinting at how much she looked forward to him rescuing her. Griselda had taught her daughters that if they wished to nourish a man's interest, they must first fatten his ego. After responding, Lustacia always put the letters and the roses from her sight. She claimed the perfume and the ink's bright shimmer made her ill. Griselda knew the truth, that they reminded her of Lyra. Annoying as it was, she had allowed her daughter this one weakness. Until now. A queen must have the fortitude to choose brutal-ity over mercy and apathy over conscience when her crown was at stake.

"You've worked hard for this." Griselda took the rose and letter from Lustacia, dropping them in the basket to carry out with the other items. Throughout these last six months of their confinement, without fail, her youngest daughter had bathed in salve and used thick paste on her hair and lashes. Both concoctions were made of smuggled starlight, brumal antler powder, and egg whites, and had the effect of silvering anything they touched. Lustacia had even put droplets of the mixture, thinned with milk, into her eyes, despite the agonizing burn, resulting in a lilac hue. Even with her tendency toward bruising, she had proven herself thick-skinned enough to do what had to be done.

Though Griselda despised that her youngest was forced to trade her rosy, freckled complexion, auburn hair, and blue eyes for a gloom-dweller's countenance, it had been a necessary transformation. The one thing they hadn't accomplished was lengthening her lashes. After trying without success, they decided instead to alter all the portraits of Lyra in her youth. Griselda sent Bartley for pigments, canvas, and brushes, having him claim Griselda's daughters and the princess needed a hobby to pass the long hours, so they were to take up painting landscapes. It wasn't difficult to mix and match colors enough to blend away Lyra's unruly, long lashes, making Lustacia resemble the child in the portrait as much as her cousin. By the time the portraits would be hung upon the walls of the castle once more, people would assume they'd exaggerated the princess's appearance in their memories, and all would be forgotten.

"At last you will reap the spoils of your labor," Griselda assured her daughter.

"Yes," Lustacia answered, wrapping a nightsky veil across her silver hair and moon-glow skin. "I've given up everything that made me myself. All for him to love me. All to be his queen. But I still have my own words, even if it's her voice." Shortly after being locked within the posh dungeon, Lustacia had ceased practicing the hand signals Prime Minister Albous had taught the real Lyra. Instead, she used the passage of time to shape Lyra's stolen voice into speech by blending it with her own without losing the trilling birdsong quality. "I'm ready to stop hiding the ability to speak. My prince will be the first to know. Perhaps then he can be proud of something I've done on my own as myself."

"We wish to watch you change the monsters to men." Avaricette horned in on the conversation, sensing they were to leave without her and her middle sister.

"Mums, please!" Wrathalyne joined in. "*Metamorphing* sounds so fascinating."

"That's metamor*phosing*, Wrath," Avaricette corrected with a roll of her eyes.

"You will both stay," Griselda insisted, gathering up the heavy pot and joining her princess daughter at the door. She knocked thrice, signaling to Sir Bartley that they were ready. "The goblins must drink the potion directly from Lustacia's hands for the bond to be complete. We don't need you there arguing and disrupting the process. Make yourselves useful. Feed the birds. We will return shortly, with your sister's most loyal subjects in tow."

The Butcher, the Baker, and Other Lawbreakers

In the center of the Ashen Ravine, the black market opened every day, four hours after the cessation course ended. It remained open during the diurnal course for six hours thereafter, allowing five more of leisure before time to rest again. Most denizens chose to use the latter for looting, liquoring up, or fornicating.

Set amidst the monochromatic haze of shifting gray ash, black twisted trunks, and impenetrable gray-leafed canopies, the market offered a welcome splash of color and vitality.

Each day at opening, glass lanterns the size of apples—permanently affixed to the thorny branches—were filled with lightning bugs from the night realm, supplied by Dregs, the hoarfrost goblin. Nigel, a retired thief, was in charge of climbing each tree to fill the lanterns, being as nimble as a mountain goat (with the beard and face of one, to match). Once lit, the glowing yellow globes dotted the trees like giant dewdrops, brightening the narrow expanse below where a dozen makeshift booths of timber, branches, and rock lined either side of the winding onyx walkway.

The older, rickety stalls shook with the shouts of owners trying to outdo one another with promises of quality and quantity. Everything from typical food and spices to wares both mystic and intangible were peddled. Illiterate shop owners had colorful banners with embroidered images to represent their wares; others, who could write and read, painted words on signs. Some shop fronts were decorated to extremes: multicolored ribbons or feathers fringing the edges to flutter invitingly when someone walked by, or sea glass and pebbles pressed into mortar forming intricate mosaics. Then there were those that were no more than wood planks slapped together—rotten spots patched up with tar. These had yet to be updated. Five years earlier, *all* the booths looked that way: gray, shabby, and moldering.

It was Stain who had started the beautification campaign, quite by accident, when she debuted at the shop with her guardians one month after her rescue, once they deigned it safe for her to be seen in disguise.

She recalled that first interaction often, how wonderful it had felt to finally belong to something . . . a community, however strange it might seem to those on the outside.

"Ye hang the memories on the pegs, facing out, so may-let patrons be intrigued enough to stop," Crony had told her when they'd first arrived at her booth. Stain's job was to fill the lower pegs, as she was too short to reach the higher. Luce took care of those.

She'd hung only a few of the sparkling glass tokens before noticing people shuffled by without stopping. They veered to the shops selling enchanted potions and ensorcelled weapons—completely overlooking how magical memories could be. Having lost her own, Stain had wanted to make patrons stop. To make them understand.

She couldn't shout and tell them what they were missing like other shopkeepers did. And Crony and Luce seemed too busy stocking the shelves to notice.

She'd had some flowers in her pocket that day, having plucked them from the garden before they came. She liked keeping bouquets hidden on her person for their gentle, pretty fragrance. She might look grimy and unkempt, but there was no reason she should smell the part. The flowers were also a reminder that the burning in her fingertips yielded beautiful results, making the recurrent pain more bearable.

Taking out five wilting blossoms, she crawled up on the booth's counter beneath their sign: NOSTALGIA RETOLD: BENEFICIAL MEMORIES FOR THE CURSED & BROKEN. She glued the fragile flowers in place between the slabs of wood with squishy mud.

Luce and Crony stopped stocking to watch, and soon, others paused, too—for a moment. Then they turned again and went shopping elsewhere.

"It be a good try, wee one," Crony encouraged her, patting her fuzzy head. The witch's murky eyes held a soft twinkle. It was the light of affection, but Stain wanted more. Although the old witch's smile had the power to wilt plants and inspire fear, Stain had grown rather fond of it.

"A very good idea indeed," Luce agreed. He offered a sly glance to Crony, one Stain had seen pass between them when they were teaching her things about the world outside their ravine. "Perhaps you simply need to think *bigger*. Say this stall were a kingdom. Would a wise monarch bestow attention and wealth upon only the palace?" He pointed to the sign. "Or would they spread it all around every corner in the vicinage, so it could be seen even from a distance, to catch the eyes of other kingdoms, possibly lure away their own populace with the desire to be part of something so powerful, beautiful, and unified?"

Stain considered his insight, and at closing time, after all the other shopkeepers and patrons had left, she shared a plan with her guardians.

Crony wrinkled her brown forehead upon hearing it. "Aye, that be a big undertaking with some painful sacrifice. Ye up for it?"

Stain nodded, and Luce grinned in approval before shrinking to his fox form. He kept watch around the abandoned market, running in and out of the trees and booths to be sure no one witnessed Stain using her gold fingertips to feed the mud she'd spread all across the booth. The fiery burn was worth it, for the blooms took root. Not only that, by opening time the next day they'd multiplied—a riot of red, fuchsia, blue, and apricot petals covering the skeletal booth from top to bottom. Their sweet perfume overpowered the usual funk of decay permeating the marketplace.

Crony had record sales that day; patrons crowded around her memory booth, as it couldn't be missed. If a patron didn't see the blanket of bright colors, they smelled the enticing scent. Everyone was captivated by the enchanting flowers they assumed the witch had conjured, asking to buy them. When she said they weren't for sale, they instead bought everything else lining her shelves, even her chimes for "kinder sleep." The long cylinders of glass—strung together with wire to hang over one's bed—were captured memories of bedtime stories and lullabies. In the past, they'd been shunned by the jaded criminals. However, something about seeing the flowers flourishing in a wasteland—strong in spite of their frailties—softened even the hardest heart that day, making everyone nostalgic for gentler times.

Soon it became a competition to see who could have the most colorful and eye-catching booth; to see who could draw the most patrons. Even now, none had beat Crony's record, but their attempts made for a much prettier hub, and in return, happier shopkeepers and patrons. And the best reward of all had been Crony's smile. It wilted an entire line of flowers on their booth that day, but it had been worth it for the memory.

Every memory Stain had revolved around Scorch, Luce, or Crony, having lost all others to amnesia. That big gaping hole inside her and her past forced her to never take life for granted. To make each experience bigger, brighter, and bolder, so she could fill that emptiness with meaningful things.

Today something smelled meaningful on the air as Luce and Stain arrived at the break in the tree trunks that formed the market's entrance. However, the strange, underlying scent faded beneath the aroma of fresh-baked cookies, the stench of body odor, and the sticky-spice of black-current mead.

Scorch stopped at the thicket's edge and pawed his front hoof through the ash.

"Good day then, donkey." Luce offered a haughty bow to the Pegasus and strode in, an unspoken summons for Stain to say her good-byes.

Scorch's ears lay back; he looked ready to blaze the entire market down. He was always grumpiest when time to part ways.

Stain placed herself between the Pegasus and the entrance. She felt everyone's eyes on them, aware of how odd they appeared: the puny foundling "boy" and his massive, wild companion. She barely came to Scorch's chest, yet he had restraint enough not to tromp over her when she stood in his path. Though Scorch never wanted to speak of his past—that time before he'd found his way to this ravine—the Pegasus must have been preyed upon aplenty, for he trusted no one . . . other than her.

Stain repositioned the pouch's strap on her shoulder and asked him the same question she did each time she left to work: *If I allow you to come in this once, would you behave?*

He snorted and smoke curled from his nostrils. *If by behave, you mean torch the stalls to the ground, set fire to the screaming crowd, and raze their embers with my hooves, yes.*

She grinned. *We could stay together if you would at least pretend to be civil. It's all about diplomacy. Luce has been teaching me—*

Being civil isn't what's kept me alive and free, is it?

The scars upon his glossy black hide—people's attempts to shoot him full of arrows tied to nets, or slice him with a sword to slow his canter—attested to that fact. Stain had seen the hungry way the ravine's denizens watched him. So much fire within him, boundless and regenerative. Should someone manage to bottle it, they would bid a fortune at one of these booths. Yet somehow, he always escaped then took to the air to heal. That's how his magic worked. The act of flight—either in the ravine where the gray-green canopy stretched highest, or over the ocean in the wide-open skies—sutured his seams. Should his wings ever be broken, it would be his downfall. No one knew his weakness but her, and she'd go to the grave with it.

She removed a glove to rub his downy muzzle. *Have a good day then.*

He blew a charred breath across her. The warmth spread to her toes, much like the cinnamon cider Crony made on the stormiest days, when rain managed to drizzle through the canopies.

Stay clear of the moon-bog, Stain scolded. She then spun toward the onyx walkway, about to head for Luce some ten stalls down where he strung glassy memories on pegs in Crony's flower-coated shop.

Scorch nickered and Stain looked back.

Don't you sense the change on the air? We should explore.

Yes, there was that meaningful scent again. Something that smelled musky like Scorch's equestrian hide, but raw instead of roasted. Similar to the scent of rain, yet different. Starker and more brittle. She couldn't quite place it, but now that she stopped to focus, her every sense stood on end, as if reaching for the answer.

The problem with living here, so isolated from the kingdom, was the absence of town criers. Most denizens stayed to the periphery of Eldoria if they ventured out at all, and it was rare for the ravine's brambles to allow anyone to enter unless they had a stench of death or vice about them. As rumors were more exciting than fact, any morsel of news that made its way in had already been chewed up, spit out, and chewed again—into a tale fascinating enough to justify the telling. Once it hit the marketplace, it was as unrecognizable in its origins as a lump of masticated meat.

There are strange horses about, Scorch offered the answer without Stain even asking. *From the night realm . . . the crust of ice is stale on their coats. Ten riders; three females, seven males. They may be assassins, if the oily scent of eel is anything to go by.*

She did a full about-face. *You know all of that from one sniff?*

His inscrutable dark eyes stared down unblinking at her, assuring her of the folly in such a question. She shouldn't be surprised; he'd known she was a girl since the moment they met. Of course, she'd always assumed that was because he could hear her voice in his mind as she could his.

Wouldn't you like to see who they're out to kill?

She bit her lip at the baiting query. Scorch knew she hated violence almost as much as he reveled in it; but he also knew she could hardly resist the opportunity to see a Nerezethite in the flesh.

She'd come to believe that the night realm must be her home. She couldn't belong to the day, in a place that would burn her alive should she ever venture out of the shade. Who she was and how she'd come to be here were the real mysteries. Mysteries she'd been trying to solve, though it was difficult while keeping a low profile.

Somewhere out there, she must have a mother and father or siblings . . . someone who missed her, not just an unseen enemy who had hated her enough to see her dead. But it was fear of facing said unseen abusers that kept her cautious. That, and Luce and Crony. To date, they had never allowed her to wander close to the overgrown cave—the Rigamort entrance to Nerezeth tucked at the farthest end of the ravine. But Stain knew of it. And what *they* didn't know was how often she and Scorch trekked over, weaving their way through the labyrinth of thorns surrounding it. They went to observe. To wonder. To contemplate. One day, she would plunge inside that cave. It was a matter of convincing Scorch to accompany her. He, who raged into every situation headfirst and unafraid, seemed skittish to go within. She assumed stepping into a land cloaked in ice might threaten his flame, though there were other dangers to consider.

In the market, Dregs sold the preserved corpses of cadaver brambles and rime scorpions. The hoarfrost goblin regaled tales of the gore and blood that went into capturing them to anyone with an ear. However uneasy the dead creatures made Stain, they also made her sad. They were familiar somehow, and she wondered if she might ever see any alive.

Why spend the day toiling with a flea-bitten fox—Scorch interrupted her musings—*when you could walk in the shade of a grand Pegasus, or climb the trees alongside him as he flies? I always give you splendid adventures.* His eyes lit brighter on a dare. *Just think, we might even trail the Nerezethites back through the Rigamort. With them forging the lead, I could be tempted to venture within. And you can find those answers you seek. Come along.*

Stain's pulse leapt at the offer, though she didn't quite trust he'd follow through unless it would somehow benefit him. In the past, she'd asked him many times to seek answers for her by flying over Eldoria. He insisted he could only soar in the open above the ocean, that to go anywhere else would risk his freedom.

Stain glanced over her shoulder at Luce. *He's given me a tithe. I must stretch it into five and complete today's barter if I want to earn time off.*

All these tricks he has you perform are beneath you.

He's teaching me to negotiate. It makes me better at my job here.

And the flowers he forces you to grow . . . in spite of the torment it brings you. What of that?

Luce says when someone has the ability to inspire happiness or beauty, and restore balance, they should use it. Even if it hurts a little.

Scorch's gaze lit to the soft orange of guttering candles. *A lowly dog is not the master of man.*

Stain smiled at his vanity. *Nor is a horse. Human responsibilities aren't to be taken lightly. Unless today I might be a Pegasus, vicariously? If I can ride you and we fly together to spy on the ravagers . . .* She liked that idea. To be safe upon Scorch's back would offer anonymity. Being high overhead, out of reach but with a bird's-eye view.

Scorch shook his elegant neck, loosening the embers fringing his mane to drift toward her. Stain's temporary bout with hope faded. She anticipated his answer even before he thought it, as they'd had this conversation countless times: *Only when the sun and moon share the sky, will I carry you.*

She popped the airborne embers like one would an ensemble of soapy bubbles. She barely felt the heat. *And then you'll belong to me, my beastly brawn, and together we'll solve the riddle of my past.*

Scorch's nostrils flared as fire-bright as his eyes. *There's as much chance of that as of the fairy tale coming true, tiny trifling thing.*

She'd heard snippets of the fairy tale spouted about the marketplace. A princess in Eldoria's palace was to marry a prince from the night realm. The prince had sunlight brewing beneath his skin, and the princess was formed of moonlight and could sing like a bird.

According to lore, should the two unite, they would have power enough to reconcile the sun and the moon.

Stain pretended to share Scorch's cynicism—cracking bawdy jokes at the absurdity. However, deep in her heart where no one could see, she longed for it to be true. For then she could at last fly with Scorch, outside in the open night skies, escape this barren exile under the trees and the hollow past that seemed to always mock her here upon the ground.

Perhaps she could even coax him to give Luce a ride. She'd only accompanied Luce and Crony to steal memories in the ravine a few times before Luce started insisting she stay home. He hated for her to see him eat the corpse's heart, liver, or lungs so he could retain his sylphin beauty. Though he tried to hide his shame and longing, Stain sensed it, just as she sensed how he missed flying.

She understood. Not being able to admit missing something was very like missing something one didn't quite remember having. Both left an emptiness that couldn't be filled.

I have a theory. Stain contained a wave of sadness by teasing Scorch. *The prince has come to claim his princess. That's the ice you smell.*

A princess so delicate she can't sleep upon a feather bed without bruising. So cowardly she won't leave her castle walls for fear of the thistles and bees that surround it. Instead, she waits for someone to come and bleed for her freedom. I hardly see why a roughened night prince would want such a tender maid to share his throne of thorns.

Stain tilted her head. *It's said the princess has the voice of a nightingale . . . that she's beautiful as a swan.*

Scorch grunted. *Does a falcon seek company with a swan amidst the lilies of a pond, or sing duets with a nightingale? Or does he soar through the storm alongside his equal, the hawk? Walking the same rocky path. Swimming the same choppy currents. Sharing courage enough to face a thicket of briars with nothing to gain but pain and flame. That's the true measure of a companion's worth.*

Stain smiled then. In spite of his constant condescension, Scorch valued her scars and all the things that made her difficult to look upon. Humans could learn a lot from animals, as they looked with their hearts instead of their eyes.

The rumors have an appointed day and hour, she teased again. *Now that the princess is old enough to reign, they say time is near.* She raised her brows, telling him without words that he'd best be ready to pay up.

They also say time flies. As do I. He turned then to head into the trees, gracing her with a view of his spark-gilded tail swatting against dark flanks—as if she were a gnat pestering him. *I'm bored of this parley. I'll not mourn your absence today. Perhaps I'll not seek you out again at all.*

Perhaps, Stain answered, pulling her glove back into place. Then she turned and grinned, knowing he'd threatened the same for five years. He'd be back to report whatever he found on his adventure when the shops closed for the day; this time, he might even have some answers for her.

Stepping into the marketplace, her boot soles slapped the slick black walkway. She passed stall after stall, enacting her boyish gait. Crony's and

Luce's reputations alone would've been enough to protect her, had anyone seen beyond the masquerade. But no one cared to look any closer: scarred skin that appeared grimy no matter how hard she scrubbed, due to a daily dose of sun protectants; shorn hair that never grew, greasy from a paste of crushed blackberries which left a residue even when clean. Not to mention breasts so small that binding them was unnecessary as long as the clothing was baggy.

Stain didn't mind not catching anyone's eye. Being mistaken for an unkempt boy had fooled whoever dropped her in this wasteland to die and gave her an advantage, should she ever discover who *they* were.

Stain hurried past the first five booths where edible fares waited for purchase. The scent from Brannigan's Breads and Cookies made her mouth water. The booth's banner was a golden loaf stitched in thread upon a blue swatch of cloth. Her meager breakfast had left a hole in her belly, but she hadn't time nor payment for filling it. Contrary to past bartering tasks, Luce hadn't given her any gold, sterlings, or coppers—the three forms of payment preferred by the retailers.

Today her pouch held one item alone, vendible only to a particular recipient. Haggling without traditional currency added another challenge alongside having no voice. Luce maintained that her limitations needn't limit her; that by using her mind and listening skills, the observations she'd garnered of each shopkeeper's personal interests over the years could make her the wisest diplomat in the marketplace.

Now Luce was putting her to the test.

"Fresh sugar cookies, little sprout." Puppy-eyed Brannigan's yipping voice taunted her. The baker had once bred greyhounds for a nobleman in Eldoria, before he'd been caught racing them illegally to line his own pocket. Since then, he served the lowest of the low, adapting recipes he'd used for dog biscuits. Surprising how good they were. "Two sterlings for a dozen. Have some silver weighing down your bag?"

She averted her gaze, moving onward as three more booths passed in her peripheral. One was a candy shop with elaborate white-and-red peppermints twisted in the shape of skeletons. Blood and Crème Confections was run by a bald, cross-eyed butcher known only by the name Vice. He'd lost his business after stocking his meat hooks with his murdered partner's remains. Then came a cheese-and-liquor stand under the keep of Alyse, a portly woman who held a steady discourse with her two dairy cows tied alongside the booth—selling only to whom they approved. Next stood an herb dispensary owned by a woodland dwarf named Winkle, who, after being cast out of the castle as the royal ratcatcher some years ago (he'd offended the king's sister by chasing a rat into her chambers where it scampered across her bare feet), now pilfered wares from village gardens by disguising himself as a large rabbit.

Stain paused at Edith's Edibles, where dried vegetables and fruits, salted meats, fried mealworms, and honey-glazed beetle larvae were the specials. Some might cringe at the menu, but tastes varied as much as people's appearances. Old Toothless Edith knew this better than anyone, having worked for the royal kitchens some thirty years ago, until she and the finicky princess had a falling out. Edith was caught incorporating less than savory ingredients into Princess Glistenda's breakfast for spite, and was thrown into the dungeon and plucked of all her teeth for her trouble. After serving a five-year sentence, she came here to stay, deeming herself too ugly to face the world again.

Stain glanced down the line where Luce leaned inside Crony's booth, forearms relaxed atop the counter. No mistaking the expression on his celestial face: *Get to it then.*

Soon the walkway would be crowded with shoppers, and bartering options would dwindle. Stain's nose crinkled and she eyed all twelve booths. Luce had given her a difficult puzzle: only one piece to start with, and five chances to grow it. Her end goal was to purchase a special item from Dregs—Luce had already specified what it should be, and it was something the hoarfrost goblin wasn't likely to part with for cheap. Unless she could find the perfect payment with which to negotiate . . . something Dregs couldn't resist.

A half smile tugged at Lyra's lips. There it was, displayed on a shelf at Percival's Frills and Footgear—a prize Dregs would desire with all his frosted little heart. Now to bargain her way to it. That's how the game of diplomacy and barters was played.

She opened her pouch's flap. Inside was an enchanted handheld mirror that could make a person see either their inner beauty, or if they had none, their demons. It was from Crony's stash—one of many magical tokens stolen off corpses over the centuries. Stain hated to let it go; many a time she'd held it up for herself at home.

She did so now, standing directly beneath a lightning-bug lantern to watch the transformation only she could see in the reflection: a rag-tag boy becoming a girl with long silver hair and luminous moon-kissed skin—free of scars or smudges.

Shaking her head, she chided herself and tucked the mirror away again. She'd once told Scorch what she saw in the mirror. He had threatened to crush it beneath his hooves, telling her that entertaining perfect, pretty fantasies would make her weak and gullible.

This looking glass would mean nothing to a goblin, as the magic worked only on people; that's why Luce had chosen it. To make Stain think . . . who would be most tempted by such a prize? She turned back to Edith's Edibles and stepped forward.

Edith's gummy smile greeted her—a gaping hole of slime and empty sockets amidst a wrinkled saffron complexion.

"Mornin', boy. Thomthin' caught your eye on my shelvth?" A whistling lisp edged her words, a flaw that made her reluctant to speak. But with Stain, who couldn't even make a sound, Edith felt comfortable enough to be herself without fearing ridicule.

Stain nodded, pointing to a jar labeled: Cow Cud Crackers. The snacks were as repulsive as they sounded—flat, misshapen, and the greenish-black of tobacco spittle. True to their name, the main ingredient was predigested balls of food taken from the mouths of cattle on the way to slaughter. Stain couldn't imagine who, other than a cow, would wish to eat such a thing, but it was that very logic that made this the ideal wage for her next stop.

"They be five copperth for a dollop," Edith insisted, her small eyes sharpened. She hadn't moved toward the jar yet, obviously noting that Stain's pouch didn't jingle as she wrested it open. "Ya ain't got the meanth to pay, boy. Go bribe your keeper for coinage." She jerked her thumb toward Luce, who was still watching. He tipped his head Edith's direction, delivering a seductive smile. Stain had watched that expression put many a woman in dizzy, happy stupors for days.

Edith, to the contrary, choked back an embarrassed grunt and bowed her head, shoulders hunched, as if she wished to crawl beneath her booth's counter. Her reaction made this exchange all the more gratifying, knowing it would bring the old woman some happiness.

Just as Edith turned to Stain with "No money, no deal," on her tongue, Stain held up the mirror, aiming the reflective surface her direction.

A soft flash of light bounced across Edith's face, indicating the glass clearing, then a moment of disbelief before Edith's jaw dropped and her graying eyebrows lifted. She touched her cracked lips, tracing a smile. Blissfulness softened the sad lines around her eyes. "Ith that . . . me?" She reached for the handle but Stain pulled back, pointing to the crackers and then the mirror.

"Yeth! Yeth. A bargain. I'll bargain with ya, boy." Edith scooped up some crackers and dropped them into Stain's leather pouch. In exchange, Stain offered the mirror. She walked backward on her departure, smiling while Edith whispered to her reflection as if it were an old friend she hadn't seen for years. When the shopkeeper turned and batted her eyes at Luce, Stain had to suppress a laugh.

After the first trade, it took Stain close to an hour, going from booth to booth, following the strategy she'd laid out. Her second stop was Alyse's Dairies and Brews, where she bartered with the cow cud crackers for a wheel of cheddar; Alyse's doe-eyed advisors could hardly tell their owner not to make the trade, for what ruminant beast doesn't love chewing cud? Next, Stain stopped at Winkle's. The dwarf had a falling out with Alyse weeks earlier when he'd accused her of smelling like a dairy farm; both she and her heifers were so offended, he could no longer buy cheese there. This posed a unique problem, as his rabbit costume was old and fraying and he'd been patching it up with rat and rodent hides. Having nothing to arm his traps of late, Winkle was eager to take the wheel of cheese in exchange for a handful of anise, which Stain then carried across to Jeremiah, owner of Potions, Elixirs, and Magical Necessities. Amidst shelves stacked with wands, chalices, and cauldrons were bottles of magical liquids. Jeremiah used anise for a special fragrance one could wear to ward off evil eyes and ill thoughts. In a metropolis filled with stinky, angry degenerates, this was a product high in demand. Being a businessman, Winkle had raised the price of anise to an outrageous amount, and Jeremiah had been unable to afford it. He'd run low on supplies and could no longer make the fragrance, which in turn made everyone angry with *him*. Now, with Stain's help, he had a supply again, practically for free. He would've been a fool not to trade for the plume agate Stain requested. She took the gemstone to Percival's Frills and Footgear where the bare shelves gathered dust. Having lost his wife to another man months earlier, the artisan had also lost the ability to design new magical accessories. It was rumored he might sell his booth and retire. When Stain presented him with the agate—a stone whose mystical properties were known to boost creativity—Percival instantly had an epiphany for a new line of bronze-spiked necklaces that could double as nooses for unfaithful wives. Thrilled to have his muse back, he handed over the requested pair of shoes without question. Stain basked in her victory.

Had Percival known who they were for, he'd probably not have been so agreeable, considering Dregs was the one to introduce Percival's wife to her new lover in the first place.

Stain flaunted the shoes, dyed the yellow-green of fresh figs, by waving them in Luce's direction. He was busy with a customer, wrapping up a memory that had been activated by Crony days earlier to form a stained-glass portrait of a child and father on a fishing trip. Still, Luce managed to cast her a sidelong glance and shake his head, reminding her the ultimate prize had yet to be won.

Stain wedged herself in a small space between two stalls, ducking out of the now crowded fairway to slip off her boots. The chartreuse shoes magically conformed to whomever wore them, which meant they'd be as perfect for Dregs's little feet as they were for hers. She left her own boots hidden in the nook, then tromped three booths down, where a sign, black with silver lettering, welcomed customers: DEEP IN THE NIGHT—DARK CURIOSITIES FOR DAY DWELLERS.

Dregs's booth was the most morbidly fascinating by far. He sold items smuggled in from Nerezeth: salamanders that once affixed themselves to a wearer's feet and ankles, forming the most beautiful rainbow-scaled slippers; crickets that once sang chirping symphonies; and shadows that in the night realm followed one's every move like a second skin. The morbid part was that these things were now dead. People of the day realm didn't trust the night's creatures, and wanted them only as empty trophies to place upon a wall or lock within a box for when a visitor needed to be entertained or an enemy to be threatened. Thus, Stain's challenge: to bargain for a *living* supply of one of Dregs's most popular items: moths. He kept them hidden under the counter, waiting to be smothered for fresh displays.

Dregs cocked his head upon seeing her, and the icicle growths upon his chin caught a sparkle of light from the lanterns. "If it isn't the Stain, here to pull at the reins."

She nodded in greeting and pointed to the counter, making a downward motion to signify the living items underneath.

Dregs puffed through the long, crooked tip of his nose. "White gold only is currency enough, should you wish to see my breathing stuffs." He was playing games, knowing that though Luce and Crony had a bevy of stolen wealth hidden away, they rarely spent it.

Narrowing her eyes, Stain stomped the soles of her shoes upon the ground seven times each. In an instant, the soles thickened. Stain's stomach rocked as she grew taller and taller, until she loomed over the booth, level with the sign at the top. She pointed to a picture of a flying moth painted in silver ink next to the lettering.

Dregs gaped, then clambered atop his step stool to view her feet over the counter.

"Pedestal shoes in the shade of chartreuse . . . how did a boy such as you come by such a coup?"

Stain shrugged, then tapped her toes seven times, deactivating the soles so they shrank and returned her to the proper height. She gestured again beneath his counter.

Dregs salivated, his glossy marble gaze stuck on her feet. "Were I to step within and stand, I could walk as grand as any man." His sharp-toothed smile split wide open.

The greed in his eyes inspired Stain to raise her price. Luce would be impressed if she could bargain even more from the goblin than originally planned.

She held out two fingers.

Dregs snarled, but she knew she'd won. She took off the shoes and stood barefoot, the onyx walkway slick and warm beneath her bare soles. Dregs grabbed the heels and placed them on his own feet, giddy. After growing tall enough to look Stain in the eye, he withdrew three jars from their hidden spot under the counter. "Three from which to choose. Two is the price of the shoes."

In one, crickets climbed their glass walls—a black wave clambering atop one another to reach the holes punched in the lid. Crony was always commiserating over missing the sound of cricket songs. Stain couldn't resist the chance to make her smile, so she pointed to the insects, fully intending to choose the moths as her second option. Dregs waved twiglike fingers over the two remaining jars. Inside one, moths fluttered in a frenzy of activity. Stain started to point to them, but hesitated, intrigued that the final jar was wrapped in black fabric. She peered within a peephole cut in the side, seeing shadows clinging to the opposing edge under the lid.

"Midnight shadows, they are. On hold for the castle afar. The princess requires special attire. I'll send to Nerezeth for mores, should you claim these as yours."

Stain had never seen a real shadow—that she could remember. Once, while gardening together, Crony had mentioned their history. After the world split beneath its magical curse, shadows became indentured to moonlight and candlelight, a completely different creature than the patches of darkness here in the ravine. Shade was cast by sunlight, and was the warden of Stain's prison, for to venture outside of it would burn her alive. Crony had told Stain that one day, she would see shadows for herself and understand the magnitude of their differences, for shadows offered freedom where shade offered only respite.

Stain had always wondered what that meant.

She shot a glance to Luce, who was busy with a line of customers. Taking a deep breath that filled her nose with myriad odors from the milling crowd, she weighed her options. She wanted to pick the moths, not just because Luce specified them, but to save them from being smothered. Yet she had only one choice left.

Luce would be angry, unless she could convince him that midnight shadows, so rare in the day realm, must have more value. With that, her decision became clear. She tapped the cloth-wrapped jar.

Dregs' frosty eyebrows raised and his shoes lifted him taller so he was looking down on her. "Ah, be you careful with these, if you please. A touch of the sun and they'll come undone. Tuck them into a dark room where they can loom; light a flame, and they'll join you in a game."

Stain nodded a thank-you as he handed over the two jars. Before she could even take a step toward Crony's booth, a familiar voice shouted inside her mind: *Danger. Kill. Fly.*

Her heart jumped into her throat. Scorch was in trouble.

Gloved hands trembling, she stuffed the two jars into the pouch slung over her shoulder. In too much a hurry to grab her boots, she sprinted out of the market and scrambled into the trees—her arms and legs straining as she leapt from one branch to another, the fastest mode of travel in the denser parts of the forest—not daring to look back when Luce shouted her name.

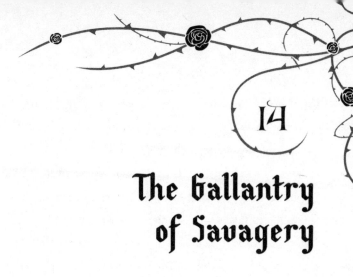

14

The Gallantry
of Savagery

Over the past several years of disuse, the thorny maze that camou-
flaged the cave opening from the Rigamort into the Ashen Ravine
had grown even more thick and winding, so that even Alger and
Dolyn were intimidated by the tangles. Though it limited the already muted
light filtering through the canopy overhead, Prince Vesper appointed himself
the lead. At least the black, twining palisade with spurs as big as an eagle's
talons would assure no tender-skinned Eldorian would dare pass this way,
which meant no unwanted encounters. The prince was still feeling weak after
having drained some golden blood to paint streaks across the Rigamort's
rocks and walls—giving the stags sunlight to absorb until he could send a
new supply.

Before venturing through the labyrinth, the troop trussed their horses in
barding again. Then they resumed riding single file through the slim openings. Vesper soon came to see they weren't to be as sheltered as he'd hoped. As
the lead, he should've paid closer attention, should've noted the faint scent of
smoke, or glimpsed the subtle orange flashes illuminating small openings in
the gnarled labyrinth from far in the distance. But he'd been too beguiled by
how familiar the surroundings looked here, in a place he'd never been: a dim,

hazy world he'd only envisioned through lore shared by children at play or details offered by Nerezeth's assassins and sun-smugglers.

Uncountable pathways sluiced the maze, most leading to dead ends. Yet the troop trudged forward, having no occasion to stop and turn about, all due to Vesper. He knew exactly when to duck, where to turn, or how to swivel Lanthe's reins to avoid false routes in the circuitous brambles and forge safe passage. It wasn't a memory. It was a learned rhythm for the path that had no sense belonging to a prince from the night realm who had never set foot in the ravine.

So preoccupied with this anomaly, he didn't see the boxy clearing until he and Lanthe stumbled onto it. He hadn't expected it to be there; it clashed with that strange intuition guiding him. He realized it was freshly made: brambles burned to the ground, smoldering cinders blending with the gray ash.

From left to right, towering vines crackled with sparks. Some crashed into one another with loud, snapping thuds—having lost their supportive infrastructures—and closed off extra pathways. The noise and movement spooked Lanthe. Vesper settled the stallion enough to coax him into the clearing, only to find himself surrounded by impenetrable tangled walls with only two openings. One, the pathway where his companions would soon siphon through behind him, and the other a few feet ahead where black smoke masked any chance for a visual.

The clearing, narrow and rectangular, left little room for the others; possibly one rider and horse could fit alongside him. Vesper raised his hand, halting his companions before they could enter. Suffocating heat filled his lungs and melted the paint on his face. He held tight to the reins and pressed his knees firmly into Lanthe's ribs to calm the stallion's nervous, dancing hooves. The horse's ears flattened; there would be no going forward until the smoke dispersed. But Vesper suspected his mount's reaction was to something other than the remains of the fire, for he sensed it, too.

Within that pitch-dark cloud that blocked the opposite entrance, something pulled at Vesper's sunlit blood—an aching, visceral tug—like a lodestone called to metal. The sensation made his thoughts fuzzy, bewitched. He *had* to get through, to find what had razed the vines and thorns—even if it meant going afoot.

The prince motioned to Cyprian. His first knight entered the clearing and together they slid from their saddles, ankles sinking into the ash. Their boots provided coverage up to their knees, which would aid their trek through the thorns once they plunged within.

Cyprian drew his sword and Vesper unsheathed the knife at his waist, deciding a smaller weapon might be easier handled in this cramped space. He took the lead. He felt rather than saw Cyprian cast a glance back at the others, no doubt sending silent assurance to Selena that he'd watch over her brother. Vesper had caught the worried expression upon her face—clear even beneath the thick smear of sun protectant coating it—when she'd stalled on the edge of the opening. Nysa must have sensed her mistress's tension, for she began to bark. Vesper would've just as soon asked Selena and Nysa to accompany him . . . his sister was better with a dagger than Cyprian, who was more a swordsman. But as third in line, Selena had no room to enter, and dismounting inside the path would be complicated.

Vesper's ears strained for sounds beyond falling vines, popping sparks, and Nysa's yipping. Inching forward, he heard something panting. He proceeded, led by that all-encompassing pull.

Smoke curled around him, stinging his eyes and nostrils. Without warning, something huge crashed out from the path. Caught off guard, the prince and Cyprian floundered rearward. A bugling roar shoved them against their mounts, who reacted with squealing neighs.

A magnificent black beast crowded in: hooves, fetlocks, and mane alight with embers. A horse, but so much more. Its wings spanned so wide it couldn't open them fully in the tight clearing. Vesper swallowed a gasp and held his knife up, as ineffective as threatening a wildfire with a dewdrop.

He'd seen flying horses in paintings and historical scrolls. When he was young, irresponsible, and angry, he used to dream of riding a Pegasus into the stars, away from his kingdom's responsibilities and all those who feared or judged him for his differences.

Yet he'd never heard of one that could breathe flame.

He and his lieutenant exchanged awed glances. "Weren't they said to be extinct?" Cyprian asked under his breath.

"Either the scribes were misinformed," Vesper answered, "or this is a breed yet undiscovered."

The beast pressed forward, intensifying Vesper's need to get closer. The gold-plated flesh in his torso, arm, and leg vibrated, as if being hammered flat. He ground his teeth and took a step.

"Your Majesty, no!" Cyprian tugged him back. His first knight struggled to brandish his sword, but he couldn't risk their own mounts skidding around them through the ash. Their barding wouldn't stand up to the slash of a silver blade.

Vesper's lungs filled with dust and smoke. He coughed, shaking himself out of the trance. He captured Lanthe's reins and backed up the horse, putting himself between the stallion and their winged attacker. Vesper's veins stung, as if his blood rebelled against moving away from the Pegasus, but he continued, indicating Cyprian do the same. It was a maneuver the mounts were familiar with, having learned it to escape cadaver brambles along cramped trails.

Once Lanthe's tail reached the path's opening, Selena handed off the wriggling Nysa to Luna, who was seated on a horse behind her. Selena then coaxed Dusklight's head down and vaulted herself onto Lanthe's hind-quarters. She scooted into the saddle, then reined him in and backed him all the way onto the small trail where the others made room. Without losing a beat, she did the same for Cyprian's horse. She then motioned to everyone to back up farther, allowing space for Vesper and Cyprian to enter the path on foot.

Snorting black soot from its nostrils, the Pegasus whipped one wing down to hide the smoke-filled passage that led out of the clearing and into the ravine, then used its body to force Cyprian onto the other trail with the waiting troop. The first knight dropped his sword, but he hadn't time to retrieve it before the Pegasus pawed it with a front hoof; the blade spun atop a spray of cinders and ash, coming to rest a few feet from Vesper.

The Pegasus lifted its head high. A flame huffed from its mouth and nostrils. Cyprian turned his back and barely had time to drive everyone farther inside before the fire engulfed the front of the path. More vines fell and shut off the opening.

Vesper turned back, cornered by the Pegasus. The beast's movements were agile and precise, not ravening and mad. From the other side of the thorny wall, Nysa barked and Vesper's troop shouted, but he couldn't make out their words.

The Pegasus reared and whinnied—a threatening and victorious sound. It was a male. Perhaps he was territorial, and they'd stumbled upon his den. The beast dropped his front hooves into the ash beneath him, raising a clap of dust that mingled with the fresh smoke.

His eyes ignited with sentience and strategies far beyond instinct. Rearing again, the Pegasus came down within inches of Vesper's head. The prince dove, rolled through the ash, and dropped his knife in exchange for Cyprian's fallen sword. He brought the long blade up and felt a jolt. In the same move, he twisted his torso so the beast's hooves came crashing down upon his ossified abdomen.

Every bone in Vesper's body reverberated like a metal gong being struck. His rib cage hummed, shaking his heart, but he spun to his feet. He stood, panting. Sweat beaded the edge of the eel-skin hood fitted snug over his hair. He lifted the sword high to fend off another attack. A fiery sludge drizzled along the blade's edge, so hot it melted the silver. Vesper realized he'd made contact in the same instant the Pegasus did.

The beast grunted and backed up, plugging the one way out of the clearing. His left wing hung limp where it joined his muscular shoulder. The black feathers shimmered with the same molten ooze that coated Cyprian's sword: blood.

A moan of sympathy shuddered through Vesper's throat.

Glancing once at his wound, the Pegasus's eyes lit to a furious red, and he lifted his head high, prepared to release a rain of fire.

Vesper crossed his arms over his head, having nowhere to run. His eyes closed instinctively to shield from the brilliant flash of light. But instead of being engulfed in flame, he heard a small crash to the left.

The prince's eyes snapped open to see a gangly boy plunge out of a fresh-made gap, breeches ripped up to his knees and shirt hanging in shreds beneath a vest. His dingy skin and even his buzzed, dark hair sported punctures where thorns had gouged him on his way in. Blood slicked his unshod feet, yet he seemed oblivious to any pain as he shoved Vesper back and stood between the prince and the Pegasus.

The beast stomped and grunted, a froth of cinders flecking his mouth.

"Step back, son," Vesper said, grasping the boy's scrawny elbow and readying the sword. "This is no ordinary creature."

The boy shook him off and tramped forward three more steps, eyes locked on the winged horse. There was a mental tug-of-war taking place; Vesper had been on the outside of enough silent conversations over the past few years to recognize one.

With an ear-shattering bellow, the Pegasus spun and thundered down the path he'd been blocking, swallowed by smoke. The boy stood frozen, watching after him. Vesper stepped up, and the lad's head barely came to his chest. So small to be so brave.

"Thank you, son." Vesper placed a gloved hand on his slender shoulder. "Let me help you now. We have food . . . water . . . clothing and shoes to spare."

The boy grabbed the prince's wrist with his own gloved palm, spun, and slammed his head into Vesper's chest. The prince's golden shin gave out and he fell backward. He struggled to catch a breath as his attacker pried the melting sword from his fingers and flung it aside.

The boy's lips, strangely pretty beneath their smudges, were pressed tight—as if holding in screams. He used his hands, signing to Vesper: *I am no one's son. And I don't need help from one who makes a living of savagery.* Then he scrambled back toward the path to pursue the Pegasus.

Intrigued by the boy's knowledge of the ancient language, Vesper lunged and caught his ankle. His hand slipped in the blood smears, but managed to hold on and topple his opponent onto his back. The boy landed, a gush of breath bursting from his lungs. He struggled—kicking, biting, scratching.

"Hold still!" Vesper gritted his teeth as he dragged him closer. He'd had an easier time taking down the cadaver bramble. Of course, he didn't wish to break or harm this particular adversary, so he reined in his full strength. But what the boy lacked in brute strength he made up for in speed and wiles. He was matching the prince move for move.

Vesper took a cuff to the chin that left his skull ringing. "Would you stop? I simply want to talk to you!"

The boy snatched Vesper's half-buried knife. A toothy grimace glared white against his grungy face as he lashed out with the blade. A canine snarl broke from the smoky pathway. Vesper only had time enough to leap to his feet as a red fox dashed in, fangs bared. The boy stood and tucked the knife in his vest. Growling quietly at his side, the fox backed toward the path. Sooty clouds hung heavy in the opening, a black fog waiting to swallow them. As the lad ducked in beside his pet, he cast a final glare at Vesper.

The prince couldn't move. Those eyes, peering out from the darkness, shifted to an amber so bright they illuminated a thousand lashes, a quality the prince had failed to notice earlier during the chaos. Now the lashes were all Prince Vesper could see: so long and feathery they resembled the lacy, crystalline deposits of water vapor frozen in mid-drizzle upon branches and shrubbery in Nerezeth.

No one in the day realm had eyes like that.

"You don't belong here," Vesper murmured.

Huffing, the boy kicked a plume of ash toward him, then sprinted into the dark passage, the fox following at his heels.

Vesper stood in the floating ash. Awareness came back in increments: the scent of the beast's blood—metallic and scorched along the melting silver sword; a slight itch across his skin where the golden plates slowed their thrumming; the taste of ash coating his lips; the nicker of horses, the call of jackdaws, and Nysa's growling barks; the sound of his troop hacking at their thorny enclosure.

Dolyn, Leo, and Luna broke through first with axes in hand. Next, Nysa scampered out alongside Selena and Alger, with Thea and Tybalt close behind. Black soot smudged everyone's silvery-white hair, eyebrows, and pale flesh.

"Are the others all right?" Vesper asked, lowering a hand to scratch the spaniel behind her ears.

"Cyprian was burned," Selena answered.

Vesper cursed and started toward the opening.

Selena stopped him. "He's all right. Luna is wrapping the wound."

Vesper nodded. Luna had bandaged his own wound earlier. Her experience as a field nurse was already proving beneficial.

Selena managed a self-deprecating smirk. "Cyprian will be furious that I told you. He hopes to hide his injury. He wanted me to find you, so I'd stop fussing over him."

Vesper shook his head, attempting an answering smile. "I highly doubt that's true. Since when has Cyprian balked at your attention?"

She bit her lip and her white lashes fluttered down. Vesper wondered what had happened between the two during the interim while he was separated from everyone.

"And the horses?" He dragged off his hood and released his dark hair. Right now, he was more than Selena's brother. He was their leader in this foreign land, and they'd almost all ended up as kindling.

"They're good enough. Just spooked."

He watched Nysa snuffle around the clearing. "Did any of you see what took place in here?" He lifted the sword that had disintegrated to half its size.

Leo stepped over. "Cyprian won't be happy about that."

Vesper fought a bought of sympathy. The sword had been a gift from Sir Andrian. Cyprian's father had recently passed away of the same sickness that killed Vesper's own. When the molten blood started oozing toward his hand, Vesper dropped the blade again.

Luna nudged the sword's handle with her boot toe. "We were watching as best we could through the slits. A *Pegasus?*"

Vesper raised his eyebrows. "It would seem."

"And who was that poverty-stricken child?" Luna asked, weaving loose silver hairs back into her braid and wiping smudges from her neck.

Vesper rubbed his bruised chin, still mystified by the lad's courage. *I am no one's son*, he'd signed. "An orphaned stripling. Unable to use his voice. His wrists and ankles were as small as twigs, yet he staved off my death by simply standing there."

The boy had proven himself a worthy sparring partner as well. There was a spindly confidence to his movements, like the small luminous spiders that occupied places of honor and reverence alongside the crickets in Nerezeth's castle. Vesper's family and subjects always took care not to step upon the royal bugs. Yet here was this boy who appeared to have been trampled again and again and somehow kept going. Finespun as glass and tough as iron. A mix of qualities that intrigued Vesper beyond reason.

"What's this?" Selena wandered over to the jagged opening the boy had made. She lifted a pouch that was dangling from one of the vines. "Must've slipped off in his struggle to plunge through."

Vesper took it. Opening the flap revealed two jars. Upon seeing their contents, his mood turned somber. "That was no common boy. He walks through brambles without shoes; he faces flame without cowering; he commands untamable beasts and signs in the ancient language. And then this . . ."

Selena took the pouch back and looked for herself. "Shadows and crickets, smuggled in from Nerezeth?"

Vesper tensed. "He stole my knife, but it looks like that's the least of his crimes." He waved Alger, Leo, Thea, Tybalt, and Uric over. "Follow his trail. Go on foot and we'll see to your horses. He had the eyes of a Nerezethite, which means he can see in darkness. Perhaps he's a scout, paid to lead smugglers into the night realm."

"You think he has something to do with the stags?"

Vesper didn't want to think ill of the child. "He saved me from being burned to death—even while under the impression I was an assassin. There's good in him. I can't see him as the one who fatally wounded our gatekeepers. He was furious that I harmed the Pegasus. Still, it's possible he knows *something*."

Alger, Thea, and Leo started toward the opening that led out to the ravine where Tybalt and Uric already waited. At last the soot had cleared away.

"Wait." Vesper scooped up his sister's pet. "Take Nysa; she can scent the fox. I suspect if you find it, you find the boy."

Selena reached for her pet, but Vesper passed the dog off to Leo. "I need you here, Selena. We'll set up camp . . . surround it with rocks to stave off quag-puddles and gather some twigs for a fire. Cyprian can use some nourishment, and the horses have earned oats and rest. There's a cascade of fresh water running down a steep embankment of rocks, just on the other side of that passage. It leads to a small tarn where we can fill our skins. There are even fish we might roast for dinner."

"How do you know all that?" Selena asked, but before Vesper could search for an answer within himself, Leo interrupted.

"What of the witch?" he asked. Distracted by the dog's licking tongue, he hadn't heard the question on the table.

"Thana is watching over her," Vesper answered. "If you happen to run across them, try to apprehend the witch and bring her to camp for questioning. But do not cross the threshold to her home. According to Dyadia, it's accursed with violent magical wards. Whatever happens, be back by the cessation course. We'll resume the mission when the denizens are sleeping."

"So, the boy is our priority for now?"

"Yes. Let Nysa concentrate on the little thief, before his scent is gone." Vesper chose his words carefully, trying to justify his sudden change in priority. Truth was, he needed to find the orphan for himself, to absolve the confusing emotions awhirl within him. "The boy might offer aid in what's happening at the Rigamort, considering his smuggled items. I intend to know who he is, what he's about, and where he's from, before this day is over."

Leo nodded, bid his wife good-bye, and left with his group.

As others guided the horses through the clearing and into the exit passage, Cyprian joined the prince where he crouched beside the sword handle—all that was left of the blade.

Vesper gripped his friend's shoulder, careful to avoid his neck and collarbone where bandages covered his burns. "I'm sorry, Cyp."

His friend did an admirable job suppressing his disappointment as he sheathed the handle. "I've never seen a beast like that. What other mystical secrets does this forest hold?"

Vesper had no answer, for he was keeping a secret himself: the effect the Pegasus had on him; how the beast had beckoned to his own blood, how even now he could feel that telling prickle spread through his left arm. Like golden vines, the metallic shimmer expanded where his wrist and the back of his hand showed between his sleeve and glove. He would have to make an incision and drain the poison before it petrified and left his fingers completely useless. Vesper's dagger had been stolen, so he needed Selena's, and he'd need her assistance closing the incision—too private a procedure to ask help of anyone other than family.

He'd soon have a new scar.

Vesper clenched his jaw against the brittle, creeping sensations, determined to understand how the Pegasus had the power to affect him. Since the orphan stripling seemed to have a mental connection to the beast . . . he might be key to that as well.

Vesper assured himself these were logical reasons for this urgency to retrieve his small rescuer—to prioritize this vexing fascination for those lips and eyes, for that fighting spirit, over finding the witch and getting to the castle.

Madame Dyadia would say the fates had set the boy in their path for a purpose; that there was no such thing as an accidental meeting where the prophecy was concerned. But what role could a ragamuffin thief possibly play in reuniting the sun and the moon?

15

Charitable Secrets and Merciful Lies

In any other part of Eldoria, a man carrying a bleeding, bedraggled boy who wriggled to break free would raise eyebrows. In the ravine, it was little more noticed than having the same "man" run alongside that boy's ankles moments earlier as a fox. A metropolis filled with villains had a unique code of ethics: apathy was a courtesy everyone extended without question, in hopes the same would be passed on to them. So, as Luce carried Stain past men and women going to and from market, or off to spend their lucre at the Wayward Tavern—located in the hollowed-out trunk of the forest's widest tree—no one even glanced their way.

Upon their escape from the labyrinth, Luce had morphed into his human form and, without a warning, lifted Stain and pinned her between the edge of his rib cage and his hip bone—much like he toted large sacks of ash from their home after Crony had swept the floors. Luckily, he'd kept Stain facing the same direction as him.

Put me down. Signing from this awkward position wasn't easy. She jostled with his every step, causing her shoulders to jerk and making it difficult to form her fingers into anything legible.

"I will not."

She sighed at the resolve in his voice, resigning herself to his brisk, bumpy stroll over ambling tree roots and around quag-puddles. Urgency gnawed behind her sternum, so much more agonizing than the ache in her shredded feet. She needed to get to Scorch. She'd wounded his pride, and that lesion would fester and spread even faster than the slash to his wing if she didn't find him soon.

I wish to walk on my own beside you. This is humiliating. Please.

Luce directed a grimace her way. "You were fool enough to go gallivanting about without your boots, but I'm not fool enough to turn you loose just so you can chase your fancy donkey."

His mention of Scorch pricked Stain's heart deeper, as if a thorn had wedged within it during her tear through the labyrinth. Her eyes stung, but no relief would come. Much the same as her hair wouldn't grow, she hadn't shed a single tear since she'd first awakened on the lumpy mattress in Crony's house, no matter how sad, confused, or brokenhearted she felt at times. Perhaps she'd cried so hard on that day someone tortured her and left her to die that she had no tears left in her body. Yet that didn't stop her soul from weeping when someone she loved was in pain.

He's wounded, Luce. He's bleeding.

"Dammit, Stain. You're bleeding, too. He can wait."

Until when?

"Until I get you home and have Crony dress your wounds. All you needed was more scars. Top it off by the fact that you didn't even get the moths. Shadows and crickets! What did you think to accomplish with those?" He cursed under his breath.

Stain fell limp, bobbing along with Luce's gait, letting his scent of feathers and fur soothe her panicked state. He'd been so angry when she told him she lost the items from market. Why did he care, considering he was unhappy with her selections anyway?

She suspected he'd wanted the moths so he might watch them fly, to live his lost ability vicariously through them. For that reason, she could tolerate his harsh scolding.

"You know, we didn't save you all those years back just to watch you rip yourself to shreds again. You've no idea the crimp you've made in the plan."

Those words gave her pause. She was used to being at the whipping end of Luce's tongue. From a sylph's perspective, grumpiness was the equivalent of chivalry. And it wasn't the first time he'd referenced saving her. Yet he'd never made it sound as if there were a motive. A plan, in fact. She readied her hands to insist he explain, but he took back the conversation with an annoyed snarl.

"Whatever possessed you to leave the market and attack a group of strangers in the first place? You're in rare form today."

Stain dropped her arms. Form. What form *should* she take? She had no idea who she was, or where she came from. Perhaps she belonged with those strangers. Yet she no longer wanted to be of the night realm, after having seen their cruelty firsthand—a hunger for violence woven within the very fibers of their costuming: the assassin's hooded face painted with smears like a melted skull with empty sockets; his skintight assassin's uniform that shimmered like scales along his tall, masculine frame—appearing lethal as a black snake; and his silver sword, tainted with her dearest friend's blood. Today she'd learned how little those of the night realm thought of life. Which left her to surmise that she was dropped here to die because their kind didn't know how to care. No wonder no mother or father was looking for her if Nerezeth was her home.

Oh, they were a tricky lot . . . appearing to be kind and helpful to lure their prey into their trap. Like the ravager, when he managed a voice that somehow seemed familiar, that soothed with deepness and gentle words. He'd offered her water, shoes, food. She'd known better than to fall for it.

Trust no one on royal business—either of the day realm or the night. Scorch had taught her that, as had Toothless Edith and every other nefarious neighbor who shared this forest. Royalty and the like were as dangerous as sunlight.

She cringed, thinking upon the Night Ravager's last words to her: *You don't belong here.*

Her eyes had given her away. They rarely glowed in this place, as the shade wasn't dark enough. But surrounded by tangled walls and sooty smog, it made the difference.

She'd been foolish to look back, but his own eyes had captivated her. They were wrong for a Nerezethite's—yet they were made of night. As mysterious as the shadows she'd bargained for at market, and as all-encompassing as the wave of crickets climbing the walls in their glass jar. His gaze held both wisdom and confusion—twisted like the ravine's trees that divided their roots and trunks between the moon and sun.

She wondered how striking the contrast would be against silver hair and bluish-white skin, when not covered by his uniform, gloves, and face paint. Then she bit back a groan, disgusted by her own fascination.

"Did the ravager say anything to you before I got there?" Luce asked, as if he stepped inside her mind and watched her thoughts pass above him like clouds.

Stain allowed her hands to sway, answerless. He was angry enough already. What would he think if he knew she'd actually lost all sense upon seeing Scorch's blood and screamed at an assassin in sign language? Though the ravager couldn't possibly know what she said, she'd gone one step farther and threatened him with his own sword before stealing his knife. The flat side of the cold blade still pressed against her skin where her ribs wedged under Luce's arm.

She couldn't even entertain the possibility that her careless, spiteful reaction might have put them all in danger.

"Crony should be here. Where is she?" Luce let the question hang as he stepped out of the thicket of trees and onto their home's isolated plot. As he stepped across the framework that separated the bedrooms, she prepared her muscles to launch.

Luce was too quick. He dragged the talisman from around her neck and over her head, pocketing it in his red jacket in the same moment he deposited her atop her mattress. She bared her teeth and he offered a wry smile as he dropped her boots beside her with a *thunk.*

The shoes would be of no use now . . . no crossing the threshold into the yard without her talisman. Luce had effectively imprisoned her without walls. Sometimes she hated his sly, clever ways just as she admired them.

Her eyes darted around the four rooms to put a plan together. Some way to distract Luce, pick his pocket, and break free.

She removed her gloves. Luce's slender shoulders strained the fabric of his jacket as he turned his back and lifted aside the curtains covering Crony's shelves. After years of being his ward, Stain was immune to his charms—the one advantage she had over most women and men in this forest. However, he *wasn't* immune to her charms. His affection for her was of a parental sort, far more powerful than lustful attraction. She'd rely on that.

Luce splashed some water into a cup, then upon finding a tin of healing ointment and thin strips of muslin—bleached and gathered into rolls—he came to sit cross-legged on the ground beside her mattress.

He offered her the drink. She sipped, widening her eyes until her long white lashes fanned high, knowing how the pleading expression affected him.

Setting the empty cup aside, she signed with her scarred hands: *Wouldn't Crony rinse the wounds with hot water first? And might I have some mint-and-lavender tea to ease my pain?*

It was perfect. A fire. Something to heat Luce through so he'd take off his jacket.

"I suppose Crony *would* boil water. Once again, you're forcing me to be nursemaid. A role I've no desire to play." Luce's jaw twitched, an annoyed gesture that only enhanced the dangerously beautiful lines and angles of his face. "For that, no ambrosial tea for you. Something bitter, something medicinal. An elixir of persimmons and fish oil to cleanse your innards as well as your outwards is what you'll be drinking."

Stain offered no argument, resolved she wouldn't be here long enough to partake in said refreshments.

He lit a small flame in the fire pit and placed a kettle on the iron hanger atop it. The scent of smoke and roasting wood escalated her need to find Scorch to the point it itched beneath her skin.

While waiting for the water to boil, Luce returned to sit across from her. The flames lit the greenish, hazy surroundings. His red hair and suit flickered in vivid hues.

"You never answered my question. Did the ravager say anything to you?"

Stain decided a half-truth would serve. *He offered me food, water . . . clothing. He believed me a boy. Called me son.* This admission made her snarl. Until today, it had never bothered her to be thought of as boy.

Luce sighed. "Son . . . and then you kicked ash in his face on our way out. Not exactly the best first impression."

Stain shrugged. *What difference do impressions make? It's not as if I'm to see him again. It's not as if it matters.*

"It matters more than you know," Luce whispered under his breath, fisting the rolls of bandages in his lap.

Why? He can't possibly be behind what happened to me. Though she wasn't sure precisely how long she'd been in the world, she sensed that she and the ravager were close in age. *He's not old enough to have left me here all those years ago.*

"Age aside, assassins are a dangerous lot. Wouldn't want them coming around and causing trouble." Luce's orange eyes narrowed and he ground his pointed teeth, a sure indication he was lying. He looked more canine than human in moments when he felt cornered.

Stain shook her head. *There's more. Something you're not telling me . . .* Her hands paused as she thought back on that moment years ago when he carried her out of the brambles after she first met Scorch. She'd so easily forgotten what Luce had said, overlooked its significance. Having him carry her shredded body again just now brought everything full circle.

She forced out questions, although she feared the answers: *You once said that you wouldn't have me costing you your wings again. What did that mean? Luce . . . why did you lose your wings? Did it have to do with me?*

Sweat beaded his brow. He loosened the top buttons on his white shirt, exposing his talisman necklace. Then he peeled off his jacket and draped it over one knee. "You're not to blame for any of my losses. I made feckless choices because I could fly so high in the clouds, I was immune to consequences. So, I was punished by losing my ability to escape. That's all." He was placating her, tucking paper-thin replies within pretty frames to distract from the emptiness of the words themselves.

You know, don't you? The possibility made her signing clumsy and her stomach queasy. *Where I'm from . . . where I belong. You've known all these years and have been keeping it secret. If you care for me at all, Luce . . . you will tell me. Now.*

His expression softened. "We found you in the lowlands, shaved, broken, and spilling out of a handmade coffin, about to be eaten by shrouds. We had to bargain for you. That's all I can say. You must understand . . . not every secret is meant to harm. Sometimes a past is obscured for charitable reasons. For protection. Perhaps the reasons aren't so insignificant as one person, but even bigger. Others who share the world."

Stain clenched her fingers around the bandages that had come unrolled between them. They *bargained* for her? With what? His wings? And he made it sound as if her past had been hidden purposefully. She held her breath and studied the sparkling glass tokens hanging about the room—final memories of the dead.

Perhaps of the living, too.

She gestured to the trinkets: *Do any of those belong to me?*

Luce's jaw muscles spasmed as he debated the response.

"Shushta yer trap, ye prattling cur!" Crony's shout carried across the path leading to the front of the house. "Ye said enough already!"

Luce swiveled around to meet her stare. Both of them startled when a white crow dropped from the branches above. It swooped over Crony's head then into the rooms, large wings stirring gusts that disturbed the fire and caught strands of Luce's hair. The creature landed on the cedar chest, taking up half of the lid. It was beastly, its one eye as bright pink as the sky after the flash of twilight when the sun returned.

Luce leapt to his feet, dropped his jacket, and lunged at their grotesque guest. Stain yanked his jacket over, fishing out her necklace. She stuffed it, along with the tin of ointment and bandages, into her vest.

Caw-caw! the crow screeched, escaping Luce's clutch.

Only it wasn't a screech or a caw . . . it was a shrill, wordless lamentation—like wails sung by the dead and dying. Stain slapped her palms across her ears. White feathers fluttered down in a dreamy sequence as Luce chased the bird, and in the muffled silence, Stain wondered if that's what snow looked like upon falling. Had she known at one time? Had that memory been taken from her along with the others?

A dog barked in the distance and prompted Stain to stand on her tender feet just as Crony crossed the threshold. Stain's eyes held her guardian's muddy gaze, and like the first time she awoke to the witch's blindfolded, slumbering face, she couldn't see the goodness and affection for the murkiness there.

You lied. It wasn't . . . amnesia. Stain's hands moved in such a spasmodic manner her accusations came out disjointed. *My memories. You took them. Sold . . . or hid? Where? Why?*

Her cheeks prickled with heat as she awaited an answer.

Crony averted her gaze and tipped her skull staff toward the crow, the flames in the fire pit glimmering off her black horns. "Thana, be ye gone, old bird! Tell yer mistress I'm minding me own, so she should do the same!"

Luce, who'd managed to catch the crow by its tail feathers, released it. It soared up, up, up, into the trees with thudding flaps until the canopy swallowed its hideous cries.

Luce watched with a strained expression. Stain wasn't sure if the reaction was one of envy, or of remorse for all the secrets. The loose feathers still drifted, as if carried by an invisible force. Stain reached up and caught two, her eyes burning—a cruel tease to empty sockets.

Her life was a lie. She'd known that already. But she never realized Crony's and Luce's lives were lies, too. For they'd both been lying to her. She could have no revenge, because in every way, they'd been her family. They'd made her trust them. They'd made her *love* them.

She crushed the feathers in her hand and tossed the clump toward Luce, feeling as lost as his wings. Catching up her boots, she leapt across the threshold before either of her shouting guardians could stop her. Unless he transformed to fox form, Luce would never catch her. And if he tried, she would take to the trees.

She heard the dog of earlier barking once more, but it was distant. Just to be safe, she altered her route and stopped to slide into her boots. Forcing the leather over her damaged feet intensified the stabbing jabs of each puncture mark. Still, she pressed forward at a full sprint. The air stung the welts on her skin where thorns had left their mark. She'd learned long ago how to shut out discomfort, how to function in spite of it—on that day she met the one soul who had never lied to her: the beast of sky and wind and feathers and flame, who cared only that she ran alongside him—evenly matched.

The tin of ointment rattled next to the knife in her vest. She would see that Scorch would heal and fly again. Then she would avenge his wounds, as she could never avenge her own.

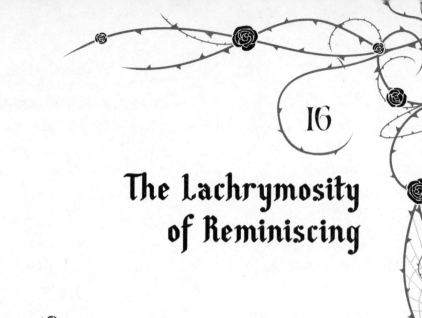

16

The Lachrymosity of Reminiscing

Somewhere in the distance, a dog barked and a crow keened in answer, loud and earsplitting—a discordant symphony of the natural and unnatural. Crony hoped wherever Dyadia's nettlesome bird was flying, it would lead the prince to Stain. But Dyadia didn't yet know the truth of the girl's identity, which meant the prince didn't know, either. And without him, how would the princess ever find her way to Eldoria's castle to claim her fate? Wasn't he supposed to be the lure to lead her there?

Crony had never wanted to return a set of memories to their rightful owner more than now. But if she did, the world would forever remain split in half. She couldn't stop seeing Stain's wounded expression, and it scored her innards as if she'd been running through the brambles herself, turned wrong side out. Crony and Luce had agreed neither of them should take chase . . . that it would only make her run farther, harder. The girl needed time with her Pegasus. If anyone could comfort her, the horse could. They had a strong kinship, those two. Crony had attempted to offer the child such a foundation herself, but a house built on mislaid bricks is destined to crumble.

None of this would have happened if Luce had kept his muzzle shut.

The witch stared at her sylphin companion across the short expanse of their skeletal kitchen, frowning. "What was ye thinkin', dandy dog?" She was tempted to wrap him in filaments from her horns and string him up in the branches like all the stolen memories . . . those Stain assumed were her own. "Ye and yer blabbering tongue. Did the fleas wriggle themselves into yer brain and suck out all yer common senses?"

"That's hardly fair. You know as well as I that parasites are lazy. It's too far a climb from my tail to my head." Luce's smug frown looked every bit as fierce as her own must.

Her lips twitched. If she wasn't so furious, she could try a smile. See if that might bring him some humility.

The tea kettle whistled, breaking Crony's and Luce's unblinking stares.

"You know I'll have to go after her soon." Luce made his way to lift the kettle from its hook. "The cessation course starts in a couple of hours. She doesn't need to be out there in such a state."

"May-let she does." Crony found two teacups, cracked at the rims but suitable enough to hold water. She crumpled a handful of tea leaves and dried mint into each. "May-let her prince will find her now."

"She already found *him*."

Crony's body tensed. "Where . . . when?"

"She was with him in the labyrinth when I saw them."

"And . . . be he worthy of her? All that we hoped?"

Luce shrugged. "Not sure yet. They were fighting on the ground. Considering the man could easily have bested her in size, there's something to be said for his gentleness. He was dressed as a Night Ravager; I only recognized him by his dark eyes. But there was no communicating between them. Instead of bargaining for the moths, Stain had nothing but shadows and crickets in jars, and bloody good they did."

Crony thought back to the day when she'd shared the memory with Luce . . . the one where Stain was still Lyra—princess in the castle. The child had used moths to tell her aunt she would never be her mother. The first time Crony viewed it, she felt a warm flash of pride, even though she barely knew their young ward then. After Luce watched it, he suggested they arm Stain with moths so she might speak to the prince through the insects. He even arranged for Stain to get them herself by bargaining, thus keeping Crony and Luce from technically interfering. A shame that had fallen through.

"Where be the shadows and crickets now? May-let she can use them somehow, to intrigue him with their fealty to her."

"She left them behind when she ran—after spending all morning haggling for them. You can blame her pesky horsefly for everything. He had the prince trapped and on the defensive. I've known biting midges with better self-control than that half-wit donkey."

Crony snorted. "Have ye e'er considered that it's her frolics with said donkey that made her wily enough to wrestle a trained prince and match his skills?"

"Ha! Her fighting skills were honed by watching drunken brawls between our upstanding citizens here. No need to credit the Pegasus with that."

"Not so. She would ne'er have seen such skirmishes had ye been her only companion. Yer too protective. But Scorch led her into the thick of it all. Now, she be that prince's equal, just as the prophecy said. I'm guessing that fact is turnin' in our royal man's head . . . that it be makin' him think. Makin' him wonder. I'm guessing he be searching for our 'boy' as we speak. That Pegasus may be an impulsive beast, but her walk with him has served a purpose." Crony held up the two teacups so Luce could fill them. "In fact, best hope she's walkin' with him now. That ye didn't send her hiding so deep none of us can find her."

"I didn't *send* her anywhere," Luce snarled, hesitating on pouring the hot water. "Stain's always had a mind of her own. In spite that we stole half of it. If you had been honest with me from the beginning, just once shared the reason why you made your damned vow . . . why it's so unbreakable, I wouldn't have been so tempted to tell her some snippet of truth."

"Nay, ye still would've bubbled up like a pot put to boil. Ye can't resist when she bats those lashes. It was my mistake trustin' ye with any of it to begin with."

Luce tossed the full kettle into the yard with a clang, baring his teeth. The water gurgled from the spout and the opened lid, creating a puddle of mushy ash. "Well, let's have a full confessional then. It was *my* mistake that killed that girl's mother. My mistake that landed her here half-dead. Do you see why I might feel more responsible than most? Why I might feel a bit softer toward her than I care to admit?"

Crony groaned. She set aside the cups and stepped across the threshold to retrieve the kettle, shoulders slouched against the blame weighing them down. A patch of bleeding heart had withered beneath the boiling water. She gathered the bright pink flowers into a soggy bouquet. A stabbing twinge caught in her chest as she worried over the princess's own bleeding heart. In Stain's eyes, they had betrayed her. And she didn't even know the half of it.

"I haven't your wretched immortal body, old woman," Luce said, recouping her attention while he kicked sand into the fire pit to stifle the flames. Some white feathers slipped into the mix and their burned stench soured the already bitter air. "I'll die one day, from age, here upon the ground. Unless I continue gorging myself on the entrails of corpses. She was my one chance to undo the bad, to regain agelessness, and now that chance is gone. Her *faith in us* is gone. All because you wouldn't allow me to tell her who she is."

Crony stood, her back still turned to Luce. "Ye think it easy for me? Keepin' this trap shut?"

"Yes. Because of your thick gargoyle skin. You're impervious, don't you see? You're unaffected by the world around you. I've had burrs in my fur, I've had cuts on my skin. Ever since the moment I was grounded, I can *feel*. Just a prick of a thorn can incapacitate. Yet every day, that tender girl faces these things and more, going on without even a complaint. Becoming stronger instead. I was convinced she was unbreakable. But did you see the look on her face? This split her wide open, and at the worst possible time. And again, it's my fault. Can you imagine what it's like, knowing you've destroyed such a noble and inexhaustible spirit? Knowing the kind of queen she could have been? Knowing that you'll never stop wrestling the guilt until you're either cold in the grave, or you've flown so far into the sky, you no longer have to feel anything but the air and the wind?"

Crony stepped back into the house. She crossed to the kitchen and stood before him, tilting her heavy horns so she could meet his glistening orange gaze. "I know better than any. And I be more to blame than ye ever could . . . I *feel* deeper than ye ever would. For I betrayed a kindred spirit, and destroyed the world entire."

He wrinkled his perfect forehead—an expression of doubt and anguish.

"I've been too harsh with ye, frilly fox. Ye took on the task without ever lookin' back, and ye did a rouse-about job. Better than this old biddy could've did alone. I owe ye a thanks." She offered him the soggy bouquet.

He took it begrudgingly.

She gestured to the nearest upended cask. "Sit and I will share me own confession. For seein' as the girl no longer trusts either of us, there be no more risk of ye spillin' me secrets, aye?"

Luce sat, and Crony did the same on the barrel opposite him.

She wrestled the words at first; they'd been wound so tight upon the spool of suppression, it tangled her forked tongue to try to speak them. The stuttering lasted only until she remembered how tales prefer to be told: as one would a bedtime story—leading with the happy parts.

"Once upon a time, some seven centuries ago," she said, "there were an ugly, horned witch esteemed enough to live in the glittering ivory palace of Eldoria. Esteemed enough to be the mystical advisor to the king."

The words came easier as a fairy tale. They opened doors within her mind's eye that she'd locked long ago. Yet the images weren't covered with dust or cobwebs; nay, they were vivid and bright: She could see herself, walking among royalty, wearing sandals of gold and robes of white emblazoned with three stalks of wheat and a running horse in red. There was no personal sun to be celebrated as Eldoria's sigil back then. They shared every day—every summer, fall, and spring—with Nerezeth, in the same as winter and the moonlit stars painted both kingdoms' skies and shadowed their hearths. They shared also the creatures of day and night: the singing birds, the trilling crickets, the fluttering butterflies mingling with fuzzy moths. And the autumn leaves, spring flowers, drifts of snow, and summer storms swept across their terrains in equal parts, providing beauty in diversity.

Eldoria's strengths centered around their talent for farming and livestock, thus their sigil. Nerezeth, on the other hand, lived on the heavily forested lands closer to the mountainous, eastern edge of the sea, and chose a silver fish and antlers against a field of blue satin as tribute to their proficiency in hunting and fishing. Commerce was maintained via the imports and exports of each kingdom's goods and services—a balance that benefited everyone. Nerezethites and Eldorians traversed to one another's kingdoms and markets in peaceful alliance.

In that unified world, Crony had an honorable title: Madame Cronatia Wisteria, Eldoria's Royal Enchantress. She'd sworn fealty to the monarch, Kiran's ascendant of earliest Eyvindur generations, King Krešimer. Like Kiran, he was kind, wise, and noble, and she was honored to follow him. Her loyalty—to her king, the queen, and their three young princes—knew no bounds.

Nerezeth had a sorcerer of their own, Master Lachrymosa. He was at once stark and striking: a complexion of chalky white with streaks of black drizzling from his pitch-dark eyes like oil. The same pattern continued along the lower edge of his black lips, making it appear he'd been drinking a vial of ink; he wore a beard that furthered the illusion—dark curling strands hanging from his chin to his chest alongside shoulder-length hair. His deep voice flowed and rolled, sweet and carnal through the ears, like a song of honey and thunder. Though he was young—barely twenty-three years in the world—he was powerful. He had but one downfall: he begrudged his half-blood lineage. He'd been born of an immortal sorceress and a mortal royal guard who had died while serving in the Nerezethite army.

May-let his youthfulness was Lachrymosa's ultimate downfall, for had he been older and wiser, he wouldn't have considered himself half of something, instead of two parts of a whole. May-let he would even have found strength in both sides of his blood, instead of attempting to flush out all traces of humanity.

But wait . . . Crony was getting ahead of herself in the telling, for that wasn't one of the happy parts. She backtracked, returning to the beginning when things were good between both kingdoms. When two magistrates—Kreśimer of Eldoria and Velimer of Nerezeth—joined forces to rid the skies of their common enemy: the poison-spitting drasilisks that could turn anyone to stone with one puncture from their scorpion-like stingers. The only way to kill them was by beheading with a halberd's axe-like blade, a process only possible once they were grounded.

Crony first met Lachrymosa at a convocation between the kingdoms' councils. He appeared at first glance to be seated beside an empty chair, with Nerezethite's king on the other side. When Crony and her own king sat across from their counterparts, a three-eyed woman took shape in the empty chair next to the half-blood sorcerer. Master Lachrymosa introduced her as his mother, Lady Dyadia. She was there to contribute magical insight into how they might defeat the deadly plague upon their skies.

Crony had heard of her kind, descended from chameleon chimeras—a striped sorceress sharing her son's coloring, though the pattern was more elegant and subtle upon her, like a snow tiger. Even now, so many centuries between those memories, Crony still found herself captivated by that first meeting . . . by Dyadia's ability to blend into her surroundings, to be invisible. How often since had Crony wished for such a talent herself? Or at the least, to close her eyes and have the world disappear.

While working together, she and Dyadia became fast friends. Crony demonstrated the technique behind memory transference and herbal elixirs and potions, and Dyadia impressed her with the ability to enchant objects and divine prophecies through her third eye. They had things in common that no human could appreciate: laughing about mistakes made when first learning their crafts; commiserating over broken glass and shattered spells.

Crony paused. Luce, who'd been listening—enthralled—leaned forward.

"There must be more. You've yet to speak of betrayals, vows, or curses, Madame Cronatia." His elbows rested on his knees, and the wilted flowers drooped where his pants draped his shins. "Don't stop now. I've waited over a decade for this tale."

Crony ground her jaw to repress a sad smile, for how short of a time was ten years in the grand scope of things. "May-let we trusted one another too quickly with too much, Dyadia and me. She confided the fears she be havin' about her son. Worries o'er his dangerous ambitions, his dabblings in necromancy in hopes to find immortality. In return, I admitted me one fear."

Luce lifted a red eyebrow, looking entirely too wolfish to be so handsome. "And that would be?"

Crony shook her head. "Nothin' ye need know for the tale."

Giving up her immortality to grant the princess another chance at life . . . that was something she still couldn't tell Luce; it risked interference, for should Luce know, it might affect the outcome in ways Crony couldn't predict. Nay, she wouldn't chance it. She opted instead to be crafty with her words. Distract him with an emotional revelation.

"Immortals be but a distinct few. We're given the opportunity upon conception to live on the earth, or on the celestial plane, out of sight of mortals.

Only six of us walk upon the terra, each of us descended from ancient beings: gargoyles, chimeras, seraphs, or demons. Those four immortal classes were enemies, historically. So we be hard-pressed to find someone with which to live out an eternity. In the mortal mindset, to stumble upon another like yerself, to have trifles and tricks to learn and trade, it be a gift. But for an immortal, to feel as if yer long, plodding steps have been bestrewn with new paths flaunting two pairs of footprints instead of one—it be a *miracle*. Dyadia and me, we both be wise enough to hold it close, in the beginning. I cherished her. For her frightful beauty, for her mystical talents, for her maternal ways with her son—something I would ne'er experience for meself. Harrowers don't be made to have offspring. We lose that ability the moment we take the power. And we keep the curse till we be flushed of our magic, passing it to another soul. Whether mortal or immortal, monstrous or indistinct, a harrower recipient must be a willin' vessel, and ready to swear off any hope for children however long their commission. Me mistake was takin' on the power while being immortal. Eternity be a long time to live without family." Crony dropped her gaze to the flower stems curling down to Luce's shin, finding herself thinking upon the princess again, wanting so much for the girl to find her way, but unable to make it happen herself. Is that how true parents felt? "But there be a downfall to an immortal having a child, and it is far greater than the pain of ne'er havin' one."

Luce nodded. "Because they will one day outlive said child."

"Aye. That was Dyadia's greatest fear. Hard to becalm such a worry, but I heared her each time she needed to be heared. It seem to satisfy her some bit, to have a companion such as me. And on me end, none I had met in that long walk felt so much like home. Like belongin'." Crony's chest warmed in remembrance of those happier days. "Dyadia became me beloved family, and more."

Luce smiled, gentle and heartfelt. The sort of expression she'd only seen him impart on Stain. "Well, smack my snout and call me vixen. Never thought to hear something so pretty from the lips of a puckish old witch like yourself." His eyes were teasing, but his features fell to somberness. "Something horrible happened. For you to be so far apart now, to have lost one another to opposing realms. Tell me . . ."

Crony disliked this part of the fairy tale: the moral test, the downfall of the hero. Better she leap in without hesitating, better to fall headfirst—eyes painfully open, *always open*—into those final memories; better than to pause and anticipate the agony, to remember how her heart would rip anew when she relived her grandest mistake.

The final battle to save the two kingdoms from the drasilisks had been won. Between the hand signals used by the infantries so the halberdiers could carry out their lethal formations in silence, and Cronatia's and Lachrymosa's presence on the front lines combining their magics—her ability to make weapons of nightmares and his to communicate with the creatures mentally—the victory belonged to the kingdoms.

No more drasilisks were left. Their gargantuan, beheaded, rotting forms laid coiled in fields set afire. The noxious stench of their burning scales—like puss-filled boils roasting on a spigot—signaled freedom at last. A proclamation went out, and both kings sealed an alliance swearing if any sign of the destructive creatures appeared in Eldoria or Nerezeth, they would be hunted down and eradicated, for the good of all life. The people celebrated, anticipating a future without fear.

A future that was short-lived.

"Some five months later," Crony said, her voice shaking now, "the sun began to bow to the moon at unreasonable hours. The winter came early, when spring was just raising its pink-petaled head. Fear crept 'cross both kingdoms once more."

The drasilisks had preferred to hunt at night, and over time had developed an uncanny ability to call down the moon, even in midday, to darken the skies so they might feed on those out tending fields or fishing. Now, even with the creatures extinct, confusion fell upon the two kingdoms once more, though nothing fell from the sky.

King Krešimer called Cronatia to his throne room early one afternoon, when the skies were cloaked in midnight. He believed he'd discovered the cause of the strange occurrences; after having Eldoria searched and finding no sign of drasilisks, he reached out to King Velimer to do the same. However, the king had fallen ill, and their sorcerer, Lachrymosa, was serving as regent—the king's eldest son being too young to rein. King Krešimer had sent missives to the sorcerer, asking him to search Nerezeth from border to border, but each one came back unanswered. So Krešimer sent spies into their kingdom, and it was soon confirmed Lachrymosa was harboring a live drasilisk, though no one seemed able to find it.

Crony didn't tell her king that day how she'd been in contact with the sorcerer's mother via a one-eyed albino crow. It would visit weekly, perched upon Crony's window to converse, as if Dyadia were sitting right beside her. Crony didn't want her king to doubt her loyalty to Eldoria, for that had not changed in spite of her friendship with a sorceress from the opposing kingdom. And she wasn't hiding anything of import, as Dyadia had refused to confirm or deny her son's guilt during those unconventional visits.

On a gloomy day, the sky heavy with dark clouds, Eldoria's infantry prepared to march into Nerezeth with intent to behead the beast and the sorcerer responsible. They planned to leave within the week. Crony had received another message from Dyadia, this time in a note tied to Thana's scaly white leg. The sorceress pled for her to come to Nerezeth's palace in the depths of the forest posthaste, but to keep it secret, for her son had made a tragic error.

Crony left before the infantry, telling King Krešimer only that she was to investigate the strangeness in the skies by meeting with Dyadia.

Thana flew above her during the three-week-long journey, as if to ensure she came alone. The albino crow took her leave once Crony arrived at the black castle and was escorted alongside Dyadia through the glossy, obsidian halls. Dyadia dismissed the guards then grasped Crony's hand and spoke casually, as if catching up over tea. Her forced composure made Crony uneasy, but she played along, sensing the depth of Dyadia's pain, knowing somehow that her son was dying, seeing it in her eyes. Knowing more, with every step, why she had been called to the sorceress's side. Though dread filled her heart, she followed on.

They walked down a sloping staircase that led into the dungeon, past cells rife with the scent of urine and body odor, and the moaning of prisoners. When it looked as if the corridor stalled at a dead end, Dyadia magically manipulated a row of stones, coaxing the wall to open another set of stairs. These led deeper into the earth, into a passage almost a full league beneath the castle.

Though Crony had no fear of the dark, her spine tingled with a bleak premonition, compounded by the all-too-familiar scent of puss-filled boils somewhere within the dripping, moldering dampness.

Dyadia spoke an enchantment that echoed through the small chamber, and torches lit. Orange, flickering flames painted shadows across the stony space—revealing an alchemist's lab. In the center of the room, on a dais, laid her son's supine body, cloaked in his blue satin robes. And in the far corner, sat a nest bigger than two bales of hay. Within were five leathery eggs, split down the middle, as if they had stopped mid-hatch.

"Drasilisk offspring." Crony croaked the revelation, unable to look at her friend for fear of what her face would show. That explained why a full-grown drasilisk had not been found; eggs were much easier to hide. She forced herself to meet Dyadia's weary feline gaze. "Regardless of their immature state, yer son broke the alliance."

Dyadia stood by the dais, her hands covering her son's closed eyes. "The queen had asked him to use his necromancy to find a cure for King Velimer.

He dabbled deeper than he ever had and stumbled upon the drasilisk secret. You musn't tell anyone. He would have to be beheaded for such an offense against your king and the alliance, or there would be a war . . ."

"There already be one brewin'." Crony stepped closer to Lachrymosa's prone form. "The soldiers be but a week behind me and I be sworn to me king to keep the world safe. As yer son is to his. What he be thinkin', doing such a thing?"

"The heavens are eternal. He thought to draw from that power, to use the link the creatures have to the moon to find a cure for the king."

"Nay, he finally found a means to become immortal himself, or so he thinked."

Dyadia turned away. "He spoke to a drasilisk's spirit," she began, her voice breaking in intervals, "and it told him of a nest of eggs . . . he concocted a determinate elixir with some scales he had saved to find their whereabouts. It transported him to the cliffs by the ocean where he found them hidden. They . . . were the only survivors. My son connected himself to the nestlings mentally, climbed inside their minds. Stole their link to the moon and learned how to manipulate it himself." She spun to face Crony. "I tried to reason with him, to warn him of the dangers, but he wouldn't listen. A few days ago, they began hatching. I thought he would come to his senses then, but he was emotionally attached and convinced they felt the same, that he could raise and control them. And not only would he be immortal, but ours would be the most powerful kingdom." Her slitted pupils dropped to the hem of her swishing dress. "I tried to intervene for his own safety, for everyone's safety. I cast a spell upon the eggs—a quietus thrall—to fool their minds into think-ing they were already dead, to prevent them from growing strong enough to break out. In my haste, I forgot the most crucial precept: that it should only be conjured in a sacred place of life and death, else the recipient's spirit grows fearful. Once a spirit gives up faith, all is lost. I didn't mean for it to be fatal, but they're dying."

Crony leaned across one cracked egg and shuddered as a glint of firelight reflected off deadened eyes and glimmering coiled scales. "How ye be sure?"

"Because my son is part of them now. He can't disconnect. I realized it when he fell to the floor and struggled for breath. He's dying, too. At his mother's own hand—" Her voice cracked and she clutched her chest, as if she could feel her insides tearing apart.

Crony shielded her own chest with her staff, putting up barriers. Her friend grasped her wrist, tears streaming down her beautiful striped face, several leaking from the empty socket in the midst of her forehead. "You must know what I need of you."

The witch's stomach turned and twisted, torn between pity and self-preservation. "And ye know why I can't be givin' it."

The sorceress fell to her knees and gripped Crony's ankles, her fingers too fine and elegant to put a dent in Crony's thick, rough skin. Was she as calloused inward as outward? So much she could say no to the one who meant most to her in the world? Was she such a coward, she couldn't trade her immortality for another's son? Didn't that make her no better than he in his search to live forever?

"Please. My love . . . my life, everything I have is yours and always will be. But I cannot live with killing my child. *Please*," she sobbed. "You must bid him back."

The memory became too real, and Crony stalled the narrative for fear of saying too much to Luce, or worse, that the acid rising in the back of her throat would seep into her tongue and render it as mute as little Stain's. She met her sylphin companion's gaze. He waited, silent and mortified, for the end.

"I deemed me dearest's son unworthy of bein' saved," she told Luce, her vocal cords no longer cooperating, cutting her voice to a whisper. "But even worse, I kept it quiet in me heart. I knew, to bring him back from the brink, I be bringing back the drasilisks with him. I knew he had to be destroyed to save the kingdoms." Crony didn't tell Luce the ugliest part, that she was a coward who justified her cowardice by telling herself it was a black-and-white choice. By convincing herself there was no gray. "I pretended I be willin' to help him, only to get close enough to steal his last few breaths and lock the memories he'd shared with the creatures in me own mind, so I could break their hold o'er the moon. That I did, with Dyadia standing there beside me, trusting me, thinkin' I was to save her only child's life. Thanking me as I was takin' his last breaths away."

Crony's tongue prickled on the admission, each word stinging like a shard of glass. "She knew what I'd done in the same instant I realized the catastrophe me thievery had caused, for in breakin' Lachrymosa's connection to the creatures and his hold over the moon, I left the heavens in an uproar."

Neither she nor Dyadia had expected what happened next, that the moon would fall from the sky, still tied to the threads she'd severed. That it would tear through the earth and drag Nerezeth down with it. As the castle walls began to shake, Dyadia met her gaze and Crony saw agonized perception. She would never forget that look.

Crony had started up the stairs as debris tumbled from the ceiling all around—running from her guilt, from her fear, from her self-deprecation. But she couldn't outrun those final memories she'd stolen from Lachrymosa. One of which she could ne'er share for its power and potency, as it was still tied to the moon. It would stay locked within her for the entirety of that long lonely forever she'd chosen over a man's life and her dearest one's heart.

Dyadia followed Crony through the corridors as they passed confused royalty and guards alike. Thana was waiting when the giant doors opened to reveal the drawbridge leading to a landscape in turmoil. Trees, hills, and rivers shivered as if they were painted on flimsy parchment and set aflutter on the wind. Thana screeched at Crony and flew to her mistress's side where Dyadia stood at the threshold. Crony stepped off the bridge and looked down on them when the castle began to sink and the world shook. Trees crumpled forward as if bowing to the moon as it glided into the open seam of the earth—as it magically converted to smoke and clouds, then siphoned through the crack. Then it was gone, pulling with it all of Nerezeth's terrain, the forest, the castle in the same fashion.

Crony and the landscapes that belonged to Eldoria were untouched. Somehow the moon knew who belonged to it, to the one who'd been controlling it. Every creature that loved the darkness, and everything that had ever been a part of Lachrymosa's territory, slipped away and took form again within the belly of the earth. There to stay, along with Dyadia and all her righteous rage.

When the dust settled and the sun beamed down—hot and accusatory on Crony's back—all that indicated Nerezeth had ever stood beside Eldoria was the crack between realms, still glittering with broken magic that would form the ravine. At first, the kingdoms had no contact with one another. Eldoria despised Nerezeth for taking the moon. But in time, after hearing of the harsh conditions the night realm endured, Eldorians came to feel superior. They believed Nerezeth deserved their eternal night for their sorcerer's vile actions. In turn, Nerezeth hated the day realm for their apathy, and envied them their sun.

Thus, blind prejudice was born.

"I stayed here"—Crony indicated the ashy terrain around their skeletal home—"as the twisted trees grew 'round me and the sins of others crept down the trunks to swallow me bare feet. I left all me possessions in the castle behind, let the king believe I was swallowed by the earth that day. I couldn't return to me kingdom, for by then they believed I betrayed them by siding with Dyadia, and may-let I had. For I'd made a new vow to her. In those last minutes when I be seein' her face through the castle's drawbridge, afore the bubble of magic formed around her palace and all those homes . . . afore every citizen and creature were dragged again' their own will into the moon's pull . . . we had our last words. I begged her forgiveness. She refused . . . said

I chose Eldoria o'er her precious son; that there be no forgivin' a sin so vicious. I told her it was for the world, for the greater good. But she knew me heart, and the cowardice and fears lurking there. And she knew me sworn loyalty to King Kreśimer. She made me vow I would leave all kingdom politics behind, ne'er interfere again, for look what I had wrought. I agreed, and vowed as she said, and in her anger and bitterness she added a curse upon me head. That I could ne'er close me eyes so long as I walked the bright, sunlit earth. That I would have to always be seein' the world's undoing. And should I interfere again in either kingdom's politics, the world would ne'er heal. I felt the curse take hold when me eyelids thinned to transparency. Now ye see why I can't stop seein', and ye know why me interference is forbidden."

Luce's face contorted with compassion, a reaction Crony had never expected—an unworthiness compounded by her recent understanding of the depth of a parent's love for their child.

"Wait," he mumbled, his eyes alight with cunning perception. "So, the grimoire I found hidden within the tunnel . . . ?"

She nodded in answer. He opened his mouth again, as if needing to air out the many facets of this revelation, but was interrupted by the bark of a dog at the edges of the thicket.

They both leapt from their seats and turned to see a brown spaniel and Dyadia's crow leading five Nerezethite soldiers.

"Ready your weapons!" said the man at the head, drawing out a sword.

A woman came forward and paused beside the garden. Her purplish eyes glinted with an odd mix of trepidation and authority. It appeared she'd been warned about crossing the threshold. "Cronatia of the Ashen Ravine, you are under royal order by Prince Vesper to accompany us to Eldoria's castle and face Regent Griselda and Princess Lyra. You are to account for the murders of King Kiran and his first knight, along with the princess's cousin Lustacia. Also for the malicious misuse of your magic against the kingdom, causing its subjects and citizens to be imprisoned within their homes over the last five years. Will you come peacefully?"

Luce tensed as if to defend her, but Crony whispered, "No interferin'." She didn't tell him that should she fight back, she could be killed prematurely, before her part was complete in all this. "This be in the hands of the fates. Keep to our code. Find Stain and tell her of me imprisonment. Tell her I be sorry for hurting her, and that she made every day brighter just by bein' here. But don't force her hand. She must be makin' choices of her own accord."

Jaw clenched, Luce dropped the flowers and transformed, scampering out the opposite side of their home as a fox, his talisman dangling from his neck. The spaniel began to take chase, but was caught by the female soldier. Crony looked around at her belongings, stopping on the cedar chest. The contents of the two boxes—Lyra's memories and Griselda's conscience—would be safe with her nightmare wards. Luce would return in search of weapons. And he would find Crony's note, waiting to be read.

The old witch stepped over the threshold and laid herself prostrate, allowing her captors to bind her, giving all her faith to the crafty nature of prophecies. It appeared the prince wouldn't be luring the princess to the castle after all.

17

A Collection of
Corpses and
Consciousness

In the ravine's lowlands, where the ash thinned and the shade deepened, the Shroud Collective prepared to feast. It had been a long famine—three full weeks—since their last taste of flesh. Soon their suffering would end. The page boy who escaped five years earlier was about to stumble back into their keep. From this distance, he appeared to be in much the same state as when he first arrived in a pine box: shredded clothes matching his torn skin, deserted and broken. The perfect candidate for luring into their lair. Mistress Umbra began casting out her siren's song—a whispering enticement meant to trick those walking the path overhead, meant to sound like whatever their heart wanted most to find. The page boy would take the bait. He was too lost to do otherwise. The mother shroud gathered her children within the clearing, each amorphous silhouette conforming to the black, gnarled trees that hid them. Innumerable glowing white eyes blinked between branches, awaiting attack.

Stain paused along the steep pathway, perking her ears at a rustling down below. The ash within the ravine muffled most sounds, like a thick layer of downy feathers. The ravine's lore echoed within that silence . . . a tale she hadn't thought of in some time: those who came to live here brought their sins and shed them upon the trees. The wickedness, having nowhere else to go, transformed to a sentient moss that slunk to the ground and decomposed every wild, beautiful thing to ash.

Had she been so wicked, in her past? That someone had shed her here like a vile sin? Or was she once beautiful until left to decompose and rot in the wastelands?

With the absence of wind, birds, and skittering bugs, the quiet became deafening. She'd been calling for Scorch in her mind to fill the void, to no avail.

Before ending up here, she had searched their usual haunts: the market where they frolicked in the after hours when everyone closed shop (Scorch was fascinated by human customs and items, much as he tried to deny it); the *lofties*, where the ravine's dense canopy reached to monolithic heights so high Scorch could fly without even stirring the ash below; and the quagmire-quarry, where they held contests to see who could outrun the most puddles. Scorch had the advantage of wings, but Stain learned that climbing trees worked as well, since a living puddle—no matter how agile—was repelled by wood and stone. Over the years, she had tied with Scorch in only three matches, and only because he allowed her to, according to him. Every other time, she had to tolerate him mocking her lack of wings and extra legs. Today his arrogant jibes would be music, if she could only see him safe.

She'd circled around the tarn of clear water where they liked to go fishing, only to stop in her tracks, hidden behind a trunk. Though she didn't see the Night Ravager, his crew had set up camp there—close to the labyrinth of thorns where Stain first encountered them. Scorch hadn't been anywhere in sight, so she slipped away undetected, ending up here at the ravine's entrance.

If she couldn't find her friend, perhaps she could at least find herself.

She licked her lips and tasted blood, which reminded her of the drying spots that dotted her clothes. The healing ointment she'd brought promised a numbing comfort, but she wasn't sure how much Scorch's wing might need.

The tin and bandages were no longer tucked in her vest. They were now residing in a bag she'd found earlier at the marketplace. The nightmare wards set upon Crony's booth to prevent anyone stealing wares after hours held no sway over Stain. She fingered the talisman at her neck and swung the bag against her thigh, causing the assassin's knife to clink against the kinder sleep chimes she'd plucked off the shop's pegs. Stain had always liked the bedtime stories and lullabies that played out across the cylinders of glass, and decided if Crony wouldn't give her memories back, she had every right to steal some from the shop's supply. She required them, after all, for her plan—as dangerous as it might be.

The rustle again. It came from her destination: the lowest clearing surrounded by a circle of black trees in the distance—down the steep decline and past stumps and burbling quag-puddles. She'd always avoided the lowlands. Even Scorch had abided that rule, wary of the repulsive creatures subsisting there. Yet today the valley held an irresistible pull.

Crony and Luce had made Stain believe she belonged with them; but all the while they'd been hoarding the only true *belongings* she ever had. Even her rescue had been a lie. There were reasons . . . ulterior motives, mysteries that made up her entire existence, that they'd either sold on the market to degenerates and criminals, hidden out of her reach, or given away as a bargaining tactic.

She'd never been able to view all the trinkets hanging in the house; without Crony's magic animating them, it was no better than looking through a glass pane: a transparent backdrop to a colorless, unseeable past. Luce admitted they'd found her lifeless body spilling out of a coffin, about to be eaten. They'd had to bargain with the shrouds for her release, though he didn't say what they bargained with.

It was said that Nerezethite sun-smugglers used to come to Crony's shop and purchase memories to trade for their lives on the chance they should get trapped by the voracious creatures.

Shrouds craved humanness in all facets: flesh, spirit, or memories.

It made sense that Crony and Luce might have given the shrouds Stain's past in exchange for her future. If so, the creatures had absorbed details about her prior life into their shared consciousness, the very details her guardians didn't want her to know.

She moved the bag's strap higher on her shoulder. The kinder sleep memory chimes tinkled against one another—animated and tempting. She would offer them as a trade to the vaporous corpses: fresh memories for stale information.

Stain took a step sideways as a sudden wave of dizziness smeared her surroundings to mottled blacks, pale greens, and grays—as if she were trapped in a cylinder of spinning glass herself. Fear collided with hunger and heartache, and she sat upon the path. She stretched her legs, avoiding the sticky liquid sunshine that dotted the trunks beside the briar curtain. Her feet cried out, aching to be released from their prisons of soles, heels, and laces. But it was her heart that was truly trapped, entombed within a body scarred from head to toe, yet as nondescript as a pile of bones. She had been hoping Scorch's need for her help would outweigh his anger. But in truth, she needed *him* now. She needed his cynicism and wisdom to talk her out of doing this.

Elbows on her knees, she cupped her temples and shut her eyes, willing the world to stop spinning so her disjointed thoughts might do the same.

Scorch, where are you?

She took her favorite memory of him and spun it like a web within the dark swirl of her consciousness, hoping it might capture Scorch's own thoughts, remind him of their bond, and bring him out of hiding.

※ · I · ※

In this memory, Stain and Scorch had snuck out during the cessation course, as the best adventures were had while most everyone slept . . . when the hazy, greenish-gray world belonged to them alone. A group of thieving minstrels had passed through the ravine, and a gala was in full swing at the Wayward Tavern. Stain had peered within the tree's opened windows where the musicians played fiddles, lutes, and percussion instruments. Dancers in fancy dresses and suits—with threadbare hems and tarnished embellishments—filled the hollowed-out trunk. The scent of ale and a comingling of warm food and body odor wafted out with the music.

The rhythm made Stain's feet warm and twitchy. Much like walking, or signing with her hands, dancing was a skill she'd retained, though she couldn't grasp its origins. She wriggled in her boots and swished the hems of her breeches, pretending she wore a wide-swinging skirt with a fringe of lace. Her nose wrinkled as she attempted the fancy steps.

Scorch nudged her away from the window. They walked out of view of the tavern until the trees surrendered to a small clearing. The music reached across the hazy distance.

What were you doing there, with your feet? Scorch asked. *And why was your nose crinkled?*

Stain shrugged. *I was concentrating . . . pretending to dance in a ballroom. To spin among candlelit sconces, under an ornamented ceiling, alongside a graceful partner. That would be a grand adventure.*

His tail snapped in derision. *Rather more like a waste of time.*

Of course, you wouldn't understand. She wriggled in her boots and swished her hems again. *Horses can't dance.*

His ears flattened. *I can dance as well as any man.* Whickering, he shook hundreds of embers free of his mane until they lifted in the air. His wings flapped, stirring half of them to drift upward, imprinting their glow on the velvety canopy overhead. The rest of the lights floated around them until their surroundings resembled an arbor made of fireflies.

Scorch huffed. *There's your ballroom.*

Stain gasped, marveling at the beauty of it. She reached up to blot appreciative tears from her cheeks, but none were there—regardless that her eyes pricked.

Scorch lowered his long neck and bent a lithe, graceful foreleg in a bow worthy of any gentleman. Then, he pranced within the circle of embers, keeping time with the music—his tail flared out elegantly like a flag of silk, his legs stepping high.

So awestruck by his expertise, Stain simply gaped.

I'm too graceful a dancer for you, then? He asked, paused in mid-prance. *Pitiful. A human game, yet I beat you at it like any other.*

She shook her head, unwilling to be bested. After a proper curtsy, she spun to the music alongside his prancing hooves . . . spinning and spinning until her surroundings blurred and the embers streaked inside her eyes to ribbons of yellow-orange light. Giddy and breathless, she fell on her back into a plume of ash, laughing.

Scorch trotted up and snuffed her fuzzed head. He then sat on his hindquarters to gawk at her. *Humans are strange creatures. Moved to tears by emotions. Moved to laughter by physical exertion. And you, tiny trifling thing, are the strangest of them all.*

She took that to mean she was the most human of all, and thanked him profusely, only to laugh again when he assured her it was nothing to be proud of. But she *had* been proud, for even if she didn't know where she belonged, she knew with whom she belonged.

❈·‖·❈

Stain's chest tightened on the memory; reliving it alone only made her feel lonelier. She no longer knew with whom she belonged. She wasn't the foundling boy she pretended to be. She wasn't the companion to a harrower witch and sylph team who robbed the dead and gave their memories life. She couldn't remember Eldoria or Nerezeth—only the in-between.

She had no identity; nothing that could serve as compass or beacon in this dry, powdery, gray world where she had never fit. Even the crooked shop owners had histories: places they'd come from, purposes to serve.

Her closed eyes prickled—refusing her the satisfaction a few tears might offer. Tasting the salty flavor of heartache upon one's lips was what made the pain one's own. Without that experience, even her losses felt as if they belonged to someone else.

Stain opened her eyes to find her dizziness gone. Standing, she stomped both her feet so the torn skin along her soles and ankles would throb. The pain grounded her, assured her the one true friend who helped her feel anchored and strong was still out there.

Scorch . . . I want to help you. And I could use your help, too. Where are you?

She caught a breath upon hearing what sounded like a muffled whinny from below. What if he had wandered within accidentally? He might be dazed if he'd lost enough blood, or even feverish. She didn't know how a Pegasus's body or mind reacted to trauma if he couldn't fly to heal. The shrouds were known for playing tricks on the mind, yet she couldn't dismiss the possibility her friend was trapped down there and needed her. Her desire to find him, and to find herself, trumped all caution.

Crouching, she used exposed roots and low-hanging branches for anchorage during her descent. A stray quag-puddle—souring the air with its putrid stench—lapped at her heel, but she rolled her hips to the other side of a tree, sending the burbling murk off in another direction.

She arrived at the bottom sooner than expected, and only then did her caution return in the form of countless white, piercing eyes. She didn't see Scorch anywhere. Clenching the bag at her shoulder, she reminded herself of her other reason to brave this cursed lowland, and stepped forward as vapory, black silhouettes glided out from behind the trees to surround her.

Her shapeless captors stirred the thin layer of ash covering the ground, causing a misty effect. One skimmed closer, faded to a washed-out white, as gauzy as the clean muslin bandages in Stain's bag. This shroud grew lithe-limbed and slender, morphing to a woman's torso and face. Black, bony obtrusions appeared, giving the impression of a beak and horns.

The creature leaned across Stain and breathed the scent of must and decay. "Our lost boy has returned."

Bitter regret knotted in Stain's throat; if they thought her a boy, they hadn't absorbed her memories. Crony must have them hidden away, meaning Stain had endangered herself for nothing.

"I am Mistress Umbra, mother of the Shroud Collective. We are your ancestors. Those who lost their minds to the promise of darkness and rest centuries ago. You have two choices: become one of us and strengthen our cerebral framework, or offer your flesh for us to consume. Should you not choose, we choose for you."

Stain pointed at her throat, indicating she couldn't speak.

"Ah, have you lost your tongue? Fret not; I can look into one's heart, read their deepest desires. But there must be nothing between us but flesh." Mistress Umbra's phantasmal hands became a half-dozen jagged twigs that reached for Stain's clothes.

Stain stepped back, causing the mother shroud's fingers to miss their mark. A gust of wind bristled the shaved hairs along Stain's neck. The ring of vaporous creatures tightened around her, pushing her forward.

Mistress Umbra siphoned in and out of her children, one part ethereal, and the other substance. "Foolish boy. Do you not realize there's no escape this time? You haven't your pets to protect you. No rime scorpionsss," Mistress Umbra's beakish mouth hissed. "No shadowsss."

Stain hadn't expected that information. Scorpions and shadows . . . protecting her. Her mind reverted to Crony's cryptic allusion in the garden, about shadows offering freedom. Had she, in her half-dead state, somehow brought such creatures into the ravine with her? Where were they now? Had they been captured by Dregs and mounted as displays in his shop?

Remorse tightened in her chest as she thought upon her abandoned jars of earlier. She had to return to the ravager's camp and steal them back.

The wispy shrouds expanded to a wall of solid soot around her, leaving no opening. Meeting Mistress Umbra's beady gaze, Stain pointed to the path above, indicating she wished to leave.

"We have captured you," the mother shroud said, "thus we own you. We need but choose whether to absorb your mind and memories, or gorge upon your flesh."

Stain's throat grew dry. She signed out of instinct and desperation, having no expectation of being understood, for who could possibly read the strange language shared by her, Luce, and Crony?

You didn't capture me. I know you to be tricksters, but I chose to brave entering. To seek answers. I've no memory for you to consume. Your lair is as much my birthplace as it is yours . . . the place where my identity both ended and originated.

To Stain's surprise, the circle of shrouds drew back, their eyes dimming as they turned to their mother.

"How do you know the old language?" Mistress Umbra asked, her beakish nose tipping sideways, as if weighed with curiosity.

Stain gasped in disbelief. Her fingers grew more eager with the next question. *Old language?*

"Ancient."

Where did it come from? Who first used it? Stain asked these both as questions and wondrous epiphanies. There were a people somewhere with whom she could communicate.

"Its origins are vague. We know only that it abides within our consciousness." The mother shroud waved a twiggy arm to encompass her children. "Our eldest souls brought it with them after the moon dropped from the sky. They remembered it from a great war involving deadly beasts. It harkens back to a time when there was no ravine . . . no split in the earth. No collection of disembodied corpses craving everything they've lost."

That was Stain's cue. She opened her bag and dragged out a chime, holding it up. The glassy cylinders glistened faintly in the stagnant, shrouded miasma surrounding her.

I propose a trade . . . fresh human memories for my freedom.

She forwent asking for any further information. Given that the multitude of white eyes pierced her through—as though surmising how she might taste—securing her present seemed much more crucial than any past ever could.

Mistress Umbra took one look at a mother and daughter singing nursery rhymes in the jingling glass and laughed—a thick, frothy sound, like the gurgle of a stray quag-puddle. "No, child. There will be no bargain. These memories sing of sleep and cessation. The search for rest is what trapped us here. We have *slept* long enough. What we wish for is to live, to experience. To wake . . . *eternal.*"

The mother shroud's refusal spurred her children to rise, bobbing in front of Stain with cavernous mouths open, their cold breath rife with the stench of blood and death. Stain suppressed a soundless scream and dropped the chimes while holding tight to her bag.

Mistress Umbra sidled close enough her beak touched the tip of Stain's nose. Her ghoulish beauty sent a chill through Stain's spine. "Many long years ago, a sylph man fluttered in and took a prize from us. A princess of Eldoria that we marked as our own."

Stain sucked in a shocked breath. A sylph. Were they speaking of Luce when he still had his wings?

"In the bargain, he left us a part of her, to experience the robust flavor of her sins. But it escaped our watch. Then, you came to fulfill that emptiness. We felt the same draw to you, as you were also from that castle."

Stain tensed. *From Eldoria's castle? How do you know?*

"We recognized the page boy's royal vestments; only two other witnesses realized you were wearing Eldoria's traditional habiliments. A shame those *two* have been keeping that secret from you."

Stain stood her ground, though the reminder of Luce and Crony's betrayal made her want to sink.

"You came today in hopes to understand who you are. I will tell you." Mistress Umbra stretched tall as a tree. Stain craned her neck to look up at her and lost her balance, landing on her rump. "You are payment for a debt long overdue. We've thought of you often, wishing to see inside your mind and understand how a boy of Eldoria's courts merited the fealty of Nerezeth's creatures. Day and night, together, here in our wasteland. When you first came, we had hoped to absorb your memories, your identity, your power; for our need to conquer and assimilate roils as deep and dark as our hunger for flesh."

The shrouds whipped around Stain's head, slapping her with fallen leaves and bits of ash. Their gusty passage swiped at her eyelashes, stirring them so they tickled unsettlingly.

"However, mostly dead and broken as you were, the old witch thought you valuable. So she promised us recompense should we turn you over." The mother shroud snarled. "She gave us an important memory from a dying knight then vowed to send that marked princess to us again, so we could share the memory with her. For it will *break* her. Thus, we released you, as the promise of vengeance is sweeter by far than any other flavor. But five years have passed, and all we have to show for our patience is the bouquet of roses that rested upon your chest in your coffin." Two of the shrouds sank into the ground then returned with a bouquet of withered black roses held between their nebulous forms. They tossed them toward Stain. She picked them up. The perfume was powerful and stung her nose, triggering a ripple of familiarity. Not from a memory, but from a dream she'd had just before waking the first time in Crony's keep. A dream of lavender petals and golden ink on black pages. "As you have no memories to share, your mind has little to satisfy our consciousness. Thus, we'll settle for your tender flesh to appease our appetite."

Stain's pulse lurched. The shrouds hissed and gathered so thickly, they blotted out the canopy overhead until there was nothing but blinking white eyes and gaping, hollow mouths. Stain drew up her hands to protect her face, pleading in silence. Her eyes squeezed so tightly, she didn't realize her fingers had lit up until she felt the burn. She peeked, seeing the golden glow and that the roses had revived in her hands, the petals soft and velvety again—as if freshly plucked.

The shrouds pulled back to make room for Mistress Umbra. Her twiggy fingers took the bouquet away. "You've sunlight in your hands, boy . . . another fascinating anomaly. But not enough to save you. Not enough."

The shrouds advanced and siphoned into her skin, their blackness spreading alongside her veins in jagged trails. She felt herself becoming vaporous, her heart slowing its beat.

If you're done entertaining your playmates, I could show them some real *light.*

Stain's body stiffened at Scorch's voice in her mind. He sounded out of breath, yet strong.

Help me, she pleaded.

As you say, tiny trifling thing, but you will owe me a token of service. Things are going to get hot. Protect yourself.

She forced her body into a ball—a monumental effort, as her limbs and torso felt as insubstantial as air. The moment she'd covered her head with the canvas bag, rescue came in a rush of hoofbeats, heat, and harrowing shrieks. An uncomfortable pulsation stretched beneath her skin and out her fingertips as the shrouds abandoned her. They dispersed behind their trees, leaving Mistress Umbra to fend off Scorch's fiery attack alone.

Stain coughed in the smoky aftermath, her body aching again. She welcomed the pain; it meant she was solid, alive. Scrambling to her feet, bag in hand, she positioned herself behind Scorch.

The Pegasus's powerful muscles twitched, though he listed toward his left wing where it dragged the ground. The other wing, healthy and strong, thudded, stirring gusts that fed the sparks in his mane and tail until they flickered bright as torches. Damaged as he was, there was no question he would be the victor. Shrouds were nothing more than darkness incarnate. Scorch—with his flame and wind—was their enemy inasmuch as shade fled from sunlight.

With a low, grunting nicker, he ignited the tangled roots leading to the circle of trees, setting trunks and limbs ablaze. The shrouds wailed and sank beneath the ground where the moss and ash protected them.

"You want to know who you are, *girl?*" The mother shroud was submerged up to the waist within the gray powder as she slowly descended the way of her children. "We tasted your fate, beneath your flesh. You are riches and poverty. Life and death. You are more and less than you ever dreamed. But you have challenges yet to face. In the end, you will have to prove hard enough to wrap yourself in spikes, yet tender enough to walk amongst stars without crushing their fragile legs. You will need to have hair of steel and tears of stone. Only then will you find your true self again." Her head disappeared into the ground, the ash funneling in her wake.

Panting, Stain could do nothing but stare at the blank spot where the creature vanished. Possessing Stain's body must have given the mother insight, for she had recognized Stain as a girl. Did that mean all her riddles were true? Steel hair. Stone tears. Wearing spikes and wading through stars? How could such things be in anyone's future?

Scorch whickered, the equivalent of clearing his throat.

Stain looked up. *Thank you . . . and I'm sorry.*

The Pegasus puffed a cloud of smoke in answer.

They stood there, surrounded by firelight and cracking wood.

She wanted to hug him for his timeliness—for saving her—but he was too proud for such emotional frippery.

What foolishness led you here? He asked, flicking his tail in an annoyed gesture.

I thought you had stumbled into their trap.

You should've known better.

How? You wouldn't answer me! Shutting your mind to mine gave my thoughts a wide vastness in which to wander.

He stomped a hoof, managing to look majestic in the process. *You came here for something more. The creature said you were seeking yourself. What did she mean?*

Stain disclosed all she'd endured today after they parted ways—how she'd been betrayed by those she considered family.

I told you. You can never trust humankind.

Stain's fingers clenched tighter around her bag's straps. She'd known better than to expect sympathy. *But I am humankind, yes? Or am I something else?*

You are like me. A rare peculiarity. Covert as the wind. Unidentifiable. Forfeit and untamed. I came into this place like you. I awoke here in a ring of smoke and flame. If there was anything before that, I remember none of it. The difference is I embraced this oblivion as a benefit and moved on without looking back.

What? This time, Stain stomped a foot. For her, the gesture was much less elegant as she winced against the throbs shooting through her shredded toes. *You always said you didn't wish to speak of your past. Not that you couldn't remember.*

I don't *wish to speak of it. It bores me. I don't need family. I don't need history. I simply need to be. In the moment, living and free.*

The heat and smoke swelling around them burned Stain's eyes. *But I do need those things. And you knew that. If nothing else, it would've helped me not feel so alone.*

I'm on your doorstep each day. Waiting for you. Walking, flying, running with you. I am your cure for loneliness and all the family that you, in your weak human-ness, will ever require. Am I not?

Stain wanted to argue, but in all their years together, this was the closest he'd come to admitting affection for her. There was a proverb she'd once heard . . . something about not looking a gift horse in the mouth. Since she could never seem to make *this* particular horse understand the human side of things—that being family should mean more than playing together and having adventures, that there was the expectation of sentiments spoken in earnest, hugs and kisses given freely, and aid offered without bargains—she shrugged, the closest she'd come to agreeing with him outright.

Good. Now that you're done pitying your lack of self, let us leave this place before the Shroud Collective returns. His dark eyes reflected the holocaust. Once the tree trunks extinguished, the flames would find no other kindling along the barren ground.

Scorch did an about-face, and Stain followed where his wounded wing dragged a path through the ash. She took the incline in silence, wordless and riddled with confusing thoughts. Who was the marked princess the creatures spoke of? And did Luce help with that girl's escape like he had hers? Why had Stain been wearing an Eldorian page boy's clothes when dropped here?

So deep in her musing, she barely noticed they'd reached the top. No wayfaring puddles had crossed them, deterred by the scent of charbroiled wood and smoke.

The Pegasus's hooves clopped onto the onyx pathway. He paused and bent his glossy black neck, waiting for Stain to catch up. His eyes scolded her the moment her foot met the trail.

She clenched her teeth. *I know, I owe you a service.*

He huffed through his nostrils and shook his mane in a nod.

In the dim light, Stain caught sight of the molten blood dried upon the hinge of his beautiful feathered wing. *Let me start by treating your wound.*

She reached into her bag, pushing aside the ravager's knife to find the ointment. The knife's handle poked out and Scorch nudged her hand away to lift the blade between his teeth. He dropped it at her feet with a clatter.

This is all you need to treat me. Only by draining the Night Ravager of his blood will my wing be healed. You will repay your debt by helping me see him dead.

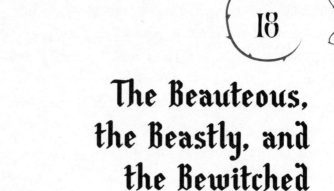

18

The Beauteous, the Beastly, and the Bewitched

The way to the fishing tarn was mostly deserted when Scorch and Stain took to the lofties. Stain had unrolled and tied her bandages into one long, sturdy strip. After wetting it for fireproofing, she'd wrapped the length around Scorch's back and belly to bind his limp wing in place along his rib cage. When she finished, it folded against his side like the healthy wing did naturally for easier maneuvering through trees and thickets. Stain also insisted on using the ointment, although Scorch deemed it a waste, as it wouldn't help him fly.

It was hard watching him stay grounded; he almost always flew in this tallest part of the forest. And if it was hard for her to watch him, she could only imagine how difficult it was *being* him. She would've chosen another route, but they needed to avoid her home.

Stain wasn't ready to encounter her guardians yet. She had plans to storm the threshold later and drop the shroud's riddles at their feet. By having bits of truth to reason with, by demonstrating her need to know herself—a desperation so profound she had faced the collective alone—she hoped to shock and shame Crony and Luce into confessing the rest.

This had to wait, though, as she had a service to fulfill. A service that made her stomach wobbly. She watched her boots trudge through the ash. Just a few hours earlier, she was contemplating recompense for Scorch's wounds. But now, after having faced her own near death, she reconsidered.

Distracted, Stain barely looked up in time to see Toothless Edith and Dregs leaving the Wayward Tavern a short distance ahead. Scorch's every muscle tensed beside her.

Hide behind the brambles there, she insisted, giving his chest a nudge. He grunted, but obliged.

Her acquaintances were in rare form. Dregs walked tall as any man with the pedestal shoes that matched his hat, escorting Edith, who was dressed as fine as any lady in a velvety gown Stain had never seen. She'd pulled her hair into a bun and even had lipstick in place. She spoke loudly to Dregs, no longer seeming to care about her lisp.

"Thain!" Edith hollered. The old woman waved a lace hanky Stain's direction. "Beth trade I ever did make!" She had the mirror in her other hand, keeping it turned on herself as she spoke. Tilting her head, she admired her face, her features blissful if not beauteous.

Dregs spun in his high heels. "I second that, and tip my hat." He tapped the felt brim that shaded his bulbous eyes. "My booth is at your disposal, should you ever have another proposal."

Stain nodded a thank-you and hoped they'd be on their way.

"Wait. Did ya fall inthide a fire hole, boy?" Edith dragged her gaze away from the mirror long enough to look Stain over from head to toe. "Ya be a bit more torn than usual, and thkorched to boot."

"Scorched indeed, and his clothes are but weeds." Dregs flicked the icicle-shaped growth at end of his long nose, as if in thought. "Earlier, there were night soldiers and a dog nearby . . . five we saw, with intent in their eye.

Walking the wood and headed that way," he pointed the direction Stain and Scorch had avoided. "Be a dangerous lot to engage in horseplay."

She forced a shocked expression to assure them she'd be cautious. An out-and-out lie. The fact that there were five of the soldiers walking about on foot with the dog meant Scorch's plan had just been simplified by half. That would leave only five at the Nerezethite camp with their mounts. And since neither Dregs nor Edith had mentioned ravagers among the wanderers, the assassin must be one who stayed behind.

Both the goblin and the old woman suddenly shifted their gazes across her shoulder, wearing horrified expressions as Scorch lumbered out from behind the brush—his mane and tail glowing hot, embers alight in eyes wild with rage and resolve. Against Stain's bared nape, warm gusts stirred from his healthy, flapping wing. Even with the other wing pinned back, he posed a formidable threat.

They're harmless. Leave them be. Stain placed a hand upon his velvety muzzle as he towered beside her.

They dared speak my name.

They didn't. They were referring to my scorched clothes, and you know that. They're guilty of nothing but enjoying life for the first time in some while.

He snorted. *They're in our way. Send them off, or their last taste of life will be the lick of my flame upon their charred tongues.*

Wearing an apologetic frown, Stain waved good-bye to her friends— insistently. As if waking from a trance, the two stumbled toward a thicket that opened in the direction of Crony's, their retreat not nearly as refined as their entrance.

Scorch trudged onward and Stain followed, prisoner to a promise she wished she'd never made. The cessation course would soon be underway. It made her stomach lurch to think of attacking the ravager and other four soldiers in their sleep.

The trees drooped lower once they abandoned the lofties. A rainstorm brewed outside, and the fresh scent of moisture mingled with a tapping across the leafy canopy offered an oddly tranquil backdrop to their murderous venture.

Scorch avoided a patchy opening where the rain rolled from one leaf to another. Normally, Stain would have to duck around such a space herself, as sunlight filtered in. But with it cloudy, she was able to walk under the miniature waterfall. She lifted her face, washing off the blood caked on her lips, cheeks, and forehead. Water beaded along her lashes, coating them like dew gathered upon spindly webs. She followed next with her arms, rinsing her wounds as well as possible with the sparse supply.

How she wished to be outside in truth. To actually stand in the storm. To feel the rhythm of the drops race along her skin, to see them fall from an open sky in sheets—a glimmering dance of crystal in the sunlight.

Sighing, she sipped some droplets to appease a niggle of hunger. Then she dragged the ravager's knife from the bag and caught up to Scorch. She wished the assassin's blade could be used to catch a fish dinner rather than to take a man's life.

I've never killed anyone, Scorch. She sent her companion the thought, so hesitant it would've been a whisper had it been spoken aloud.

He didn't slow his pace. His only acknowledgment was the swish of his tail. *Not that you can remember, you mean.*

Stain poked the knife's point into her thumb's tip, indenting the pale flesh. Her sunlit magic pooled beneath her skin and warmed the silver blade to a reddish heat. The resulting burst of agony caused her to tuck the knife away in the bag. She shuddered. *I give life to the flowers smothering in the soot. Surely, I can't take a life. I was just a child when I came here.*

A baby serpent's venom is deadlier than that of his parentage. We are all born with a will to survive. In some of us, you and I for example, that will is greater than most. *A grave injustice was done to you . . . someone abused you. You are made of life and death, according to the mother shroud. I would like to think you had a taste of vengeance before being cast aside. And if you didn't, I'll see that you have revenge one day. Whoever hurt you will answer to both of us. And now I should like your help to get the same satisfaction.*

Stain grimaced. *He cut you only once.*

It's more than that. I smelled my death in him. Then he attacked me, proving me right.

Stain clamped her teeth. *You speak of the instinct to live. Yet you won't acknowledge that the ravager cut you for that very reason . . . to protect himself. To protect his companions. You were the one who instigated the attack.*

Upon this, Scorch paused, his left wing tugging awkwardly in its binds. His ears lay flat against his head. *The danger called to me from within the thorny maze. His blood asked to be spilled before I even encountered him. I had no choice but to act.*

Stain moved around his powerful flanks and twitching muscles, getting ahead. She walked backward to watch him, knowing every root and gurgling pit by memory. *And he reacted. There are consequences to everything we do. Will you ever step outside of your beastly brawny stubbornness and learn to stop and reason for that?*

Scorch's eyes lit to orange. *There is no place for reason within a beast's heart. Instinct is my master. You would do well to remember* that, *and squash these tender emotions that weaken and blind you. Had you acted on instinct earlier, you would've stepped aside while I trampled him, and we wouldn't be having this argument now.*

He started forward again, his silver hooves plodding through the powdery groundcover. She spun to follow at his right, reaching up to grasp his dark mane when the ground grew uneven and sent shooting pains through her toes and ankles.

He moved closer and curled his healthy wing around her. She leaned her temple against his shoulder, feeling tendons grip and slide beneath his satiny coat. The scent of horse musk intertwined with smoke to fill her nostrils.

Am I not your friend, tiny trifling thing? he asked as they loped in synch with one another.

Thunder rolled in the sky, shaking the leafy roof above her wet head and the ground beneath her weary feet. *Yes. The dearest one I've known.*

Because I've never lied to you.

She captured a black curl draping his neck and twisted it around her finger-tip, stirring sparks to scald her skin. *Other than withholding your absent past.*

Scorch released a sooty puff from his nostrils. *I told you I didn't wish to speak of it. That was no lie.*

Stain clucked her tongue, the only sound of derision she could make.

And I'm not lying now. Scorch flicked an ear, ignoring her. *There is danger in this man.*

Well, he is *an assassin.*

No. He's something more. A personal threat to me. I tasted it. I scented it. Something in his blood wants to bind and suppress my flame. If it's too much for you to stab him in his heart, then lure him out of camp—away from his companions. I'll see to the rest.

Their mental conversation ended as the aroma of roasted fish marked their arrival to a grove of trees around the campsite. Stain's mouth watered and her stomach grumbled.

Hush. Scorch sent the silent demand while leading them to a spot behind a scattering of thick, wide trunks that enabled a view of the camp-front without being seen.

Stain was about to argue that she had no control over her stomach's protests when he interrupted again: *Wait here. I'll scout a plan of attack.*

Stealthily, he slipped from tree to tree until he reached the labyrinth, where the thorny walls—tightly bound and towering all the way up to the canopy—offered camouflage with tiny openings for peepholes.

To free her hands, Stain looped her arms through her bag's straps, hanging it secure at her back. She then peeked from behind the tree. There were three enclosures set up in the distance: two, set apart beside the horses that had been relieved of their armor and fixed with feedbags upon their muzzles— more serendipity, as they wouldn't smell Scorch and panic. Since there were six mounts, it reasoned that the scouting party Dregs had mentioned had returned for their horses, but only four left again. The caged birds she'd heard screaming during the chaos in the labyrinth must have also gone with the scouts. Stain hoped they had the dog with them, too.

In the two farthest tents, the flaps were shut, and snoring sounds drifted out.

The third enclosure, straight ahead, was propped next to the fishing tarn: a tall embankment of rocks tapering to a wide circle of stone beneath an opening in the canopy. The basin captured rain and dew, never drying up. Water trickled into it now with a soft, rhythmic patter. Sporadically, fish leapt out and plopped back in with a splash.

This tent's flap remained open, and Stain saw her leather pouch from earlier, which meant they had found her jars of night creatures. Her mind scrambled for some way to get them back. Moving carefully from one tree to another revealed more of the scene. The silhouette of a man in a white shirt and black leathery breeches—tight enough to conform to his sinewy, masculine lines—sat within the opening on a blanket. Beside him crouched a moonlit girl dressed in a soldier's uniform. A long, silvery-purple braid curled from her nape to rest in her lap like a pet snake. She had bandages, reminding Stain of those holding Scorch's wounded wing in place . . . her hands grew clammy at the reminder of how wrong this day had gone.

In the distance, the girl held a dagger over a campfire where the remains of their savory meal burned in the flames—fish scales and bones turning to ash. The girl's silver blade burnished red, and the man mumbled something under his breath. He rolled up his left sleeve, exposing a metallic golden sheen along his forearm—either a vambrace or some similar piece of armor.

Everywhere else, his skin was the deep red gold of burnished copper, beautiful, but bearing no resemblance to a moonlit-kissed Nerezethite. He appeared instead to be of Eldoria, bronzed by the sun. So why was he riding with soldiers of the night realm?

Soundless, Stain eased from behind one tree to another and another, utilizing the dense growth until she was a few feet from the edge of the tarn. She stopped when she could feel the water droplets as they splattered and hear the man and woman as they spoke.

"I'm ready, Selena," he said, gesturing to the dagger. Stain recognized the ravager's voice at once. Although young, like she assumed, in other ways he looked very different than she'd expected.

His hood had been removed, and thick hair—as purply dark as the winter plums Dregs offered for purchase on special occasions—hung to his shoulders in messy waves. The skull-face paint was gone as well, revealing high, angular cheekbones with a long, aquiline nose that suggested regality. A straight, pale scar, raised and thin, started beneath his left cheek and ran to his strong jawline, disrupting his smooth complexion.

"Would you rather I do it this time?" the girl named Selena asked.

"No, dear sister . . . I still have use of my hands. It's enough you have to watch." His forehead was wide and expressive under tendrils of disheveled hair, and thick, black eyebrows punctuated his words, furrowing or rising in cadence with his deep, soothing voice.

He cringed, sliding the red-hot blade along the golden vambrace on his arm. Only it wasn't armor; for where the dagger's sharp edge skated along the surface, fine hairs raised in its wake as if magnetized. That metallic shell was his *skin* . . . a part of him, like a crab's carapace.

This man was under some sort of bewitchment.

Stain covered her mouth as the knife stopped where the shell surrendered to natural, soft flesh on the back of his wrist. There the blade sank in, cutting a long slit. She expected beads of bright red to swell at the site, but instead, a stream of gold drizzled free—as radiant as the liquid light that clung to the trees at the ravine's entrance.

A man who bleeds sunshine.

"Do you wish to use it for ink?" Selena wiped the golden blood from the dagger, then drew a small vial from one of the three saddlebags beside her. "I brought a quill and parchment." She placed a stack of black paper next to him.

"No need to write anymore," the man answered. "By tomorrow, I'll speak to her in person. At last I'll know her."

His sister positioned the vial to capture the glittering stream at his wrist. "You know her already. You've been exchanging notes for years."

"Yet she feels like a stranger. Doesn't feel right, for a marriage. Do you remember Lord Father's pet name for our lady mother?"

Selena beamed—a smile that transformed her delicate features from pretty to stunning. "His Northern Star." Using a bandage, she blotted away some lustrous blood that had overrun the vial's mouth. Her silvery eyebrows arched. "Perhaps their great love gave us unrealistic notions of romance?"

"Perhaps. But *you* will have what they did. Cyp confessed his affections today, when he thought you were both to die in the fire. And you didn't for a moment question if it was sincere, nor did you hesitate to return the sentiment."

"He told you?" Selena's face flushed, making the bluish veins behind her thin skin more prominent. "He should've waited. We've more important things to think about on this journey."

The ravager grinned gently. "Cyp told me because he knew I'd be happy for the both of you. There's no shame in celebrating the discovery of love, especially between friends. You've walked alongside one another for years on the same terrain—carried one another through the loss of your fathers. You've shared goals and secrets. You always find middle ground, ways to compromise, even when you disagree. Friendship is a measuring stick for love. Would that my intended and I had such a tool to gauge our relationship. It would ease the responsibility of consolidating two such different kingdoms."

Stain's ears perked at the words *intended* and *consolidating kingdoms*. This was the night prince, come for his princess in Eldoria's castle—wearing a disguise. How careless of her not to suspect . . . not to question . . . having played at masquerades for so long herself.

The prince's sister drew back and corked the small vial now filled with effulgent liquid. "I think, because our people no longer practice arranged marriages, it's harder for you. But even if a betrothal is nontraditional, the love that grows from it can still be real and true."

He chuckled—a cynical gesture—and pressed a piece of gauze against his incision to slow the seeping driblets. "Ah, good to know. For there's nothing traditional about my love story, to be sure." His full lips pressed tight. "A flawless, fragile lady is supposed to be my missing half—to complete me— scarred and hardened as I am. Yet I know nothing of her. So often her letters feel rehearsed. As if she's writing what she believes one of her station should say, or what she thinks I wish to hear. Yes, I want the romance . . . the poetry. But those are ideals a king can set aside, if only his queen will speak from the heart—as one confidante to another—responsibilities and status notwith- standing. I want my partner's thoughts and feelings, in earnest."

"That's reasonable. Be patient. You've never even seen her face. I predict, the moment you meet and spend time together, all pretentions and doubts will fade. As Madame Dyadia said, you will know her by her voice."

He sighed. "Once I hear her song, from her lips instead of a seashell, only then will I know that my people and I can be cured." There was a ragged edge to his voice—as if he'd been holding out for such a moment for an eternity. "The truth of it? Only then will I know the foretelling was worth believing."

The man turned his face to the fire, hiding doubts within the long shad- ows cast by his cheekbones and dark eyelashes. Stain ducked behind her tree, peering through a juncture of branches that brought her to his level. How profound, to see that dark gaze up close—as inscrutable as a blackbird's. How had she overlooked that detail earlier? She'd been too busy comparing it to night shadows and crickets.

His lustrous blood attested he was truly forged of sunlight. All this time she and Scorch had made a mockery of the fairy tale. She'd never dreamed the descriptions could be taken literally: a prince with the eyes of a raven, to marry a princess who spoke like a songbird.

Stain cupped her barren throat. Ever since the day she'd awoken in Crony's home, she'd accepted the inability to make sounds or speak. Yet the fairy tale had always left her covetous for a voice. Now, seeing those details coming to life, the envy heightened, coating her tongue with a briny-bitter taste.

It was just another reminder of how different she was from others in the world. Everyone other than Scorch . . .

She glanced at the thorny maze in the distance where a glowing spark glimmered behind some tangled vines.

"At least there's one small triumph today," the prince said, recouping Stain's attention. "No more hiding behind ink and parchment." He pushed aside the stack. The movement loosened the gauze on his arm and spurred a few remaining droplets to smear upon the paper's black surface, a bright and glittering counterbalance to the darkness.

Stain slammed her eyelids shut, her mind flashing to that odd dream of golden words upon black pages from years earlier. Opening her eyes, she studied her fingers, thinking upon their scalding, bright magic. Somewhere inside her was the missing detail . . . the explanation for why she had sunlight beneath her skin like this man. She cursed Crony and Luce for stealing those answers, for leaving nothing but a residue to cling to.

Shaking off her anger, she looked up once more. Princess Selena stitched her brother's incision. It oozed red now, as if his blood had been cleansed by the draining. She tied off some black thread and cut it. Before Stain could blink, his skin had healed to another scar—absorbing the stitches in the process. More magic.

"I wonder how many that is now?" The prince patted the raised white welt. "Perhaps enough I can double as a patchwork quilt." The edges of his mouth twitched. "Let's play a trick on the castle's seamstresses . . . hang me on the wall naked beside their finest creations. See how long it takes them to notice."

Stain stifled a surprised laugh at his wit. Her own scars stared back at her, providing an intimate awareness of how desecrated he must truly feel. Though some of her wounds had been made through experiences and adventures she chose, there were others inflicted upon her, robbing her of any choice.

Princess Selena laughed, as if buoyed by her brother's momentary lapse into humor. "You might've got by with it in your youth—bedeviled, rebel prince that you were. I can think of several maids who would swoon at the prospect of such a sight even now." Clucking her tongue, she tucked all the articles away in the bag, including the papers. "However, I hold you to a better standard. That behavior would be entirely unbecoming of the king."

The king. One half of the couple who would return unity to the heavens. Stain's heart sped, keeping rhythm with the rain drizzling into the fishing tarn. It hit her suddenly: she'd attacked royalty, offset an honorable quest to mend their realms. And now, aware of the prince's condition, seeing his humanness, she felt even sorrier for her preconceptions—for judging the Nerezethites without knowing intimate details of the realm's traditions.

Cloth rustled as the prince opened another saddlebag and a cylinder of unusual silken fabric unrolled, revealing feathers, fur, and lace that swirled like rippling water in a cave. Within the pleats rested a handful of treasures: an ornate hairbrush of pearlescent opal with steel bristles, an amethyst-jeweled hairpin, and a ring whose setting consisted of a miniature lavender rose. This too was magical, as the blossom somehow thrived without soil, water, or roots. Its perfume—so potent it reached Stain even without a breeze to carry it—reminded her of the blackened bouquet from earlier . . . those withered roses the shrouds hoarded as a macabre keepsake from her entry into the ravine. Another similarity between her and the prince. They shared sunlight somehow . . . scars . . . and a history with these strange flowers.

Confusion surged—a woozy sensation. Her knees weakened. She gripped the rough tree bark to keep from reeling.

Compose yourself. Scorch's voice ignited in her mind. She sensed his return, behind her where the trees thickened. *You need your wits about you so we can execute my plan.*

No, Stain answered as the prince leaned closer to the fire, his complexion waxen and drawn, as if siphoning the golden solvent from his body had weakened him.

Yes. Scorch grunted low in his throat. *He's unsteady now. It's the perfect opportunity.*

We can't kill him. Her heart pounded in her chest as the thought flickered between her and her winged companion, hot and bright as the blaze reflected in the prince's deep, haunted eyes. *He's royalty.*

Could that be why Luce had been so upset with her earlier? Had he known the ravager's true identity all along?

What have I told you about royalty? Scorch's response was gruff. *They are the vilest of all humankind. Selfish, power hungry. Cruel. They'll kill anyone who threatens their status, even their own subjects.*

Stain tightened her stance. This prince didn't seem selfish. And cruel? Earlier, when she first met him, his words were kind and noble—offering her help. Now they centered around concern for his people and the broken skies, inasmuch as himself.

We must act now.

Stain ignored Scorch's snarling command and the faint smell of smoke curling around her—focused instead on the quiet conversation still taking place between the prince and his sister.

"I just don't understand how it's all to be." He held the ring up to the campfire, pinching the rusty-brown band that matched the color of his forefinger and thumb. Firelight and shade alternated along the whorl of lavender petals, brightening some to a satin sheen while darkening others to velvet depths. The jewelry was tiny in his large, slender hand. "How my marriage to Lady Lyra will align the moon and sun so both kingdoms can benefit. How it can cure my poisoned blood and save our people. Can magic be so strong?"

"It was strong enough to separate the heavens, to keep you alive in spite of the sun's taint." Selena traced the intricate lines of the hairpin. "Strong enough to capture a princess's teardrops in this pin and harden her hair to bristles of steel for this brush. We must have faith it can ameliorate all the wrongs. Put things back to right."

Stain touched the corners of her eyes . . . as dry as they'd been since she could remember. Then her hand slipped over her forehead and caressed the downy fuzz from her crown to her nape, once silvery-white, now a shade of blackberry not unlike the prince's own. Something inside her woke—a stir of jealousy, knowing that she would never have use for such beautiful items since her own hair didn't grow? Or something more?

"Faith," the prince's growl stole her breath. "Faith in a prophecy—nothing but an amalgamation of words arranged prettily upon an ice cavern's wall. Belief that every event is a stepping-stone. That everyone we meet serves a purpose." He rewrapped the gifts in that dark, swirling fabric and placed them inside the saddlebag. "The prophecy has colored every decision we make . . . every challenge we stumble upon. At each crossroad, we stop and wonder. How do our wounded stags figure into this? Our dying people? How does that boy we seek—bleeding, scarred . . . so poverty-stricken he has no shoes—fit in? What of the ancient mystic that Leo's team is taking to Eldoria's castle as we speak, or our reserve of midnight shadows and spiders they took to break through the enchanted honeysuckle walls?" He clasped his sister's hand. "Selena, by hanging our confidence upon magic, we're shirking our own accountability, our capacity to reason and surmise. You met the prisoner yourself. You heard me interrogate her. She's nothing like Dyadia said. We all saw her humility, her gratitude when we shared our food with her, the gentleness in contrast to her ugliness."

Selena pursed her lips in thought. "She was very respectful to you. To all of us, in spite of her captivity."

The prince closed the flap on his saddlebag, his expressive eyebrows pinched tight. "I made a mistake, sending her to be punished on mere faith. We haven't any proof of wrongdoing . . . not even the box marked 'princess - revolution.' Nothing other than an albino crow's word and Regent Griselda's suspicions. Enough of *faith*. It's time we take control of fate and make things right on our own. Whether or not Luna and Nysa can track the orphan boy, we leave for Eldoria when the cessation course begins. I wish to consult with the princess as soon as possible. Even a horned harrower witch merits a trial—a chance to defend herself."

Albino crow . . . harrower witch . . . punishment and trials. Stain's fingers dug deeper into the bark's crevices as the words spun in her brain.

Scorch huffed. *As I said. Royalty is not to be trusted. You've heard what happens to those who end up in Eldoria's dungeons. Your toothless friend from market is a prime example. I assure you, the punishment is far worse for those who practice magic outside of the Regent's requests. Had the prince already been dead, your precious Crony wouldn't be in danger now.*

Stain squeezed her eyes shut as Scorch's truths sliced her to the core.

Everything that had transpired between her and her guardians earlier— their betrayal of her memories, their lies—fell away in light of Crony's predicament. Dregs had mentioned seeing the soldiers. Stain hadn't given it a second thought . . . but it was she who led the troop there. An albino crow had crossed their threshold, magical enough to bypass the nightmare wards. And Stain heard the dog barking when she left. She led them straight to her family, then abandoned them. And unless Luce had escaped, he was captured, too. Or worse. She gasped on the thought, a burst of air that proved too loud.

The prince and his sister scrambled to standing, their tense bodies turned her direction.

"Who goes there?" the prince called out. He wavered on his feet, still unsteady.

His sister coaxed him to sit beside the fire. Drawing out her dagger, she shouted toward the other two tents, her gaze never leaving the surrounding trees.

A loud rumble of thunder broke overhead—an ominous portending. Pulse skittering through her wrists, Stain crouched low and dragged the bag around to her chest. Her spine ate into the bark. Her hands clamped like iron bars across her lips. Every nerve prickled beneath her skin, every bone stiffened to near breaking. She was voiceless, incapable of pleading Crony's case; and she, too, would be captured and placed in chains.

Fabric rustled as the other tents opened and their occupants leapt out. Rushing footsteps, crackling leaves, shuffling ash—growing ever closer.

Witless mite, Scorch snapped. *Once again, I must save you.* Glowing, orange sparks drifted in the greenish haze around her. *I'll catch fire to their tents and set loose their horses to draw the others away. When he's alone, you slash his throat. No hesitation. You owe me that.*

Yes. Stain agreed, dragging out the knife. But she had her own plan. The prince mentioned searching for the boy . . . for her. She would lure him to the moon-bog where she first met Scorch. It was close—and the perfect place wherein to trap someone unfamiliar with the terrain.

The prince must live to be Stain's bargaining chip. For surely the prophesied king's life was valuable enough to trade for a lowly witch's safe return.

19

The Murkiness of Fate and Other Illusions

The storm must have been enchanted . . . or so most Eldorians believed. Other rains had drenched their skies over the past five years, yet these were the first to feed the honeysuckle plague more rapidly and vigorously than sunlight itself. Within hours of the rumbling thunder and splattering raindrops, the pink blossoms swelled to the size of cabbages, calling more stinging bees to their syrupy pollen. The foliage and thistles tightened around every cottage like a bristly green fist, in the same as it held the castle's courtyard, walls, and towers, effectively nailing all doors and windows shut. The thoroughfares—which had worn the green cloaks for years—undulated and rolled, resembling the spiny tongue of some mythical lizard and making it impossible to walk upon.

Citizens huddled in their dimly lit homes—weak from lack of physical labor and play, malnourished from lack of hearty food, chilled to the bone from lack of sunlight upon their skin. They peered out of slits in the vines covering their windows, watching for the arrival of the night prince and his infantry of spiders and shadows. A prayer went up to their golden sun, that together with their princess—a ghostly figment occupying the palace dungeon—Prince Vesper could bring back their freedom to walk outside.

Prejudice had been traded for tolerance, a by-product of harsh experiences shared. Even those who once laughed at the ill fate of Nerezeth, buried beneath blizzards that muffled all sound and barren of fragrant flowers, were looking forward to snowflakes falling silent from moonlit skies—as winter evenings would mean a land untainted by cloying perfume and the constant buzz of bees.

Griselda's royal spies, armored infantrymen with axes hung at their waists and white gold lining their purses, hacked through the honeysuckle vines to forage for news of the kingdom's state, and the condition of people's spirits. Upon learning that many commoners believed there was no longer a princess—as in all these years she had not been seen even by the castle's twenty-some inhabitants—Griselda smiled. At last, people were at their most disparate, providing the perfect opportunity to introduce the queen-in-waiting she had so diligently crafted.

Griselda sent word by her infantryman, back to the castle keeps and cottages, that the princess was to make an appearance in the highest southern tower just before the wink of twilight. As every townsperson with a westward-facing window or door used axes and gardening shears to widen their line of sight, Sir Erwan did the same for the tower's dormer.

Griselda dressed herself, her two daughters, and "Lyra" in their finest tight-laced court gowns, fur-lined mantles, and cone-shaped hennins. Though Griselda despised the beribboned headdresses, today was about tradition and propriety. So, accompanied by her two trusted knights, Regent Griselda led her family in a royal procession. They started at the bottom of the dungeon's staircase and wound up toward the turret's dormer window—the very one from which Lyra had looked down upon her kingdom through blue-tinged glass, years ago.

The procession grew longer as they ascended each flight—council members, subjects, and servants attaching to their tail like a gemstone rolling up hill and gathering moss.

Anonymous whispers bounced off the white marbled walls and floors.

"See the princess's star-struck beauty," said one.

"I'd forgotten how silver her hair and lashes," said another.

"She practically glows with moonlight and grace," said a third. "We needn't have worried. Nerezeth's dark prince will worship her upon first sight. Told you she'd grow into her own, didn't I?"

"She's more than grown into her beauty," said a fourth—the words erupting from the end of the procession on a booming bass. "She's grown in diplomacy, wisdom, and fairness under the council's written disciplines, and is now fully prepared to rule our kingdom. Perhaps she might offer us a blessing, in her special language?"

This voice Griselda recognized even before seeing the cropped black hair and intelligent green eyes among the assembly. Of everyone they needed to convince, Prime Minister Albous would be the most difficult. He was the one soul, still living, who had spent more time with Lyra during her last few months than anyone else. Though he hadn't *seen* her in years, he hadn't forgotten his special rapport with the small princess—a closeness that would be difficult for Lustacia to emulate since she had stopped practicing the ancient sign language. The most she could offer was a greeting, and two or three phrases . . . certainly not a poetic blessing.

Thus, Griselda chose that moment to unleash her final, most brilliant deception.

She tapped Lustacia's elbow. Responding with a slight nod, "Princess Lyra" turned in front of the turret door to face the assemblage. Opening her pale, purplish lips, she released a nightingale's warble that echoed through the corridors—silver and pure.

Her audience, adrift atop the mellifluous notes, grew as silent as stone. The princess beckoned with her palm upturned and three fingers curled—a regal gesture that might've been mistaken for a hand signal. Her flaring sleeve stirred at her wrist, and the shadows that had been darkening the floor and walls alongside her and her sisters and mother peeled free and hovered in midair. There were but five—one for each goblin smuggler Griselda's spell-chant, brumal-blood potion had warped and reshaped. They were half-lights now, dimmed to only a portion of their customary mass— mere wraiths in a world of solidity. However, it was that vaporous form that allowed them to swoop and shudder with such ferocity they appeared to be a multitude of shadows.

The audience ducked and gasped, no longer mesmerized, but afraid.

"The day of fate is at last upon us," Griselda said as the goblin-fray darkened the cathedral ceiling like a gathering of storm clouds. Turning to face Lustacia, the regent dropped to her knees. Wrathalyne and Avaricette exchanged wry glances and knelt beside their mother. "Soon, the moon will rise and cleanse our kingdom of the plague. It is time we join Princess Lyra's shadow attendants in celebration, and give allegiance to our queen."

As one, each person around them dropped to their knees, including Albous and the members of council.

Griselda's pride kindled bright as hand signals were all but forgotten for the princess's authority over the shadows. No one would dare question her daughter's legitimacy now.

Their princess humbly dipped her head. The translucent, beaded veil erupting from her hennin's tip gilded her silver hair like a layer of frost. The picture of elegance and majesty, she turned and strode into the turret.

"Our royal family wishes privacy as the princess first reacquaints her kingdom," Griselda insisted. She and her daughters followed at Lustacia's heel. The "shadows" swept down, blocking anyone who would enter, until Sir Erwan and Sir Bartley took their places outside the closed door under which the shadowy creatures disappeared.

As their sooty forms seeped into the turret like black smoke, Griselda made a wide berth to avoid the half-light goblins' annoying antics. Avaricette and Wrathalyne squeaked and grumbled when the cursed beings sniffed them and swirled in and out of their gauzy gowns. Though Griselda had managed to change their forms, she'd been unable to curb their obnoxious personalities.

"Mums!" Wrathalyne screeched, tucking a fallen lock of auburn hair beneath her hennin. "When we finally turn them back to goblins, will they still be so clingy and *vexalatious*?"

Avaricette snorted and withdrew a half-gnawed sweetmeat from her pocket. "Vexatious, you imbecilic ninny."

"Oh? If I'm a ninny, you're a toad."

Avaricette popped the confectionery between her lips and winced upon biting down. "For an aspersion to be effective, it must make sense. Goats are illiterate, as are you. How am I like a toad in any way?"

"Your lack of teeth."

Avaricette slapped a palm over her cavity-filled mouth and shoved her sister with her free hand, who in turn shoved her back. The goblin wraiths whirled around them gleefully, egging it on.

"Enough!" Griselda shouted, then gentling her voice, called to her youngest, who already stood at the window, waving in a dream state at any who could see her through the blue-tinged glass. "Princess, please contain your most loyal subjects."

With a sigh, Lustacia motioned the wraiths over. They sank into the floor, becoming imprints of her movements once again, like any good shadow. Griselda settled at her daughter's side and opened the rain-streaked window enough to let in the joyous shouts and applause from below.

"Hear how they adore you, daughter. You have won your kingdom's heart. This is a day of victory."

Lustacia frowned.

Griselda clucked her tongue. "Just because you look the part of a gloom-dweller, doesn't mean you have to share their dour moods."

Lustacia shook her head, closed her eyes, and inhaled a deep breath.

Honeysuckle drenched the humid air—so potent and sickly sweet it burned away all other sensory cues from the palace garden adjacent to the tower.

"I miss the flowers of my childhood," Lustacia said—the lyricism of her voice cushioning the ears like a lullaby. "The licorice sway of pink carnations, the vanilla brush of violet heliotropes, the powdery flutter of white gardenias. None can be seen, smelled, nor heard through those wretched thistly vines. I can only make out the sylph elm now." She glanced over her shoulder across the room where her sisters snooped through dusty trunks for forgotten jewels or treasure, then turned again to the cursed kingdom outside the window. "The leaves are changing color. That was Lyra's favorite thing to watch for. At last it's come, and she's missed it."

Griselda scowled at the attempt to guilt her for robbing them of childhoods, for cutting short her niece's life. But her scowl softened as she noted for herself the fringed leaves of vivid yellow overtaking the red that billowed out from the glistening, encroaching vines. She'd been waiting for those leaves to change, too. Hoping they might lure Elusion back to the castle and her bed. An air sylph's charm was always good to have on hand.

Lustacia wound a silvery strand of hair around her finger, growing dreamy again. "There's a path that leads to the sylph elm where the vines don't grow. It must be the tree's own enchantment, acting as a barrier. Your brother . . . our uncle. The *king*. He used to tell us a story about when the leaves changed, that a cursed sylph—"

"Could win back its wings and return to the skies?" Griselda huffed. "A farcical bedtime tale."

"Truly?" Lustacia put her back to the window, steadying her lilac gaze upon her mother's face. "More farcical than this?" She gestured to herself, and to the illusory shadows at her feet. "I agree with Wrath. Return the goblins to their original forms. They've played their part."

Griselda clenched her jaw. "Every time I believe you've wizened enough to be queen, you disappoint me with that misplaced sense of mercy. Good that you'll have me as your counselor."

Lustacia hid her profile behind the beaded sweep of her veil. "I think my counselor should be someone with a conscience."

The words were meant to cut, and indeed something coiled within Griselda's chest. It was, however, more like a snake preparing to strike than a wounded creature curling upon itself for protection. "You're not *thinking* at all. You still have to convince the prince you're Lyra. After that, you'll have to convince his entire kingdom. This will be impossible if no shadows respond to you. And these are the only ones who ever will, unless you've managed to befriend one or two in the dungeon over the years?"

Lustacia worked the hennin from her hair and tossed it down. The goblin shadows reflected every defeated motion. She rubbed her head, fingers digging into her hairline. Rolling her shoulder, she moved out of view of the cheering audience. "I abhor everything we've done. It pains my head to think of it."

"Yet, you went along with it all."

Lustacia's eyes filled with tears. "Out of obligation. You stole hope from the man I love. And now it's up to me to give him empty promises. All those letters he's written. He's sincere, perceptive, and kind, but so broken; he expects me to have some missing piece of him, to make him *whole*. You took that away. She's gone forever, as is his chance to live. He's coming here so I can watch him die of a terrible curse." Her tears fell in clear streams.

Griselda plucked her own hennin off, fingers massaging the knots in her hair above her temples. They'd been stinging almost nonstop today. "Best you learn to curb your weeping. Unless you first stain your face with blackberry juice, so your prince will mistake them for the lines of your tears. And enough with the gloom and doom. *Because* Lyra is gone, you're the only one who *can* save him. That gives you all the power."

"How can save I the prince, when I'm not his other half? Here you are promising the sun and moon to our subjects, when I can't even command a shadow. Even if no one else can see through me, the prophecy's magic might. Have you ever considered that, Mother? Even once?"

As if on cue, the sky dimmed as the sun surrendered to that dusting of twilight, heralding the start of the cessation course. Everything looked foreign and distorted in the temporary darkness, the honeysuckle plague taking on the semblance of a swarm of drasilisk nestlings in mid-hatch. For one breath . . . one heartbeat . . . Griselda harbored doubt.

Then the sun brightened again behind its swarm of clouds, and returned the world to perfect clarity, resolving the scene to all that Griselda had wrought through conspiring and trickery—confirmation of her control over both magic and fate.

She removed her gloves, revealing the glossy bluish-white tint upon her palms and fingers, the residue of the brumal-stag murders she couldn't seem to wash away. "I was told years ago that the heavens' splendor would be returned at my hands. Thus, I etched my own path. As you said, there is no Lyra now—*at my hand*. And of every lady in our two kingdoms, you're the only one with the physical traits specified by the prophecy—*at my hand*. All you need to cure the prince's cursed heart is her songbird voice, and you have that as well—*at my hand*. Just as these things have fallen into place, so shall the sun and moon. Whatever I must do to see it done, I will. Have faith in me, in this opportunity I've given you. You are the real princess, for I have made it so."

A sudden knock at the door startled a yelp out of Lustacia.

Griselda gloved her hands and put her headdress in place. "You may enter." She flashed a glare at her daughter. "Stop being so skittish. There's no one who can stand in our way now."

The door opened enough for Sir Erwan to step within. He swung it shut behind him. "I intercepted a missive sent via jackdaw. Prince Vesper's troop captured the harrower witch. They're bringing her here to be questioned by the council. They should arrive within two days."

Lustacia gripped her mother's arm, her expression a mix of horror and haughtiness. "It would appear, Mother, that your '*no one*' will soon be deposited at our castle gates."

A chill skittered through Griselda's chest as all her blood drained into her feet.

❄ ·I· ❄

Inside the Ashen Ravine, cinder and flame rained down—a storm more ravaging and violent than the rains outside.

The attack happened so quickly the prince had little time to react. A bugling roar cracked and the Pegasus broke through the trees, galloping toward the camp. Sparks trailed his hoofbeats. His mane, tail, eyes, and nostrils glowed with an incandescence both blinding and searing. One giant, lone wing spread out—a harsh slap of feathers, tendons, and hollow bones that shoved Vesper onto his back.

Braying in triumph, the Pegasus veered left toward the horses, scattering Vesper's companions in the chaos. Fire lit the farthest tents and smoke filled the campsite—billowing black curls that converted shouts to hacking coughs and snaked across the horses, spooking them. Eyes wild, the six mounts strained until the lead ropes snapped free of their branchy anchors. Before Vesper's companions got to their feet, the Pegasus rounded up the loose horses and drove them toward the thorny labyrinth.

Prince Vesper rolled to his stomach, squinting through soot and heat. His head buzzed with grogginess from the draining of his blood. He half-crawled, half-dragged himself toward the fishing tarn and the water flasks. They couldn't hold enough to staunch the fire, but their contents would stifle the sparks along the edges of the blankets Selena and Dolyn were using to smother flames.

Cyprian and Tybalt drew swords and sprinted after their mounts. Vesper tossed the water flasks in his sister's direction, then stumbled toward his open tent, determined to get his sword and follow the two men. He'd barely dragged the hilt toward him when his blood sang again, that strange reaction to the winged beast. The thrumming spread through his metallic shin, forearm, and abdomen, rocking the bones behind them—making it difficult to move. In this state, he would be artless with weaponry, but he refused to be completely useless. If Cyprian and Tybalt could hold off the Pegasus, he could lasso their mounts.

He found a coil of rope, then gave a shrill whistle. Lanthe responded, darting out from the herd before the rest plunged through the labyrinth's entrance. The Pegasus drove the others inside—into the boxed clearing Vesper had faced earlier. The winged beast pivoted, then kicked his back legs. The entrance vines snapped at the impact of his flying hooves, falling and tangling—effectively locking the horses within.

Whinnying, the Pegasus raced past Cyprian and Tybalt, razing them with his wing to knock them off their feet. The beast slanted a glance into the trees next to Vesper's tent. The same intelligence sparked in his eyes that Vesper had seen earlier. The Pegasus switched his tail in a loud snapping motion, almost as if impatient, then disappeared into a thicket the opposite direction.

Lanthe arrived, stirring up ash with his hooves. Vesper stood, swaying, and prepared to vault onto his back.

The boy came out of nowhere, armed with Vesper's stolen knife. His willowy body barreled into the prince's chest before he could mount. Lanthe reared in surprise, skittering backward. The prince's metallic shin torqued and he lost balance, but managed to catch the lad's sleeve and jerk the knife from his hand. Growling, Vesper dragged the orphan down with him, both of them plopping into the ash with a thud. Head-butting Vesper in the shoulder, the boy twisted free and ducked into the tent. On his way out, he sneered down at the prince—holding the saddlebag with Lady Lyra's gifts and the leather pouch containing the jars of night creatures—before Vesper could shake off the humming within his metal plates and get to his knees. The little thief lunged toward the trees, looking back at Vesper for several beats, the expression on his gray-stained face unmistakable: *Catch me if you can.* Then he was gone.

Lanthe pranced forward again. Vesper picked up his knife and tucked it in the empty sheath at his waist. He stood, dragged himself up to the stallion's withers, then swung a leg over his bare back.

Selena and Dolyn had the fire under control and sorted through the seared wreckage for anything salvageable. Farther away, at the labyrinth, Cyprian and Tybalt chopped at the maze's entrance with their axes. The horses nickered within, overwrought but slowly realizing they were safe.

Vesper's gaze followed the path the Pegasus had made, marked by the flickering cinders left in his wake. This had been a plan. All of it. The Pegasus and the orphan worked together to steal back the lad's jars of crickets and shadows. The princess's gifts must have caught their eye while they spied upon the camp. The opal hairbrush, amethyst hairpin, and panacea ring were priceless and irresistible to a thief; but Vesper wanted them back for more reason than that. The pack contained the hooded lacewing cloak of nightsky that the princess would need to safely make the trek out of her castle to Nerezeth's palace.

Fearing he'd lose the gifts, and even more fearful that he'd lose the boy should he hesitate, Vesper shouted. "The orphan stripling stole the princess's gifts! I'll return once I have them in hand."

Selena rushed his direction. "Wait until we free the mounts! Let us accompany—"

Vesper kicked Lanthe into a gallop before his sister could finish. He drove the stallion into the trees, ash swirling around them in time with the thrilling pace. Vesper and his mount ducked under low-hanging branches and leapt across noxious quag-puddles, guided through the dim haze by the slip of the boy in and out of the trees ahead. Even when he lost sight of the thief, Vesper found their way again, led by that same inexplicable intuition that had carried him through the labyrinth earlier.

Soon, the ash gave way to a wet, thick sludge. A thicket of interlaced briars rose in the distance to form an enclosed dome, hunched and dark like a mud-slicked wolf. A sense of impending danger bristled Vesper's nerves. Something bad had happened here. The sight alone made him feel trapped. He struggled against the sense of being stuck . . . pulled under . . . drowning. But he pressed on, his resolve stronger than the cryptic foreboding.

Lanthe slowed to a trot, ribs rising and falling rapidly where Vesper's thighs and calves straddled him. The stallion came to a stop at a slit in the brambles where the boy had vanished within. Vesper's odd instinct told him there was a bigger entrance somewhere, large enough for a horse, but were Lanthe to venture forward, they could both get trapped within the bog.

How he knew there was a bog inside, Vesper couldn't say. It was the same strange knowing that told him there was a fishing tarn earlier. Though the stench of dead and dying things might have sparked the idea this time.

Dismounting, Vesper slapped Lanthe on his flanks—a signal to the horse to go home . . . or in this case, to find someone he knew. The prince watched as the stallion trotted in the same direction they'd come. Lanthe's sense of hearing and smell would lead him back to the camp, and Vesper's troop could use the horse to find his whereabouts.

Plunging through the thin opening, Vesper gripped the knife at his waist and raised his metallic forearm in front of his face like a shield. His boot soles sucked in and out of the mucky ground. Thorny shrubbery snatched at his clothing, piercing through. Aside from the reek of decay that burned his eyes and coated his tongue, he hardly noticed; it was no different than being home and facing the Grim. There was even a similar glow like moonlight guiding his footsteps.

He wound through the brambles: left, right, and left again. When at last he broke through, he was face-to-face with the thief. An odd, silvery-blue glimmer emanated from the bog, gilding the brambly surroundings and the boy's appearance. Aside from new burn marks upon his torn clothes, he was cleaner now and donned a pair of boots. His long lashes glistened, as silver-white as hoarfrost, and his scars stood more prominent against his scrubbed, grayish-tinted skin.

The pouch with the night creatures rested across one shoulder. The prince's saddlebag hung from his other hand, swinging precariously above the gurgling bog. The slimy surface rippled as a snakelike projection resembling a fern leapt out, trying to snatch the pack.

Vesper's nerves prickled beneath his skin at the dangers within that oddly glowing murk; he could almost feel them wrapping around his neck. He had to get out . . . had to find a way to reason with the thief so he could get them both to safety.

He swallowed against the tightness in his throat. "What is your name?"

The boy furrowed his brow.

Vesper raised his hands and prepared his fingers, hoping he hadn't over-estimated the orphan's knowledge of the ancient language. *My friends call me Vesper. And you are?*

The boy drew the pack away from the water so it hung on his elbow, his expression awed. His hands trembled as they lifted and formed a response. *You know how to speak to me.*

The prince smiled. *Yes.*

An expression, akin to surprise, twitched the boy's pretty lips and he pointed at himself and signaled: *Stain.*

Vesper nodded. *That's all right. We're both a bit of a mess, aren't we? I've been wanting a bath all day.*

The boy snarled—an airy, frustrated sound. *My name is . . .* He dropped his hands in mid-sentence and glanced at the bog, as if considering whether to cast the saddlebag in after all.

Vesper signaled: *Put the treasures down, please.*

With a shrug, the orphan dropped the saddlebag behind him on the other side of a pile of rocks.

Thank you, Vesper gesticulated. *I have questions, and you appear to need some funds. I'll pay you for answers.*

The boy grimaced. *No answers until you give my mother back.*

Vesper raised his brows. He'd been wrong, assuming the boy didn't have a family. "Your . . . mother," he spoke aloud, forgetting to use his hands.

The lad positioned his thumbs at his temples, like horns.

"The witch?" Vesper asked. "Is she the one who taught you the ancient language?" It made sense. As an immortal, she'd been alive from the time of the drasilisks.

The boy moved his hands and fingers so fast, Vesper had to concentrate to read the words: *No answers . . . no bargain . . . no trade until you bring my family back. Safely. Then I will give you your treasures and let you leave. I want your word, Prince.*

"So, you know I'm royalty," Vesper answered, hoping the lad wouldn't notice him inching closer.

Which means nothing. You're no better than the ilk that tossed me out of the castle like rubbish.

Vesper stopped in his tracks. "Which castle would this be?"

The boy's mouth gaped slightly, those unique eyes widening. He'd disclosed more than he'd intended.

"Eldoria's palace," Vesper reasoned aloud. Hedging forward again, he kept his gaze locked to the stripling's. "I know you didn't come from mine. I would never forget someone with your pluck and talents—nor would I forget such a face. But you're a contradiction, aren't you? Your eyes . . . they're born of stars and moonlight." Vesper tried to suppress the appeal those epicene features held for him. "Why were you tossed out of the castle? Were you spying on the princess?"

The boy's long lashes quivered—like the downy barbs of feathers on the wind. Vesper's fingers itched to touch them, to see if they were as soft as they appeared. He had closed enough space that he wasn't more than an arm's length away. All he needed to do was reach out. He bit back an oath, resolved not to lose himself to the oddly tender compulsion.

The thief stepped backward until his heel scraped against the rock pile. *I . . . don't know.*

"You don't know," Vesper repeated, picking up the hanging threads of their conversation. "For which question is that the answer?"

The boy gulped a breath and his fingers clenched the pouch at his shoulder. He dropped his hand to respond. *Both. I remember nothing before waking in this ravine. Nothing of my life, or what I was doing. Only that Crony took me in.*

Vesper wrestled a wave of sympathy. "So, in the time you've known the witch, has she shared her plans for the 'princess revolution'? Do you know of her conspirings against the castle? Tell the truth, and perhaps I can help her."

The boy's face changed, the grit and resolve softening to a sincere frown. *She's not just a witch. She has a name. Crony. She's my family. And she's never once mentioned your precious princess in the five years I've known her.*

"Five years." Vesper mouthed the words. That was around the time he swallowed the sunlight . . . around the time he lost some crucial part of himself. This couldn't be by chance.

The marshy bog gurgled again and a shimmer from the movement reflected on the thief's face, reminding Vesper of their dangerous surroundings. Determined to resolve this discussion at camp, the prince leapt forward.

His captive lurched backward and stumbled across the pile of rocks. Vesper lunged to catch him before he busted his head. The stripling reached back for Vesper's left arm and found balance atop the rock pile, making them the same height. His pouch slipped off and the jars crackled as they broke upon the rocks.

Neither the prince nor his captive reacted, too intent on what was taking place at their point of contact. As the boy gripped Vesper's metallic forearm, the shell of infected flesh began to soften. Vesper's coppery skin showed through—an imprint of the boy's warm grasp.

Warm. Vesper couldn't remember how long it had been since he'd had any feeling in that part of his arm.

Their gazes met, and in those lilac eyes, Vesper saw moments he'd never lived, yet somehow knew existed, for they had altered him profoundly: the flash of dusk igniting that gaze to amber . . . eating apples from the palm of that small, grimy hand . . . an unconventional dance beneath a leafy sky.

Then, he saw a shock of fire, thorns, and pain.

The boy winced, stretching his mouth in a soundless scream. His fingertips lit up with golden light—an effulgence that matched Vesper's sunlit blood. It spread along the thief's arm and flashed through his entire body—a surge so dazzling it rendered Vesper blind for an instant. His breath hitched and he pulled back.

When the prince's vision returned, the boy appeared ill. He stepped off the rocks and sat. The glow in his body withdrew, converging in his hands. His drab complexion paled to an even sicklier hue as he dug his fingers into the slimy ground.

Flowers sprung up from the mud—blooms of crimson, bright pink, blue, and orange appearing around the boy's torn fingers. Like a beautiful contagion, more blossoms followed, spanning the sodden distance between him and Vesper. Varicolored petals opened around the prince's boots before continuing through the thicket, climbing the twigs that formed the domed roof, and overpowering the stench of the bog with a heady perfume. Vesper's mind spun. He stood beneath a vivid, ambrosial rainbow, in a softly glowing world that had once been colorless and stagnant. It was as if he'd fallen through the earth and landed within Neverdark, back in his childhood when the arboretum still brought him wonder and awe.

Speechless, Vesper studied his metallic arm where it retained the imprint of that small hand. It was as if the boy had cured a part of him by absorbing his sunlight and sending it into the ground. Their eyes met once more, but before Vesper could say a word, a huge crash broke through the bramble wall closest to him.

The Pegasus barreled in and looked from Vesper to the boy—now slumped over bent knees, panting. Armed with nothing but his knife, Vesper spun to face the beast. The Pegasus reared up, eyes, mane, and tail ablaze, hooves aimed for Vesper's head.

Vesper ducked left. He slipped in the mud, squashing flowers as he fell, and landed inches from the bog. The hum of his blood became a voltaic buzz, pulling toward the beast as if magnetized. Vesper fought it, trying to put distance between them. Still clutching the knife, he bent one knee and pushed up, but the snap of a bracken caught his arm. With a jerk, the vicious fern dragged him off the banks and into the deep. His liquid surroundings undulated between luminous and murky. He kicked out his good leg so he could surface. He choked on the taste of decay then capsized as the Pegasus plunged in beside him, fully submerging them both.

Vesper opened his eyes in the silver-blue depths. Smoldering feathers, hooves, and flame surrounded him. His legs tangled with the stallion's, his hair enmeshed with the barbs of the opened wing. Vesper took his knife and aimed for the beast's heart. The instant the blade found its home with a meaty thrust, a lancing agony ruptured within Vesper's own chest. Air escaped in a gush of bubbles. A brilliant light detonated with a loud blast in his head, as piercing and agonizing as cannon fire. His skull seemed to shatter on the implosion. He surfaced for an instant, sipping another breath, but was dragged under again.

Vesper fought the Pegasus's sinking body, its tail having wrapped around his neck. Everything around them blurred. Amidst that suffocating myopia, the past collided with the present. In his mind, Vesper returned to the ice cavern under the sorceress's spell, his body broiling with sunlight. In that moment of destruction and creation, when Madame Dyadia rent him in half and trapped his pain, rebellion, and pride inside a new vessel, he'd struggled to put a name to it. Now he could see it clearly: four legs, hooves, and a body of shadow with wings of flame. A Pegasus.

Vesper tugged at the snare constricting his windpipe, trying to stay focused. Those sweat-drenched dreams over the past five years had been his only ties to his missing piece: the taste of steam, the scent of burned wood, the running, running, running alongside a trusted friend—a girl who masqueraded as a boy—here in the Ashen Ravine.

The epiphany slammed into him. With wildness born anew in his heart, he stared, unflinching, at the truth. There was no dying Pegasus dragging him down. There was only Vesper himself, whole again, alone in the depths with a bracken around his neck—holding him captive beneath the sludge. His lungs begged for breath. He wrestled the binds, wanting only to get back to her . . . to *Stain*. His playmate, his confidante, his tiny trifling thing.

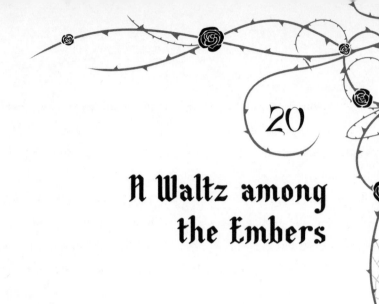

20

A Waltz among the Embers

Slumped on the rocks, Stain watched orange and red bubbles rise from the moon-bog and burst in midair. In the wake of Scorch's plunge, a churning, chaotic and violent as a monster's heartbeat, rendered everything beneath the surface imperceptible.

She didn't have to see to know that the prince and the Pegasus were fighting, fully submerged. The fools would drown if she didn't stop them.

She attempted to stand, but her surroundings spun. She fell back onto the rocks and clenched her fuzzy scalp with aching hands. Sowing a thicketful of flowers had left her more depleted and agonized than she anticipated. How had she done it? Never before had her sun-power covered such a distance, and so swiftly. Then rationale prevailed, and she *knew*: it happened because she touched Prince Vesper's arm; his curse infected her, rushing sunlight through her entire body. She'd had no choice but to channel it somewhere, the ground and brambles her only options.

She would've pulled free of him sooner, before the sun's intrusion, but she saw something in those penetrating eyes: a glimpse of those times she'd felt most alive—most like herself. When she'd waltzed in the embers, when she'd fed Scorch a handful of apples, that first glimpse of identity through his eyes. She would've embraced any agony to be there again, to remember. But those were moments made with Scorch—so how had the prince revived them?

The bubbles expanded in the bog's depths and sloshed a glowing wave against the banks. A tangle of thick, dark hair surfaced, then jerked beneath again. Scorch's tail or the prince's head . . . she couldn't be sure with the pain blurring her vision. The gnawing, burning throbs that often pooled in her fingertips ran all the way to her elbows and shoulders. Even her bones felt hot, aching through to the marrow.

She curled her chest over her knees, fighting a bout of nausea.

Scorch was going to kill the prophecy. The Pegasus had rushed upon the scene. He took one look at her and deduced she'd been hurt at the prince's hand. As always, he'd assumed the worst and attacked.

In her state, she had been too weak to stop him. What would she have said, anyway? That when she'd touched the prince, every moment that followed had spun out of control? That at the same time, the event seemed orderly, as if it had been laid out, brick by brick—a bridge between two paths that never should've crossed?

Never *could've* crossed.

Yet they had.

Magic was at work in the prince's destiny, but why would it involve her? She was no one. Unless . . . unless she was more than she'd dreamed, as the mother shroud had said. There must be some explanation for the parallels she'd seen between her and this man—for the way their skin-to-skin contact had been so all-encompassing it bordered on combustible.

Clearing her head with a breath of charred decay and flowers, she shoved her sore palms against her knees and stood shakily. This wasn't the time for introspection. She had to save the prince from Scorch's bestial temper, for it was her doing that brought them both here together.

Dragging through the sludge's suction, she struggled for balance on her way toward the bank. At the edge, she gripped a bramble vine between its thorns. She bit back the bile rising in her throat, wanting to avoid another wound, another scar. She'd suffered enough pain today—emotionally and physically. Yet that hadn't stopped her in the past, and it couldn't stop her now. She prepared to tie the thorny rope around her waist as she had all those years ago, so she could dive in.

A chorus of sound from behind gave her pause. She looked over her shoulder. An invasion of chirping black crickets hopped out from the rocks. She'd forgotten about the jars breaking when she'd dropped them. A whirl-wind of shadows followed the bugs—having no reason to hide in this dim, barbed thicket.

She barely had time to react as they surrounded her and forced her to drop the brambly vine and retreat from the banks. The shadows nudged with gusts of chilled air and the crickets rubbed their legs, composing a song so high-pitched she had to step back to save her ears.

She wasn't afraid; not for herself. The shrouds had said such creatures were once her protectors. Even with their presence so new to her, she sensed they were trying to keep her safe.

What they didn't realize was that by shielding her, they were endangering their night prince. Her chest tightened on the thought, bewildered as to why she cared. It was Scorch who was her dearest friend. So why was she driven to save both of them with the same desperate need? She wanted to believe her desire to help the prince centered around Crony's welfare, but there was more. She'd heard him pour his heart out to his sister—witnessed his humanity and vulnerabilities. He was a good man.

Let me through . . . she pleaded, craning her neck to see around her creep-ing, boisterous protectors. *They'll kill each other.*

Their barricade didn't relent. They had pushed her several foot-lengths from the bank when a muffled roar bulged the bog's surface; a swell of fire and water thrusted her back and thudded her head against the ground. Everything went dark.

The sound of rhythmic chirrups roused her. She groaned, unsure how long she'd lain there. A headache pounded the back of her skull. Her eyes struggled to open, but bog sludge had tangled her lashes—making the effort near impossible.

Yet she *needed* to look. Something was lying beside her, large, warm, and breathing. Long, silky hair tickled her cheek and the featherlight movements along her scalp felt like a horse's muzzle. With a start, she realized it was crickets crawling across her head. She launched to a sitting position and spit on her hands, rubbing her eyes until her lashes came free.

She blinked. Her surroundings resolved to clarity. The prince was sprawled out, unmoving on the ground beside her. Drag marks pocked the mud, as if he'd been thrown from the bog and crawled over to her before collapsing. The shadows bowed in a circle around him.

Stain swished them away and they drifted toward the crickets, expanding their radius yet refusing to leave—forming a ring around both her and the prince.

She leaned in for a closer look, transfixed. Wet locks of plum-black hair covered his face, so thick only a glimpse of closed eyelids could be seen where his spiky lashes broke through. His sopping shirt, torn and singed to rags, revealed a trail of dark hair that started between his collarbones and faded to flaxen threads upon another metallic carapace. This one glimmered across his abdomen in the bog's glow. Like his forearm, it was as if a layer of gilt had been painted across ripples of muscle, transforming him, bit by bit, to a statue. His finely cut chest, shoulders, arms, and face appeared even darker when juxtaposed against the sporadic plates of bright gold and hundreds of white, raised scars—ossified reminders of the pain he'd endured throughout his young life.

His chest rose and fell, the rhythmic cadence of his heartbeat kicking beneath his sternum. Stain had seen other men's torsos bared, but none of them so close to her age. None shared this man's unique imperfections either, or suffered his debilitating curse.

Curiosity overcame caution, and she lowered her hand, her fingers skimming that path of coarse hair along his chest, careful not to make contact with his flesh for fear of the effect it might have on her own. She paused atop his shining abdomen, where the hair yielded to stiff flaxen strands. These clutched at her fingertips like thistles. Radiant light seeped up each strand and into her fingers. Stinging pinpricks spread all the way into her knuckles. There on his forearm, her imprint still remained. She considered trying to help him . . . wondered if the resulting agony would be worth it. What would happen if she attempted to draw all the sunlight from his body and grow a thousand flowers in this ravine? Would it kill her?

Scorch would insist she not even try, that royalty wasn't worth it. Perhaps he was right. This man had endangered Crony, and possibly Luce—intentional or not.

The prince's eyelashes twitched, as if he could sense her mental debate and the brazen inquiry of his body.

She jerked her hand back, her face warming.

Scorch . . .

His name had niggled on an afterthought, but now it punctured like a knife, leaving her exposed to the quiet stillness.

Stain leapt to her feet and looked across the shadow guards, seeing nothing more than brambles. The flowers had either all been burned away by the explosion or were aglow with embers that would soon snuff out.

The prince was here, so where was the Pegasus? Her stomach tightened anxiously. Taking a step, she dislodged something beside the prince's limp hand and crouched to pick it up. His dagger, or what was left of it. The handle gave way to a stubby shank, melted by voltaic blood.

Scorch's blood.

That blade-sharp awareness hacked at her heart, robbing her of breath. Stain scrabbled toward the marshy banks. The shadows tightened their barricade, but she fought against the gusts—leaning into them in an effort to break free.

Fingers cinched around her boot from behind. Even through the leather, they were fire-hot and strong. She nearly tripped adjusting her stance. She glared over her shoulder as the prince groaned and rolled closer.

"Wait," he murmured so low she struggled to hear.

Growling, she kicked at him while screaming with her hands. *You stabbed him and left him to drown!* She lunged toward the swampy pit.

He sat up with some effort, hand gripping her torn pant leg to secure a tighter hold. "No." The word came out in a rumbling moan, as if he was trying to remember how to talk. An odd glow lit his dark eyes, almost like a spark. "There'll be no wrapping yourself in brambles to swim those depths again."

Stain cocked her head. How did he know she planned to do that? That she'd ever done it? The huskiness of his command reminded her of Scorch's voice, making her more desperate. *I have to go after him!* her fingers shouted.

"Absolutely not. Once in a lifetime is enough." His words came stronger now, gathering momentum. "Twice could kill you. I know of what I speak." He winced and grabbed his chest with his free hand.

Twice could kill you? What was he talking about? She didn't care. She had admired his strong heartbeat only minutes earlier. Now, she wanted to rip out the source of his life's blood. *You know nothing!* she signed.

"I know you won't find him." He let her go and stood, towering over her as he took deep, measured breaths. She was trapped—between him and the shadows there was no clear path to the bog. His muscles spasmed beneath his shredded shirt as his hands fisted and released; he seemed preoccupied with the movements, lifting his arms and studying his fingers in the soft light. The shreds of his shirt flapped open, and a golden flutter crept along his sternum like veins of gilt. He turned away before she could make sense of it. His back faced her as he observed the drag marks from his body leading out from the muck.

The shadows no longer obstructed the view of the bog's surface. They hovered around her and the prince, as if unsure who to defend or who to block. The crickets took up chirping again, their song even more riotous and chaotic than before.

Stain shoved the prince to get his attention. He turned—those sculpted cheekbones scrunched somewhere between bewilderment and disbelief.

I would sense if he was gone. Her hands yelled at him, though her eyes prickled. She cursed the tears that refused to break free. *My heart would know. Now move!* She jabbed a shoulder into his chest. The golden plate at his abdomen thrummed aloud, but he didn't waver; he seemed stronger now than when she'd bettered him earlier today, which was contradictory to the way he kept wincing as though hurting.

"I didn't say . . . he was gone." His features settled to pained resolve.

She darted around him, determined to dredge the depths of the bog however long it took. To bring Scorch back.

Vesper caught her around the waist and spun her. He dropped to the ground, dragging her with him. She landed on her knees beside him, their faces level.

"Do you know what I am?" he asked—breathless, as if unsure himself.

I know what you're not. A noble prince. Her hands accused, stirred to a frenzy by worry over her loved ones and the danger he'd put them in.

"I'm a man," he said, again preoccupied with his hands and arms.

You're a murderer. And you should be the one drowning! She lashed out with her fists.

As if anticipating her reaction, he caught a wrist in each hand, keeping her shirt cuffs between his flesh and hers. The flickering intensity returned behind his eyes as he squeezed his fingers, testing their strength.

"Do you feel that?" he whispered. "I'm touching you."

Stain's throat dried, for there was no question what she felt. A feverish heat burned through the cloth on contact, different than the intrusion of his golden plague. A heat that made the rest of her cold and desolate; every nerve beneath her skin became a field of dormant seeds, aching for a sip of that warmth so they could bloom to life.

Bewildered by her body's reactions, she shoved against him, hard. He retained his hold on her while trying to stay balanced, but the momentum of her push landed him on his back and dragged her across him. She pounded his chest, rage rising for all he'd done to her loved ones. He pinned her wrists where his shirt bunched in wrinkles between them, as if to stop the onslaught. Her breath caught at the smoldering sensation of their skin almost touching, at soft curves yielding to hard angles and planes.

He lifted his head, his mouth at her ear. "Show me how fierce you are, tiny trifling thing," he mumbled, low and raspy. "I predict, this time, you can convince me to let you win."

She stilled. Every muscle—held coiled and ready to spring—went supple beneath those lips hovering along her lobe, beneath those intimate words he had no business knowing, beneath a scent that couldn't belong to any man: feathers, singed grass, and sweet clover.

She propped on her elbows to study his face. He studied her features in turn, enthralled—an arrested expression, as if he were the one floating atop waves of incredulity. Then he smiled in wonder, a stunning flash of white teeth amidst the blur of stubble darkening his jaw.

What did you call me? Perched on her elbows, she couldn't sign. So she asked the question with her thoughts, never expecting an answer.

Tiny trifling thing. The answer tapped her mind, though the prince's lips didn't move.

She strained to look over her shoulder. *Scorch!* He had to be here. It was his voice reaching out. But from where?

The prince squeezed her wrists. *I'm here beneath you, Stain.*

Her attention snapped back to the prince. He didn't know her name. She'd tried to tell him earlier, but he'd misunderstood . . .

It's me. Look as an animal would, with your heart and not your eyes.

She scrambled to sit up, resisting the urge to run her fingers through that tangle of dark hair spread out behind his head like a horse's mane, to test if she knew its texture. Those thick, wavy strands seemed out of place, framing a human face both strange yet familiar. It was as if she'd seen him every day without realizing, in the elegant curves of Scorch's silhouette trotting through the tree trunks, in the imprint on her vision when lightning flashed through broken leaves and she closed her eyes to retain Scorch's winged profile of shadow and cinders on the back of her lids.

The prince reached up to sweep his knuckles across the shorn hair at her temple, still avoiding her bared skin, as though worried he'd infect her again with sunlight. *I know you by your voice . . . just as she said I would.*

Stain tilted her head out of his reach. *She, who?*

His hand still hung midair. He seemed reluctant to drop it, so it stayed there, waiting for another touch. *Do you realize how long it's been? Since I've been able to speak from one mind to another? Five years. Yet it wasn't, was it? For the part of me I thought I'd lost was here all along, with you, having silent conversations. Arguments . . . debates. Sharing secrets, adventures, and laughter.*

No, only Scorch talks to me like this. It's only been Scorch! She slapped his hand aside and backed up more, grasping at any logical threads to weave into an explanation. Had he absorbed the Pegasus's memories somehow when they fought in the bog? Did the moonglow beneath the murk have something to do with these inconceivable circumstances?

The prince sat up and cupped her knee, not allowing her to escape. "I *am* Scorch." Sincerity tugged at his regal features—his dark brows heavy with that same weighted somberness he'd used when discussing his role in the prophecy with his sister. He believed what he said was true.

No. It's impossible . . .

His exasperated huff reminded her of the Pegasus—of all the times she'd act "too human" and he'd snort in frustration. "If it's impossible, then how do I know that your nose wrinkles just like that each time you concentrate?"

She patted the bridge of her nose, feeling the crinkled skin for herself.

"And how do I know that when you look within Crony's enchanted mirror, you see your true self. A *girl* . . . with long, silken hair and no scars."

Her jaw dropped.

He paused, frowning. His fingers brushed at the rags of his shirt, as if he felt something crawling there. He bit back a growl. "How do I know that you long for sweet words and sincere emotions, and that you weep without tears each time it rains outside because you're unable to escape this prison and run through the open skies?" A cough interrupted his extraordinary observations. He cringed, but continued. "How do I know you saved my life in this very bog when you were already bleeding and broken? That in your darkest moment, when you'd lost yourself, you found me."

Her eyes swelled, burdensome and scratchy, filled with cruel sand. She picked up the melted knife and offered the only explanation she had. *You killed him, trying to defend yourself.* The admission sliced into her bones. A body-wrenching sob tore from her chest. *You absorbed his spirit. The bog must be enchanted.*

The prince's brow furrowed in sympathy. "I didn't kill him. I conquered him." His newfound strength seemed to be waning; he suddenly looked tired. "I *am* him . . . your beastly brawn that you waltzed with in the embers, that you fed from your hand. I've been him all along. Or he's been me. I can explain—"

A dog's bark at the thicket's opening interrupted.

"Prince Vesper! Majesty!" Several concerned voices called, followed by the nicker of horses. Stain choked on a startled breath as the cocker spaniel bounded in. Twigs snapped beneath the dog's paws on its journey through the brambles.

Knowing the prince's entourage would be close behind, Stain dropped the knife and clambered to her feet.

The prince tried to stop her but fell to his knees and gripped his chest. "Wait . . ." he groaned.

She wanted to wait, but all her bravery, all her fierceness, was sunken with Scorch's corpse in the bottom of the bog.

We'll sort this out. The prince used Scorch's inner voice again, tearing through her mind like a stampede of hooves, leaving ragged imprints on her heart. *Stay with me . . . please.*

Too many thoughts surged inside her. One rose above the fray, but instead of buoying her, it dragged her down.

Her dearest friend was gone, his essence somehow locked within a beautiful prince who belonged to two kingdoms, a princess, and a prophecy she had no place in. She couldn't stay . . . couldn't belong with him now. All that was left was to get her family back—someone with whom to stand, someone with whom to hold hands as the sun and moon came together when the prince married his songbird bride and tore Stain's heart in twain.

She held his gaze, seeing Scorch look back from those anguished, fire-lit eyes. It was too much. Her crickets and shadows had retreated already, taking shelter in the saddlebag free of broken glass—hidden safely alongside the princess's priceless gifts. Spinning, Stain grabbed the strap before making her escape, desperate to keep and protect the only companions still within her reach.

The prince's fading pleas pounded both her mind and ears, but she didn't turn back. Instead, she took a hidden pathway. She retraced the trampled vines left by a Pegasus five years earlier as he thrashed his way out of these brambles, victorious in his freedom—a freedom won at the scarred hands of a nameless little child no bigger than a speck of dust. Which was exactly how small and inadequate she felt right now as each painful step carried her farther into the empty unknown.

Part III

*In Which the Rose
Becomes the Thorn*

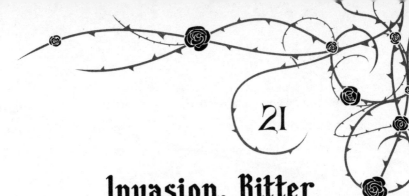

21

Invasion, Bitter and Entrancing

The trees, black as pitch and stooped like withered old giants, waited to greet Stain when she plunged out of the bramble thicket. She was careful not to be seen by the prince's entourage as she traded muck for ash. A masculine wail ruptured the stillness, punctured her eardrums and heart with the precision of a lance, and stopped her in her tracks.

It was Scorch . . . no, *Vesper*. Somehow, the two were entwined and unreachable to her. Another agonized wail resounded, and the prince's plea pounded through her: *Stay with me . . . please.* Her hands clutched a tree limb, forcing her legs to stand still when all they wanted was to run to him and help.

When another cry rung out, she put one foot forward but stalled as a banshee's screech overrode the echo. Up above, the monstrous one-eyed crow skimmed along the canopy like a ghostly vision. Stain ducked behind the trunk. She clutched the saddlebag, convinced the bird was seeking her for her thievery. Once it descended and disappeared into the other side of the brambles, she relaxed, relieved more for Vesper than herself. His already cursed body seemed to be reacting to Scorch's invasion. The odd, enchanted crow could help him in ways Stain never could. Soon he would be riding beside his entourage—with Scorch nestled quietly in his mind—to meet his princess. He would leave all the horrors of the ravine behind and embrace the extraordinary destiny for which he was born.

Stain swallowed against that growingly familiar taste on her tongue . . . the vinegary brine of envy. It burned now, more acidic, thinking of how so much that once belonged to her was being claimed by Eldoria's castle.

She stood wearily and made her way through the trees. Though she'd seen this view for as much as she could remember of her life, it looked foreign now. The thick, leafy canopies seemed to curl inward as if to chew her up.

It made her dizzy to look at them, so she dropped her gaze. She wandered in a fugue, her mind as hazy as the powdery terrain she stirred with each plodding footstep.

Despite the ash's stench of decay, her stomach cramped, hunger tunneling its claws deeper, another hollow she needed to fill. She had the skill to forage for food, but was too tired.

The desolation of her walk confirmed the cessation course had begun. Everyone was sleeping. The forest was quiet—spreading its contagion of restfulness.

Stain's pace slowed. Luce haunted her thoughts. He and Crony had a code, and Stain hoped he'd kept to it, that he'd escaped when their precious companion was taken and was planning a way to save her.

Stain didn't expect that he'd wait for her help; he'd probably already left. With her frailties, she couldn't make the trek to the castle under full exposure of the sun. Even wrapped in clothes, and even with it cloudy outside, her flesh would blister and broil as if she stood naked in a fire pit. She knew from experience that the balm protectant Crony made only worked on faint, muted light filtering through small holes in the canopy.

If there was any way to get to the castle on her own, she'd take it.

Lifting the saddlebag higher on her shoulder stirred ripples of movement inside. The night creatures ... Dregs had said something about the shadows while she was at his booth ... that they had been meant for the princess, for attire of some sort. But how could clothing be made of shadows, and to what end? In honor of the night prince? Stain knew so little about Eldoria and its history, she couldn't begin to guess.

The princess went into hiding years ago, shortly after the king's death, when several inhabitants of the castle were murdered by an evil enchantment—though no victims were given names here. The threat to the princess's life was so egregious that she withdrew into the dungeon. Then an infestation of barbed honeysuckle vines, meant to protect the palace, had spread into all the nooks and crannies of the kingdom. It was rumored that shadows might have the ability to shrink the gargantuan honeysuckle plants. That was why bringing the moon back meant so much to Eldoria.

Stain's eyelashes grew heavy as if carved of iron. Her lids drooped and her steps slowed. Her bones felt like iron, too, so heavy it hurt to lift them.

She barely noticed the stench of the burbling quag-puddle skidding her way. Its progress split a path through the ash, sending the powder flying on either side. The sentient spume caught her before she could leap out of its way. Her foot began to sink. Gritting her teeth, she wiggled out of the boot just in time to watch it being swallowed. Before the puddle could capture her bare foot, she hopped to the right and squeezed into a ring of closely woven trees. Their overgrown roots formed a nest that no puddle could penetrate. Spewing out a grumbling belch of bubbles, the quag left the way it came. Letting the saddlebag slide, Stain curled up, heart thudding from the close call. She rested her cheek against the leather. Everywhere else, knotted roots jabbed at tender, bruised flesh.

Loneliness crept into her sleep, fashioning dreams as empty as her stomach. She wasn't sure how long she'd dozed when something wet shoved against her nape and snuffled, jolting her awake. She turned to find the fox beside her—wearing a snarl that looked suspiciously like a scowl.

She mimed the words: *Are you a dream?*

His pointed ears lay back and he sneezed a layer of dust from his nostrils. The spray spattered her forehead, assuring her he was real.

"Do you have any idea how long I've been digging through this cesspool of slag for you?" Luce's silken baritone snapped out of his whiskered muzzle like a whip. "Dregs and Edith said they spotted you out frolicking with Scorch. Crony is in danger, yet you've been off with your donkey, wasting precious time."

Stain threw her arms around the fox's neck and buried her face in his fur, wanting to drown in his mix of animal dander, man, and flight. *I'm sorry, Luce. I love you. I'm so glad you're alive!* She couldn't risk losing her hold on him to sign the words, and there'd be no hearing her otherwise.

Only Scorch could . . . only Vesper would . . .

Her eyes squeezed shut against a fresh swell of loss. She held on to Luce for dear life—longer than she'd ever hugged him, and tighter than she'd ever dared. Hunger, exhaustion, and emotion shook her body from the inside out.

Luce's canine spine twitched. His tail brushed her leg and red glitter and silver smoke spun around them both. She hugged him throughout the transformation: as his long muzzle shifted to masculine features—sharp cheekbones, nose with a shrewd, pointed tip, and a stern yet pretty mouth; as shoulders, slender and solid, came into being to cradle her temple.

When she finally opened her eyes, they were both on their knees and his arms held her—a warm, comforting wreath of human flesh and bone. Together, the two of them filled the nest of roots. She snuggled into the shirt that was just moments ago a white strip of fur between two forelegs. His talisman of braided hair, the one that matched hers, pressed into her cheek. A reminder of Crony. A reminder of family and safety.

"There, now . . ." Luce's voice held a note of bewilderment. He stroked her scalp, bestowing a tenderness he rarely showed. "We hurt you, but that was never our aim. The secrets we kept were meant to help. One day soon you'll understand."

She gave no answer, but her body settled into a melting numbness. Once she stopped quaking, he stretched her to arm's length.

"Let's have a look." He gently examined her, studying the new burns, scrapes, and punctures. He winced, his orange eyes glimmering bright. Glancing at her clothes, he flicked a glare to her face. "You've no business being out in the ravine in such a state."

Stain assumed he referred to her lost boot and looked down. Her vest was almost completely burned away. Underneath, her damp white shirt—threadbare to near transparency—hugged her skin. Humble as her attributes were, her femininity was unmistakable. The rips in her clothing must've been a result of the explosion in the bog. Too much was going through her mind when she roused to even consider her appearance. She'd been preoccupied with finding Scorch and distracted by the prince: touching him as he slept . . . arguing with him when he woke . . . laying across his chest with nothing but threads separating their flesh.

Gasping, she folded her arms over her shirt.

The points of Luce's teeth broke through his downturned lips. He peeled off his jacket and draped it over her shoulders. "Did anyone see you, other than your Pegasus?"

Stain didn't know how to answer that.

"Dammit. Tell me. Does anyone know you're a girl?"

The ravager, she signed, moving only her fingers and keeping her arms in place. *The prince,* she corrected.

"Wait, you know he's a prince? And he realized you're a girl?" Luce's fox ears perked forward; he almost seemed thrilled at the prospect.

Stain nodded, confused by his reaction. *But he would've known anyway. Even if he hadn't shredded them . . .*

Luce's cheeks burnished as red as his hair. "The prince did that?" He gestured to her ragged clothes hidden beneath his jacket.

Stain nodded, but before she could explain the explosion, Luce interrupted.

"The prince *ravished* you?" There was nothing silken about the sylph's voice now. It was the sound of a storm: thunder, hail, and cracking gales. "I will maim him. And then I will kill him."

Stain shook her head and stirred her hands to action. *No. He's noble . . . important. He's the prince of the prophecy.*

"I'm well aware. That's why I intend to maim him first. Then once he's served his purpose, I'll kill him. Nobility is just as vulnerable as any other human. I've experience in the matter."

She meant to ask for details—if he referred to the Eldorian princess the shrouds had mentioned—but he was already on his feet. Fed by his anger, his otherworldly incandescence bathed the roots and tree trunks in celestial light.

You're misunderstanding. Stain attempted to reason with him. *The prince didn't mean to do this. It was an accident. Scorch . . .* She stopped then, her shoulders slumped. There was no reasonable way to finish that explanation.

Luce snapped his fingers. "I knew it! I told Crony that flying donkey would be the undoing of everything. He fought with the prince again, and you had to break them up. I hope His Highness got another good stab in. It's time that jackass learns some manners."

Stain scrambled to standing. *Never speak another word against Scorch. There will be no more.* She forgot her modesty and dropped his jacket, freeing arms, hands, and fingers to unleash an erratic stream of words. *No more influence from his lack of manners. No more distracting me from my work. No more frolicking with him through the ravine when I should be tending flowers. We'll never be together again!* She sobbed—an airy scruff that scraped her windpipe. *Scorch is gone. He and the prince . . . they're . . . everything is gone. Are you happy?*

Luce dropped to his knees, squeezing her shoulders. His sudden change in mood disturbed her as much as the admission itself. "The prince *died*? No, no, no. That can't be. Did they kill each other? Stain, what happened out there?"

She tried to explain, her fingers taking Luce where her mind feared to tread. *I don't know . . . it's hard to . . .* She fisted her hands, then made another attempt. *He's not dead. Neither of them is dead. They're just . . . together.*

"Together?"

Their spiritual coalescence was still too raw and confusing to put into words. Besides, to dwell on the loss would only get in the way of what needed to be done.

We're wasting time. Isn't that what you said? I know about Crony . . . she's being taken to Eldoria's dungeon. Recalling the questions the prince asked her, Stain sought her own answers. *Is she guilty of conspiring against the princess? Does she harbor ill will for her?*

Luce blinked, as though to extricate himself from the dangling threads of their abandoned conversation about Scorch. "Ill will is the furthest from what Crony feels. And the only thing she's ever conspired to do is what's right." He frowned, as though remembering their companion was a thief who'd stolen more than just memories from the dying. "Well, at least where it concerns the princess."

Then you have to get to the castle and plead her case. The prince means to see her have a fair trial.

"Best intentions aside, there hasn't been a fair trial in Eldoria since that bloodthirsty regent—" Luce curled his nose, like a dog scenting something foul. His gaze dropped, as if he couldn't look her in the face. "Since the king's death. I'll be breaking Crony out of the dungeon before any trial."

So, you have a plan?

"Yes." He stood again. "Along the Crystal Lake's banks, there's a way to avoid the honeysuckle plague. It leads directly into the dungeon via a secret tunnel—a shortcut. I know where the door is hidden, and I've a key to unlock it."

It was more than Luce's height making her feel small now. It was her inability to leave this wasteland. *Can I do something from here? I want to help. I would give anything to accompany you . . .*

"If you want to come, then you will. Crony's depending on it, in fact." He gnawed at his lip, obviously rethinking. "She'll want to see you, I mean to say. You don't realize how important you are to her . . . how much happiness you've brought into her life. With the flowers; with your smiles; with those eyes that seek good and beauty in everything, and that brave heart that wishes to help others see the same. You are her family. She needs you."

Stain stared, overwhelmed by the unexpected praise. He held her gaze for a beat before looking away. She sensed the rest of what he couldn't say—that he shared Crony's sentiments himself.

Hands twisted into silent knots, she glanced down. The sweetness of Luce's faith nestled behind her long lashes, warming her eyes. For hours, her head had been telling her that Crony and Luce would never hurt her intentionally; now her entire self believed. In time, they'd explain their lies. The only truth she needed to know today was that they loved and depended on her as much as she did them.

Luce cleared his throat and burrowed his hands in his pockets. "I've a way to transport you through the sunlight safely. Dregs uses boxes lined with nightsky to bring his live shipments here. It'll be a tight fit, but you're young and spindly. He'll even provide the wheeled cart that goes with it."

Stain cringed. She wasn't sure what nightsky was, but what concerned her was being shoved within a coffin again . . . the same way she arrived years ago. Though she couldn't remember that grim journey, the thought suffocated her—made her lungs tight and the puncture marks on her skin pulse as if they were tiny mouths gasping for air.

Forcing her fingers apart, she asked: *When do we leave?*

"After we gather some weapons from home. I suppose I'll piggyback you, considering you're shoeless again. Oh, and I've arranged for an army."

An army? Stain's stomach interrupted with a loud growl, distracting Luce from her question.

"When was the last time you ate something?"

She shook her head, signing again about the army.

Luce lifted the saddlebag at her feet. "Yes, yes. Storming the castle requires reinforcements. They'll meet us at the ravine's entrance. Where'd you get this bag? Is there any food inside?" He dug through the contents, sending shadows and crickets deeper inside. He looked up, gaping. "You got them back."

Stole them back . . . along with a few other items. She wondered how the prince would react once he realized; if he would despise her for stealing from him again. Or, if through Scorch's sentience, he would somehow understand her desperation—for the Pegasus knew her, within and without.

As for Luce, he seemed unconcerned that she'd stolen from Nerezethite royalty. He placed the saddlebag on the ground and withdrew that odd fabric wrapped around the princess's gifts. The brush, hairpin, and ring tumbled free into the bag, inhabiting pockets of darkness alongside the night creatures. Curiosity sharpened the sylph's features upon noting the treasures, but he was otherwise occupied—riveted to what unfolded in his hands: a hooded cape lined with rainbow-colored fish scales and embellished with violet-black feathers, silvery fur, and glistening cobwebby lace. It surged in his grasp, reaching toward Stain. Eyes wide, he released it.

Stain caught a breath as it floated toward her. The feathers, fur, and lace draped her form, arranging itself into a regal cape. Once settled, an ethereal darkness seeped across her like a cloud invading the sun—a cooling, velvet obscurity. Soon she was eclipsed by the hovering haze; it was somehow sentient, anticipating and following her every move. From her scalp to her fingertips and all the way to her half-booted feet, not a glimpse of skin or clothing showed through.

She viewed Luce from behind the screen, mesmerized by how it muted his luminous skin and bright hair while still allowing her to see with clarity. A bitter tang stamped her tongue, as if she'd tasted a similar compromise in the past—relinquishing vivid colors for the freedom to stand in the light.

Luce circled her, observing from head to toe, his expression somewhere between fascination and pride. "Well, well, well. You could not have bagged more suitable plunder. It appears you won't be stuck within a box after all. Today, you take your first step into the sun."

※·I·※

Not far off, in the moon-bog's bramble thicket, there was another who faced the sun, although the prince didn't step within willingly. Agonizing thrashes of fever and gold threatened to sweep him under. The scent of smoke, singed clothing, and blistering skin turned his stomach. He lay there, unmoving, convinced that embers embroidered his bones—and if he dared jostle, his very skeleton would disintegrate to ash.

Each inhalation of air tasted of soot and scalded his lungs. To withstand the torment, he kept his eyes pressed shut and teeth clenched, limiting exchanges to one or two words per smoky breath. He lost his ability to mentally connect again, for it took all his concentration to hold still.

He wanted his sister to know of his miraculous discovery. *I found my equal,* he wished to say. *Her voice lives within that part of my mind I thought I'd lost. The prophecy's wrong. She's not a princess. She's the antithesis of all that's pampered and frail—mighty and scarred as a battle-worn blade; feral and cunning as a wolf; a foundling, a thief, my most loyal friend. She's the only one who can cure me. I need her. Find Stain!* But he was left alone in his mind with the empty, unanswerable echoes, powerless to spend the effort.

His troop knelt beside him, though not too close. The heat emanating from his feverish body singed the brambles beneath him. Only Dyadia's wretched white crow could touch his smoldering flesh with its beak.

"Stain." Vesper sloughed the word off a tongue and lips as dry and cracked as winter bark.

"Why does he keep saying that?" Cyprian asked, weariness weighing down his voice.

Leaning over her brother's right side, Selena gasped. "Oh, moonlit skies . . . no. The plague is infecting his eyelids! If we can see it, he can't look past it. All he sees are glittering stains of gold—" A sob silenced her.

Vesper growled at her misconception. "*Thief.*" It expended such effort to push any sound beyond his stiffening vocal cords, he could merely whisper.

Selena stroked his hair with a gloved hand. "Your welfare is more important than stolen gifts. We'll find the boy and bring him to justice, once you're cured."

"*Her,*" he mumbled. "Find . . . her!"

Cyprian clasped his shoulder with a glove. "We are, Your Majesty. The princess is only a two-day journey from here. We'll get you there. Please, just hold on."

"Her voice." Vesper sipped a breath tainted with smoke and embers. "Inside." Another scalding breath. "My head."

The crow poked and prodded, an uncomfortable intrusion against the chaos roiling beneath Vesper's skin. The bird was checking for any remnants of flesh still malleable. Dread chased that thought as the *ping* of metal greeted his ears from taps gently applied to his chest, his neck, his chin.

"Dyadia, we need you here!" Selena demanded. "Not this callous sack of dusty feathers. Come to us now!"

A flutter gusted beside Vesper's ear, then a woman's croak of pain. Following an icy burst, the sorceress possessed the bird's body. Vesper peered long enough to see Dyadia's cat's eye scouring him, having taken the place of the bird's pink iris. He let his lashes seal again as blinding vines of gilt crept across his vision. The shocked murmurings of his companions, noting the flaxen hairs overtaking his eyebrows, dragged him deeper into despair.

"You found him like this?" Dyadia's question broke through in place of Thana's blood-curdling caw.

Selena tried to answer but a sob caught in her throat.

"Yes." Cyprian took over. "He's been trying to speak, but we have to piece-meal what he says. It makes little sense. Something about the thief and the Pegasus and the bog. Luna tracked signs of a struggle imprinted in the mud. Horse hooves and Vesper's boot prints leading to the edge, then drag marks leading out, made by a man's hands and knees. He's singed from head to foot, yet wet. We think they both fell into the bog, but only Vesper came out. It appears he killed the beast, and the boy attacked him out of anger. There are signs of them rolling on the ground then tracks signifying the thief escaped that way."

The crow tapped Vesper's hardening chest. "There's been a surge of magic here. It thrums through his body. The bird's beak never lies. Our prince, our *king*, is whole again."

"What?" Selena asked, sniffling. "I don't understand."

"Years ago, I cast out part of him to slow the sun's infestation. He defeated it here today . . . reabsorbed it. But too soon. This was meant to happen in the princess's presence, so her moonlight could cleanse his blood. Now the plague is twofold. We've little time before it claims his heart and lungs."

"Stain!" Vesper forced out the wail on a gust of fire-tinged air. The taste of smoke choked him. His windpipe tightened against a cough and locked the pressure within. The muscles in his body began to spasm involuntarily.

"Tybalt, Dolyn!" Cyprian's desperate shouts launched everyone into action. "Help me get the prince onto Lanthe. We ride to Princess Lyra immediately! If we hurry, we'll arrive only a half day behind our companions."

"No," Dyadia said. "His betrothed will have to come to us. Give him the draught I sent. The valerian and passionflower will control his pain. I must convince his mind and body that he's dead. A quietus thrall is the only means to hold off the sun's invasion, but the spell is ancient and temperamental, and must be conjured in a sacred place of life and death. Somewhere familiar to the recipient, in which their spirit can take sanctuary. I'll perform it here at Nerezeth, inside the shrine. Bring him at once. I'll return to my body and await you. Send Thana with a sealed missive for the princess and her regent. Tell them Lady Lyra is required at his side . . . the nuptials must take place the moment they arrive in the night realm."

"We can't go the shorter route . . . the avalanche sealed the Rigamort's entrance," Selena said, her voice heavy with frustration.

"We've no choice but to head for the iron gate," Cyprian agreed. "If we hurry, we can make the five-day trip in three. We move now!"

There was a rustle of feathers and footsteps, then a glass vial touched Vesper's mouth—cool and smooth. A soothing liquid, flavored of fruit and sour wood, trickled down his narrowing throat. Darkness blotted his pain; drowsiness suspended his senses. Relieved, he tried to say thank you, but his lips wouldn't comply. They were petrified.

Vesper realized with horror that it was too late. There would be no marriage, no reconciliation of sun and moon, no saving his people from their illness. His worst nightmare had come true: he was a man of metal and stone.

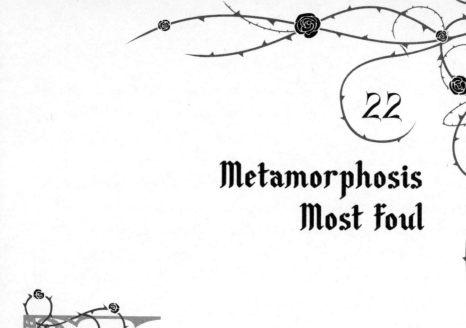

22

Metamorphosis Most Foul

With Eldoria's cessation course underway, heavy drapes had been drawn to block the unrelenting sunlight—more from habit than necessity, as the honeysuckle vines managed to obstruct most windows in the castle at present. The glossy marble halls and corridors mirrored the bluish glow upon Griselda's hands as candles winked from beneath their tinged-glass domes like wily accomplices.

Carrying her gloves as a precaution, she kept her footfalls light upon the floor while making her way to the lower wings. She rearranged the hennin upon her head, warmed by a sense of smugness. She had kept the secret of the witch's arrival for two days. And then fate once again smiled upon her, bringing the prisoner to the castle while everyone slept. No one on the council even knew about their prisoner yet; no one had been apprised of the contents within the jackdaw's sealed missive but Griselda's daughters and her two loyal knights. The ambitious soldiers, stationed at the outer bailey and gate, all hoped to win an honored place within the king and queen's guard once "Lyra" married Prince Vesper. Thus, they had agreed to their regent's command—to hand off the witch to her first knights upon arrival—without question.

After a momentary brush with panic, Griselda had come to realize she couldn't have timed everything better herself. She'd already sent her daughters to bed within the chambers where they'd been staying—free at last of their underground imprisonment. The queen's posh room belonged to Lustacia now, as the entire kingdom did. Avaricette and Wrathalyne had been quick to take advantage of their own inflated status by claiming Sir Nicolette's room as theirs and working every servant to the bone over the past two days redecorating for them.

Two hours ago, when the witch first arrived, the Nerezethite guard named Thea apprised Griselda that Prince Vesper and the rest of his entourage should be close behind.

So, as Sir Bartley and Sir Erwan led the prisoner to the dungeons, Griselda put her soldiers to work with their axes alongside the four heavily dressed Nerezethite escorts, suggesting they use their supply of spiders and moonlit shadows to carve a path through the honeysuckle vines and bees in preparation for the prince's appearance. Griselda's maneuver served a dual purpose: keeping Prince Vesper's subjects preoccupied while she questioned, then silenced the witch; and staunching any chance that the night realm's eight-legged vermin would be brought within her castle walls.

Now alone, Griselda took the spiraling stairs into the bowels of the castle, following the torches Erwan had lit for her. As much as she despised darkness and shadows, she celebrated. This was the final loose thread, then no more traversing the dusty subterranean like a begrimed beetle.

Upon reaching the end of the dungeon's corridors, she pushed the cornerstone to open the hidden underground tunnel. Inside, she pulled a latch. *Clicking* and *clacking*, the entrance rearranged itself into a solid wall, closing the tunnel off.

Gripping her lantern, she plunged even deeper beneath the ground. Sir Erwan bowed upon her arrival as she turned a corner—the torch beside the locked door casting fretful lines across his yellowish-brown complexion. She glanced at the darkness where the tunnel continued to wind out of sight. Somewhere at the end, less than a quarter of a league, it opened to the enchanted outlet that led to the Crystal Lake and the Ashen Ravine beyond.

Nostalgia curled through her; it seemed so long ago that she'd come here with Elusion; but that wasn't the fond memory she embraced. It was the moment she sent her niece's corpse through that tunnel that warmed her. Griselda's one regret was that she didn't dump Lyra's remains within the ravine herself . . . that she didn't get to see the shrouds feast on her ghastly flesh.

She cleared her throat against the suffocating stench of loam and subsoil, her attention on Erwan again. "Has the prisoner spoken?"

"Not a word. Even when I chained her up. The Nerezethite escorts said she was silent on the journey as well. It seems she impressed the prince with her humility and cooperation." Erwan shrugged. "They suspect he might want some say in how we handle her arraignment."

"A shame she's going to attempt escape with a conjuring flame . . . that she'll destroy all the cells beyond recognition before he arrives." Griselda dragged a pouch out of one pocket. She placed the mixture of saltpeter, wood ashes, and tinder-bat dung into Erwan's leather glove. "Use utmost caution. When combined with the vinegar, it will form an incendiary so potent, anything it's been brushed upon becomes flammable. Wood, fabric, plants, dirt, or stone. Whether wet or dry, it will spark." Their ultimate goal was to bury the witch alive in the hidden tunnel while making it appear as if she'd been trapped beneath fallen stone in a collapsed cell. "Once mixed, brush it everywhere in the cells—floor to ceiling—then spread a line to the secret tunnel's entry. It's the only way we'll precipitate a cave-in. Take care not to get any upon the stairs or your feet. Leave a pathway from which we can walk out."

Erwan's brow furrowed to a worrisome scrawl. He was always squeamish about handling potions or elixirs. "You mentioned wanting some for the sylph elm in the garden. How much should I set aside?"

Griselda shook her head. "I made a batch earlier. I've already coated the trunk. It is not to be ignited unless I give the command, and only if he refuses to cooperate." She had warned all the soldiers to watch for a red-haired man too beautiful to be fully human; told them as little as they needed to know, but enough that they would guard their ears against his persuasive voice. Elusion wouldn't dare attempt to enter Eldoria as a fox, for his pelt would be a precious temptation to any self-respecting hunter. She couldn't deny the spark in her blood, knowing upon his arrival they would either resume their past partnership or she'd burn his wings to ash.

"So, I'll retrieve you when I'm ready to torch the dungeon." Erwan began to leave, but Griselda grasped his elbow.

"A torch won't suffice." She showed him two orbs, aglow with swirling turquoise light. "We'll toss these from the stairway. I've altered a recipe, using our accursed honeysuckle petals and liquid sunshine. Only the purest strand of moonlight can extinguish the flames these will birth. No water, sand, or any commonplace means can stop them. The blaze will burn until it's eaten anything and everything combustive around it." She dropped both orbs into her pocket once more.

Erwan's chin tightened. "It could take some time to assure all is well coated. Should Bartley give me a hand?"

"He's overseeing the honeysuckle slashings." She took off her hennin and patted her hillock of twisted braids, searching for the knots beneath. Pressed against the hat's base, their itch had become unbearable. She glared at Erwan's obvious interest in her lumpy hair. "One of you has to watch the gloom-dwellers. Should they get too warm in the sunlight while wearing those mummified costumes, they'll need to come in and rest in the guest wing. Can't have them wandering down here." She smiled. "Of course, should they find their way before the flame is ignited . . . well, that's completely out of our hands, isn't it? The witch has already murdered many of Eldoria's own. Should a Nerezethite be captured in the fray, it will only confirm how dangerous she is. Considering her immortality, keeping her buried will prove wisest for everyone."

Erwan's gray eyes clouded, sure indication he was attempting to think for himself instead of blindly obeying her command. "Then, it would no longer matter what secret memories she holds. Why question her since she'll be silenced? She might refuse to speak, or use sorcery to rattle you. Go to bed, make it appear you've been asleep for hours by the time the cave-in happens. Wash your hands of this, put on your gloves, and call it done." At that, his gaze fell to Griselda's clenched, tinted fists.

Glaring, she tucked her gloves into her empty pocket, keeping her hands bared. "A lazy man's logic, which is why only a woman can do the job. One must not rest until the trophy is won and mounted upon the wall. I need to be sure she hasn't imprinted Sir Nicolet's final memory on someone else. And what have I to fear of a harrower witch's sortilege? She knows nothing of potions or poisons that can alter a life . . . she only deals in the dead and dying. Once she sees the enchanted blood staining my skin, she'll know I've harnessed powers beyond her own. For that, *she* should fear *me*. Without having an ounce of inborn magic in my fingertips, without needing a guide, I've won the thrones of two kingdoms."

Griselda stopped short of admitting the role Elusion's grimoire played. However, she'd be sure to share that detail with the prisoner. The witch should know her loyal fox was responsible for her eternal entombment. It was a knife twist too delicious to resist.

"Get started on the preparations. I'll need you to help me box up and carry out the keepsakes and magical stock before we destroy the entrance to the dirt room. Apprise me when you're done slathering the cells."

"Yes, Your Grace."

Upon hearing his mechanized exit into the dungeon, Griselda opened the door and stepped within, assailed by each and every fragrant panacea rose sent to Lustacia over the years. Other than the moth-eaten gowns covering

Prince Vesper's letters, withering bouquets, and her dead niece's keepsakes, dirt dominated the room's motif—floor, wall, and ceiling.

The prisoner crouched in the middle of the floor, wrists and ankles locked within joint shackles staked deep into the ground. If not for the torchlight gleaming off the iron chains, she'd be practically invisible. From her muddy eyes to her scaly toes, everything about her exuded the same unremarkable brown of dust. With her awkward posture, she favored some oddly horned turtle that might topple at any moment and get stuck on its back.

Griselda smiled and perched her lantern atop a wooden crate. "Here we are again, *witch*. Me, standing over you—chained up and at my mercy like a vagrant mongrel."

The prisoner flitted out her forked tongue. "The name be Crony. And I've no need for mercy. I'll still be standin' when yer naught but a pile o' bones for me to gnaw upon."

Griselda's fingers fisted. "Immortality aside, you're forgetting the interim. I can make this portion of your eternity miserable."

"I forget nothin'. Not me own thoughts, or the thoughts of another. I recognize yer knight's voice. Erwan be his name. I remember his face, just the way he looked through Nicolet's eyes, the instant he hammered his skull with an iron mace."

Griselda shook off the chill that coursed through her blood. "So, you overheard my conversation with my knight. Eavesdropping doesn't speak to your acumen; it speaks to your desperation. The quicker we do this, the quicker I release you back into the wilds."

"We both know ye not lettin' me go this time. And the wee princess not be here to convince ye. Pity. Would like to have seen her now that she be a lady, to thank her and her shadows and bugs, afore ye bury me alive."

Griselda flinched despite herself, remembering how Lyra had bettered her that day in the dungeon cell. How she'd left her in the darkness, alone and frightened. "She's sleeping. And she's long outgrown her sympathies for the likes of you, along with her affinity for playing with shadows and bugs."

"Did she, now? Don't be soundin' like the princess of the prophecy . . . silver-haired, songbird, friend of all things shadowed and dark. Of course, it be barmy, expectin' she'd be just as the foretelling dictates. After all, prophecies find their true, clear way, even if the details get muddied."

The thud in Griselda's chest belied the calm she forced into her features. "Enough blathering. You know the fate that awaits you. But you can do something charitable first. You can win deliverance for your friend Elusion."

Crony's serpentine face sagged, as if taken aback.

"Yes," Griselda taunted. "He's here and I'm holding him prisoner. But, as you seem to be somewhat aware, I've a fondness for him. Should you cooperate, I'll allow him to claim his wings again. I believe that means something to you?"

The witch's head bowed, as if defeated. "Aye, it do."

"So, I'll give you my word. Tell me all the details of Nicolet's final breath, and assure me no one possesses that memory but you, and your friend reaps the benefits."

"He came alone then, did he?" The witch rearranged her spine with disgusting popping sounds, as if growing tired of the squatted position. "Straight up to yer castle gates and into the hands o' yer guards?"

Griselda shifted her feet, a dirt clod crunching beneath her shoe. "Yes. Who else would've accompanied him, and how else would he have arrived? It's not as if he can flutter down from the sky . . . yet. So, do we have an accord? The details of Nicolet's memory and its whereabouts will buy Elusion his freedom and true form. You can win him the ability to fly again."

Crony's muddy eyes flickered with something akin to amusement. "I took *two* breaths from Nicolet's dyin' corpse, not just one. So there be two memories ye need have fearin'. The first is the other half of the memory I shared with yer constable, and will damn ye and yer faithful knights for yer brother's and Nicolet's murder. The second will destroy ye alone, in ways ye never imagined. One I've locked safe within meself, but the other I shared with the Shroud Collective, who be a very talkative lot. Up to ye to find out which memory be where."

Grinding her jaw, Griselda kicked dirt into Crony's face. "You care so little about your sylphin friend?"

The witch blinked her transparent lids and grit crumbled out from the corners of her eyes. "Ye be a masterful liar and strategist, Regent, but Elusion be even better. He'll arrive under yer nose. And it will be yer own feathers that get ruffled and singed, not his wings upon a tree."

Griselda twitched with rage. "If you weren't immortal . . . I would kill you with my bare hands."

Crony sighed. "Aye, if but this were a fairy tale, we'd all get our druthers and wants."

Griselda spun for the door, her face and ears burning. "I hope you'll be at home here, amidst the mildew and decay of unwanted, forgotten things. For this will be your eternal tomb." She began to open the latch, then remembered the final knife twist. "I'll tell Elusion, once he arrives, that he has himself to thank for your burial. The book he gave me has served quite useful."

"The *Plebeian's Grimoire*." Crony's chains jingled. "It prefers to be called by name."

Griselda turned. "What? How would you—"

"I do be at home in this place," Crony interrupted, eyeing the shelves and the small crates lining the walls. "Always knew I'd return; is why I kept bits o' me tucked away here and there . . . awaitin'. One's past always be a mirror to their future."

Griselda shook some dust off her skirt's hem, trying to make sense of the witch's senseless chatter. "Your past *here*? Our time together five years ago meant so much to you? How I wish I had the choke pear . . . fond memories, hearts and roses, and all that sentimental rubbish."

"Ye do appear a bit flimsy without the razor extensions to yer hand. That brumal blood upon yer palms be a beggarly substitute."

"Yet it's easier to hide," Griselda answered, refusing to be shaken. She took out her gloves in demonstration.

"Aye. Hands can be hidden. Shame ye can't say the same for horns." Crony tilted her head, her own horns catching a flutter of firelight from the torch on the wall.

Horns. A gush of ice water sluiced through Griselda's veins as the knots upon her scalp tingled. She leaned against the door, the latch jabbing into her lower back. "It can't be."

"What else could it be?" Crony chuckled, dark and taunting.

Griselda thrust aside her gloves and parted the braids piled atop her head, revealing the bumps beneath. Blindly, she felt where prongs had formed since she'd examined them last. She gasped and stumbled to the corner opposite the witch, whipping a gown off Arael's mirror—the one her brother so painstakingly glued back together after Lyra's clumsy attempt to find herself at the age of twelve.

There was no mistaking, even in the jagged reflection. The growths upon Griselda's head, though no bigger than butter beans, were identical to the brumal stag antlers she'd so diligently crushed to powder over the past six months. Her jaw dropped—every question, every expletive of disbelief, locked within her chest. "What sunless perdition is this?" she managed to whisper.

"*Now* ye be askin' the right questions. And I be the one with answers. After all, it be these hands who conjured this very tunnel and the room we be occupyin' . . . that invoked the enchanted doorway leadin' here from the Crystal Lake. And the creature that guards it be crafted of a dying man's nightmares . . . stolen, as ye might've guessed, at these hands. Allow me to introduce meself proper." The witch waved her withered palms in a flourish as grand as she could manage with shackles. "Cronatia Wisteria—Eldoria's enchantress, at yer service."

Griselda couldn't tear her gaze from the mirror. "You lie. There's no such name in our kingdom's history . . ."

"Ah, but there's no denyin' there be an anonymous enchantress who served King Kreśimer, aye?"

Griselda's chin dropped. Luce had suspected this room belonged to an enchantress. And hadn't Prime Minister Albous mentioned something of the sort when he started teaching Lyra sign language? That he'd seen a reference to such a being under the castle's employ, centuries before, when they still had a night sky? By the title, Griselda assumed it referred to some exquisite sorceress, not a hideous, gnarled old hag. But there wasn't a description, and all other mentions had been blotted out.

The only reason anyone's name would be blotted out was for betraying the royal kingdom. Crony's admission years earlier in the dungeon: *The debt I owe not be yers. It belong to King Kiran's royal seed.* It never occurred to Griselda to analyze those words, to think of them as anything but empty insults about her lack of a crown.

"May-let ye still don't understand. The *Plebeian's Grimoire* . . . found for ye within this very room . . . be mine." Crony's words swept the moan that rose to Griselda's tongue back into her throat where it lodged within a rise of bile. "Though to be fair to our air elemental, he didn't know me as its author back then. In fact, he didn't know me at all."

"A mistake . . . ?" Griselda mumbled. "Elusion gave me *your* book . . . completely by mistake?"

"Nay. That be fate. The mistake is on ye. Ye chose not to respect the rules of spellcasting. It be a give-and-take. Every grimoire has a hand that writ it. And that hand holds the key to cipherin' all its secrets and edicts." Crony's murky eyes strayed to Griselda's head. "The recipe calls for antlers culled beneath a new moon."

"But . . . I made the smugglers follow that instruction to the letter . . . each time."

"Fool. That not be referrin' to an actual moon. It be what we call the brumal stags' seasonal molting, painless to the creature and in step with its species. Had ye understood the language of magic, the reciprocity of nature, ye would ne'er have butchered a peaceful animal for yer own gain. It be as easy as gatherin' the molted antlers off the ground. See, a poison be released when a wild, enchanted being is attacked. Though it's buildup be slow, in the end, it's a grand penalty for any spellbinder's impatience and ignorance."

Griselda sobbed, her head pounding as the horns pulsed and grew before her eyes. They were now as long as her pinky. "Is there a cure? You owe a debt to me! You betrayed Eldoria!"

Crony's silhouette sat flat on her haunches. "Nay. I betrayed meself and one I loved, and the whole world suffered for it. As for yer predicament, ye need only some practice to wear horns with grace. I'd offer to tutor ye, but afraid I don't be likin' ye enough." She smirked—a horrific expression Griselda caught in the mirror. It sent her to her knees, face-to-face with her own warped image. "Take yer medicine, Regent. Ye be reapin' the rewards of dabbling in things beyond yer ken. Or may-let beyond yer kin*ship*. Would've ne'er happened, had ye had a mentor. But ye were too strong to need help from anyone, aye? Such arrogant frippery. Don't ye see? It take more strength to humble yerself and reach for another's wisdom, than it do to plummet into the unknown without gripping the proffered hand for anchorage."

Griselda's eyes burned. Lustacia's complaints about headaches over the past few months. Could it mean . . . ?

"And now ye be wonderin', as well ye should, if the moonlit princess ye carved of lies and lineage will share yer penalty for this error in judgement. The answer be yes."

Griselda swallowed against that thickening lump in her throat. It tasted gritty and foul—like the putrescence of overturned graves. She smacked her lips, trying to cleanse her palate.

"Be that regret upon yer tongue? Hard to know, I'm sure. As ye've no conscience to guide ye in the sampling of sin and remorse."

Griselda's chest caved on a choking groan. How did the witch know about her missing conscience? Elusion must've told her. Or had the shrouds mentioned it when she'd handed off Nicolet's memory? More importantly, how did she know about the princess being a fake, that it was one of Griselda's own daughters?

Griselda's sagging lips formed the inquiries, but her tongue wouldn't comply. Hand trembling, she reached toward the glass to touch her hideous, horned reflection, slicing her finger on a serrated edge. The vision of her blood—red and glossy—grounded her. Whatever this curse, it was limited to her outer appearance, not her inward workings.

"Antlers can be cut off as easily as a wart," she assured herself aloud.

"Not so easily, as they be a part of the skull. May-let an axe would prove effective. But I doubt yer princess will concede to such gory tactics afore the nuptials. Isn't the coronation to take place first? What will her betrothed say, when there be no balancin' a crown on her uneven head? Upon finding she be responsible for maiming his treasured gatekeepers, do ye think he'll still wish to wed her?" The witch clucked her tongue. "All along ye be sure ye pulled it off. Ye ne'er once considered the prophecy might be bidin' time, awaiting the perfect moment to right all ye've put wrong."

Griselda slumped; was it true? Had she failed? Lustacia had experienced the strange headaches *after* her. The buildup was slow. Perhaps there was still a chance, if she could expedite the wedding. Have it *before* the coronation. Every Eldorian bride wore flowers woven through her hair, which would cover any bumps. Griselda could widen her own hennin for the ceremony . . . that would hide her sins long enough to see them wed. Then afterward, she would find a spell to reverse it all. Eldoria's trio of mages owed their fealty to their queen. Surely they could help.

She veered her gaze to the witch who was chortling softly as if she'd won.

It was then Griselda saw it glistening in the soft light: a seam of black wetness along Crony's wrists and ankles where the cuffs sliced into her hide. Sucking in a breath, Griselda spun on her knees to face her. "Your hide has softened." Her trembling, cut finger pointed to the witch's raw skin. "You bleed just like me."

It took only a moment to formulate the plan: break off a shard of glass from the mirror and plunge it into Crony's heart—but the door pushed open with a *screech* before Griselda could move.

Erwan's face greeted her from the other side, drawn and panicked.

The regent hurriedly arranged her braids atop her head to hide her horns. She put on her gloves and stood, bolstered by the witch's vulnerability. "Have you finished already?" she asked, prompting the reluctant knight to speak.

"There's been a delay, Your Grace. A creature . . . a snowy cyclops crow . . . it brought word that the prince is on his way to Nerezeth—dying. The gruesome bird flew through the corridors, seeking Lady Lyra. Its infernal screeches awoke her, along with everyone in the castle. The council members and servants are all risen now, preparing with their families for the journey. Prime Minister Albous . . . he's leading Nerezeth's entourage down here to collect you."

"I will go out and meet them on the stairs."

"But our plan . . ."

Griselda's attention strayed to the baldric at his side and the sword within it. "The plans have changed. It would seem our witch is no longer immortal. Thrust your blade through her heart. Her corpse can rot here. All minds are on the prince now. Cronatia Wisteria was once forgotten . . . blotted out from the pages of Eldoria's history." Griselda shot a glance toward the broken mirror behind her, then sneered at the witch's image looking back from the glass. "Her future is a mere reflection of her past." Upon gathering her fallen hennin and stepping across the threshold, Griselda dug into her pocket and handed one fiery orb to her knight, along with two final demands. "Do not leave until she takes her last breath. Then once she's dead, ignite the sylph elm."

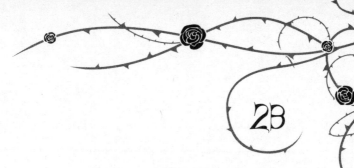

28

The Wonderment of Pebbles and Decay

L uce's army was both small in number and made up of misfits from the dark market.

Toothless Edith and Winkle, the woodland dwarf, came along due to their extreme dislike of Regent Griselda, having butted heads with her when she was a young, spoiled princess. Winkle, who barely came to Stain's waist, had braided his long moustache into his beard to emulate whiskers that complimented his bunny suit. The small wooden box tucked beneath his left arm contained rats, as indicated by the scratches and squeaks within. He planned to turn them loose in the regent's bed. Edith was dressed in a clean tunic and breeches like Stain. In one hand, she held her enchanted mirror. In the other was a basket covered with a cloth too thin to smother the stench underneath—worse than moldy cabbage and skunkweed combined. The paste, made of cow cud crackers and fermented dung beetle saliva, would be stirred into Griselda's next meal.

Neither knew how or when they'd enact their plans, but anything they might do to belittle, terrorize, or frustrate Griselda along the way—such as helping a prisoner escape her keep—was high on their priority list. Dregs, walking tall in his pedestal shoes, came with a more selfless motive—shocking as that was for a hoarfrost goblin. His cousin, a smuggler named Slush, had some long-standing business with the regent, of which Slush never gave details. He and his crew had planned to meet Dregs the previous day for a drink at the Wayward Tavern, to celebrate the conclusion of those dealings. When they failed to appear, Dregs suspected they'd crossed the regent and been thrown into a cell alongside Crony. He had come to free them and send them back to Nerezeth.

The sunlit journey out of the ravine—one that Stain never imagined she would take—was bittersweet. The sky rose above her, endless and beckoning. She wanted to run toward the banks of the Crystal Lake at breakneck speed, wanted Scorch to be there alongside her. Instead, the day's many losses and what awaited in Eldoria tainted the experience. Still, being outside the oppressive forest in the open air, daylight, and soft grass, her footsteps lifted higher, freed from gray billows of ash.

Stain's body pulsed with energy—beyond what the quick supper of cheese, bread, and tea Luce had thrust upon her at home could've sparked. Sound became a living thing in the meadow all around her. Fluttering butterflies, chittering squirrels, gurgling water, and most of all, trilling birds. Their melodies charmed a sympathetic twinge within her throat, running deep into the dip between her clavicle. Unable to follow their notes with her own vocal cords, she fell into a quiet despair. She was as voiceless as the wind, yet held none of its power to alter the world with its presence.

The colors renewed her sense of wonder, momentarily. No one ever told her that one could *taste* color. Even muted behind the nightsky, green became the flavor of moss, fresh rain, and spring flowers. Blue was next, riding a lake-scented breeze that caused the nightsky to stick to her eyelashes before the magical cloth remembered to change positions and hover freely around her face. The rainbow-scaled fish that leapt in and out of the lake formed a prismatic tang upon her tongue. And then followed white, as clean as the plumed wings of swans, guiding them down from the sky to float atop ripples left in the fish's wake.

She passed Luce upon their arrival. Her fingers raked his, the nightsky molding around their joined hands for an instant until she pulled free. She shared his ache to fly, an even deeper yearning now with her Pegasus gone.

Luce readjusted the bag upon his back and started forward once more, going slower so their three accomplices could catch up.

Stain braved sliding down to the margins where gray and pink pebbles crunched beneath her feet. Their pale shades tasted of comfort, warm even through her boot soles. And then she noticed it, the most extraordinary flavor of all: yellow. Sunrays imprinted their shimmer on her cape—comforting like a sip of spiced cider, a horse's musky hide after a brisk run, or her fingertips in that moment before they sizzled, aglow with the promise of life. She impressed that moment of true light upon her heart . . . on the chance she and her companions might be thrown into the dungeon, unable to ever sample the delicacy again.

On the other side of a small hill, the castle came into view. In earlier years, Stain had climbed trees to see out of the ravine's sunken bowl, glimpsing Eldoria through tightly knitted branches and thick leaves. Back then, the honeysuckle growth had only begun and the kingdom remained resplendent with its sparkling white fortress skirted by well-kempt cottages, plentiful farms and gardens, and busy thoroughfares. Today the castle still jutted from the epicenter, but its gleaming windows, glittering walls, and elegant towers and turrets were smothered by nettled, drossy vines; the same plague strangled every cottage and thoroughfare like a rumpled green skirt. The honeysuckle—a deep, bloody pink from the rain—hung in clusters like plump leeches, sucking away hope and freedom. And the jarring buzz of bees could be heard even from afar. Instead of a thriving metropolis, Eldoria now resembled the ruins of some ancient, forgotten place fallen to hazard and woe—an architectural boon of mankind reclaimed by nature in its most unnatural form.

The kingdom's isolation affected Stain as if it called to her, as if it *belonged* to her. How she wished she could thrust her fingers into those bristly vines and renew the beauty and majesty that lay dormant beneath. But that honor belonged to the prophesied prince and princess. She had no part beyond this moment: rescuing Crony and seeing her safely back to the ravine where they would live in seclusion for the rest of their days. Yet she longed for a role in grander schemes. Interactions with the people of this land. A life of consequence like the one spread out at the tender, privileged feet of the princess.

At last, Stain and her companions arrived at the doorway to the secret tunnel leading into the dungeon. Though instead of a doorway, it was a deep, dark pit. An untrained eye couldn't see it, hidden as it was by an outcropping of mossy rock slanted like a roof at the edge of the lake. The hole—brimming with water—favored a wishing well and had the same proclivity to prey upon a mind's fancies. Stain peered within then leapt back when a sea serpent's scaly coils rippled, stirring a formidable wave. A giant head surfaced with fangs opened on a hiss—as chilling and fetid as a demon's breath—that plastered her hood to her skin.

"You'll need this to clear the way," Luce said, withdrawing a hand from his pocket.

Me? She mimed the word with quivering lips.

"I can't open this door. You have to do it. Drop the key onto the serpent's tongue."

She shuddered at the thought of facing the fanged creature alone. But Luce wouldn't pass off the task unless he had no choice. He wanted to save their friend as much as her.

Trembling, she held out her upturned palm.

Much like the doorway wasn't a doorway, the key Luce dropped into her palm was little more than a pebble. Leaning over, Stain held her breath and waited for the snake's reappearance. Its head lifted and its jaws unhinged.

Stain tossed the pebble onto a forked tongue the size of a shovel. The serpent clamped its fangs shut and submerged once more.

Stain stood beside Luce, her skin chilled with nervous prickles, wondering what would happen next. She hadn't long to wait before the entire scene below resolved to steam. Once the mist cleared, all the water had dissipated. A glistening white stairway came into sight, winding far into the dark pit, formed of the serpent's coils now hardened to a statue of salt. Either the snake had been an illusion, or a shifting, spectral guardian who had an appetite for stone and once satiated, repaid the favor with safe entrance.

Luce admitted to not being sure either way, and when asked by Stain where he got the pebble, cryptically replied, "It's a typical piece of rock, soaked in a mixture of brine along with a bloody thorn pulled from a mongoose's paw, and a few other arcane ingredients. I found the recipe upon the pages of a grimoire years ago . . . perhaps I'll show you one day, should that book ever reach its rightful owner again."

Luce lit a torch and led the way. Stain took the first few steps down behind him. As soon as she was out of the sun's reach, she lifted off her hood. The cape's nightsky elements withdrew into the silk—leaving her face and hands bared once more. From there, she took the long stairway with her four compatriots as the cape's lace hem swished freely at her ankles.

Luce was quiet. Stain knew his moods well and dreaded what he must: that Eldoria's mages had already imprisoned Crony in some perpetual form of torture, leaving them helpless to intervene.

The three shopkeepers—descending in single file behind Stain along the grainy serpentine stairway—didn't share her and Luce's trepidations. They tittered on about their hopes to make their way into the upper levels of the castle to catch a glimpse of history.

"Always hoped to gander a peep at the fabled princess," Winkle said, his voice so high and shrill it made the squeaks within his box grow louder in competition.

Edith whistled through her gums. "Dregth, tell uth again of your couthin. How he'th heared the printheth thinging."

Stain tried not to listen, didn't want to relive a goblin's claim of being entranced by the beauty of the princess's nightingale songs, and the otherworldly glow of her hair and flawless skin. It made her stomach clench to imagine the sun-prince at last acquainting the moon-kissed princess of his destiny with a Pegasus prancing inside his head.

The tail end of Dregs's soliloquy recaptured her attention: "—see them both today, even if hidden in alcoves or under furniture is our only way. Can't miss this exciting time of history and boon, when at last the sun will welcome the moon."

Stain fisted her hands under her cape. She could've been content to continue her humble, sequestered masquerade in the forest had Scorch still been at her side . . . had she not, this very day, greeted the sun without him there to share it. She missed his austerity, and how he always put things in perspective. He would've convinced her she didn't need silly, petty indulgences such as a home beneath endless, bright skies, or the enchanted gifts within the saddlebag across her shoulder, or a prince's touch lighting up every nerve with a fascination so acute yet foreign it made her want to learn more about him. That was most ironic of all, considering said prince now held Scorch trapped in a coppery citadel of human flesh, sinew, and bone that she had no hope of invading.

If she hadn't lost Scorch's grumbling voice and comforting presence to Vesper, she wouldn't have unlocked the restlessness she'd always kept hidden away.

Or was it Vesper himself who had unlocked it? Watching the prince from behind a tree; glimpsing his poet's heart as he spoke to his sister of wanting a love built on friendship; observing his struggle to be a fair ruler against everything the prophecy or others dictated he do; and admiring his courageous battle against a curse that seemed to somehow be spreading beyond his scarred, broken flesh and into his people.

His earlier wails rang within her memory, and shame vibrated her bones. She'd been a coward to run, to not return when he called for her. True, she owed her utmost devotion to Crony, who had saved her all those years ago. But her inability to face seeing him again had played as big a role as loyalty. She could conquer any physical discomfort the world could dish out, but the pain of heartache made her shrink away like water droplets sprinkled along the edge of a raging fire.

Luce took the final step onto the dirt floor that opened into the tunnel. He drew Stain to him and shushed the chatty shopkeepers by waving his torch in their faces. Edith's sunken lips pinched to a small knot, Winkle snuggled deeper beneath his rabbit-ear hood, and Dregs slapped a hand across his mouth, causing the icicle growth at the tip of his nose to quiver like a violin string.

"Do you hear that?" Luce directed the question to Stain.

She strained her ears. Though she didn't share his keen canine senses, the muffled moans were unmistakable. She answered: *It sounds like someone crying in the distance. Crony?*

"I hope not, for that soul is in grave despair." He looked Stain over. "Take off the cape and tuck it in your bag. Your legs need to be free, to run or fight."

She nodded. The cape sloughed off reluctantly. She rolled it up with reverence, hesitant to part with it as well; she'd forever remember the gift it had given her today—a sunlit stroll across a meadow that filled the hollow places in her heart, if only for a while. After tucking it gently into the bag, she glanced up at Luce.

Pressing a finger to his mouth, he jerked his chin, indicating they follow. Together, they crept toward the weeping wails.

It took five turns to find the source, a jaunt that seemed forever as with each step the sound grew louder. At last, they arrived at a door set into the dirt wall. Luce deposited his torch inside a hole level with his eyes. He tried the latch quietly, and leaned an ear against the wood. His nostrils flared once, then he stepped back and dragged Stain with him, out of earshot.

"Crony is within," he whispered, barely discernable over the occupant's weeping. "Her scent is strong, but there's another I don't recognize. And I hear chains."

Can you pick the lock? Stain gesticulated. When Luce's only answer came as a frustrated hand raking through his hair, she looked over her shoulder for Winkle—their famed thief. The trio of shopkeepers peered around the bend from some distance behind. Stain scowled at Luce. *Some brave army you recruited.*

He cocked his head upon reading her words. "I never listed bravery as a requirement. They each have their own agendas that will motivate them when the time's right. But this isn't that moment. We have to make our move quietly. Breaking or picking the lock would alert the guard. We must find another way to open the door, from the inside. Any ideas?"

The guttural sobs grew louder behind the barricade. Stain's shoulders sunk. She signed: *Do you have a pebble I can eat to turn me into steam?* She was being facetious, though a part of her hoped he did.

"That's what we need . . . something that can siphon under the door's seam into the room and let us in. I'm fresh out of magic. What about you?" One of his red eyebrows quirked. The torch flickered across his face and stirred shadows in her peripheral along the threshold.

Shadows. Stain remembered the moon-bog, her shadows from market trying to protect her . . . how they bowed around Vesper, obeisant to him. The mother shroud's curious musings, wondering why a child such as herself had merited the fealty of Nerezeth's night creatures.

Fealty meant devotion.

Maybe they were devoted to anyone from the night realm. If so, wouldn't they obey a command from her, if she was truly from Nerezeth?

She lifted a finger, stirring the darkness in the crevices and corners of the door, teasing it. *Will you help us get inside?* She held the question in her mind, for surely creatures of transcendence and obscurity could hear unspoken words.

The shadows elongated, wrapping around each of her fingers. She pulled them out, coaxing them like she'd seen the candy maker stretch taffy at Blood and Crème Confections. Soon she'd managed to amass a swarm that oozed from her hands all the way to the floor like fingernails made of tar. She moved her arms, and they moved with her, stirring the dirt at her feet into dusty clouds.

Edith gasped from around the corner, and both Dregs and Winkle mumbled in awe.

As for Stain, she gawked, astonished. The prince's saddlebag shook at her shoulder. Responding to the movement, Luce opened the flap. The midnight shadows filtered out and joined the others now swirling away from Stain's fingertips to fill the tight passage and play games with the firelight.

"Masterful," Luce whispered as shadows whirled around him and gusted through his clothes. Sharp white points appeared at the edges of his smile, glistening in the reflection of the torch.

Before Stain could respond, the shadows seeped through the keyhole like black smoke; with neither a *click* or a *clack*, the door swung open. The unmistakable scent of panacea roses leaked out. Stain shrank back, reminded of the death bouquet that once shared her coffin. If the shrouds were honest about her Eldorian page boy clothes, her sojourn to death had originated here, and her enemy could be anywhere in this castle, waiting to finish what they started.

She gripped Luce's elbow at the horrific thought.

He stretched out his arm to insist he go in first.

The bag hanging from his shoulders blocked her view until he stepped in far enough to open a line of sight.

A torch on the room's wall illuminated the scene: A knight convulsed on the ground in full sprawl, a sword gripped in his hand. Crony, seated beside him with white lightning sizzling between her horn tips, held him within a nightmare thrall.

Stain almost clapped in relief.

"Took ye long enough," Crony spat, her swampy gaze shifting to Luce.

"I had to find this one." Luce gestured to Stain with his chin, revealing his profile. "And to gather up your boxes from the chest. As to that, the note you left was no easy read. *Chicken* scrawlings would've been more legible."

"Aye, ye would know, bein' an expert on poultry. Foxes spend as much time in henhouses as soldiers do brothels, from what I hear."

Luce barked a laugh, and Crony grinned, but something deeper passed between them . . . an unspoken exchange, somber and meaningful. It was the same look Stain had watched cross Luce's face as he'd read Crony's note back home before shoving two small boxes and an assortment of weaponry within his bag. Stain had been curious about what the note *and* boxes contained, but Luce refused to tell her.

"Is this one of them?" Luce broke the tension, pointing to the wailing man whose eyes rolled back and forth beneath closed lids.

Crony scoffed. "Aye. This be Sir Erwan. One of the regent's most trusted knights."

Luce snarled. He appeared ready to rip the man apart. He'd obviously been about to take a sword to Crony. But why? She was immortal. What good would it have done? It would've made more sense had Crony been in magical bonds, set by the mages.

"You couldn't have planned this better yourself," Luce spoke again.

"Yet me hands touched none of it, which be best of all."

Tiring of their cryptic conversation, Stain nudged Luce aside and dropped her saddlebag on the way in. She met Crony's gaze, saw it brighten with affection, and answered with a tremulous smile. *I'm so relieved you're all right.*

"Thank ye for comin' for me."

Stain wanted to hug her and mend everything between them like she had with Luce in the forest. But first, they needed to get out safely. *There's little time,* she signed, then turned to Luce. *Your secret tunnel is not so secret. If one knight knows the way, more will be coming. We must leave.*

Her guardians exchanged glances and then looked back at her, as if awaiting her next move. Crony's chains jangled, and Stain understood. They had no key. She motioned the shadows toward the shackles.

The witch calmly watched the pitch-black tendrils siphon in and out of the keyholes, snapping the chains free. She covered her wrists with her cloak's sleeves and her ankles with her hem before her muddy gaze strayed to Stain. "Ye have somethin' to tell me, wee one?"

The question fell easily from that serpentine tongue, not out of curiosity or shock for the miracle Stain had just performed, but prideful, like a compliment.

The shadows are my friends. My . . . attendants. Having answered Crony's query, Stain's hands dropped to her sides.

Attendants. Crony had once said that Stain would one day know shadows and understand how they offered freedom where shade offered only respite. Had she been speaking of this moment? Of today?

Stain bounced a questioning glance to both her guardians.

Crony looked up at Luce who raised his eyebrows.

The shopkeepers peered around the door frame.

"Ye three," Crony said from her seat on the ground, "stay in the passage and close the door. It is for ye to keep guard." She pointed to Edith's basket and the squeaking box under Winkle's arm. "We've somethin' more important to attend than yer petty pranks. Don't leave till I say, or I put a nightmare ward on each o' yer houses and leave ye homeless forevermore. Be we clear?"

All three looked at the frenetic currents between her horns then down at the sobbing, catatonic knight, and nodded. Dregs's was the last face they saw as the door clicked shut.

"Lock it," Crony directed Luce.

He did as she asked, dropped the bag from his shoulders next to Lyra's saddlebag, then returned to help Crony stand.

What are you two doing? Why aren't we leaving? Stain shaped her questions while taking a tally of the room. Ratty old dresses covered unseen items along the dirt walls. Shelves hung in place, as if growing out of the dirt like roots. Dusty jars filled with items, magical, herbal, and revolting, lined the wooden slats. But it was the mirror that enchanted her . . . luring her closer. Long and oval, it showcased her entire form. And though broken, it held her reflection more fastidiously than any mirror she'd ever seen.

She couldn't look away from the girl with dark fuzz covering her scalp; her wide eyes, glinting between lilac and amber in the shifting flames; her long, white lashes casting a lacework of shapes across her gray-tinted, scarred cheeks.

The mirror held something beneath its lacerated surface, a part of her she hadn't known existed.

"Shadow attendants, aye?" Crony asked in the background over the knight's moans, though Stain was too distracted to answer.

"Don't worry," Luce responded in Stain's place. "She came to that realization on her own. And she brought her crickets." Luce led Crony to the wall.

The witch's bones popped as she leaned against a shelf. "So, all we be missin' are moths."

Stain furrowed her brow. *Crickets and moths and shadows.* She rolled the words around in her mind, wondering what was so important about each one. Why they gave her a sense of security, of acceptance. The more she thought upon them, the dustier the room grew, as if a haze rose from the walls. Stain blinked in disbelief as that haze became a rush of brown moths flapping in the small space, dancing with the shadows in the torchlight. It was if they'd been hiding there, blending with the dirt for ages . . . waiting for her to call upon them.

Joining the moths, her crickets dug their way out of the half-opened saddlebag and hopped around the room.

Stain released a soundless moan as Luce and Crony looked on with quiet calm—inscrutable. The white lightning that bridged the witch's horns snuffed out, and the knight stopped weeping.

"Wake up, pig. There's something I'd like you to see." Luce kicked the man, eliciting an *oomph*. Scooping up the sword, Luce handed it off to Crony then jerked the man to his feet. The crickets scrambled into the corners and into the hems of old gowns, followed by the shadows and moths.

The knight swayed as Luce turned him to face Stain. The man stared at her eyes then rubbed his own, blinking hard.

"No," he murmured. "Those lashes. It's not possible . . ." His complexion drained to a greenish hue. He spun toward Crony. "Return me to the nightmare! Please! Please, anything but this!"

Unnerved by his reaction, Stain backed closer to the broken mirror.

Luce forced Erwan around again. "Afraid not, rotter. This is your nightmare now." After locking the shackles around the knight's ankles so he had to face Stain, Luce stepped into the corner next to Crony.

All the shadows rose and thickened until Stain could no longer see her guardians, providing a darkness so deep the torchlight circled only her and the knight. It was if they stood on a stage—as if they were performers in some grand, disturbing drama. The crickets began to chirrup softly, an eerie musical accompaniment.

After attempting to escape his shackles, the knight fell on his knees at her feet and pressed his face into the dirt floor. "I won't look. You can't make me. You're not here . . . you're not real. It's impossible! I watched you die . . . watched the cadaver brambles mangle you. I shut the coffin on your corpse myself; we carried you away—" He gagged.

Stain's legs weakened, her body numbing. *It was you?* Her hands hung at her sides, unable to form the question. Yet her accusation echoed—carried on the flutter of moth wings hidden around the room: *You, you, you.*

The knight cried out and slapped his hands over his ears, burying his face between his arms.

Stain's barren throat prickled. Kicking a plume of dirt at his head, she forced him to lift his nose for a breath.

She stared down on him as the moth's wings continued their mantra: *You, you, you.*

"A witch's trick," he mumbled on a groan. "You aren't her. She had no voice. And your hair's all wrong. Too dark. It was silver when I shaved it. One doesn't forget hair like that. One doesn't forget . . ."

Stain gripped her scalp to ward off a chilling sense of violation.

The knight grabbed the corner of a gown—one that hid a rectangular shape. "You're a ghost. Gone. Dead. Nothing more than paint and mildew." The drape slipped away, revealing a portrait underneath, veiled in white dust.

Hand trembling, Stain cleared the powdery haze. There, staring back at her, was the girl she'd seen each time she looked in Crony's enchanted mirror . . . the one with long silver hair, lilac eyes, glowing pale skin, and no scars. Except this girl had shorter eyelashes, and she wore a crown while standing beside a kingly father.

This girl was a princess, something Stain could never be.

The crickets chirped louder, shuffling out from under the sheets, each of them coated in white dust. They hopped onto Stain's pant legs and clambered up. Their movements comforted her, even as their bristly legs and feet crept along her neck and shoulders in waves, forming a cover all the way to her scalp, stopping at her temples and brow. Next, the moths slipped free from their hiding places and fluttered about her head.

Watching in rapt wonder, the knight's eyes widened. Then he screamed, ripping his hair out in bloody clumps. "I was following orders! It wasn't my idea, I swear it . . ." Tears and snot streaked his face, transforming the dirt upon his cheeks to mud. "Majesty, I beg you; have mercy!"

Majesty. Stain's shadows pressed in around her, a gentle persuasion to turn back to the broken mirror. This time, she viewed a long mane of white crickets and a crown of moths. And she saw her true self at last: a murdered princess, resurrected.

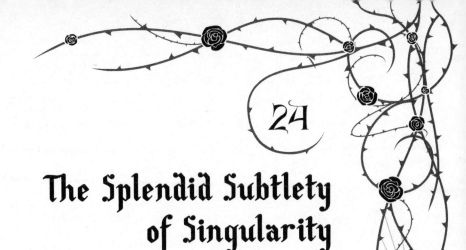

24

The Splendid Subtlety
of Singularity

The room fell to pitch-black. Stain's shadows whirled at her command, their gusts snuffing out the torch and leaving only her eyes reflected back from the mirror, slicing through the darkness like shards of voltaic amber.

She spun as the shadows piled upon the screaming knight. *Bury him,* came the thought unbidden. *Bury him like he'd tried to bury me.* If she had the power, she would've carried him to the ravine, let his sins fill the forest's lowlands with enough ashes to reach the sky.

Eat him alive.

Upon her charge, the shadows pounded him with isolated bursts of wind, shredding his uniform, ripping at his hair, tearing the loosened bloody tufts from his scalp. He struggled against the shackles at his ankles.

Stain ground her teeth and stepped closer as the crickets slipped off her head. Hopping along the ground, they migrated with the moths to find safety under the discarded gowns.

He wants to stand . . . help him. Stain waved an arm and lifted it high.

Her shadows jerked the knight up so he hovered on bleak gusts of air, nailed in place by the chains at his feet. He begged for mercy again as the shreds of his surcoat twisted around him. His arms flailed, his head bobbed front to back. Spotlighted in the dim glow of her eyes, he looked like a wooden puppet frayed by too much play . . . loved to the point of rot and ruin. She wondered how much real damage her shadows could wreak, if they had the power to tear him apart at the seams.

The violent thought both frightened and tantalized her.

Scorch's harsh wisdom returned, having burned its brand upon her heart: *"I would like to think you had a taste of vengeance before being cast aside. And if you didn't, I'll see that you have revenge one day. Whoever hurt you will answer to both of us."*

How she wanted him here now, to show her the way to brutality. Her mouth stretched on a soundless, frustrated wail and the shadows reacted, tugging the knight's upper torso back and forth in midair like an inverted pendulum. If she allowed them to drop him, his skull would hit the ground with a cracking thud.

"Ye need him alive." Crony's voice broke through, a bright beam piercing the savage murkiness of Stain's thoughts. Her guardians had been whispering in their dark corner throughout her rampage, but so intent on revenge, she pushed them out of her mind. As if to bring clarity full circle, the torch relit, revealing Luce and Crony standing beside it—sympathy shifting over their features with each flicker of firelight.

"Let the man speak, wee one."

Stain commanded the shadows to unlock his shackles. Luce stepped through the receding gusts of wind to lift the knight by his torn surcoat. He held him pressed to the wall—the torch inches from his head—hot and imposing.

Sobbing, Erwan covered his muddy, bloodstained face with his fingers.

Luce exchanged glances with Stain, his eyes as bright with bloodlust as hers had been moments before in the mirror. "She has every right to vanquish him." He directed the statement to Crony. "If she needs to keep her hands clean, let me be the executioner." Gripping Erwan's hair, Luce jerked his head to one side to expose his jugular. "You can get her answers from his final memories as he dies."

Crony placed a hand on his tense shoulder. "Nay. He must be the one to give them willingly without me usin' me memory magic. It be the only way."

The knight stopped sobbing then, at last realizing he might yet live. He collapsed in Luce's hold, limbs limp and forehead resting on the slyph's shoulder. His fight with the shadows had cost him his bodily functions, and the urine dampening his pant legs commingled with dirt and rose petals to form a moldering malodor.

Luce crinkled his nose. "You disgust me, and that's saying a lot, considering I've the standards of a flea-bitten dog." His jaw twitched and he met Stain's glare. "What say you, Majesty? Do I release this maggot, or hold him for you as you enact your fury? I will do as you bid."

Lyra took a breath. *Majesty.* Luce said it differently than the knight. Not with fear, but with veneration. It calmed her, renewed that part of herself that had always hated violence, despite that she'd been abused and lost her memories.

Her attention returned to the royal portrait. This father was kind. She could see it in his gentle mien. His coloring reminded her of Vesper: russet complexion and dark gaze. The princess who barely came to his waist was vastly different—a colorless face and winter-shade eyes, her gauzy gown pale against the vivid depth of his velvet surcoat, gold belt, and crimson stockings. Yet the child was smiling. She knew she was accepted and loved, and there was no mistaking by whom. Paternal ownership warmed the king's own smile as he looked down on her—a genuine pride obvious even in the torchlight.

That king wanted his princess to have a wondrous future . . . to be revered for her heart, for her soul. To earn her subjects' devotion. Even without remembering him, the image said this much to Stain. This king wouldn't have given in to brutal passions.

But who *was* this king? If Stain was a princess . . . which princess might she be? Sir Erwan said she didn't have a voice when he'd cast her out, and since a songbird princess lived within these ivory walls already, who did that leave? Was Stain a cousin, a sister?

She knew nothing about the royal family's history.

Crony was right. She needed answers . . .

Who am I? Stain signed the question to the knight, her fingers wobbly.

"Tell her," Luce interpreted the hand signals, "her given name."

Erwan's head lolled off Luce's shoulder. The man let it hang there until Luce shook him. "Answer, swine, and answer truthfully. Elsewise, I'll turn you back over to the shadows and feast upon what's left of your carcass after they're done skinning you alive."

Erwan answered hoarsely. "You are . . . Lyra of the House of Eyvindur. The one true daughter of King Kiran and Queen Arael. The princess of the prophecy."

Stain clamped a hand across her lips. Eldoria's king and queen, rumored to be kind and noble rulers, had died years ago. To know she was theirs cut deep—severed the threads that had held together any hope to find her parents one day, any chance to feel what is was like to be in their arms.

Her throat swelled with suppressed sobs, yet even in grief, she grasped the full scope of the knight's confession. She was the true princess of Eldoria.

Not Stain. *Lyra.* She wrapped herself within the name, wearing it like armor, drawing strength from the power behind it; strength enough to face all of the truth.

Where? She pointed to her throat, fury and agony simmering just below the surface. Her shadows drifted closer, held at bay but ready to act.

Luce shoved the knight's body higher against the wall. "Lady Lyra wants to know what became of her birdsong voice. I'm rather interested in that detail myself."

The knight covered his neck and stared at Luce's snarling teeth, obviously fearing his own throat's fate should he answer.

Lyra bid Luce to release the knight and step back. Cursing, Luce conceded.

Erwan slid to the floor and cringed at the imposing shadows. "It was stolen from you with an enchanted device . . . and given to another." He braved a glance at the gowns draped around the room. "These dresses hide your keepsakes. The lots of your life from the time before you left. They were stashed here because she couldn't bear to look upon them, to face what she'd taken from you."

She? Lyra mimed the word between gritted teeth, moving into the light so the knight could see her lips.

"The other princess, Lustacia . . . your cousin who took your place. She went along with it, but only for love of the prince. She has regrets, unlike . . ." The knight slumped, the emotional and physical stress taking a toll.

Luce growled. "Spill the names of any accomplices, and we'll let you rest."

"Sir Bartley, the Regent Griselda, and her three daughters—your aunt and cousins." Erwan murmured the last part in Lyra's direction, his head dropping into his hands. "But everything was done at the regent's command."

A growl curdled low in Luce's throat. "Ah, there's more than one singing bird in this castle. Though the regent will be none too happy when she hears how prettily you crooned today. And I get to be the one to tell her."

"She's not here to tell!" Erwan shouted, flinging his hands from his face. "They've already left for Nerezeth; the wedding is to take place upon their arrival. Only a handful of Eldorian guards stayed behind to watch the castle . . . none of whom know anything about this. Should you tell them— they won't believe you. They've already seen and heard the princess of the prophecy; she has all the traits. Looks enough like the child in the portraits to convince anyone. She even has shadow guards. And they're too far ahead. You'll never catch up . . . never make it to Nerezeth in time to plead your case before the wedding."

Luce forced him up again so they were nose to nose. He sneered, sharp white points pressing into his lower lip. "I will if I fly."

Lyra took a broken breath, wondering what she could possibly have done as a child to warrant such treatment from her own family. She sought Crony's tender muddy gaze, her roughened arms, her scent of myrrh and decaying flowers.

Crony stepped forward and cradled Lyra's chin in her withered hands, waiting.

Why did my aunt hate me so? Lyra signed. *To take everything from me?*

Crony drew her close. Lyra melted into her. Crony's scabrous fingers smoothed her scalp, catching upon the fuzz. "Some people harbor so much thorns inside, it strangles out all the beauty. The kingdom under yer aunt's keep—smothered by nettles and vines—be a reflection of her heart. A rosebush with nary a rose. It weren't ye that caused it. It were her own dark devices and hatred that drived her. That ugliness be makin' its way out as we speak. It'll be what vanquishes her in the end. Have faith in that."

Lyra snuggled deeper into the embrace. Her shadows sank to the floor around her. The crickets and moths crept out to join them.

"You'll never win . . . the regent always has an alternate plan," Erwan grumbled.

Luce cuffed the side of his head, eliciting a yelp. "That's why I'm here, lump. To be the crimp in all her plans." He tossed a glance to Crony. "Now? Are we done? Is he mine?"

"Aye, he be yers. But I'd rethink killin' him. Take him with us to seek out the sylph elm. We need yer wings and can't afford any holdups. Though the castle be mostly abandoned, we may happen upon a guard or two. He can be an asset."

Luce lifted Erwan's face. "Yes, an asset. All you need is motivation." He caressed the side of the knight's face as a lover would, then lulled his voice to that silken cord of persuasion. "I'm intimately aware of Lady Griselda's charms. How she excels in controlling the men of her life. Look at all she coerced you into doing. She'll never take the blame without dragging you down, too."

Erwan caught a breath—captured in Luce's spell. "I tried to tell her she was growing too brash," he answered. "She never listened."

"Of course you did," Luce agreed through a sneer. "No doubt you'll lose your head over this. Wouldn't it be delectable, if first you could have the upper hand just once? Go out like a man. Shake her tree and rattle some branches. What say?"

"Yes, a man." Erwan's response was threaded with a dreamlike quality. "She needs to see me as a man."

Stain had seen Luce use his sylphin charms before, digging into a victim's mind to discover their hidden desires. Erwan had obviously harbored hostility against Griselda for drawing him into this dangerous plan, and the regent's mistreatment of him nurtured the grudge.

Luce's ability to persuade and entice made him all the more dangerous in his aerial form, when he could be heard without being seen, when he could trick his prey into thinking he was their own inner voice. Were he to get his wings back today, to become ethereal again, he would be a formidable ally for Lyra's rise against the fake princess.

But why were his wings here? Had the regent played a part in his punishment? Did it have something to do with Luce saving her from the shrouds? Why would he have saved her in the first place? The woman appeared to poison every life she touched. But still reeling from her own discoveries, Lyra couldn't find the strength to ask such questions.

"Ready to go?" Luce asked his victim.

Erwan nodded, entranced.

Luce glanced Lyra's way. "You are not alone. We're with you, to the end." He tipped his head to Crony, then dragged Erwan across the room and flung open the door. The three shopkeepers toppled in, having had their ears pressed to the wood.

They scrambled to their feet and gawked at Lyra.

"Ya ain't no boy, you're a long-lotht printheth!" Edith was the first to speak. She turned to Winkle. "She one of uth! She wath wronged by Lady Grithelda."

"We'll avenge you, Highness!" Winkle squeaked and bounced around the knight in a fit of rage, his bunny ears wriggling.

Dregs gawked at the shadows, crickets and moths surrounding Lyra, his bulbous eyes round as tea saucers. "A child of the day realm holding sway over the night's helm. Indeed, our slates be writ by the fates."

All three of them exchanged stunned glances, then dropped to their knees. Upon forcing the knight to kneel, Luce did the same.

Lyra stepped forward. *Thank you*, she mimed, wanting more than ever to shout—in grief, in fury, in gratitude.

Crony waved to the open door. "Dregs and Winkle, ye two go with Luce. I be behind ye shortly. Edith, stay outside the door. I've a proposal for ye."

Everyone left, leaving only Lyra and Crony. Once the door clicked closed, Lyra spun, bidding her shadows to whisk through the room and drag the tattered gowns from the items hidden along the walls. She touched all they unveiled: more portraits—some of her queenly mother with a bump in her belly that would one day be her, then others of both her parents, young enough to be newly wed, looking at one another adoringly, as flawless and beautiful as polished copper statues; a small tower of panacea roses—stems tied with silver ribbon and petals withering and curled; and a stack of black parchment letters, each with the title *Princess Lyra* and a date written in golden ink on the front.

Lyra examined her golden-tipped fingers. Only hours before, the prince had spattered his sparkling blood upon matching papers in the ravine. She walked to the pile and lifted one. The royal seal of Nerezeth—a silver-wax crescent moon beside a nine-pronged star—was broken on all the letters.

They'd been opened, read and answered by someone other than her. Someone pretending to be her.

Feeling Crony come up from behind, she turned. *I saw the mother shroud today.* The words tumbled from her hands. *When I ran away from you and Luce, I went to her lair seeking answers of my past. She predicted this . . . that there was more to me than I knew. She said to know myself, I'd need to have hair of steel and tears of stone, that I'd need to prove hard enough to wrap myself in spikes, yet soft enough to walk through stars without crushing their legs. What does that mean? It all sounds impossible.*

Crony's transparent eyelids widened, indicating more interest than surprise. "I've ev'ry faith ye can do the impossible. Ye proved it by yer will to o'ercome death when I found ye."

You knew all along. This is why you and Luce taught me about the outside world, about being diplomatic and making peace with others. You knew I was heir to Eldoria. Why did you take my memories, Crony? Where are they? Why do you keep them from me still?

Crony averted her gaze, regret weighing upon her serpentine features. "That be the only way I could bring yer soul back from the dead, by pilferin' yer memories of being alive. I can't be sayin' more than that. Might it be enough, that Luce and me saved ye and cared for ye?"

Lyra squeezed her fingers into knots, then nodded. After everything that had happened in this room, she understood there was something beyond the witch's power that held her within its thrall. A nightmare of her own that she couldn't outrun.

"Good." Crony caught her hands. "I be seein' that ye'll get yer past back. But first, ye must win all that's yers in the present. Ye must be strong enough to claim it without yer memories. Remembrance be yer reward in the end."

Lyra clenched her teeth, inspecting her reflection again: scruffy-headed, gray-tinged scarred skin, dusty tunic and breeches.

How am I to be a queen, when I know nothing of ruling? How am I to prove I'm a princess to any kingdom . . . the *princess, no less? I look nothing like the prophecy dictates. And I've no nightingale's song bursting from my lips. I'm unremarkable in every way.*

"Ah, but ye can learn to rule, when yer heart already be wise and merciful. And ye can spit and polish to look the part of royalty. That be yer advantage o'er yer impersonator. No matter what be on the outside, one can't change their innards. Ye are Prince Vesper's singular match, for yer strengths balance his own, just as the prophecy say. When it come down to it, that be more important than any external shell, aye?"

Lyra caught a sharp breath. Scorch had said similar words, all the years they ran together. Her dear, precious Scorch . . .

As if reading her pained expression, Crony drew closer. "Are ye thinkin' of all ye be leavin' behind in the forest?"

Lyra sighed, forcing herself to relay what she could hardly bear to remember. *I'm not leaving Scorch behind. He died . . . but he didn't. His essence united with the prince when they both fell in the moon-bog. There was some dark magic at work.* She felt ridiculous trying to explain. *It doesn't make sense. But it's true . . . I lost him already.*

Crony shook her head. "May-let ye only thought ye lost him. May-let the magic was within the prince himself, and ye gained them both." She withdrew a black letter, not from the pile, but from her cloak. It was addressed to Lyra, like all the others, and was dated three years earlier.

Lyra took it, raising a puzzled brow.

"Sir Erwan and me had a bit o' time in this room alone, awaitin' rescue. When the knight was in his thrall, I bade him into handin' me some letters." She shrugged. "This one I found most interestin', more so now."

Lyra ran her fingertips along the golden script. The ink leapt up in response, as though it was magnetized and her fingers were metal. It lit her skin, warming it with needlepoint stings—an encroaching sensation that filled her from head to toes. She broke loose and the ink fell back onto the paper, reshaping the words:

My Dear Princess Lyra,

> *I hope this finds you well. I was encouraged to hear*
> *of Prime Minister Albous's work with you on your*
> *signing. I understand what it's like to be hindered in*
> *communications with others. Since the moment of my*
> *curse, I've lost the ability to speak mentally, mind-to-*
> *mind, with my people. Perchance one day I may learn to*
> *use your ancient signings myself—for my subjects, and for*
> *you and me, so we might communicate easily. You asked*
> *in your last note how I came to be cursed two years ago;*
> *it was an arrogant impulse. The day my lord father died,*
> *I swallowed sunlight to become powerful enough to heal*
> *my people on my own; instead, I almost followed my king's*
> *eternal passage to the stars. Nerezeth's sorceress saved*
> *me. I had a dream while under her spell, that something*
> *hovered above me with wings of shadow and fire, but then*
> *it slipped from my view before my ensorcelled mind could*
> *reason it out. When I awoke, I felt incomplete. The only*
> *thing that gave me peace was your song; upon hearing it, I*
> *knew that finding you would make me whole again. So, in*
> *return for this great gift, I hope to make you stronger and*
> *able to face the sun. These letters are written in my blood,*
> *rich with sunshine. We've found that it has the ability*
> *to desensitize Nerezethites to daylight. And as you are so*
> *alike them in that way, I'm hoping touching these letters*

will enable us to share a dance upon my arrival to Eldoria.
To not only join lives, but to join hands as an example to
our kingdoms.

Yours in both night and day,

Prince Vesper

Lyra froze as bits and pieces of the prince's explanations in the moon-bog made sense: *The part of me I thought I'd lost was here all along, with you, having silent conversations.* Vesper had said he didn't kill Scorch; he'd been so sure of it: *I am him . . . your beastly brawn. I've been him all along.*

Gasping, Lyra looked up at her guardian.

"Aye, there indeed be magic at play, wee one. But it started five years afore, when his spirit split in twain."

Lyra folded the letter, overcome. It was too much . . . too much all at once.

Crony picked up a wilted rose and sniffed it. "Our arrogant Pegasus seem to have a carin' side after all. It remained in Nerezeth with the prince. A boy who learnt to speak in sign for a girl he'd yet to meet, and drained his blood letter after letter, just so he might touch her."

Lyra couldn't respond. She'd suspected the prince was a good man after eavesdropping earlier. Still, she left him when he was hurting and confused . . . she ran because she couldn't face the pain of her truest friend being locked within him, and torn from her forever.

Regret, deep and winding, strangled her heartbeat. She clutched the note tighter and dropped to her knees. One corner of the parchment curled down, exposing the script again. Ink touched her skin, tinting it gold like the prince's. She moved her hands to the withered roses piled beside her, draining the sunlight out of herself until the blooms burst with new life. Her shoulders slumped, body weak and aching from the effort.

Crony clucked her forked tongue. "Methinks ye had time to read one of these letters, afore ye were put in a coffin and left for dead. The prince shared his blood to help ye. But may-let the fates had another purpose in mind—to help him."

Crony's words struck Lyra's conscience. She asked herself again, just as she had in the moon-bog: Could she drain the sunlight from the prince and release it elsewhere, act as a conduit to cure him?

Fear skittered through her spine upon considering how weary she felt already. Would she survive such a monumental transaction? But knowing he was Scorch—the one she'd laughed, quarreled, and ran with over the past five years—made the question moot. She loved him enough to try.

I should've saved him already, she told Crony. She dragged a velvety rose into her lap, its perfume taunting and accusatory. *I just left him there. I didn't think it possible. How could it have been possible? How can any of it be?*

"Magic be boundless. Consider how the prophecy found a way to unite its prince and princess, in spite of others' meddlin' hands. How it give ye time to know one another . . . to become helpmates, friends—"

Equals. Lyra's fingers finished Crony's thought. *What if Vesper marries the imposter before I make it there? He doesn't know I'm Lyra. He thinks she is, that she'll heal him. What if I've lost him already?*

Her guardian took her hands in hers. "As a foundling girl, ye loved a horse who all along was a boy. And now that ye know, yer afeard of that love bein' one-sided enough he'd marry another over ye? That horse still live within him. He'll crash through walls, shatter bones, and defy his destiny to be with his quiet, orphan girl. Ye had the courage to save him as a Pegasus. Tell me, what lengths will ye go to, to save him as the man?"

I'll do anything. Lyra's latent ferocity reappeared. She rubbed her nose, feeling as inept as Vesper about how the two of them could possibly fix the disjointed skies. *I've moonlight in my blood, and the prince has sunlight in his. Is this how the sky will be united? When I save him?*

"The pieces'll fall into place as they will. All ye need do is concentrate on helpin' the prince." Crony smiled then—that turn of wormy lips and pointed teeth that brought soldiers to their knees.

Yet it was that smile that gave Lyra strength to stand, her legs no longer shaky. It was that smile that had built her up from a nameless orphan to a member of the forest . . . one who served a purpose and had a family. And today it would give her strength to be the princess Vesper and their two kingdoms needed.

She hugged Crony again, long enough to feel their heartbeats hammering between them. Forcing herself to break the embrace, she signed: *Thank you for saving me; for giving me a home. Such a great sacrifice for a free-spirited harrower witch and a sylphin fox.*

"Nay, it be a great *honor*, wee one." Her rough fingers tilted Lyra's chin high. "Hold yerself up as the princess ye be. If ye believe it, so will they." She motioned to the pile of letters. "Now learn the prince's side of yer beast's heart. Then clean yerself and prepare. When Luce returns, ye two will leave for Nerezeth."

You mean when Luce returns, we all leave, right? Lyra gesticulated.

"I've me own role to play, here in this realm." With that, she stepped over to the shelves on the wall and took down several jars. Placing them in a box on the ground, she returned her attention to Lyra. "It will work out best this way, ye'll see."

Lyra sensed something ominous in the response. As the witch started toward the door, she turned one last time to look at Lyra.

Lyra moved her fingers: *I'll see you soon . . .*

Crony tipped her horns to one side then limped out.

I love you, breathed Lyra before the door closed. Knowing Crony hadn't heard, Lyra commanded her crickets to squeeze under the threshold and follow the harrower witch. She had bargained them for Crony, so they belonged to her; they would stay with her, sing to her, and keep her company until Lyra and Luce returned.

That gave Lyra some small comfort.

Clean up . . . prepare. She stripped down and washed off with the water supply in her saddlebag, rubbing herself dry with rose petals. The clumps of discarded clothing and gowns, frayed and moth-eaten, awaited. After looking for some fresh undergarments, she sought the dress her mother had worn in the portrait as a young newlywed queen. Nose tickling from the mustiness, Lyra stepped into the gauzy, torn silk, the same pink shade as pebbles at the Crystal Lake. She tucked the talisman of Crony's hair beneath the neckline, then covered the gown with its velvet tunic, as emerald green as the grass she'd walked on today. Embroidery and tattered lace bedecked the neckline and hems—like sprawling vines and withered petals. At one time there were beads and gems, but they'd been plucked away, leaving frayed threads.

This gown used to be spectacular, yet looking at herself in the mirror, scarred and scalped, with dirty boots upon her feet in place of elegant slippers, it fit her better as lovely rags. Disrepair complemented her peculiarities in the same way perfection would've detracted from them.

Humility warmed her cheeks, giving the veins beneath her skin prominence even through the gray tinge. She looked nothing like her parents, and never would. All she could hope for was to look like herself, that one day the grayish tinge would wear away so her moonlit complexion could glow again. Her flaws stood out vivid against the gray. Each scar had a story to tell, each bruise and scratch were the beginning of another—evidence of a subtle strength. Perhaps *that* was the true reflection of her mother and father.

She mimed a mantra while sorting through Vesper's many notes: *My prince. My kingdom. My life.* Her battle cry, silent but empowering. The moths took flight around her, echoing with their wings: *My life, my life, my life.*

At last she understood her calling, her identity. She would make her parents proud . . . reclaim what had been stolen, save the night realm's prince, and unite the sun with the moon—whatever it took to see it all done.

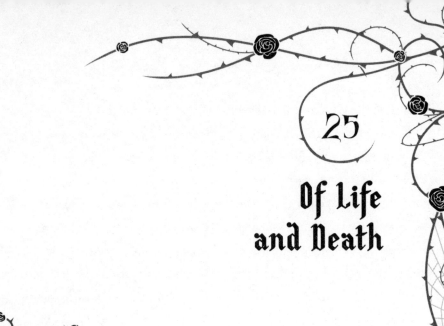

25

Of Life and Death

Eldoria's military—over two hundred strong—escorted Griselda and the princess's retinue to Nerezeth's iron stairway on regal blood-bay stallions. The infantry wielded halberd blades to cut paths through the honeysuckle for the wedding entourage. Upon arrival at the stairway, half the soldiers stayed at the base of Mount Astra, camping outside the panacea rose hedgerows to await the new king and their queen's triumphant return. The other half accompanied the entourage across the night realm's snowy terrain and to the obsidian fortress. Queen Nova sent her own infantry—though scanter in number due to illness—to meet their Eldorian guests and assure they had safe passage down the stairs and through the Grim. She opened her drawbridge without question, the welfare of her son her upmost priority. There was a blood pact upholding the peace, and once the marriage took place, their kingdoms would be united under the same sky again. Both Nerezeth and Eldoria needed this union, making the threat of war an obsolete and pointless consideration.

Back in Eldoria, where the real princess waited in her hidden room of dirt, forty guards occupied the palace's outer bailey, postern gate, and battlements—using axes to clear away bristled vines for temporary walkways in the sunlight. The commoners sat inside their cottages, looking through any opening in the honeysuckle plants cloaking their windowpanes, hoping soon to greet the soft glow of moonlight that would kill the plague.

Inside the ivory castle, curtains were drawn and the corridors and chambers abandoned. Silence wreathed the halls, interrupted only by the banshee cry of Thana somewhere up high in the towers. There were five guards holding vigil at the doorway to the royal portico garden. Griselda had stationed them with swords drawn, insurance against her fear that only Elusion could derail all her hard work and wicked machinations now.

The regent was right to be afraid.

Crony found Luce hiding where the north and east corridors intersected down the hall and around the corner from the garden's entry. An entranced Erwan along with Dregs and Winkle were hidden alongside him. The shopkeepers had their heads together, positioned beneath a candlelit sconce while looking within Winkle's box and whispering.

Crony leaned against the cool, marble wall, wishing she'd had her staff for the walk here. Those bothersome shackles and chains had left her ancient bones stiff.

Around the corner and in the distance, the guards talked amongst themselves. They debated a variety of subjects, from which of them might be appointed to the queen and king's royal guard to how beautiful the princess had looked in her wedding trousseau and what a shame she had to cover up with nightsky for the walk to Nerezeth. When a disturbing caw drifted from far overhead, talk fell to why the night sorceress's giant crow still frequented their palace.

They couldn't possibly know what Crony knew: that the bird was seeking *her*. She would call the one-eyed beast herself, when the time was right.

"What be the plan?" she whispered to Luce. She would've offered to lock the guards within a nightmare thrall, but her frail body hadn't the strength to attempt one again so soon.

Luce leaned close and motioned to Winkle's long-eared hood. "Our resident bunny is to send the guards on a chase. Erwan says their top priority is to keep the castle undefiled while the regent is away. She doesn't want to return to any infestations. Obviously, I'm included on her list of vermin."

"So, we send 'em runnin'. Then we're in?"

Luce shook his head. "Our worthless knight doesn't have a key to the garden." He glared at Erwan, who could barely stand on his own, drifting in and out of consciousness. Luce had him propped against the wall. Candlelight flicked across his mud-and-bloodstained face. "Dregs will have to use his shoes to reach the window."

Luce and Crony both peered around the corner, observing the beveled portal glass high above the garden door where soft streams of sunlight slanted in. With a solid push, it would swing open to allow fresh air into the castle.

Crony frowned as they withdrew into the adjacent corridor again. "It be small. Even a goblin won't fit through there."

"No, but a fox will. I'll hitch a ride with Dregs, slip in, and unlock it from the other side."

"There be the honeysuckle bristles."

Luce shrugged. "Erwan said a pathway was cleared for the regent a couple of days ago. I doubt it's fully grown back yet. And if it has, small matter. If a little girl can face a coffin full of cadaver brambles and scorpions, I can face a few thistles in my fur."

"Thistles the size of sewin' needles." Crony glanced at the trail of crickets coming up behind her. "A shame these tiny bits aren't as adept at opening locks as the shadows, aye?"

Luce gave her a lopsided grin. "How did they come to follow you?"

She suppressed smiling back. Though Luce had grown accustomed to her gruesome expressions, Dregs and Winkle hadn't built up the tolerance. And were Erwan to witness it, he might be shocked out of his trance. "Our girl decided I needed an escort of me own."

Luce's grin turned winsome. "Eldoria's gain will be our loss."

Crony lowered her head, her horns weighing heavier than she cared admit. Or may-let that was her heart dragging her chin down. "Ne'er thought I'd see the day we'd be nostalgic for our parentin' years."

"Speak for yourself." Luce stood tall and straightened his lapels. "I'm no parent. I'm rather more . . . the dashing uncle."

Winkle and Dregs chose this moment to glance up at them and snicker softly.

Luce snarled. "What are you laughing at? Ever seen what a fox can do to a rabbit?"

Winkle smacked a hand across his whiskery facial hair.

Crony snorted. "Don't be cross, me comely cur. They be seein' anew yer soft spot for our ward. And yer sentiments be premature. Yer to see her through to the end, as ye promised."

"About that." Luce twisted his lips in thought. "When I'm in flight, I become a spirit . . . wind and air. Even should I have my wings"—his features shifted to contained eagerness, as if at last grasping the glorious possibility—"I can't carry her unless she's small enough to fit in my pocket. I can only carry myself and the clothes upon my back. Am I to fly ahead and forestall the nuptials?"

"Nay, ye go together. Ye can use yer wings and sylphin talents as a distraction when ye get there; clear the way for our princess to heal her prince."

Luce peered around the corner to ensure the guards remained preoccupied, then retreated back into their hallway. "But if we don't fly, how will we get there in time? It takes days, and that's by horse."

"Edith. A minute ago, in the dungeon, I gifted her one of Lachrymosa's final memories. It be havin' nothin' to do with kingdom business, so me hands be free of interference."

"You gave her a memory weave?"

"Only containin' a small spell. The most important memory still be occupied here." Crony thumped a fist against her skull. "The sorcerer had a determinate elixir. It homes in on a subject's locale and transports ye directly to their side in a blink of an eye, if'n ye have a sample of said subject to add to the brew. I boxed up the ingredients she be needin', and she have the prince's blood upon his notes. Edith be in the tunnel with our princess now, preparin'. She'll be ready, upon yer arrival."

Luce's orange eyes shimmered. "So you told Edith all of it? That the tunnel, the gateway, and the room once belonged to you?"

"She knows all she need be knowin'." Crony felt a tug of nostalgia for past days. She missed using her magic for the royal family, using it for good. Had she her druthers, she would've been the one to take Lyra to win her throne. She would've seen King Kiran's daughter victorious. It wasn't to be, but she still had her part. And Thana would help her accomplish it.

Luce's red eyebrows furrowed. "Are you convinced of Edith's ability with spells and elixirs? What if she accidentally turns us into toads?" He brushed his forehead with a thumb. "I doubt even I could make warts attractive."

Crony rolled her eyes. "She be a cook—adept at readin' recipes, at mixin' and stirrin'. And she have a respect for nature and givin' back what's taken. That's all she be requirin'. In fact, when this be done and behind ye, see that she receives me grimoire. It be hers now."

"Wait . . ." Her companion's features took on that canine quality—a feral mix of wariness and suspicion. "Are you saying Edith's to be your *successor*?"

"Aye, she be inheritin' me harrowing skills very soon."

"You really are leaving then, like you said in the note? Why? And where? It's too late for you to join the other immortals in the heavens. You made that choice long ago."

"There may be a way for me to reach the heavens yet," Crony answered cryptically.

Luce's expression looked like an open wound. "Were you even planning to say good-bye? A proper one, I mean. A messy half-hearted letter doesn't measure up when we've had each other's backs for so many years."

"Enough talk. Let's be hurryin' this plan along." Crony had chosen not to tell Lyra that Prince Vesper was at death's door. The child had enough to process as it was, and enough pressure upon those wee shoulders to prove heself. If only Crony could do more; if only she could intervene . . . tell Luce all she knew of Griselda's crimes, tell him of the proof growing from the wretch's very head, the brumal blood staining her hands. That accursed vow of noninterference had become the bane of Crony's existence.

"I want to know." Luce held his voice to a strained whisper, bringing the witch's mind back to the here and now. "Will Stain . . . *Lyra* . . . and I see you again when we return?" He gripped her wrist gently.

Crony gasped as he touched the raw places made by the shackles.

Scowling, Luce pushed up her sleeve and rubbed a finger across the lacerations. "What is this?" he murmured. "You're bleeding?"

"Did you hear that?" one of the guards down the corridor said. "Around the corner back there, coming from the east hallway . . ."

Several pairs of boots clomped their direction. Luce nudged Winkle, and the dwarf tipped over his box.

Ten rats scurried out, their claws clicking on the white marble. Winkle shooed them the right direction with his bunny paws, his long ears wriggling with the effort. Shrill squeaks and wiry tails led the way as the rats shot around the corner toward the guards.

"Two things left undone," Erwan murmured out of the blue, slowly waking from his trance. "Prove I'm a man."

Crony cupped a hand across the knight's mouth. Luce gestured with his chin for Winkle to head back the way they came, toward the dungeon and the hidden tunnel—his part done.

Winkle wished the rest of them luck, then bounded off, his hopping feet indiscernible over the melee of stampeding rats, clanging swords, and shouting guards still out of sight in the adjacent hall.

"Grab the rodents! The regent'll have our heads if those things stay loose!"

"Get it . . . that one, there!"

"Those three are going for the upper level. If they make it to the regent's chambers, she'll grind us up for meat pie!"

"I've got one! Ouch . . . ah, drat! He bit me. No, he's off to the kitchen!"

"Split up!"

Five sets of boots clomped away from the intersecting corridor, taking the stairs—both up and down. Empty echoes rang in their wake.

Luce turned again to Crony, wearing a troubled frown.

"The prince be dyin', Luce. He be under a sleeping death to hold off the curse till he can be cured. And as his soul's other half be our girl's beloved Scorch, she'll ne'er forgive us if we cost her the chance to save 'im."

Luce's jaw sagged open. "The flying donkey . . . is a *prince*?"

"*The* prince," Crony corrected.

Looking more frazzled than she'd ever seen him, Luce glared at Erwan, who was still mumbling about being a man. Crony nodded, unspoken confirmation that she had the knight in hand.

Luce shifted to fox form. He shook off the cloud of sparkles clinging to his whiskers and muzzle as he trotted behind Dregs, tail dragging the floor. The goblin stopped at the door, grunted as he hefted Luce's furry form into his arms, then stomped the soles of his pedestal shoes seven times.

Higher and higher they lifted, until the goblin stood face-to-face with the window. Balancing Luce upon one shoulder like an infant, Dregs swung the beveled glass on its hinges, inviting the sickly-sweet scent of honey-suckle in. Luce twisted around and hooked his front paws over the opening then dragged himself through, his tail's tip the last thing to be seen as he fell inside.

Crony winced upon hearing the resulting yelps, sure he'd landed on a thistle or twenty. She kept her gaze on the window. Seeing red glitter and smoke, she breathed a sigh of relief.

Dregs shrank back down and headed for the stairs to seek his cousin Slush. As he passed Crony, he tilted his chin her direction. She nodded her gratitude and he slipped out of sight.

The garden door flung open, revealing sunlight filtering through a tunnel of thick, bristly vines along with the chronic hum of bees. Luce, picking off several burrs embedded in his sleeves and pant legs, motioned Crony in. Bracing Erwan's shoulder blades, Crony pushed him across the threshold then followed, Lyra's crickets in tow. Luce shut the door and bound the latch with several vines to keep the guards at bay should they return. He then took up the end of their trio, careful not to step on the bugs.

On all sides and overhead, vines, thistles, and cabbage-sized pink blooms smothered wrought-iron benches, dried-up water fountains, and a variety of flowers. The sad, scant heads of marigolds, heliotropes, and gardenias twisted in odd directions, subsisting off what little sunlight they could find. Bees, too busy to care about the intruders, buzzed to-and-fro gathering nectar. It was a struggle to breathe in the thickly sweet air as Crony pushed Erwan forward where the vines opened to a curving path. The trail led directly to the sylph elm rising high and proud.

"It's the most beautiful sight I've ever seen," Luce said behind her, referring to the bright yellow canopy just a few feet away. Upon the lowest branches on the right side, two vivid crimson leaves stood out, easily within reach to anyone standing beside the trunk. They swayed as if on a breeze, though no wind could breach the vines surrounding them. Luce squeezed Crony's shoulder. "They're calling to me. I've waited so long," he whispered.

"Aye, ye have." Releasing her hold on Erwan, Crony patted Luce's hand.

As if the knight had been waiting, he leapt forward, digging into a pouch beneath his surcoat. "Two things left undone," he said, coherent now. "Burn the tree." He withdrew an orb, the size of a marble and alive with pulsing turquoise light. Before Crony could reach out to stop him, he tossed it toward the sylph elm.

The ball hit the trunk, burst, and erupted into flame. Instantaneously, the blaze rose high—bright turquoise, pink, and white hot—spreading from leaf to leaf, making its way up the canopy far too fast for any earthly fire. Luce's wings flapped, trying to get free from their branches.

"No!" Luce nudged Crony aside and stumbled toward the elm.

"Kill the witch," Erwan said beneath his breath. He withdrew a dagger from his boot and lunged for Crony. Luce tore his gaze from the burning tree. Snarling, he leapt between Crony and the knight. The two fell to the ground and rolled: a blur of red hair, a torn white surcoat, and a shiny silver blade.

Grunting, Luce got the upper hand and snatched at a nettled vine, wrapping it around the knight's neck. He tightened the noose while Erwan struggled, his angular eyes bulging.

Crony turned to the tree. Embers gathered at the edge of the wings. Her companion yelled for her to stop as she hobbled straight up to the trunk—now nothing but kindling. The flames lapped at her once impervious hide, peeling it away in foul-scented blisters. The heat singed her hair, charred her horns, and caught fire to her cloak. Her transparent eyelids offered no reprieve from the brilliance. Unable to see, she reached up and swatted at all the leaves within reach, hoping to free the wings.

A gust fluttered by her head as she collapsed, blind and in agony. The sound of flapping gave way to the bone-snapping crack of the knight's neck, then Luce's exultant shout. Even without sight, Crony knew the wings had found their home. The crackling flames silenced, the fire burning itself out. Smoking wood and soot intertwined with the honeysuckle perfume.

Crony throbbed all over . . . as if the flames still lapped at her. She tried to move, but couldn't. She'd never known all-encompassing pain or how debilitating it could be.

On the other side of her sightless eyes, Luce dropped down next to her, his triumphant cries breaking into a wail. "Why?"

"That fire were enchanted, born of sun . . . nothing could've stopped it but purest moonlight. Ye ain't have that, nor do I."

"You know that's not what I meant! What were you thinking?"

"Ye chose me o'er yer wings." Her parched words raked from her throat like shifting ash.

"Because you're no longer immortal, you foolish old bird. I was trying to save you, and you made it all for nothing!"

She sought him with her hand, sighing when she felt the swoop of ethereal feathers at his shoulder. "Nay. Ye made a selfless choice and the fates rewarded ye. I no longer be immortal, but ye are ageless."

"We were both supposed to be rewarded; we went into this as partners, remember?" On the other side of the black void, she could hear him shrugging free of his jacket. Her naked body shuddered as the cloth covered her sticky and blistered hide. "Tell me how to help you." His voice wavered, his hands running across the cloth, gentle as raindrops. A cool wind soothed her skin in their wake. He'd changed to his celestial form, no doubt fearing his corporeal touch would cause more damage.

"Go to our princess." Her throat tightened, her breaths rattling in her chest. "See this done so she have the life she be born to."

"You expect me just to leave?" The wind rushed over her faster now—driven by frustration. "What am I to tell her when she asks of you?"

"That it finally be dark, me dandy dog. That I remember now, what it be like to close me eyes and have oblivion. But ye wait to tell her until the prophecy be completed."

He growled. "It wasn't supposed to end like this."

"This be the only way it can end, me doggish dandy."

There was a strangled inhalation. "Your penalty for bringing a life back from the brink was death. You've known since the day Stain came into our lives . . . yet you never told me."

"And yer ne'er to tell her neither. Not all the days of her life. Now go, or everythin' we've done be for naught."

Luce howled—the hapless cry of an animal snared by a steel trap and forced to chew off a limb. Gusts of air burst through the garden, shaking the vines and leaves all around her, stirring the dust beneath her. She didn't have to see to know when he'd vanished; she could feel his absence in the silence. In the stillness. Even the bees stopped buzzing, chased away by the smoke. With each piercing breath, with each pound of her heart and rush of blood, her skin mourned. She wasn't sure how she could hold on long enough, but she had to.

Around her smoldering ears, a tender chirping song erupted. *Crickets.*

She would've smiled had she any lips left. She once told herself it would be worth it all, so long as she could hear their symphony in the darkness one last time before taking her final breath. Little Stain had made that possible. "Thank ye, wee one. Ye see to yer part, and I'll see to mine."

The cheery chirrups comforted the witch's heart, gave her the strength to concentrate on Thana . . . calling to the bird with her cracked, sand-paper voice.

In moments, Thana's spine-curdling caw answered alongside a beating of wings overhead. The gentle peck of a beak prodded the jacket covering Crony's chest. "Aye there, wretched beast." Crony's tongue tasted of smoke and nectar. "Call to yer mistress. Tell her I kept me hands clean. It all be done by fate. I be at death's door. She be me eyes now. Everything must befall at the proper time." Crony hoped Dyadia would at last open her mind and heart to her. They had unfinished business. She'd like to make peace before it ended.

The large bird nested along the crook of her neck, its downy feathers a welcome torment against her raw flesh. The crickets sang louder as Crony waited, as if they could see Lachrymosa's final memory stretching within her skull, pressing to get out. May-let, even more, they could sense the alignment of things; very soon now, all would be as it was in that golden time before Crony stole away a sorcerer's dying breaths and tore the world in twain.

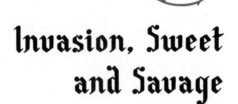

26

Invasion, Sweet and Savage

ithin Neverdark's latticework shrine, Prince Vesper had been laid upon the dais, cradled by a cushion of moonflowers and twigs. A canopy of glassy cobwebs, attached to four wooden stakes, hung a few feet above him, sparkling in the ceremonial luminary's starry light. Fragrant curls of cinnamon incense comforted and anchored the prince's spirit to his inert body. Dressed in royal robes, fur-trimmed tunic, stockings, and boots, he was regal and elegant; those who kept vigil commented on how he favored his kingly father of bygone years, but only in form. For all intents and purposes, Vesper appeared dead, or rather he appeared to have never been alive to begin with.

He looked more like a tribute—a gold-gilded likeness of Nerezeth's evening star—from his toes to the lovely bow of his upper lip. If not for the untouched flesh between his eyebrows, along his straight nose and reaching to his nostrils, forestalled from surrendering to the curse by Dyadia's quietus thrall, there would be no hope to revive him. As it stood, hope was all Nerezeth had, and even those who had once considered him bedeviled prayed for his recovery. They could no longer deny his sacrifices, starting with that first sip of sunlight. However rash, the action was one of a monarch-in-the-making—a king who would one day love his people even more than himself.

Crowds had congregated around the shrine since the prince's arrival—Nerezethites of all walks praying to the stars for his health. The final observance, consisting of over seventy commoners, had recently been cleared out. Now none remained in the arboretum other than two of the prince's most trusted men—Lieutenant Cyprian and Lord Tybalt—who guarded the shrine's entrance.

A regiment of five watched the heavy exterior door to Neverdark's iron edifice itself, waiting outside in the snow and biting wind to usher Eldoria's princess into the world of manufactured sunlight and astonishing botany. Her entourage had arrived at the obsidian castle some half-hour earlier, where "Lady Lyra" delighted everyone with her ability to speak—having learned to shape words and sentences with her singsong voice while in seclusion over the years. Most surprised of all was Prime Minister Albous. When he tried congratulating her in their ancient sign language, Regent Griselda quickly pulled him aside. She requested his help as she and her two daughters joined Queen Nova in the throne room to oversee the placement of Eldoria's colors around the dais for the coronation.

In the meantime, Selena, joined by a half-dozen Nerezethite guards and Eldorian soldiers alike, escorted "Lady Lyra" to the shrine, where Madame Dyadia was to meet them shortly to awaken the prince. Once inside the arboretum, Selena and the night guards took off their heavy furs, accustomed to the balmy gardens and meadows brushed with soft violet-gold light. The Eldorian guests paused to admire the landscapes. Fragrant and colorful foliage stretched out for several leagues in every direction, interrupted only by the wooden-and-wire edifices of the jackdaw aviary and the livery where the royal birds and horses—their coats and feathers tinged with a soft purplish hue—ate, trained, and frolicked within their enclosures. In a distant pasture, Eldoria's blood-bay stallions had been turned out to graze.

The springtime atmosphere convinced Eldoria's princess to stay within her nightsky suit, as she claimed to be leery of the fireflies afloat overhead—fed with the same mix of pollen and sun that had cursed the prince. She had learned to play her part and play it well. Under her mother's guidance, she'd packed her "shadow attendants" within a bag which now waited in her guest chambers. For though her goblin apparitions could pretend to shy away from light, they didn't disappear in the sun as true shadows did.

Selena led the entourage across a winding path and the footbridge, unaware that it wasn't the true princess's footsteps crossing over enchanted rocks and steaming water beside her . . . unaware that the glowing moonlit complexion, silver hair, and songbird voice belonged to another, who was in fact only moments away from arriving.

Back in Eldoria, within a humble dirt room belonging to an equally humble witch, Luce had returned, this time in his ethereal form—translucent and untouchable. While Edith completed the elixir, he swooshed about the walls, refusing to allow Lyra to corner him. Each time she asked of Crony's whereabouts, the higher in the room he spun. Only when Edith finished her task did he materialize, with his red, feathery wings swooping high behind him. Lyra touched the feathery appendages and her fingers skimmed through, appearing on the other side as if the wings were a mirage. They were beautiful, but instead of being elated to have them again, her guardian was stoic—tragedy written in his eyes and carved into every ageless feature.

Lyra signed: *You are a creature of flight and capriciousness again. This should be the happiest moment of your life.*

He ground his teeth, holding his emotions at bay as he always did. "Crony gave up something precious for these wings."

What did she give up? Lyra asked, but again received no answer. Luce's silence pained her enough she hugged him until his muscles relaxed . . . until Edith brought over two vials of smoking, amber liquid that smelled as pungent as rust and as salty as the ocean.

Before taking her vial, Lyra made a promise: *As queen of Eldoria, I will use all my resources to win back whatever Crony lost. She saved me, and mothered me. You and I will have ample time to show her our gratitude. She'll outlive us all. Take heart in that.*

Luce only clinked their vials together and told Lyra to drink to their success.

She downed the magical elixir in the same instant as her sylph guardian—each holding the other's free hand. Before she could blink, she dissipated to a thousand particles, as if she were made of butterflies, leaves, dandelion fluff—all things that careened and floated on the wind, lightweight and care-free. There was a rush of warmth, and then a slash of cold. When she came together once more, she and Luce stood toe to toe in a latticework dome with glowing white spiders scrambling along the floor or hanging from the ceiling on tendrils of web. Even though Luce still had his pack with the mysterious boxes on his shoulder, Lyra searched for the saddlebag's straps atop her own, and was relieved to find her treasures had made it as well.

The two had materialized behind a Nerezethite banner; an emblem's silver seams showed through on the back of the shimmery black fabric: a large star along with a crescent moon and three smaller stars. Overhead, crisscrossed slats formed a roof. Light from outside painted Lyra and Luce in blocks of violet gold. She threw a grateful glance to Luce who still winced from the bitter, metallic flavor that coated their tongues and made their throats itchy. He had insisted she wear her lacewing cloak for protection, in case they ended up in the midst of a thorn thicket. Considering the soft glow that warmed her face through the nightsky mask—much like the sun at the Crystal Lake—he'd been wise to do so.

Glimpses of meadows and gardens showed through the trellis at their backs. A floral-scented breeze wafted in and tugged the hem of her cape, car-rying the sounds of birds, horses and cattle, waterfalls and gurgling brooks. Her senses . . . her heart, they brimmed full, savoring this flavor of life—everywhere. It was beautiful. Thousands of fireflies drifted like glimmering dust motes along the roof and outside, reminding Lyra of the dance she and Scorch had shared so long ago beneath a rainfall of cinders. Though in truth, she'd been dancing with a prince . . . her betrothed, and neither had known it. She hoped they'd get the chance to relive that moment. A pang of worry echoed within her like the gong of a warning bell.

She oriented herself; the fireflies were insects, not sparks of flame shaken from a Pegasus's mane. She'd read about the arboretum in one of the prince's notes earlier while waiting for Luce to return. Vesper had explained how the manufactured daylight nourished spring flowers and fall harvests, yet also rationed out sickness to certain members of Nerezeth's populace. She hadn't expected to land in that very place, inside a latticed bower.

So, where is he? She turned to Luce with the question. Her hands froze in midair as the breeze caught a corner of the banner and revealed the dais in the center of the enclosure. She pushed Luce aside for a better view.

No. Her breath caught.

The prince was all but a statue now, laying upon a bed of twigs and petals. But that wasn't him, not truly. As both the man and the Pegasus, he was stalwart, alert, wise, and witty. To see him so silent . . . so immobile . . . provoked a tearing sensation behind Lyra's sternum. A large luminary reflected a celestial pattern along his golden face—high cheekbones, full lips, and strong chin. The bright stars dimmed as they crossed the only flesh that remained dark, soft, and flexible upon his forehead and nose. Guilt pricked anew when she realized what she had seen in the moon-bog: the glittering flash beneath the shreds of his shirt had been his chest surrendering to his infected blood. His heart and lungs couldn't be far behind. If she'd only stayed, he would never have come to this state.

Eyes hot and stinging, she started forward, swiping the flag aside so she might reach him—to touch his nose, to search for the warm rush of breath.

A snap of wind shoved her back and flung the flap into place in front of her.

"Stay hidden." Luce's whisper tickled her ear.

We don't have time! Lyra shouted with her hands. But Luce had already abandoned his bag on the floor next to her feet and shifted from corporeal to ethereal. *He may be two breaths from death and you're flying about like a summer breeze.*

"He's not. He's under a spell of preservation."

Though the explanation gave her hope, she had to force herself to wait, to allow him to think strategically for her, since in this moment her emotions ruled.

She squinted, trying to keep track of her sylphin accomplice's movements. It was like watching the atmosphere itself—that combination of sunlight and water when the beams splintered apart to craft the sheerest rainbow, except this rainbow was shaped like a man—barely discernible except to those who knew how to seek life in hidden places.

"Don't make a sound." Luce's coaxing voice trailed upward, indicating his rise to the domed roof. The fireflies parted for him. "You're about to have company."

Through the slats, Lyra caught sight of two women being escorted by guards and attendants a few steps from the entrance. One she recognized as Vesper's sister, and the other Lyra's false counterpart, judging by the nightsky draped over her lacy orchid gown. A long, flowing train encrusted with pearls and gems showed beneath the cape's hem. Only a princess bride would wear something so glittery, so splendorous.

Lyra thought upon the regal rags beneath her own cape.

This was the cousin who'd so callously taken part in a scheme to murder her and steal her throne—endangering both her kingdom and Vesper's, not to mention Vesper himself. *Lustacia.* The name tasted pungent on Lyra's silent tongue. Her entire body twitched, impatient to confront her. Yet how does one face a past without any prior memory to stand upon?

Lyra couldn't even picture her rival's face. It was impossible to see clearly through the nightsky, which formed a mask. Lustacia and Selena spoke as if they were old friends. Lyra wondered if Vesper had shared portions of the letters her cousin had written in her name. Lyra itched to expose every lie. She owed her cousin all that she'd given Erwan earlier—and more.

An angry heat climbed her cheeks and a new batch of shadows she'd never met—those that darkened the outline beneath the prince's dais—hedged closer while staying outside the patchwork of light.

"Not yet," Luce murmured from above. His airy presence stirred some anchor webs and their spiders. "We don't want to draw attention until you've healed your donkey . . . *prince.*" He amended the latter to appease Lyra's scowl. "Defeat his curse, and no one can deny you're his destiny and Eldoria's true heir. We must have irrefutable proof to countervail your cousin's prophetic characteristics—the ones you're missing. The ones they've already seen and heard in her."

The ones she stole, Lyra mimed. Teeth clenched, she directed the shadows to stand down . . . to wait. They shrank back obediently. Luce swept outside, encircling both Selena's and Lustacia's forms like a gust of wind before returning.

"Your imposter yearns to walk through the wildflowers," her invisible companion whispered, so close his breath pressed the nightsky to Lyra's face. "Like you, she's been hidden away so long, she's missed being outdoors and visiting Eldoria's royal garden. I'll lure her over to pick a bouquet, and encourage the entourage to follow for her protection. However, I sense her desire to see the prince is greater than her need for fresh flowers, so I'm not sure how long it will hold. I'll get you as much time as I can."

With that, he left again. There was a flapping of hems, tunics, capes, and surcoats, then the entire party veered to the left where red, yellow, and blue wildflowers bobbed in the distance beneath a grove of elms. Once only their backs could be seen, Lyra leapt from behind the banner. She carefully cleared a path through the spiders and asked the shadows to keep watch. Pulse racing, she stepped forward—fearing the burn and singe that awaited her flesh and blood . . . more frightened than she'd ever been, even when she'd first lost her identity and stormed a bog to save a winged horse.

The dais came to her waist. She knelt, her hands trembling as she held her thumb in front of Vesper's nose. As his faint breath warmed her skin, she sighed in relief. Her hand lowered to smooth the thick tangles spread around his head—only the ends remained dark and untouched by the brittle golden plague, and those were every bit as soft as Scorch's mane.

Vesper . . . Can you hear me? she asked of his mind.

No answer.

She'd read several notes in the tunnel, and her respect for his human side had grown. How lovingly he described his family and his people; how much he hurt for the ill, especially the children; his affection for his world and all the creatures in it—from the lowliest cricket, to the brumal stags that were enchanted to share his thoughts and guard the hidden borders, to his horse, Lanthe, a precious gift from his father; his hopes for Eldoria and Nerezeth to thrive in peace once they came together under the same sky. All this, along with poetic dreams of a future with his bride . . . so many facets from a man with only half a heart. Now that he was whole, she could only imagine his capacity to love, to reason, to rule. He could teach her so much about being a sovereign. But first, he needed to live.

I know who you are. Lyra made another attempt at mind-speak. *I've looked with my heart, and I see you. And I know who I am, but you do not. I'm the true Princess Lyra. Upon your awakening, all will be made clear. For now, just know I'm fighting for you, and you must fight to live no matter how much this may hurt. I don't know what will happen . . . how we're to unite the sun and moon, what it will take out of us. But I intend to survive, and you must as well. For your people, for your family. And for that little orphan girl who adores her Pegasus and misses squabbling with him. Will you do that?*

His flaxen eyelashes twitched and his eyes rolled beneath their metallic lids. Though she wished to see those expressive eyebrows punctuate his thoughts, they were now as pale and stiff as his lashes and hair; this was all the answer she would get, and it would have to be enough.

Looking over her shoulder, she formulated a plan. She hadn't considered she might save the prince in a place where sunlight and flowers already abounded. Where would she release the reserves, should she be able to drain him of his curse? If she tried to liberate it here in the arboretum, the sunlight would be magnified, which could hurt the Nerezethites.

Outside the iron door and walls awaited the snowy tundra, a world devoid of sunlight and flowers. A land thirsting for life and warmth. Though she'd never seen it, she'd heard tales. *That* was her destination. She glanced through the shrine's latticework. The way out across the footbridge and through the iron door must be hundreds of footsteps at least. Could she make it that far while wrestling exhaustive pain?

No more time to debate; she sat on the dais edge, close enough she could bow her head to the prince's without quite touching. Twigs and moonflowers poked her thighs through her clothes. She waited for the nightsky fabric to encompass them both, like it had her and Luce's hands on the banks of the lake. In dark, velvety increments, the penumbra crept from her to Vesper, binding them until nothing stood between their skin but clothing, as if they were encapsulated by a bubble of black soot. Everything outside became distant and hazy.

Carefully, she pushed up his tunic's furred cuffs to reveal his golden wrists and forearms. The place where she left her handprint in the moon-bog now blended with the rest of his metallic shell, as if they'd never connected. A lump rose within her throat, her regret for abandoning him in the bog unbearable now.

She pressed her fingertip to that healthy swatch of skin between his eyebrows, wanting just once to experience no sunlight between them. No barriers or pain. He felt warm, soft, and giving. The skin trembled beneath her fingertip, as if he sensed her and struggled to furrow his brow.

She leaned her forehead to his and touched noses. Upon contact with the golden shell, a slow-burning heat simmered beneath her flesh, starting at her head and spreading along her chest to her arms and feet. But it wasn't enough . . . the plague clamped tighter around him, hardening his nose even as hers touched it, as if it meant to devour him before her eyes.

No.

She would have to devour it instead.

Though it made her heart thunder to entertain such an intimate move, the prince didn't have time for indecision or timidity. She closed her eyes, cupped both sides of his face, and pressed their lips together. An invasion of liquid flame scalded her mouth and tongue, sucking the breath from her lungs, yet in its wake came an unexpected sweetness, a softening as his lips returned to supple flesh and began to mimic the movement of hers. His throat opened on a breath, and she tasted something both fruity and bitter—the residue of the spell keeping him alive, holding the curse at bay. She swallowed his relieved sigh. His cheeks softened beneath her hands and his jaws worked as he broke free bit by bit and responded to her touch, to her kiss. Then his relief shifted to a ravenous response, as he gorged himself on her moonlight.

The coolness seeped from her body, and yet she still would've drowned in the beauty of sensation, her mouth following his direction, his passion—a lovely exchange of light and dark—until the sunlight he sent back grew so hot it savaged her from within. She could no longer taste the sweetness, for she drank pure combustion: a flame cauterizing her throat and racing through every vein, setting fire to her bones.

She gasped and drew back, hacking. Smoke slipped from her lips and nostrils. Silent screams stretched her broken vocal cords. She struggled to stand and clenched her throat, almost blinded by the yellow brightness radiating from her own skin.

The nightsky fabric abandoned the prince and retreated to contain only her. She toppled backward, saved from a hard landing by the saddlebag still on her shoulders. Daylight scalded her from the inside, wanting out. It razed against every nerve ending, sending jolts of lightning into her muscles. She spasmed and writhed, unable to even crawl toward the entrance and the iron door, to escape into the snowy outer world. The nightsky seemed to understand; it responded, barricading the brilliant light beneath the surface of her skin. The shadows in the room joined the cape to fight the steam seeping from her ears . . . from her nose . . . from her mouth. The lacewing cloak wound around her from head to foot, then lifted her: torso, arms, legs, and toe tips from the floor. She managed one glimpse of the prince—bound and lifted as she was, but it wasn't enough. He wasn't yet flesh and blood; his deep coppery complexion and silken black hair hadn't returned. His eyes remained closed. Though his lips twitched, she wanted more. She wanted to hear his breath, to see his fingers move, clenching and unclenching in a fight to awaken. She couldn't leave, not until she knew he'd live . . . but the choice wasn't hers.

Her stomach jumped as she began to spin in midair, spiders causing the revolutions—hundreds of them wrapping her in their webs, to protect her shadowy cocoon from the light filtering in through the latticework. A slit remained for her eyes and nose, enough to see flowers and vines creeping in from the gardens and meadows. The spiders grabbed them and wove them into their masterpiece, camouflaging her. In the distance, somewhere around the grove of wildflowers, came a beautiful sound. It pierced Lyra's muffled ears—silvery and pure as a nightingale's song—and numbed her pain for an instant.

Perhaps she imagined the song, being enclosed within the nightsky, being carried through the shrine's entrance on a wave of flowers that glimmered with sunlight and multiplied at her touch. Yet Lyra recognized it, a soul-deep knowing: that voice that had once belonged to her. It was the song she would've been singing upon her walk along the sunny banks of the Crystal Lake, upon her first glimpse of her kingdom; it was the song she would've sung upon learning Scorch hadn't died at all, but was the man she was promised to marry; it was the song she'd be singing right now, if only Vesper had opened his eyes and looked back at her like he did in the moon-bog, with a mix of adoration, irritation, and fascination—the eyes of a Pegasus on fire.

The thought of flame snuffed out the music and any hope. Engulfing her, the agony returned tenfold; it was too much . . . too severe. Her brain broiled in her skull, a searing flash that made her question all she saw: Was she truly floating past everyone, encased by glowing flowers and vines glued together with web? Was she truly seeing her treacherous cousin and Selena race past as if she were invisible, stumbling toward the shrine upon hearing the prince cry out in pain? Was she truly only inches from the arboretum's iron door when it flung open and her tidal wave of flowers knocked over the five guards keeping watch in Nerezeth's tundra?

Perhaps it was all a dream, but dreams had never hurt so much.

A gust of frosty wind siphoned through spaces in the webbing as she felt herself, wrapped in her cocoon, being thrust headfirst into a powdery wall of something endlessly white and blissfully cold. In moments, the wall melted away to water, carrying her like a leaf on a swift current into more whiteness. Her hands escaped their binds, and she clawed at icy, thorny surroundings to slow her passage. With each touch, the world erupted into water, light, and color: petals, roots, leaves, and stems flinging out of her fingertips before the whiteness swallowed her again.

At last she'd spent all the sunshine she'd taken, leaving her hollow, aching, and weary. Everything around her had closed. Soggy and shivering, devastated by her failure, she curled up in her bundle of petals, shadows, and webs. Shutting her eyes against the vivid glowing flowers, she allowed her grief to drag her into darkness.

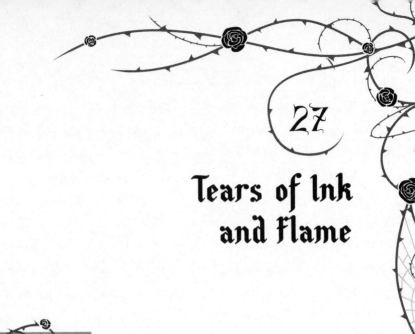

27

Tears of Ink
and Flame

The song that once rang from an enchanted seashell—upon the clear unwavering voice of a nightingale girl—resonated through-out Neverdark, tugging at Prince Vesper's spirit. When he woke, he shouted in elation and pressed his fingers to his lips. His rescuer's kiss remained fresh upon them, just as her words echoed in his mind: *I'm fighting for you.* She'd said more than that, but that was all he could recall.

The instant his eyes pried open, he sought the one who had saved him—his princess . . . his betrothed. At first, all he could see was a trail of flowers and vines along the shrine's floor; then his sister and Cyprian rushed into the entrance alongside a lady wearing nightsky over an orchid gown. She dropped a bouquet of wildflowers at her feet, drew off her hood beneath the latticework's shade, and revealed flawless moonlit skin, long silver hair, and soft purple eyes.

Vesper's breath caught and his pulse jumped. It was her: the embodiment of his youthful dreams, the exquisite princess he'd envisioned marrying and taking to his bed—as a man. Yet there was a wilder side to him now, and it remembered shorn, blackberry hair, scarred flesh, and lashes as long and sleek as the crystalized cobwebs that draped across the dais . . . a savage loveliness forged of wilderness and pain. That girl spoke with a different voice, within his head—no music, only words. Her voice grated like sandpaper when scolding his impulsiveness or contradicting his feral instincts with human wisdom, yet at the same turn it soothed like silk when his fury became too much to bear alone.

Both entities—songstress and thief—intertwined in his fuzzy memories. In hopes to reconcile the two, he took the princess's hand then molded her fingertips around his jaw.

"My darling Vesper." Her intimate, lyrical greeting should have brought him to his feet in triumph, yet he stayed flat on his back. There was no discounting the desire and astonishment on her face, but her eyes were wrong; they didn't sparkle with that fractious intellect he'd always seen looking back at him in the ravine. Only one way to be sure . . .

He pulled her down, clutched the silken hair at her nape, and pressed his mouth to hers, drinking of her until her knees gave and she swooned. She saved herself from falling by taking a seat beside him, breathless and beaming.

However lovely a princess she was, she didn't belong beside him. Those weren't the lips of the one who had given all of herself—her moonlight, her fierceness, her hope. And the fingertips stroking his cheek weren't the same as those that had snuffed out the fire meant to devour his soul.

Vesper sat up and looked pointedly at all those gathered around—his sister, his first knight, gardeners and guards alike. "She's not the one who saved me." A harsh sentiment that he couldn't contain.

"What?" The princess scrambled to her feet, appearing more horrified than wounded. "You must know that's not true! I'm your betrothed! All of the missives we've shared, the beautiful roses you've sent. The prophecy promised us a happy future. My song indeed *saved* you."

Her rebuttal, spoken in that birdsong voice, felt as rehearsed and cautious as all the letters he'd read at her hand. She lacked the fire . . . that stringent honesty and raw emotions that had broken through the most guarded corners of his mind while he ran alongside an orphan in an enchanted forest.

"It wasn't a dream," Vesper assured himself as he sat up to catch the length of hair hanging across the princess's shoulder.

She touched his hand, her features rearranging themselves to an expression of relief. "Yes, you can feel me. I'm real . . . I'm not a dream. I'm here."

He winced. "The illusion of tangible things." He lifted the strands of silver and let them fall in a lustrous cascade. "A braid of hair, a vial of tears, a snippet of song. And words on a page. But ink blurs and paper frays. Vials break. Hair thins and brittles. Songs fade once the final note rings. The only thing that lasts is trust and understanding, speaking without words spoken." Holding her gaze, he felt nothing between them other than physical attraction. He attempted to tap into her mind with silent thoughts; but she didn't answer, for she couldn't hear. "Your songbird voice is to be just that. A song without words. No more, no less."

"I've learned to speak over the years. All for you. Don't you see?"

"Oh, I see. But eyes can lie. The heart doesn't."

Their spectators gasped. The princess gawked in stunned disbelief as clear tears streamed her face.

Vesper caught one on his fingertip and held it to a strand of light. "Clear tears . . . that's wrong as well."

Baffled and bemused, he nudged his betrothed aside so he could walk out of the shrine. He ignored the audience's murmurs and the princess's sobs. He didn't turn back to comfort her. That brutality—once housed within a winged demon-steed—occupied him again, and only one girl had ever managed to gentle it.

Madame Dyadia arrived at the arboretum's iron doorway just as he was stepping out of the balmy warmth and into the frigid, blustering wind. He said nothing to her, simply led the way. A small procession followed, growing to a confused and murmuring crowd. By the time they reached the door, his queenly mother was already there, crying inky tears of happiness upon her son's miraculous reclamation of health.

❊··1··❊

Everyone within the obsidian castle was in a tizzy—from servants and royal family members to the military personnel and guests who'd been honored enough to receive invitations to the wedding and coronation. Noblemen and commoners alike congregated in the great hall where a luncheon feast awaited, the tables laden with roasted wild boar, fish pies, pears in red wine, plums stewed in rosewater, sturgeon coated with powdered ginger, and jellies and creams flavored with dried fig and fennel seeds. They drank spiced mead and hot cider while discussing the fairy tale taking place before their very eyes.

Rumor had spread quickly from chamber to chamber and turret to turret, reaching as far as to the dungeon. A handful of groundsmen had witnessed the miracle within the arboretum. Before the prince even opened his eyes, they had already raced to the castle to give details: the Eldorian princess, while picking wildflowers for her sleeping prince, had been moved to sing— and her song healed Vesper in the shrine just a few feet away, for they heard his victorious cry. Not only had she cured him of his sun-poisoning, but her voice, so pure and captivating, had triggered an explosion of glowing flowers and vines to grow, a surge of life so powerful it paraded through the shrine then plowed down Nerverdark's outer door to reach into the wintry terrain outside. Even now it could be seen: a luminous pathway of creeping myrtles, clematis, bellflowers, and wisteria. The multicolored petals and ivy led through the Grim and into the badlands, melting all the ice and drifts of snow within a two-league radius of its wake. Everywhere it touched, thorns had surrendered to blossoms that shimmered like dewdrops in the moonlight.

In the colonized province, villagers left their houses and tromped through ankle-deep puddles barefoot, for the first time in centuries able to walk outside without their furs and boots. They gathered lukewarm water by the bucketful for cooking and bathing. The sun still shied from their world, the skies were yet divided, and night still reigned. But the snow and ice were gone—at least for the moment.

Regent Griselda and her girls didn't share in the celebration. Instead, they holed up within their dark and opulent turret chamber to commiserate over the disastrous turn Lustacia's triumph had taken.

This was the last place Griselda wished to be. The glossy obsidian walls and floors reminded her too much of Nerezeth's pitch-black sky, and the white lilies in the long-stemmed vases added to the illusion—like a sprinkling of fragrant stars. Many of the Eldorian attendees found the decor exotic and charming. She, however, shuddered, haunted by the vermin that scuttled freely along the corridors and halls of this castle. The pests hadn't even courtesy enough to hide beneath furnishings or in corners.

When Lustacia and her girls first arrived in their chambers, a rash of milky-white mice scampered everywhere: upon the beds, beneath the blankets, covering the wardrobe, tables, and floors. Griselda, along with her three daughters, had clung to one another, convulsing in disgust, as Sir Bartley helped Queen Nova's chambermaids remove every one, carrying them from the room on satin pillows. That was the way here. Creatures, which in her world would be crushed beneath a heel, pounded with a book, or snapped within a miniature guillotine, were treated as royal subjects.

Foolish. Griselda rolled the word along her tongue while sitting upon a gray-cushioned chair. She peeled the hennin from her head and the gloves from her hands. "Foolish namby-pamby." She flung the aspersion at her youngest daughter.

Lustacia lay on one of the three canopied beds, sniffling and dabbing her face with the handkerchief Sir Bartley had offered while escorting them to their room. She hadn't yet been able to return it, as Bartley had left on an errand for Griselda.

The regent wondered how long it might take him to search. She still couldn't say what had inspired her premonition . . . that there was something in that empty shrine that needed to be found. Something that would give her the upper hand once more. It was almost as if her conscience had driven the suspicion, yet her absence of such a hindrance negated that theory. Perhaps, in all her dealings with potions and spell-chants, some magic had at last rubbed off on her.

Absently, she patted her head where her antlers hid beneath piles of plaited hair.

"How could you have been so careless?" She prodded her snuffling daughter to get her mind off the mutation. "Your magical birdsong voice woke the prince out of his trance. It somehow even brought life to this colorless icy expanse. Yet you manage to ruin it all by *weeping* in front of him. The worst thing you could've done! Until we can find an elixir or potion that will conjure tears of fire to leave scorched skin in their wake, you've no business *ever* weeping. Did you forget his royal family was given a vial of Lyra's sooty tears by Kiran himself?"

Wrathalyne and Avaricette, seated on the bed beside their sister, smoothed her pale, shimmery hair. Their elaborate trappings tangled with Lustacia's wedding gown—a prismatic pool of organza, lace, glittering beads, and velvety ruffles that whispered and rustled with each minute movement.

"Mums, you're being heartless." Wrathalyne twirled a silver lock around her fingertip, then dropped it alongside the other strands splayed upon Lustacia's pillow. "She just got wilted! Have some *compassiveness.*"

Avaricette groaned, her shoulders slumping. "So close, Wrath. You almost managed an astute observation. It's forgiveness. *Or* compassion. Choose one or the other. And wilted is what a flower does when it's out in the sun too long. *Jilted* is what the prince did . . . kissed her senseless then left her flushed and titillated with nary a by-your-leave. Will you ever read your lexicon, you dullard?"

"Oh, shush your mouth!" Wrathalyne retorted. "Every time you open it, your rotten teeth turn the air green with stink. Are you sure an ogre didn't crawl in there and die?'

"Would you both just stop your prattling!" Lustacia sat up and tossed the hanky in the air like a white flag of surrender. "None of you . . ." She placed a hand over her lips to contain a sob. "Can even imagine what I'm feeling."

Griselda stood and straightened her ornate gown of red and gold. The bejeweled train dragged the dark floor, making tiny clacking sounds as she strode toward the cheval mirror in the adjoining antechamber. Leaving the door ajar, she watched her girls in the reflection—each so wrapped within their own obliquities they hadn't yet noticed she'd left. She didn't mind such indifference with the older two, expected it, in fact. She'd spent all that time in isolation teaching Lustacia the social graces, while leaving her other two daughters to their own childish, awkward ways. It was unlikely either would ever capture a man's attention at this point. But that hardly mattered. Everything was riding on her youngest. It was time Lustacia took her role seriously, time she understood what was at stake.

Griselda began to unravel the black braids piled high upon her head, watching the girls behind her own reflection.

Wrathalyne leapt up, glaring at Lustacia. "Of course we can imagine your feelings, *Princess Prim*. We saw His Highness when he led that crowd in from the shrine. Those eyes, that skin . . . those lips . . . those muscles. You were mad to let him go. If I'd had that hard, royal body pressed to mine, I'd have clung on like a carbuncle to a longship!"

"A carbuncle?" Avaricette snarled. "It's *barnacle*, you nit!" Standing on the bed, she pummeled her sister in the face with a pillow.

"How dare you!" Wrathalyne's yelp was muffled by the padding crushed into her mouth. Growling, she plowed into her sister. They fell atop the mattress in a riotous melee of knobby elbows, spiky fingernails, and auburn curls.

"Ugh!" Lustacia rolled off the other side, tugging at her gown's train to free it from their wrestling limbs. Lips pursed, she pulled the bag containing her half-light goblins out from under her bed and opened the flap. Five shadowy forms siphoned into midair and hovered around her. She gestured to her sisters, whose antics had wrinkled the satiny bedspread. "I should like my linens refreshed, if you would please."

Spinning with glee, the formless silhouettes flapped the four corners of the bedspread, pulled each one up and around, then wrapped the struggling, whimpering girls within it before dragging it with a thud to the floor. Lustacia simpered at her sisters' resulting grumbles.

"Lustacia," Griselda called to her youngest, having tied a cream-colored scarf around her head. "We're not done speaking."

Her daughter's moonlit complexion—flushed almost purple from crying—caught a flicker of orange light from the fireplace as she crossed the threshold to escape her sisters and their goblin tormentors.

"Shut the door," Griselda said, tucking the ends of the scarf beneath her chin. "We need to be alone."

Lustacia leaned against the closed door and sighed.

Griselda aimed a scolding finger her direction. "I've had enough of your self-pity. Get cleaned up, find that prince, and marry him."

Lustacia gawked for all of a minute before her spirited tongue broke loose. "Certainly! Because it's that simple to make someone love you. Or perhaps you mean to cook up a love potion I can slosh into his wine. The very one you used on Father, perhaps?"

Griselda's hands fisted. The insult was subtle and well-timed. She wished she'd never told her youngest that she'd used such a potion to entrap her husband years earlier. She'd never shared the fact with her other two girls . . .

not that she felt guilt. It was rather more inadequacy. It wasn't something she liked to think about . . . that the only way she'd ever been able to win a man's loyalty was through threats, payment, or elixirs.

"Well, did you bring a potion to help?"

"I actually intended to," Griselda answered. "But the prince's impending death put a crimp in things. I had only time to gather up our Eldorian colors for the ceremonies."

"Ribbons and sigils hardly have magic in them, Mother! Make up a batch of something now, before I have to face the prince again . . ."

Griselda stifled the urge to correct her daughter. The Eldorian colors had more power than anyone could imagine. But better Lustacia didn't have such knowledge. It would only add to her angst. "I haven't ingredients or the book with me."

Lustacia threw her hands up in frustration. "Why wouldn't you bring them? Did you not consider we might need a magical boost if something went awry?"

"Use your acumen, child. If our room were to be searched, it would cast suspicion to find a grimoire within my keeping. It's safely tucked within my chamber in Eldoria."

"Then how do you propose I win his heart, considering you yourself have never had success in such endeavors?"

Griselda allowed her grimace to fully emerge this time. "I may not have had success in love, but I have transcended in lust. Lean on that. Use your assets."

"What, these?" Lustacia spread out her long, graceful arms. The slender lines of her glittery blush-pink gown showcased a small waist and hips juxtaposed against the tight curve of a youthful belly and the rise of voluptuous breasts—all the more enticing where they swelled above the beaded, low-cut neckline.

"Those exactly."

Lustacia crossed her arms over her chest, her sleeve hems fanning like lacy wings from her wrists. "I want love, Mother. *His* love. I want him to admire me for the sacrifices I've made. To know that I've spent five years of my life molding myself into the image of the girl who would make him happy, and to be grateful for it."

Griselda clucked her tongue. "You will never have that. For by telling him, you would lose him."

"And thus the chasm between us," Lustacia whimpered. "When I sang him awake and enraptured his people, I thought I had it . . . I did. I cured him, so he would be forever grateful and ravish me with poetry and passionate embraces. And when those dark eyes opened . . . oh, I could've fallen into them forever. I know I didn't imagine that spark of desire." She pressed a hand to her quivering chin. "But when he kissed me, something . . . changed. He looked me up and down like I was a stranger." She shook her head, her silvery locks shimmering in the firelight. "After all the responses I turned out for every missive he wrote . . . answering them just as a princess would. Yet he tells me I'm not the one who saved him, and leaves. Just like that! Humiliating me in front of his subjects and mine. And you, my doting mother—" Lustacia caught herself and rephrased. "My doting *aunt*, can't even offer consolation. It's always 'Get back up, dust off. Never show any emotions.'"

"Never show your hand," Griselda corrected, looking in the mirror and smoothing the scarf around the offensive protrusions above her temples.

"Quite literally, in your case." Lustacia glared accusingly at her mother's fingers—the silvery blue even more prominent against the creamy head-covering.

Griselda's dark eyebrows rose, wondering how long it would take her daughter to notice the lumps in the fabric . . . to question them.

Lustacia stepped up to share the mirror, intent only on herself. "Am I ugly, then?"

Griselda barked a laugh. "You look like one of them. Ghastly, nondescript. A vanilla cookie sprinkled with sparkly blue sugar. But gloom-dwellers are what he believes is beautiful. This had nothing to do with your appearance. You yourself said you felt an attraction, that his eyes held a spark of interest. Perhaps you simply need to work on delivering more convincing kisses."

Embarrassment deepened Lustacia's bluish complexion. Along with the tears and inordinately long lashes, a proper Lyra-blush—complete with veins darkening beneath her skin's translucent surface—was another thing they'd never quite managed.

"Wrath was right," Lustacia said. "You truly are heartless."

Griselda loosened the knot beneath her chin. "If only I were. If only I'd given away my heart instead of my conscience. Then I wouldn't be so fearful for all of our lives."

Lustacia's attention perked. "What do you mean, our lives? No one's even questioned my tears, other than the prince. Everyone else is focused on him, concerned for his addled mind. They're convinced he hasn't fully awakened from his death sleep. There's nothing . . . other than your dirty hands . . . that can cast aspersions on us. Is there?" She asked the final question with a catch in her throat, for Griselda chose that moment to whip off her scarf and unveil the prongs that were now the size of a baby's hand.

Lustacia gasped and gagged, unable to look away from the warped reflection.

"The discomfort you've been experiencing while wearing your hennin," Griselda began, her thumb tracing the antlers as she herself struggled not to gag. "That is just the beginning."

Lustacia cupped her mouth to muffle a queasy cough. Clear streams raced down her cheeks. "How long?"

"Days or weeks . . . it's hard to be sure."

Lustacia's legs went out from under her; she sobbed.

"Get up," Griselda growled, resisting an unexpected compulsion to stroke her daughter's hair and comfort her as she did when she was a child. It would only feed Lustacia's weakness, and a queen had to be strong. "The only one who knows of my condition is dead. The prince hasn't said he won't marry you. We are not defeated. After all you've endured for this moment, you would give up so easily? Do you love him or no?"

"Yes. I—I do. But . . ."

"A yes is enough. We've no time to waste. All we must do is see that the prince weds and beds you as scheduled. You saw his letters, how passionate he is about those stags who guard his boarders. He will behead us both should he ever learn of our crime. And once we're dead, he'll turn your sisters out into the wilds to die by brambles or rime scorpions. But if you're his queen, carrying his child, you can keep us all safe. We'll request a visit to the Rigamort during our stay here, before he returns with you to Eldoria for his introduction as your king. You'll say we wish to learn everything about his realm. Then we can blame these . . . things . . . on some sort of magical contagion before he ever sees the evidence."

"You truly think he'll go through with the nuptials? He wouldn't even speak to me earlier." Lustacia's skin had grown so pale her veins could almost be seen. In that moment, she looked more like a gloom-dweller than ever before.

"Neither kingdom will give him a choice. You are the only princess of Eldoria. I've assured there's no one surviving to take that title, or your crown. No other can stand with the prince to unite our skies and kingdoms. Everyone wants this marriage. Queen Nova herself is trying to talk sense into him at this moment. He *will* marry you. He dishonored you in their shrine, which I'm to understand is the holiest place in this heaven-forsaken realm. We have that to bargain with."

"And the blood oath," Lustacia mumbled, rubbing her head in search of the knots that would one day burgeon to prongs. She stayed on the floor, beaded pink organza swirling around her like a whorl of petals, and her beautiful features rearranged themselves to something akin to resolve. Though she looked like a dew-kissed rose, Griselda could see the inception of thorns.

There was her queen.

Griselda rewarded her by stroking her head. "Precisely. We can force his hand, involve our military if we must. But that would be a last resort. You have your wiles. Hide beneath the stairwell that leads to his turret . . . when everyone leaves his room, visit him alone. Remind him he must marry you to save his suffering people. He's too honorable to ignore that fact. And even more, he's a man, and all men can be seduced. You've had years of watching me shape that particular weakness to my advantage." She coiled her hair around her antlers once more. "Master it for yourself, and we will live to see you reign over two kingdoms yet."

❀ · I · ❀

In his plush chamber—within the tower adjacent to his betrothed's—Vesper slouched on the edge of his bed. He tapped the skin between his brows with the glowing whorls of a creeping myrtle he'd picked on his way to the castle. He had more company than he liked, and none were whom he wanted them to be.

"My spiritual wards have predicted a night tide." Madame Dyadia spoke from her place beside the dormer window looking out upon the courtyard far below. Her chameleon complexion and enchanted vestments, lit with the orange flicker of a lantern, blended into the gray stones framing the circular pane. Earlier, Vesper had questioned Thana's whereabouts. Dyadia claimed her third eye was keeping watch over Eldoria—to be a lodestar of sorts—for when the moon made a showing there.

As no one knew exactly how the magic was to work—if Nerezeth and Eldoria would physically stand side by side once more, or if they would

416

simply share the sun and moon at different times in their respective realms—
he agreed the portending crow was well positioned.

"When?" Vesper asked of her weather prediction.

"Soon. Upon the surface of the waters taken from the mystic cavern, I
saw snowflakes returning. By the beginning of our cessation course, they'll
multiply on icy winds to smother the flowers and vines. The thorns will be
reborn and our living rainbow will withdraw back into the cold, dead ground.
It is better we perform the ceremonies now as planned . . . ride the faith and
hope the princess has invoked in our people. Perhaps, upon your vows, this
consolidated wonder between our two kingdoms will unite us and merge the
skies at last."

"Something's wrong with the prophecy," Vesper said for the twentieth
time. He inhaled the myrtle's mint-and-honey notes, then laid it upon the
tray balanced on his pillow alongside the remains of the meal Queen Nova
had insisted he eat. The fish pie and creamed figs may as well have been
tasteless, but he'd managed to swallow enough to mollify her.

"You're making no sense." His lady mother eased down beside him, the
jeweled crickets abandoning her skirts as the fabric crushed against the edges
of his mattress. They hopped beneath the safety of his bed. "How can you
refute that it was the princess's song that saved you?"

"Her song *woke* me," he corrected. "But it didn't save me."

"There are eyewitnesses. Your own sister saw it. And how can you have
second thoughts of your bond with Lady Lyra, after the way you kissed her
in the shrine?"

"She has romantic feelings for you, brother," Selena said, standing beside
the desk where Cyprian sat. Her hand rested at the back of the knight's
neck beneath the plaited lengths of his silvery hair. "All your worry has been
for naught."

Cyprian watched Vesper studiously and added, "Selena is right. There was
sincere affection in the princess's trembling hands, in her tears."

"Tears the color of water, not ink. They look nothing like the jewels upon her hairpin," Vesper insisted.

"Her *enchanted* hairpin," Cyprian added. "Some might argue the tears were altered when they became jewels—that the color's no longer a true comparison. Either way, we don't have the pin in our keep. It's in that thieving boy's hand—"

"He's not a boy. He's a girl . . . *my* girl." Vesper gritted his teeth upon watching everyone's reaction—his loved ones' faces fraught with concern or cynicism, most likely both. Queen Nova anxiously plucked at the satiny black quilt upon his bed while keeping watch on Dyadia's distorted movements at the window.

Selena cleared her throat. "Well, I for one am grateful to see your obstinance returned, Vesper. It's good to have you hale and hearty enough to set our queenly mother's teeth on edge once more. At last I'm the favorite again."

Cyprian lifted his gaze to Selena's and a corner of his mouth quirked up.

The habit of smoothing things over with a dose of wit was something Vesper and his sibling had always shared, and he found himself wanting to smile, though it was more from seeing his sister and best friend so comfortable in their new romance than anything else.

He stretched out his long legs beneath the traveling trousers he'd donned in place of his ceremonial garb, relishing the pure red blood that coursed through him. His sister was right about his health. He felt surprisingly robust for someone who'd been flirting with death for years. His body no longer had the limitations of petrified musculature or metallic flesh. The sun's flame no longer lapped within, threatening to overtake. His limp was gone, he looked and felt like himself again—the dark prince with his lord father's bone structure, features, and stamina.

Physically, he lacked for nothing. Emotionally, he lacked patience. He was at a loss for how to explain his reservations when the only savior anyone had seen was the princess preparing for a wedding in her guest chambers at this very moment.

How could he marry a stranger when all he could think of was the little foundling who was the truest friend and partner he'd ever known?

Yet that damned prophecy said he must . . .

"Your kiss sealed the betrothal, my son. You have to realize this."

Vesper growled. "As I told Regent Griselda when she intercepted us upon my entrance to the castle, I kissed her niece to prove to myself it *wasn't* her who broke my curse. And just as I told the regent then, I'm telling you now: I won't apologize for seeking answers before I sign my life and my kingdom away."

His lady mother's hand gripped his. "We have an oath already signed—in my own blood and the princess's father's. You are not only condemning our people to die by this illness inflicted by artificial light, but you are condemning us to a war we cannot win."

Cyprian stood. "Majesty, please heed our queen. You've seen for yourself the military escort Eldoria brought. With so many of our own fallen to illness, they outnumber us fifty to one. The last thing we should be doing is challenging their sour-tempered regent over a five-year contract."

Unless you have proof that the prophecy is flawed, such that could sway both kingdoms, Selena said privately within Vesper's head so no one else would overhear. He turned a grateful glance her direction, and she tipped her head—her smile soft and encouraging. At least she was trying to understand . . . to see his side.

Vesper retrieved the luminous flower from his pillow. "Lady Mother, do you remember when we last spoke of my shadow-bride? I made her a cape, worried she couldn't embrace this world, thorns and all. I feared she would be too tender." He flipped his mother's hand in her lap to place the creeping myrtle upon her palm, then curled her fingers atop it. "You said if the prophecy is to be taken at its word, my betrothed should be capable of handling everything . . . the terrain, the creatures, the night tides, as well as me. That we should be evenly matched already, today." Vesper squeezed her hand to a fist. "I'm telling you, I've found that match. And she's not the princess."

Queen Nova broke loose and opened her fingers to reveal the crushed flower, its light faded from its petals. "Before her song's intervention, you were a statue." Her voice cracked. "Moments away from your heart turning to stone. *This* would've been your ending." She let the flower's remains fall to the floor in demonstration. "Drained of life and lost to us." Her chin quivered. "Eldoria's princess may seem tender skinned and mild mannered, but she cured you. I'm beholden to her now. Indebted to her always. I will make any compromise necessary to accept her as your bride. As should you."

"This doesn't feel like making a compromise, it feels like making allowances. The two are very different things." Vesper rose and strode to the dormer window next to Madame Dyadia, looming over the sorceress. "She's out there. Somehow, she made it here into Nerezeth."

"If there is another who's followed you from the day realm and seeks to infringe upon your foretold and sworn marriage," Madame Dyadia broke in, "she will be accused of treason. She will suffer imprisonment or worse. All present witnessed Eldoria's princess sing you alive. This other girl was nowhere to be seen."

Vesper rubbed the nape of his neck, wary of the logic. During their life together in the forest, each time Stain brought flowers to bloom, it drained her . . . hurt her. After all she'd done today, she might be half-dead. At the very least, defenseless. A wild rage thundered in his heart to think of someone harming her. He'd have to find her first.

"Cyprian, round up our best trackers and saddle Lanthe. But be discreet."

The knight's reflection stirred in the windowpane as he propped his hand at the baldric where a borrowed sword stood in place of his late father's, the other one having been destroyed by Vesper while in the form of the Pegasus.

A fact Cyprian had yet to learn. The first knight's pale hair formed a white blur in the glass as he glanced from Selena to the queen.

"Did you serve me out of pity, then?" Vesper baited without turning. "Now that I'm free of the golden plague, am I no longer your king? Must I add anointing a new first knight to this day's list of encroaching ceremonies?"

Cyprian knelt until his nose almost touched the obsidian floor. "I beg your forgiveness, Majesty. My loyalty and respect are yours to my last breath. I will see it done."

Vesper nodded and Cyprian left the room, closing the door behind him. The lantern's popping flame accentuated the muffled breathing and suppressed criticisms from the three who still remained. Vesper intensified his study of the window, beyond the abandoned courtyard where the land surrendered to vines and flowers—a tender light source competing with the moonlit puddles. A handful of royal scouts had ventured out earlier, following the trail of creeping plants to the edge of the Grim. They hypothesized, by its trajectory, that it led to the Rigamort. It may have even managed to melt a tunnel through the avalanched snow plugging the entrance. Due to the unpredictable behavior and delicate state of the brumal stags, the scouts felt ill-equipped to investigate in depth without their king's accompaniment. They returned with nothing more than that scant report.

A flurry of white flakes careened against the black sky, blotting out the stars—Dyadia's prediction of a blizzard proving true. Vesper cursed the timing. They would have to hurry before everything was swallowed up again. He scrubbed his whiskered face, grateful to feel the human features, the soft, giving flesh and bristled scruff, yet at the same time missing his wings and four legs . . . missing the ability to cover large areas in the blink of an eye.

"We'll ride to the Rigamort. Surely there will be a clue, if nothing else." He spun on his heel to make for the door, but the queen stood behind him.

Eyes lifted to meet his gaze, she hemmed him between her and the window. "*We?* You plan to gallivant about the badlands when you should be preparing for the ceremonies? Send your trackers out, fine. But your duty is here, comforting Lady Lyra and smoothing the regent's ruffled feathers. It is time you learn your place as king."

His eyebrows lowered. "It is time *you* learn my place as king." There was a hardened edge to the rebuke—a gruffness that brooked no argument. "I covet and respect your advice, but from this day forward, it will be delivered as such: *advice*. Whether in public or alone. You are not my commander, nor even my right hand. You'll always be my lady mother, but you will address me as a man to be honored, not a boy to be coddled."

Her face paled, draining the bluish softness to white. The plaits of her silvery hair, woven into her glistening crown, reflected the firelight as she placed a hand on his chest. "The coronation and wedding ceremonies, they're to take place within the hour. Please reconsider."

Her humble plea might have softened him at one time, but not now that he'd found himself again. "If I leave while the snow's still melted, I can make the trip there and back in half the time. Five . . . six hours, at most. Many of the cadaver brambles have been exposed and found dead by our scouts, much like the thorns, so there's another hurdle lifted." He placed his hand over hers. "This must be done before the night tide."

"What will the people think?" pressed the queen. "Or the regent and the princess? How will it look, you leaving in search of another girl?"

"No one is to be told why I'm making the trek. If questioned, you will answer only this: I am the reigning heir of Nerezeth who just awoke from a death sleep. If I wish to postpone the ceremonies for a few hours to gather my thoughts and assess how our altered terrain is affecting my people, none should—" He stopped and shook his head. "None *will* question me."

"Heed your words, Your Highness," Dyadia pleaded, her black-and-white stripes becoming fully visible. Vesper focused on her third eye's empty socket. "The quietus thrall may have left you hazy—inclined to delusions. If that is the case, you're endangering this hard-won peace upon nothing more than a dream."

"I did not dream her touch upon my skin, nor her voice in my head," Vesper answered. "No more than I dreamed for these past five years that my prideful and implacable half ran and flew beside her in the Ashen Ravine." He aimed an accusatory frown to the sorceress. "But you let me believe it was a dream. You withheld important details. Convinced me Eldoria's princess was my missing piece. When all along, I had to complete *myself*. It took a girl saving me again and again, putting herself at risk each time, a girl who loved me unconditionally—to lead me to that truth. And now, I intend to find her and thank her properly."

Dyadia maintained an unreadable expression but exchanged glances with the queen.

"What are you saying?" Queen Nova asked of her son, her fingers curling under his, wrinkling the open lapel of his shirt. "That you're in love with a simple urchin?"

Yes. Vesper kept the answer to himself. There was no question how he felt about Stain when they ran together in the ravine, and it was the only explanation for the emotions careening through his body and mind in this moment. But he didn't have the luxury of romance or love . . . not with the prophecy hanging over him and two kingdoms.

"Don't ever call her an urchin," he answered, struggling to keep his frustration and anxiety in check. "And she's anything but simple."

"You have an obligation to fulfill," the queen refuted. "Not to some girl who happened to befriend you in your temporary vessel when you were trapped in the Ashen Ravine. You are fated to marry Eldoria's princess."

His lady mother's acknowledgment of the magical split held no surprise for him. She was there in the cavern, watching his exiled half take form, which made it sting all the more that neither she nor the sorceress had ever told him.

"Temporary vessel? Ashen Ravine?" Selena furrowed her eyebrows. "What are you all talking about?"

Queen Nova shushed her daughter. "Vesper, please, think of our people. They are the reason we chose to omit certain . . . details."

"I *am* thinking of our people. As if I've been able to think of anything else over the past five years! My blood can no longer aid them, so I must bring the sun back. I understand that, and will do what it takes. Even if it means marrying someone I don't love. I'm simply trying to ensure that the one who truly cured me is safe."

Selena stepped into their circle, still wearing her bewildered expression. She looped an arm through Vesper's in a show of support. "I want to know what details you've been keeping from Vesper. From all of us."

Queen Nova dipped her head, feigning interest in a row of pearly crickets still clinging to her hem.

Vesper snarled. Part of him understood; he was indignant the day his lord father slipped away . . . indignant and unbending. He had done something irreversible and shortsighted. "I realize you and Dyadia were desperate to save me all those years ago. However, to sway who I loved, what I believed— all for a foretelling? No wonder my faith in this prophecy wavers more with each passing hour."

"Can you forgive us, my son?" Queen Nova asked, having the decency to look ashamed.

Vesper grimaced. "What choice do I have? You're my lady mother, and I love you." He shifted his gaze to Dyadia. "And I need your conjuring and portents." A splash of acid churned in his stomach. "But oh, to be that stallion again, to crash every piece of furniture in this room; to gallop down flights of stairs, and leave everyone who dares stand in my way in a wake of flame and fury, without a thought as to consequences." He ground his teeth, seeing the shame on Queen Nova's face creep across Dyadia's own. "You both expect me to behave as a gentleman king, after having tasted the power and freedom held within the heart of a beast." He felt Selena's eyes on him. Her fingers trembled where they held his bicep. "I fear that's impossible, because I rather liked being the beast. But, there's hope for you yet, should I find *her*. She has a way of reasoning with me, defusing my rage with honesty . . . a talent you both seem to lack."

A sudden, yipping howl rang out—familiar, yet completely foreign to his kingdom. Vesper glimpsed through the window. Beneath the haze of moonlight and beyond the castle wall, a splotch of red fur settled on its haunches and looked upward. Vesper leaned closer, forehead pressed against the cold glass. As if it had been waiting for him to look down, the svelte creature yipped again, hopped up on four legs, and shook out a long, fluffy tail. Leaving prints on the whitening ground, it sauntered toward the badlands along the flower path.

Vesper's heartbeat thumped wildly against his sternum. The ancient scrolls had told of winter wolves chasing out all the smaller wild dogs before the earth closed. Although this might appear to be an ordinary fox, it was a miracle, for wherever there was Luce, Stain would be close at hand.

"Clever fox," Vesper mumbled, thumping the glass with his finger. "I take back every bad thing I ever thought about you. Almost."

"Who are you talking to?" Queen Nova and Dyadia moved in to see.

Selena bobbed to the other side, peering around his shoulder. She gasped. "What . . . is that a—? No such creature has graced Nerezeth for centuries!"

Vesper left the room without another word, leaving his lady mother and Dyadia still staring out the window.

Selena followed him down the corridor, rushing to keep up with his pace. "I want to know what happened. What's all this talk of horses and flying in the ravine?"

"When I get back, I'll tell you everything."

"Tell me on the ride over. I'm going with you. Should I bring Nysa to help track?"

He draped his arm around her shoulders. "Leave her in the kennels. We have a fox for that." He glanced down at her, already in her traveling tunic and trousers. She'd been dressed for a fight while keeping vigil over him at the shrine. He had a poignant thought then, of his little foundling girl in torn rags and bare feet who had never had the chance to wear anything pretty. "Let's stop by your wardrobe first. I believe she's close enough to your size."

Selena looked up into his face, curiosity tugging at her silvery eyebrows. "What's her name, brother . . . this girl you seek? And what is she to you?"

"They call her Stain. She's my true heart's mate. I've no idea how to proceed . . . no idea how I'm to bind my life to another, when I already belong to her—body, mind, and soul."

28

Princess of Ash
and Thorns

Lyra awoke with a start, jolted by snuffling sounds on the other side of her sticky cocoon. A sour film of mud, soot, and soggy leaves coated her tongue. She smacked the taste away and attempted to move. Every ligament and bone crackled, as if she'd rusted all the way through. Her resultant groan silenced the odd snuffles for an instant before they resumed.

She stretched, and the nightsky withdrew into the lacewing cloak, freeing up the shadows. They seeped away to find new hiding places. Upon their retreat, an icy chill crept in, along with the sound of dripping water. Shimmering blue light pierced through the tracery of vines still swaddling her. Harsh tugs began to pull at the weave from the outside, in synch with chomping, smacking, and swallowing.

Lyra stiffened with horror. Her cocoon was being eaten. She couldn't scream . . . couldn't cry out for help. Her fingers moved instinctually, pinned as they were at her waist, though whatever beast would eat spider silk, flowers, and ivy wouldn't likely have acumen enough to read her pleas for mercy.

She twisted her shoulders to bend her elbows, then dragged her hands along her body, forcing them up the tight casing until they settled beside her chin. Sucking in a breath, she shoved her fists out of the slit for her mouth then tore away the webbing, luminous petals, and stems in clawing motions. It was like being born again . . . into a cool, dripping cave.

Her head and shoulders plunged through, and her attackers pranced back—some snorting, some growling, others whinnying nervously, their pronged heads held high. Several had glowing flowers and leaves hanging from their muzzles, half-chewed. She leaned closer for a look at the gleaming scales upon their backs and chests. One in front—taller than the others by two prongs—lowered its antlers in warning. The horns glittered in the dim blue light. Two more pawed panther-like forelegs along the stony ground, their scratching claws reverberating through her spine.

Peeling the rest of the cocoon from her clothes caused the lacewing cloak and saddlebag to slip from her shoulders. Chill bumps raised along her skin beneath her damp tunic and pants. Lyra attempted to stand. Her legs went out from under her. A surge of dizziness forced her to sit and she stared, in awe of the graceful, magnificent creatures around her. In his letters Vesper had spoken of his gatekeepers. If these were indeed brumal stags, she was at the juncture between Nerezeth and the Ashen Ravine.

Vesper. A tearing sensation scored her chest. Last she saw him, he was still dying. Prickles of heat teased her tearless eyes, but even if she had the ability to weep, she wouldn't. She must have faith. She'd freed his lips, his nose. His throat had opened enough to share breaths between them. Even if she hadn't cured him, it was possible the sorceress could've awoken and healed him. She had to find out.

She pushed herself up, propping an arm on a rock formation for support. One of the stags brayed in warning. Lyra shook off any reservations. Just like when she'd first stumbled upon her Pegasus, she felt a kinship to these beasts. The stags were partially made of moonlight like her; their scales and antlers gleamed with it. To look upon them had the effect of reviving a soul's hope and serenity.

It fed her desire to find some way to Nerezeth and take back what was hers . . . if in fact she had anything left to fight for.

Fingernails clawing into the rock, she stepped alongside it, slowly regaining strength. Glancing over her shoulder, she scrunched her nose. The source of the shimmering blue light—a tunnel on the far end—painted the cave's walls with an incandescent glaze. Her eyes lit to see even farther: the dripping stalactites and cascading streams that ran from high above to make puddles here below. Flower petals and leaves floated atop the water. The shoots and blossoms, having propelled her cocooned form into these depths, trailed all the way up a wide, winding ledge in a glowing trail. They gave off a gentle heat. They're what had kept her from freezing on the journey here.

At the highest point overhead, moonlight radiated from an opening. That had to be the entrance to the cave. She could follow the flower trail out and retrace the way she came, though she had no guess how long it might take to cross the terrain.

Hours? Days? Vesper mightn't have that long. She'd heard his cry of pain.

Considering the frigid cold outside, and all the creatures of the winter wilds that she'd seen in Dregs's booth: cadaver brambles and rime scorpions, tinder-bats and bone-spiders, it would be no easy trek. Unsettling sounds stirred overhead . . . rubbery flapping wings and scuttling, bone-tipped legs, reminding her she'd first have to make it out of the cave. She stifled an uneasy crimp in her gut and turned again to the stags. Could these majestic creatures help? But as she watched, she realized some were weaker than she felt herself.

Beyond the stags watching her with interest and wariness in their eyes, were others that appeared ill, lying upon the ground. Smears of shimmering gold, reminiscent of Vesper's blood, coated the rocks close to them. They took turns resting their heads upon it.

A horrifying thought clawed through her: what if, by introducing sunshine to their world of ice and frost and warming their cave, she had harmed them? Yet the light seemed to strengthen them—it was why they each grappled for a spot beside the rocks. That must be why the healthier stags were eating her cocoon; the flowers shimmered with sunlight, as did every single blossom that now wound around the cave.

Following a hunch, Lyra began to pluck the ones closest to her, tossing them toward the sickliest of the herd. They stretched their necks, nibbling the petals, and one by one gathered strength enough to stand and totter closer to the supply. Once she'd made a sizable pile that the stags ate from contentedly, she gathered the lacewing cloak and saddlebag, then started toward the winding ledge alone. Three healthy stags stepped into her path, blocking her. Their stances weren't threatening so much as determined. They meant to keep her there.

She shook her head. They didn't understand that she'd left her kingdom in the hands of an imposter. That she didn't know how much, if any, of her mind-speak had reached Vesper, if he'd heard what he meant to her. She dug through the saddlebag, in search of the dried apples and cheese she'd packed for their trip to rescue Crony, hoping to distract the gatekeepers with fruit. She'd only just cupped a handful of spongy bits when the stags began to bray. The entire herd turned their long lionlike tails to face her, circling a silhouette that appeared out of nowhere.

A familiar voice grumbled, though she couldn't quite place it. Lyra dropped the apples into the bag and inched forward, straining for a glimpse through the line of antlers. At the sound of stomping feet, the newcomer came into view, rising in height to tower over the stags.

Dregs's bulbous eyes spanned the cave before coming to rest on her. "Princess!"

Lyra clapped her hands over her mouth, too stunned to attempt asking how he arrived or if he'd seen Crony and Luce.

He smacked his lips and *tsk*ed. "Blasted Edith said the drink would find my kin, not land me in the brumal den."

His cryptic words wouldn't have made sense a day ago, but after using magic herself to arrive at Vesper's side, she understood. What she wouldn't give for another dose now. When last she'd saw the goblin, he was searching for his cousin. Edith must've used the same spell for Dregs. But why would it have brought him to this place?

Dregs waved a hand, trying to shoo a path through the stags. "Have you seen any goblins, dead or alive? Could be just one, or as many as five . . ."

Before Lyra could answer, threatening growls and panicked nickers rumbled through the stags, cutting the conversation short. The leader lowered his head, and with a throaty neigh, charged the goblin. Dregs yelped and lost balance on his tall heels.

He smacked the ground and the lead stag led the others to attack, claws out and antlers lowered for goring. The sickening sound of grunts and ripping cloth filled the cave. Lyra snatched her lacewing cloak and whipped it on, commanding the nightsky fabric to lift her in the air like before. The move landed her on the lead stag's back. The creature reared but she hugged its neck tight, her stomach rocking. Her aching fingers and hands cramped. They wouldn't be able to hold for long. Dregs cried out again.

Desperate, Lyra pressed her forehead beside the stag's ear, sending soothing thoughts. *We're not here to harm you . . . We're here to help your prince . . . your king. Vesper,* she offered, hoping as a night creature it would hear her somehow. *I need to get to Prince Vesper . . . Nerezeth's evening star.* Her throat cinched tight on a silent sob.

Enough, the word tapped her mind on Vesper's voice. Her heart leapt upon hearing him, though he wasn't speaking to her: *No harm shall come to these two. They're here on royal business.*

The stag stopped bucking. It panted, its ribs expanding and compressing where Lyra straddled it. The other stags gathered round with ears perked, also attuned to their king's voice. Dregs, no worse for wear other than a few scrapes and bruises, crawled out from the circle of legs and tails and clambered onto an outcropping of rock where he groused about his shredded clothes.

Lyra slid from the stag's back and dropped the lacewing cloak at her feet, looking around her, seeking him. *Vesper.* She sent up the thought, hungry to hear his voice again.

"Up here." His answer, aloud this time, echoed and drifted from the heights where he and his horse took the long, winding ledge down alongside her trail of flowers. There were three silhouettes waiting at the top, not yet following, with two horses alongside them.

Dregs leapt from his rock and scrambled forward. Standing back, Lyra gathered the saddlebag and held it to her chest like an anchor to keep from floating away on a flutter of nerves.

Did Vesper remember how she touched him? Kissed him? Or did the sorceress save him, leaving only the memory that Lyra abandoned him in the moon-bog to die?

As Vesper arrived, Dregs bowed to him. Vesper laid a hand on his head. They shared a whispered conversation, then he sent the goblin toward the cave's entrance where Vesper's companions still waited, too high up to identify.

Vesper dropped his horse's reins as the ledge leveled to the ground. He shrugged out of a fur cape dotted with snow and let it crumple in a heap behind him. With the hood gone, several strands of dark hair fell into his face—as unruly as Scorch's mane ever was. He wasn't dressed as royalty now, but as the man she saw in his tent at camp, the man who sat with her in the moon-bog, trying to convince her of his identity. A light-colored shirt and black leathery breeches conformed to lean, muscular lines and showcased a graceful stride as he approached—all limps and physical limitations gone. The burnished depth of his skin was healthy and flawless, aside from the scars he would always have as reminders.

He was cured, but by whom?

Lyra's pulse sped, hammering in her wrists and at her collarbone. The stags cantered around her in a stampede. Even the weaker ones joined the fray, though plodding slower. Their passage swished the jagged hem at her ankles. They surrounded their king with soft nickers of greeting. He fussed over each of them as one would a beloved child. Then, upon his mental command, they parted and returned to the pile of glowing flowers.

Vesper watched her, unmoving. Lyra waited, too. It was like starting over—standing on this altered bridge, trying to find her footing, wary of the rapids that waited to swallow her should she move too fast and slip off.

She attempted to hide her trembling hands by tightening her hold around the saddlebag. Then, remembering it belonged to him, she held it out.

"So, you're just willing to give those gifts up without a fight, after how hard you worked for them?" His deep, husky voice echoed off the walls. Blue light flashed across his face, his long lashes shadowing the emotions in his eyes. She didn't know what he meant; didn't know how to read him in this form. Was he teasing? Angry? Even without seeing his gaze clearly, she knew it was as inscrutable as a raven's. She was vulnerable beneath it, stripped down to her shorn head and lacy rags.

Say something, he prompted in her mind.

She struggled for a response. Everything was too big for words, too life-changing. She finally settled on *I am afraid.*

He tilted his chin. *Of this moment?*

She shook her head. *Of you.*

He frowned, as if taken aback. *Why? You know me to my bones. And I'm safer now . . . no hooves itching to trample. No flame threatening to char.*

She squeezed the bag against her chest. *You can hurt me more as a man than you ever could've as a horse.*

Ah. What if I make an effort not to be such an arrogant jackass in this form? Will that help? He raised his eyebrows teasingly.

She huffed a surprised laugh, relieved. Of course he wasn't angry. He was unsure of where things stood between them, like her. But they'd been here already—connecting beyond their differences and the inconceivable circumstances that had thrown them into one another's paths.

Reaching into the saddlebag, she dug out the apples. She dropped the bag and took a step forward with palm outstretched, the fruit balanced atop her scars.

He took a step toward her, lips twitching in an almost-smile. *So that's how it's to begin again . . . first you rescue the beast, then you hand-feed him.*

A flutter of nervous energy bounced through her stomach. So, it was she who had cured him!

Careful, you might never get rid of me this time. His flirtatious taunt circled around her thoughts.

I'm counting on it, she answered, lifting an eyebrow, though her upturned hand trembled slightly.

You do realize, I have orchards teeming with apples in the arboretum. Or perhaps you weren't there long enough to notice.

Orchard apples have nothing on these. Effortlessly now, she reprised her role from their past. *I made them special for you.* She took another step, noting his height and how small she felt now that he wasn't laid out on a dais. It was baffling—that he would seem larger than life, even as a man.

He clucked his tongue. *I think you seek to tame me, just as you have my gatekeepers.* He glanced at the stags grazing on the flowers she'd picked.

I don't wish to tame you. I seek a partnership. Her fingers squeezed the apple, then reopened. *To be your eyes in the darkness. To be your hands should you ever get trapped. To be your ears when you're flying too high to listen.*

A pained frown crimped his brow and she almost regretted saying it, but then he smiled, and she knew he understood: Although that door was closed to them now, they'd always have the past to share. And if anyone treasured memories as much as she, it was this prince who had lived two lives.

He rubbed his thumb across the whiskers at his jaw. *I'll gratefully accept the offer of your eyes, but I've other things in mind for your hands, and pretty words to speak into your ears. No more writing them in notes.* He took another step. *But first, you must be fierce enough to embrace me—body and soul.*

Her palm stopped trembling and she stretched her arm as far as it would reach. *I've already proven my fierceness is a match for yours, beastly brawn.* She awaited the expected response, for him to demand she walk the final few steps.

Instead, he closed the gap between them and caught her wrist, turning her hand to toss the apples to the ground. *That you have. Now I've something to prove to you.*

In no more time than it took for her to blink, he spun them both in a circle, his free arm snug at her waist. His touch left her breathless. They waltzed together, there upon the rocky ground, flowing despite the rough terrain. Lyra's surroundings hazed: the stags, the flashing lights—Vesper's companions now descending toward them. She recognized Luce's red hair and Selena's silvery purplish braid—both smeared in the distance, like paintings left out in the rain.

Still twirling, Vesper pulled her close so his lips raked her ear. "I told you I could dance as well as any man," he whispered. His warm breath rushed along her lobe, titillating every nerve in her body. His scent had changed—no longer singed with fire or grass, but a muskiness entirely masculine and human.

She threw her head back, soundlessly laughing. His laughter joined hers, and she reveled in the dizzy rush, giddy with relief, happiness, and desire, feeling almost as if she were flying with him at last. Their feet got caught in the lacewing cloak, and Vesper slowed their rotation to untangle them.

His features grew somber. *Luce told me all that your aunt stole from you, Princess Lyra.*

Lyra gasped. *You know . . . who I am?*

He nodded. *Even before Luce told me, I knew you were more than you seemed. That you belonged beside me. And now I know you're the princess of the prophecy. My* princess.

Lyra pressed a hand to her throat, feeling the loss of her voice anew.

Vesper placed a hand atop hers. *Voice or no voice, you were born as Lyra. That will never change. Your royal father's and mother's blood flows in your veins.*

His assurance warmed the hollow chill where her working vocal cords should've been, and hearing him speak her true name to her mind was both a thrill and a comfort.

I know nothing about being royalty, Vesper. They took all those years of learning from me . . .

"I will help you." His deep voice echoed in the cave, no longer isolated to her head. "And I'll see that you have your revenge." A spark ignited behind his eyes—the same fury that had driven Scorch to fiery rampages. "At the end of all of this, those who hurt you will answer to both of us, and will bow to you as their queen. And I promise you also, as you once promised me: I will never take anything from you that you're not willing to give."

Her eyes stung on the sentiment. Having had so much stolen away, they were the dearest words he could've said aloud. She touched him behind his right ear, a gesture that had once calmed the beast. *And for that, I will give you all that I am.*

He rested his hand on the nape of her neck, his thumb stroking her in that tender place where he used to nestle his horse's snout. "Then I will be the most fortunate man alive." He started to pull her close, but the lacewing cloak still puddled at their feet between them. He nudged the fabric aside, wearing a wistful expression. "I wanted to be there, when you took your first step into the sunlight."

You were. She smiled. *You were my first ray of light in the ravine, all those years ago.*

He smiled, shaking his head. "You know, I was too arrogant to tell you then. So I'm telling you now . . . every time I saw you, each day when your face appeared through the trees, or framed by one of those ridiculous empty windowpanes . . . you lit up my whole world. It was me that needed *you*. That's always been the case. Make no mistake. I loved the girl with my horse's heart, and now I'm ready to love her with a man's."

The beautiful sentiment curled around Lyra's body like a wisp of steam from a soothing cup of tea. It was all she'd ever wanted: words spoken in earnest, touches and kisses freely shared, helping one another without expecting anything in return.

She stroked that soft patch of skin between his eyebrows where his flesh had never yielded to the curse. *I've always said friendship has many rewards. Love is the culmination of them all.*

His gaze intensified, and he caught her wrist. With his free hand, he touched her fingertips, then outlined the scars she'd suffered on his behalf and others made in ways she might never recall. Before she knew his intention, he lowered his face to nuzzle her palm, such a different sensation than it had been in the past, his lips trailing the same path his finger had in gentle, warm pulses.

A tingle awoke along her own lips, hungry to kiss him again, with no sunlight or torment to mar the experience.

What do you remember, of the shrine? she asked.

He lifted his head to look into her eyes. *This.*

Holding her face, he pressed a kiss between her eyebrows. Then he moved to her eyelids and a contented sigh broke deep in his chest as her lashes tickled his chin. She balanced on her tiptoes, fingers woven in the hair at his nape, and led his mouth to hers.

Their lips delicately sealed. His breath tasted of honey and spiced mead. His right hand tilted her chin to fit his, his left descended to her lower back to draw her body against him, leaving no question as to his complete transformation to a man. He kissed her with gentle confidence—a reminder they still had so much to learn about one another, but that they were in this adventure together, as they had been since she could remember. Lyra fell deeper into him, into this intimate newness so fiery-sweet she ached with both the urge to gasp and to never come up for air again.

A hand gripped her shoulder from behind and forced her to catch a breath in surprise.

"Time's up." Luce tugged them apart, moving between them until all Lyra could see was the back of the sylph's red jacket and his illusory wings. "You agreed to the terms."

Flushed and breathless, Lyra turned Luce to face her. *What terms?* she signed, still tasting Vesper on her lips.

"He owes me. For all those days I made you practice with the sunlight in your fingertips. For all the flowers I made you grow despite his hoof-beating tantrums about eating into your playtime. I'm practically what saved him. So, to repay me, he's to honor my place as your guardian for the first time in our acquaintance."

Lyra peered around a wing tip to catch Vesper's gaze. He winked at her reassuringly, then gestured to Luce. "He became a spirit and whispered his demands all the way here." Vesper rubbed his earlobe and cringed. "Nothing like dog slobber to sour a pleasant trot across the countryside."

Luce suppressed a smug grin. "Better than what a certain donkey used to leave behind on his trots through the ravine. You're just jealous that I wear the wings now."

"Can't refute that." Vesper's voice was teasing, but Lyra sensed a hint of longing beneath the surface.

In Lyra's periphery, Selena and a silver-haired man—one she remembered from the ravine earlier—exchanged bewildered glances and tremulous smiles. How long had they known of their prince's alternate identity? They looked to be as astonished as she'd first felt upon realizing a Pegasus's hooves beat within his heart.

Vesper cleared his throat, and Selena and the man stepped forward.

"Lady Lyra of the House of Eyvindur," Vesper announced in a formal tone, and it made her feel something she'd never felt: regal. "This is my sister, Princess Selena Astraeus, and my first knight, Cyprian Nocturn. They are here to help arrange your passage to the castle."

Selena curtsied, and Cyprian bowed at the waist.

Luce raised his wing, cutting off Lyra's visuals of everyone as he turned to her. "First, the ground rules. I agreed the prince could have one dance with you, and a kiss. Now it's done, and until I hear marriage vows spoken and you are both crowned, you'll always have a chaperone, either me or Lady Selena. And when I'm the one chaperoning, you'll speak where I can hear—or *see*— the conversation. None of those rude silences where you disappear into your own little world together." He slanted a glare at Vesper. "I've had enough of that to last a lifetime."

Lyra never thought Luce and Scorch would stand together like comrades. If only Crony were here to witness this momentous occasion. But she'd told Lyra she had something to do in Eldoria, so it would wait until they were reunited.

Lyra's fingers formed eager questions. *We're going to Nerezeth's castle now? Everyone knows I'm the princess? It's over?*

Vesper and Luce shared a similar reaction: fists clenched and backs stiffened.

"Both kingdoms think Lustacia is the real you," Vesper finally answered, his thick eyebrows furrowed in frustration. "They heard her voice, watched the flowers come to life, and then I awoke—cured. Everyone is so preoccupied with magic, prophecies, and fairy tales, they embraced her wholeheartedly as the cause. No one saw you. Even I couldn't remember all of it. Only your kiss, your touch, and your promise to fight for me."

Then how did you know it was me kissing and not her? You never saw me.

His eyes widened, as if the question surprised him. "In the ravine, I was driven only by instinct. I learned your lips when they kissed my forelock. I learned your hands when you fed me apples; and I learned your secret voice as it gentled my rage. I'll never need to *see* to know it's you."

Once again, he'd rendered Lyra off-balance with his words. Vesper returned her silent appraisal, focused solely on her lips—a profound fascination that traced their shape like a touch.

"Get to the plan, Prince," Luce said testily.

A muscle in Vesper's jaw twitched as he looked away. "Right. Both kingdoms have rallied behind your cousin, and both are so desperate for the sky's unification they'll force my marriage to Lustacia and imprison anyone who stands in the way. And since everyone thinks I'm haunted by delusions from my death sleep, none give credence to my claims. We've no proof of your identity." He gestured to her hands. "I thought, if we could have you raise more flowers for everyone to witness . . ."

Lyra held up her fingers. The soft glow, along with the dull sting that accompanied it, was gone. Frowning, she retrieved a trampled clematis at her feet. Her touch couldn't revive its withered petals. Another part of herself now lost . . .

She shook her head.

Vesper's hopeful expression fell. "You used it all up saving me." His eyes softened and he took her hand. "For which I'm eternally grateful." His fingers squeezed hers. "But Luce says even your childhood portraits were altered. Our lack of any proof puts you in danger. Our best chance is to devise a dramatic arrival like the one Lustacia had. Since we no longer have the magical edge she commandeered, perhaps we can make people stop and wonder with a procession of unexpected creatures. You could ride with me on Lanthe. Dregs has gone to gather some goblins from the badlands. And we'll take some stags for effect." He tipped his chin to his sister. "Selena, that crag should provide cover for Lyra to assume the proper guise." He gestured to the same overhanging rock Dregs had used earlier to escape the stags.

His sister picked up Lyra's saddlebag along with one she'd carried on her mount, then took Lyra's hand. Lyra aimed a questioning glance to Vesper.

"I'm not trying to change you," he assured. "I merely want to lull the cynicism of our two kingdoms by making you what they expect on the outside. Then we'll shock them awake upon revealing your insides, which are exceptional—a strength any kingdom would want in a queen. A strength I see each time I look at you."

She smiled, for she shared the same respect for him.

Luce took up the explanation. "Some things are already in motion. If you appear looking like a royal, it will add to the confusion . . . convince everyone there are two princesses."

Vesper nodded. "I've a suspicion how they attained your cousin's moonlit skin and hair—so perfectly mirroring yours as they once were." He looked at the stags resting peacefully, and that flaming fury burned behind his eyes again. "First, I have questions for Dyadia, and Dregs is seeking his cousin for a witness. But whatever we learn, that simpering fabrication is not worthy of your crown." His brows furrowed as he rubbed his chin. "And I'm going to use that overblown prophecy to prove it. We'll discuss details after you're dressed."

Once hidden behind the craggy rock, Selena offered Lyra some leathery smoked fish and grainy bread wrapped in cloth. "Vesper worried you would be hungry."

Lyra shook her head, too nervous to eat.

Selena put the food away then helped Lyra out of her torn gown and scruffy boots. Lyra shivered in the chill. The Nerezethite's eyes glinted amber in the dimness as she assessed Lyra's goose-bumped, half-dressed form; each scar and stain lit up beneath her scrutiny. Lyra's gaze fell to her bare feet.

Selena offered a cloth she'd wet with water from her flask and Lyra scrubbed herself, though couldn't erase the stains from Crony's enchanted sun solvent. She braved a glance at her companion's flawless moonlit complexion, wishing she could explain why no amount of water would rinse her skin.

Selena placed the cloth on a rock beside them, then signed the words: *I know the ancient language.*

Surprised and relieved, Lyra signed back: *Does everyone in your kingdom speak it?*

Selena smiled. "Just those who belong in court. The council, the prime minister, and the military. Vesper insisted we learn, so when you became our queen, you could be understood and never have anyone question your authority."

Lyra shook her head. *Such a kind gesture.*

"Yes, he has turned out to be a generous and wise sovereign. Our lord father would've been proud. But he still has a stubborn side that drives our lady mother to madness at times."

Lyra grinned. *I'm well acquainted with it.*

Selena laughed. "I should say better than anyone, since you didn't even have his gentler side to temper it."

Lyra bit back a laugh of her own. She was liking Selena more by the minute. Lifting the wet cloth, Lyra demonstrated that she was as clean as she could get by scrubbing at the grayish smudges on her face and shrugging.

"I see." Selena answered. "Well, on to dressing then." She lifted a corset from her bag—an ice-blue confection with wire boning and satin ties.

Lyra arched her spine as Selena laced the back and drew it tight until the sagging bustline at last conformed to Lyra's modest curves. *I'm sorry you haven't a more pristine canvas*—she paused signing to indicate her body from head to toe—*upon which to depict a princess.*

Selena stopped Lyra's hands in midair by dragging velvety-peach sleeves up her arms. "I disagree. The best canvas has flaws and furrows . . . and tells a story of its own before the paint is even added."

Lyra pondered the lovely wisdom of the words as a feminine floral-citrus scent wafted from the fabric.

Selena secured the gown's bodice with a buttonhook. "My appraisal earlier wasn't to disparage your scars. I was admiring them. Admiring *you*. My brother told me of all the times you saved him. Of how you never shirked from discomfort or danger. I'm not sure you realize, but you kept that part of him alive beyond his heartbeat and his breath. You challenged his spirit and nurtured his soul. You helped him view the world through your eyes, and he's grown from it." Crouching, Selena adjusted the skirt—the same velvety peach as the bodice—over its attached petticoat, then arranged the top layer of ice-blue lace to cascade down to the ankle-length hem, providing glimpses of the underskirt through the lacework. "It's why he wants you to do this together . . . to get your kingdom back. It's his way of thanking you, of living up to his end of your partnership."

Lyra's fingers were swift to correct the Nerezethite princess: *He's already lived up to his end. He saved me, too. Many times, in many ways.*

Coaxing Lyra to lift her bare feet, Selena slipped silver satiny boots lined with white fur into place up to her knees, having tucked wool into the toes to make them fit. "Ah, but this is different. Kingdom politics and domestic squabbles, that is Vesper's expertise. He was born and bred into it. Trust him."

I do. Lyra's answer rustled the layers of fabric draping her arms.

Smiling, Selena pulled out a handheld mirror and arranged it so Lyra could see the final result.

The rippling blue light from the tunnel revealed details she couldn't see while Selena dressed her: blue crystal beads with a pearl center glittering all across the neckline and overskirt, the wrist-long sleeves overlaid with matching beaded lace and cinched at the elbows with peach ribbons. She had no words; it was the most dazzling ensemble she'd ever worn . . . at least that she could remember.

She nodded at Selena in gratitude.

"I'm glad you approve. It suits you." Selena handed Lyra the mirror so she could produce a peach velvet caul embellished with braided silver ribbons and pearls from her bag. A scarf of creamy white silk billowed from the back like a tail of mist and sky. "Vesper brought you a fur cape to protect from the snowfall. And this will offer warmth in lieu of hair."

Lyra stopped her from setting the hat atop her scalp . . . the mention of hair tangling in her thoughts. Mistress Umbra's prediction resurfaced: "You will need to have hair of steel and tears of stone." Alone it made little sense, but when paired with that overheard conversation between Selena and Vesper about the wedding gifts, it began to adopt a hazy meaning. Selena said enchantments had captured Eldoria's princess's teardrops in gemstones on the pin, and had hardened strands of her hair to bristles of steel in the brush.

Gem*stones* and steel. Tears of stone, and hair of steel.

Lyra dug through the saddlebag at her feet, finding the brush and pin. She held them up to Selena. *Mine,* she mimed.

Smiling gently, Selena set the caul aside and took them. "Yes, they are yours. Gifts for Vesper's betrothed." She flicked a glance to Lyra's fuzzy head, sympathy tugging at her silver eyebrows. "Would you like to fasten the pin to the cap?"

You told Vesper to have faith in the magic. Lyra gesticulated the words Selena had said to her brother, as close as she could remember them. *Magic, to fix all the wrongs and put things back to right.* She pointed to the brush bristles then her scalp: *My hair that won't grow.* She gestured to the pin's gems and her eyes: *My tears that won't flow.*

Shocked perception crossed Selena's face. She lifted the brush and scraped the stiff bristles across Lyra's downy scalp. Upon contact, the bristles softened then began to shorten. Lyra held the mirror up, watching . . . waiting. She and Selena both caught a breath as the stubble all across her scalp lost its dark tint in the wake of the diminishing bristles, and a silvery fuzz took its place. The fuzz thickened and grew to wavy strands—lustrous and long—a full head of hair that passed her shoulders within moments, continuing on until the length reached her hips.

"Oh my stars and moon," Selena whispered, her eyes bulging. She held up the brush that was now nothing but a handle. "We must show Vesper."

Wait, Lyra mouthed the request and pointed to the pin.

Swiftly braiding a portion of the shimmery strands at Lyra's temple, Selena clipped it into place with the pin. The moment Selena drew her hand back, the three gemstones leaked free of their mounting—a deep violet liquid that streamed down Lyra's face. Some ran into her eyes; the rest spread across her forehead and coated her cheeks, jaw, and neck.

Still gaping, Selena handed Lyra the wet cloth to blot the liquid. The gray tinge that had stained her skin after years of using the sun protectant lifted away and transferred to the fabric, revealing a glowing, moonlit complexion.

Lyra smiled at her reflection, seeing the girl in Crony's enchanted looking glass—the cherished daughter in the portrait with her kingly father, who hadn't yet encountered the trials that awaited her. She was the image of that princess at last, with all but one exception: every scar, scrape, and bruise remained—a tribute to the challenges she'd faced since then. A tribute to the queen she would be.

Lyra didn't notice Selena's absence until she heard two pairs of footsteps rushing up behind her. Lowering the mirror, she turned.

Luce gawked, speechless for the first time since Lyra had been in his keep.

Vesper, on the other hand, whistled low as he took her in her appearance—from her hair to the glittering, gauzy skirt that rustled between them. "Such brutal beauty." His gaze skimmed the braid that framed her face, then trailed the scars upon her forehead, cheek, and the curve of her neck. "How did this happen?"

She held up the brush handle, her eyes tingling with a foreign weight that blurred her vision. As she blinked, liquid warmth trickled down her face.

After licking the saltiness from her lips, she reached up and caught one tear that clung to her lashes. It smeared across her fingertip: violet and sparkling, and more precious than any amethyst.

The astonishment on her prince's face as he watched her through Scorch's eyes, her playmate who'd never seen her cry, gave her a rush of exhilaration.

"You've renewed my faith in the prophecy, Lyra." His body tensed against the struggle to honor Luce's conditions and not take her in his arms again.

She reveled in the moment, holding power over this one who had often bettered her in every game. She caught his hand. Pushing up his cuff, she traced the scar on the back of his wrist, the last wound he would ever inflict by draining his golden blood, and silently dared him to do the same. Abandoning all control, he traced the path of her tears—from her cheeks, jaw, and neck, then down to the beaded neckline that dipped beneath her collarbone—sending a blush of delight through her body.

"Restraint, young majesties," Luce threatened with a growl.

Vesper drew back, and Lyra smiled at him. *Now we have our magical edge.* She kept the thought private between them.

The muscles in Vesper's throat contracted on a hard swallow. "You're right."

"Want to clue the rest of us in on the conversation?" Luce pressed.

"She's not to ride with me on Lanthe," Vesper answered, his gaze never straying from hers. "She'll lead, so every eye will be turned on her. All these years, our kingdoms have hoped for the princess of the prophecy, awaited some living fairy tale to unfold before their eyes. We'll give it to them: a princess aglow with moonlight and silver—a survivor of ash and thorns— riding through the gates, triumphant, astride a brumal stag, the epitome of hope itself."

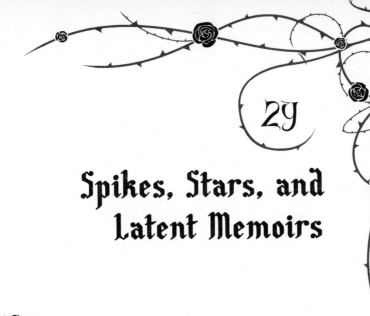

29

Spikes, Stars, and Latent Memoirs

ix hours after Nerezeth's heir apparent, his royal sister, his first knight, and four trackers journeyed to the Rigamort to prove the prince's theory behind the burst of life that had cured his blood and melted the snow, they returned with more than answers. They returned with another miracle.

Upon arrival, Prince Vesper sent his royal trackers ahead to advise the castle's heralders to blast the trumpets. Drawn by the sound, nobility, servants, and honored guests alike stirred from their feast-induced stupors and either gathered in the courtyard beneath the stars or looked out of windows at the snow-covered expanse beyond the gate.

As the procession came into view, the trumpets blared louder, shaking the castle to its icy roots. For five years, the Nerezethites had anticipated this event: the fulfillment of the prophecy—a princess to save their prince, heal their land, and align the skies.

Now there were two. One within the castle looking down from a tower, whose silver hair and birdsong voice had purportedly cured the prince and sent a rash of flowers to melt the wintry terrain; and another whose hair gleamed like ripples of liquid metal under the moon in the blizzard's fleecy winds as she rode upon a majestic brumal stag to the gates, trudging through drifts of snow so high they swallowed the stag's legs up to its knee joints. The prince and his troop of three brought up the rear on steeds, with five more brumal stags following in their wake.

Word quickly spread, via the trackers, that this latest princess—a spectacle of glittering lace, glowing skin, and lilac eyes that flashed amber in the darkness—was rumored to have been the prince's true liberator, that she crossed through the badlands after defeating the Grim with her flood of flowers and sunlight. She had scars and scratches aplenty to substantiate the claim, and had also won the respect and loyalty of the lowliest and most mistrustful of their world, which explained why a cavalcade of hoarfrost goblins walked behind the brumal stags in a rare show of solidarity.

It was difficult to refute this new princess's claim, being seated as she was astride an enchanted, untamed creature that hadn't set a clawed foot outside of the Rigamort for centuries. As most Nerezethites had never seen the solitary creatures, the vision of six inspired a mix of hope, confusion, and euphoria.

The castle buzzed with debates between Eldorians and Nerezethites as to which girl was the true princess of the prophecy. Everyone had their favorite.

But how to choose? How to be sure? Only one princess could marry the prince, and only the prophesied pairing would bring the skies together again, which was the most crucial consideration of all. Crucial enough that a death sentence was hanging in the air, awaiting whichever girl would prove counterfeit.

A convocation of the two kingdoms' councils would decide. The anticipation was palpable amongst the crowds gathered in the corridors of the great hall as they awaited the verdict being decided behind closed doors.

Neither princess attended. They were isolated to their own towers, their doors watched by both Eldorian and Nerezethite guards. One of them was an imposter, so neither could be trusted to speak on their own behalf until they'd proven their claim to Eldoria's throne by some credible means.

Credible indeed. With the convocation ended, Griselda followed Sir Bartley through the crowds held at bay by a line of guards, arriving at her chambers where Lustacia awaited under lock and key. Nodding, the Nerezethite guard closest to the door let Griselda within. Her knight exchanged an uneasy look with her but stayed outside to give her and her daughter privacy.

The moment the door closed, Lustacia scrambled from the table where she'd been eating. Her goblin apparitions pounced upon the food tray in her absence. Being half-corporeal and half-spirit, they still required small doses of nourishment. The shadowy forms scattered chunks of fish pie and smears of jellied cream across the table in their wake.

Griselda turned up her nose at their lack of manners.

"Well?" Lustacia blotted crumbs from her lips with a napkin. She had changed into a more comfortable ensemble—a navy velvet gown with simple beading about the neck and wrists. "Did you see her up close? Her gaze was so like Lyra's. Even from up here it glinted in the darkness as she rode through the gate." She wrung the napkin in her hands.

"A glint no different than every other gloom-dweller's." Griselda strode to the chair and peeled off her gloves and hennin, still unnerved by the memory of the procession, an unease compounded by the tingling of her antlers upon the arrival of the stags. "Show me one Nerezethite, other than the prince, that doesn't have those spectral, wolfish eyes."

"Did you hear her speak? If she has a voice then we'll be all right. Won't we?"

"She wasn't at the convocation; she's been locked in a tower, just as you have."

Lustacia flung her napkin down and twisted her pale hair into a side braid. "Ava and Wrath visited me earlier. The guests are saying she uses sign language with the prince and his sister. There's a mystery surrounding her origins, for she has no memories. She has white eyelashes that curl up to here." Lustacia indicated her forehead. "Add that to the fact that she goes by the name *Stain.*"

Griselda groaned, too perplexed to even attempt hiding her reaction.

Lustacia's eyes narrowed. "You used to call her that. It must be—"

"Impossible." Griselda snapped. "The poison had no antidote. I chose it for that reason. She died because no one could have stopped it. And death is irreversible. No, this is that witch's doing. She heard me call your cousin a stain when she was first imprisoned in our dungeon. The old hag must've escaped Erwan somehow, and is here pulling the strings." There had been mention of a red fox loitering around the gates earlier, though it hadn't been seen since the prince returned. It had to be Elusion, another indication of Crony's presence. At least it appeared he was locked in his vulpine form, which meant Erwan got one thing right: he'd burned down the sylph elm before Elusion got his wings. "The witch has thrown her own imposter into the mix to spite me. Some native Nerezethite who has charmed the prince, perhaps with a love-spell. But the hag made a mistake leaving this in the shrine."

Griselda picked up the bag Sir Bartley had brought in just after Lustacia returned from spying beneath the prince's stairwell—having overheard his and his sister's plans to ride out in search of someone else . . . someone by the name of Stain.

Fortunately, Bartley had found the bag in the shrine, just as Griselda had expected. Her premonition had been correct, as it had contained all she needed to prove that foul play against the real princess—her daughter . . . *niece*—was afoot.

Lustacia knelt on the floor beside Griselda's knees. "So, you gave them the box. What did they say?"

Griselda regaled the pertinent details orally, all the while mentally reliving the exchange. Attending that wretched assembly, being under everyone's scrutiny, had left a bitter taste in her mouth.

❈ · I · ❈

Prince Vesper had sat at one side of the long table with Queen Nova, Madame Dyadia, Selena, and four Nerezethite council members. He'd positioned himself directly across from Griselda instead of choosing her prime minister, her first knight, or the any of the five councilmen from her court. It was an intentional move, meant to intimidate. Like most Nerezethites, he was tall but lithe—corded muscles wrapped around elegant bones. Yet he had a presence about him, a feral confidence that made him more imposing than a beefier man of weight and stock.

The quandary was presented before the assembly. The prince laid out an empty opal handle that was once a brush, and a hairpin that had lost its jewels, claiming the girl he brought back from the Rigamort had freed the spell upon them both. Then he deferred to his mother to mediate the proceedings.

When the question fell to Griselda as to her thoughts on the dilemma they faced, she offered her well-rehearsed words:

"We are victims," Griselda said, "to the malice and mischief of Crony, the harrower witch. Everything is her doing. From His Highness's rejection of my dear niece, Lyra, who's kept herself pure for him and exchanged heartfelt letters for five years, to this imposter who's appeared at the last hour with artifacts that were meant to be wedding gifts—admitted to have been stolen. You must see, without the purported silver bristles and amethyst stones, we can't even be sure these are the same articles. I conjecture the witch is casting aspersions upon this marriage—predestined to cure both our kingdoms of their half lives of perpetual day and night—for some sort of petty revenge."

"Do you have proof of your claim?" asked Queen Nova.

Forcing herself not to cringe at the white crickets clinging to the queen's neckline like a string of pearls meant to complement her silvery hair, Griselda unveiled the box she'd wrapped in cloth. The words "princess - revolution" were scripted across the scaly surface.

Several of the council members gasped upon seeing the drasilisk lining.

"Some days ago, Queen Nova sent a missive to our castle via jackdaw," Griselda continued, "warning me of a box that belonged to the witch and held within it plans for a rebellion against my niece. It was found within your shrine today after my niece cured his curse. None else could fabricate such a piece, as drasilisk hides ceased to exist centuries ago. This is proof we've fallen prey to the witch's manipulations, for she's an immortal and was here when the monsters ran rampant in our shared sky. It also explains this imposter's use of the ancient sign language . . . for Crony knows it herself."

"I can attest to that," Madame Dyadia spoke up, an accusatory glint in her catlike gaze. "And I spied that very box through my bird's eye in the hands of Cronatia." She gestured for Griselda to pass it closer.

Griselda slid it across the table with gloved hands.

Dyadia lifted it, turning it over. "There's a spell in place. A temporal lock. It can't be opened until the proper time, whenever that might be. It appears there's some credence to Regent Griselda's claim."

The queen lifted a graceful hand to silence the council's murmurings. "I understand my son had the witch sent to your dungeons. Are you saying she has an accomplice here, in my castle?"

Griselda folded the empty cloth and laid it on her lap. "Yes . . . no. Perhaps. It's possible she escaped. She has done so before. She's wily and dangerous. She killed my brother and his first knight."

"And your youngest daughter, Lustacia," the prince offered, though it sounded suspiciously like a barb.

"Yes. I'm sure you can understand the omission." Griselda feigned a tremor in her voice. "It's painful to speak of her death. Even after so many years."

She sensed the prince watching her, his predatory glare so intense she felt her skin growing hot, as if it might catch flame. When she dared look his way, she could've sworn she saw a piercing orange flicker in those black depths—like a candle's wavering beam reflected off onyx stones. He raised an eyebrow and offered a smile. Not one of sympathy. An assured, almost smug, turn of the lips.

"Here are my thoughts on the matter," he'd said in that moment, his gaze never leaving Griselda's. "Considering it's both our kingdoms' welfare at stake, and it's my life being bound to another, there's only one means to know beyond a doubt which girl is my true equal. Everyone's been seeking a raven-eyed prince and a silver-haired princess. But we can agree that appearances can be altered. What cannot, however, is a person's very essence. The prophecy clearly states that on their own, the prince and princess are to conquer one another's worlds. I did this already, finding my way through the ravine's thorn labyrinth, surviving the moon-bog. Since no one can prove if the flower trail that led from Neverdark to the Rigamort was enkindled by a song or a kiss, I propose giving both girls one last test to see who truly conquered this realm today."

❈ · I · ❈

Griselda paused relaying her unsettling recollection of events, her throat growing tight.

"So, it worked." Lustacia pressed her to continue, bringing Griselda's thoughts back to the tower chamber. "He has doubt enough in this witch's girl to need proof from her as much as me?"

"Yes."

"Then why do you seem so rattled?"

Griselda clenched the empty bag in her hands and her mouth closed against the answer: *because it didn't* feel *as if it worked.*

The prince hadn't been surprised by her surprise tactic. It was if he'd expected her to pull out the box and slide it across the table to the sorceress. As if that very action played into his desires. Perhaps he'd truly gone mad after being locked within that death sleep.

Griselda thumped her fingers on the bag. "I'm not rattled. I'm simply . . . deliberating."

"Deliberating what?"

"How best to tell you the outcome of the meeting."

Lustacia waited, chewing on the end of her messy braid.

"The prince made the observation that the prophecy had some problematic details concerning appearances. That the only true measure of his princess was for her fortitude to be a match for his own. She must have the courage and grit to conquer his world."

Lustacia spat the hair from her mouth. "That's ridiculous! How can anyone possibly prove something like that?"

"It is tradition here, that all the royal children, and those of the military, grow up learning how to face the hardships of this realm. They're taught at a young age to withstand the sting of thorns, brambles, and scorpions by laying upon beds of nails in the dungeon."

"What?" Lustacia yelped. "You mean I'm to face a torture device? I bruise if I sleep upon a feather mattress!"

Griselda held up a hand to calm her. "There's one thing more . . . to be his 'equal,' his princess must prove she can relate to and befriend the creatures inherent to this world, those that occupy every corner of this castle. So, the cell will also be filled with vermin." Her own skin crawled at the thought.

"Oh no. No, no, no. Mother! All these years we've lived among pet birds who protected us from such atrocities! I've never had dealings with . . . *infestation*." She shuddered visibly.

"Take your half-lights as your shadow guards; once you're alone within the cell, have them protect you as the birds would. Perhaps they can even provide some cushion for you upon the nails."

Lustacia glanced across her shoulder at the smoky smears still fighting over the remnants of her meal. "How much more will I have to endure to prove myself? I'm so tired. I'm not even sure I want to be queen any longer."

Griselda lunged forward—fingers gouging into her daughter's tender shoulders. "Never say that again," she seethed through gritted teeth over Lustacia's whimpers. "You think *you've* endured adversity? I've given up everything for this! All so you could sit upon a throne that should've been mine from the beginning!"

The goblin apparitions swooped down, shoving Griselda against the back of her chair to protect their mistress. They ripped through her hair, pulling it out of its pins and exposing bits of antler.

Lustacia rubbed her shoulder. "Shall I call them off, Mother? Or should I tell them you're to be dessert?"

Griselda smoothed her tangled strands, patting them back into place against the gusts. "Perhaps you should remember that without my ingenuity, you wouldn't even have your guards. I've done nothing but empower you and your romantic aspirations since the moment you fell for your cousin's betrothed."

Lustacia bit her lip at that. She sent her goblins to straighten the mess they'd made on the table. One dipped across the surface to absorb wet smears like a sponge might do, while the others scooped piles of crumbs onto the plate.

Griselda nodded her approval. "We can't turn against one another now. We're so very close. The prince amended the blood oath with his own blood. The new contract reads that whoever passes this test will be his bride, and the other will be imprisoned—her fate to be decided by the new queen after the coronation. All you have to do is abide through the cessation course, or outlast your opponent without begging to be let out, whichever comes first. A few hours, and you'll win him and the crown, at last."

Lustacia worked her shoulder seam down, revealing where bruises had already marked her moonlit skin in the shape of her mother's fingers. "What happens if we both endure? It's said this girl has scars and scrapes to spare. She's of the wilderness, and obviously more inured to physical hardship than me."

"It's been decreed by Queen Nova and Prince Vesper that should you both withstand the night, the girl possessing the most physical attributes specified by the prophecy will be proclaimed King Kiran's heir and will marry the prince immediately. Your rival has only the skin and hair. You, however, have something the imposter can never emulate. The true princess's birdsong voice. Which means it is *impossible* for you to lose."

"Still . . ." Lustacia stood and began to pace. "Shouldn't we discuss our alternate plan? You always have one."

Griselda patted a pocket in her gown, her fingers tracing the small, round outline hidden within the fabric's folds. Yes, there was a plan; one she'd already put in motion. A last resort she hoped wouldn't be necessary. "We throw ourselves upon the dais, at the feet of the thrones and at the mercy of the courts."

"Have you gone mad? What sort of a plan is that? Neither kingdom will have mercy! Everyone wants the skies united and we've disrupted it."

Griselda shrugged. "Yes. We will be blamed not only for Lyra's death, but for killing the prophecy."

Tears gathered in Lustacia's eyes again. "So, you're fresh out of ideas and tricks. Then . . . we'll run away."

"In case you failed to notice, the prince has us under constant guard. He's even having your sisters watched now."

"But we could use my shadows; they could at least get us through the gate."

"It's a blizzard outside. The thorns have already risen up and the night beasts are on the prowl. You saw the cadaver brambles and rime scorpions for yourself, how they attacked Lyra's body in that coffin. Do you honestly think your sisters . . . or you and I . . . have what it takes to survive this wasteland for more than an hour? Where would we go, even then? We have antlers sprouting from our heads! We'll never be safe unless you're protected by the prince himself."

Lustacia sank to the floor, her face drained of color. Her shadowy defenders left off cleaning and returned to hover around her, lifting and dropping her braid, as if to comfort.

Griselda walked toward the adjoining chamber to splash cold water upon her face and contemplate the turning of events. She paused at the threshold. "Either find the courage to win the test, or find the courage to face the wrath of two kingdoms spurned. I leave the choice to you." She shut the door between them.

✳ · I · ✳

Every castle has its obscure passages. Within Nerezeth's obsidian fortress, most were accessible and used by everyone at court—servants, military personnel, and council members included.

However, there was one passage that was known only to Madame Dyadia and the royal family. It was a steep, secret stairway that led directly from a hidden alchemy lab beneath the dungeon to the throne room five flights above. As Lachrymosa's own addition centuries earlier, it had enabled his mother to bring him reports and commissions expediently from the king. Otherwise, she had to take four winding flights of stairs to the dungeon, a long trek past an abundance of cells, then gain access to a magical entrance through an impermeable wall to take another flight of stairs that eventually opened to her son's lab.

Lachrymosa's passageway cut the transit by at least ten minutes, and also had the added benefit of providing a back way into the dungeons from the lab without being seen by anyone milling through the common areas. This proved particularly helpful now, as the success of the princess test relied solely upon getting Lyra into a cell without being seen. And since so many spectators already lined the corridors, halls, and antechambers—to await that blink of dawn signaling the beginning of the cessation course and said test—any other route would've been unsuitable.

Lyra—dressed in tunic and trousers, hair tucked beneath a scarf—took the hidden passageway with Vesper a half hour before the test was to begin. Cyprian followed a few steps behind, having been appointed as Lyra's temporary chaperone by a grumbling Luce—the sylph being engaged in a clandestine meeting with Madame Dyadia elsewhere in the castle, and Selena being equally unavailable. With her own role to play in the grand deception, the prince's sister had remained within Lyra's tower chamber to await the guards who would be coming to escort the potential princess alongside her rival in a procession down the twelve flights from the towers to the dungeon.

In the meantime, Lyra, Vesper, and Cyprian passed through the secret alchemy lab and were on their way up the stairs leading to the magical entrance that would land them directly within the dungeon's corridors. As they walked by wall sconces lighting the darkness for Vesper's eyes, Lyra tried to get the image of the lab out of her head. The dusty and mildewed space, filled with rubble and debris, presented a sad tribute to the splendor that it once must have held, hundreds of years earlier beneath the hands of a masterful mage. Though Nerezeth's historical scrolls didn't offer specific details, Vesper had shared that the damage was done when the earth opened to swallow Nerezeth, killing Lachrymosa and indenturing Vesper's people to a life of eternal night and ice.

The ruins had reminded Lyra of her walk along the Crystal Lake, the first and only time she'd viewed her kingdom up close: strangled by monstrous vines and vicious flowers. How she hoped the moonlight would grace Eldoria's skies again, wither the honeysuckle plague, and return the castle to the glittering ivory beacon it once was. She wanted nothing more than to see the people outside—playing, working, living. Just as she hoped the sun would cure the sickness in Nerezeth so Vesper's people could live again.

She and Vesper had spoken at length after the convocation—over a late dinner shared with Selena, Luce, and Cyprian, who took a hidden passage to her tower chamber—about their concerns for their kingdoms and their people. They both worried as to how any union—no matter its sacred basis—could realign their skies. But as everyone had so much to lose if the magic failed, Vesper and Lyra agreed to simply love one another, trust one another, and have faith enough to aid the prophecy where they could.

Which brought them to where they were now.

Reaching the impassable wall, Vesper manipulated a row of stones, using a code Madame Dyadia had given him. The barrier opened to the dungeon and the three stepped within.

Lyra's nerves evolved to nausea, and she regretted eating that helping of plums in rosewater. The roasted boar should've been enough. It had just been so nice to have warm food served at a table in the company of people she could converse and tease with, she'd forgotten to consult her stomach until it was filled to the brim.

After passing fifteen cells, Vesper stopped.

Cyprian took a step back. "Not to pull rank, Majesty, but do keep it short, and not too sweet," he requested. "I don't wish to get on the bad side of a sylph who can sense my every desire and turn it into an irresistible force."

"For the sake of my sister's honor, I'll concede this once." Vesper smirked.

Cyprian grinned back. "You know, such a skill could be formidable in military strategies. Perhaps one day in the future, our queen might use her persuasion with her guardian . . . convince him to stay on as a magical resource?"

Lyra quirked an eyebrow. *I'll consider it*, she signed, *if you'll turn your back and give us the illusion of privacy. You can't be blamed for what you don't see, after all.*

Cyprian laughed then faced the opposing wall.

"Well played," Vesper teased Lyra. "Never thought I'd reap the benefits of civic diplomacy honed in the dark market."

She shrugged. *As I recall, you thought my bargaining lessons a waste of time.*

"Hmmm. It would appear I owe Luce a thank-you for that, too." He cocked his head in thought. "Let's not tell him."

She smiled as he searched under his royal robes to fish a set of tarnished keys from the fur-trimmed tunic beneath. They jingled on their loop as he unlocked the large wooden door.

"This is the one," he said. The hinges creaked open at his touch. The sconces from the corridor intruded on the space with flickering orange strokes, revealing everything he had prepared her to see.

Lyra's smile faded as she stood at the threshold, taking it in: the stench of must and stale body odor, the flutter of moths sweeping back and forth, black mice scampering about among hundreds of glowing spiders scuttling across the floor. Others dangled from the ceiling on silken webs. They looked like stars, juxtaposed against the dingy gray stones, and the beauty of those luminescent constellations almost coaxed her to step inside, until her attention caught on the torture device against the wall. It was opened, displaying the metal spikes lining both the lid and the bed. Just as Vesper described, it resembled a coffin.

She hardened her chin to keep it from trembling.

"I'm sorry . . . I know it reminds you of your arrival to the ravine."

She shook her head. *There's no memory. Only a foreboding dread. A knowing that I shouldn't know. If I could grasp it, I could put it to rest.*

His eyebrows knitted and he took her hand, bringing her close enough to press her knuckles to his soft lips. "Those memories will be yours soon," he said, his warm breath scented with winterberry wine from dinner. "Dyadia has Crony's ensorcelled box now. And once you win your crown—"

It will open. Lyra finished his sentence and caressed his face with her free hand, grateful for the reminder. Luce was still being obscure about Crony's whereabouts, but at least he'd shared some of the details of the note she'd left him.

Vesper kissed Lyra's wrist. His lips lingered there, at the edge of her sleeve's cuff, leaving no question that he wanted to continue—past her forearm to the bend of her elbow, along her shoulder and to her neck.

He lifted his face, eyes ablaze with a new light. *There's something I've been wanting to ask,* he said in their mind-speak. *All along, it's been assumed, but that's not fair to you. So here, with no one listening*—his gaze flicked to Cyprian's back—*or watching, I want to do this right, just between us.* He swallowed hard. *Lady Lyra, will you marry me and be my queen for life? Rule by my side in both day and night?*

Lyra studied his beautiful, somber features, awed by the sweetness of the gesture. In the eyes of the world, they were betrothed already, but for him to ask . . . to give her the choice . . . and not as a prince and princess, but as a boy and girl whose friendship had blossomed into something lovelier still, it restored some of the control she'd lost, which is exactly what she needed in this moment. To feel strong. Confident. Whole, and hopeful.

I will, she answered without hesitation, stroking his cheek.

Thank the stars and moon! He turned his mouth to her palm and kissed her there. Then he pulled her close. *Once you're mine, I'll pay homage to each scar on your body ever made on my behalf. Including any you may acquire tonight.*

Cyprian cleared his throat. "I can't see you, but I know what that silence means. To borrow Luce's insight earlier at dinner: Pillow talk, be it aloud or in the head, is inappropriate for anywhere but the couple's wedding bed."

Lyra and Vesper shared a grin.

Releasing a breath, she faced the doorway again, muscles tensed and coiled.

"You can do this, Lyra," Vesper urged. "You're the most courageous girl I've ever known. And a Pegasus has the highest of standards."

Lyra leveled an amused glance at him, welcoming any distraction.

The sudden roar of shouts and cheers burst through the upper levels, indicating the procession had begun.

"It's now, or not at all," Vesper said.

Right. She allowed him to hold her balanced by an elbow as she worked off her slippers, one by one. *So I won't break the spiders' fragile legs,* she explained.

Vesper nodded. As Scorch, he had been there when Mistress Umbra predicted Lyra's final trial to find herself—to walk through stars and wrap herself in spikes. This wasn't a surprise to either of them. But only in this moment did it finally make sense.

She handed her slippers to Vesper for him to hide, then took one last look at him. That flame still glowed behind his dark eyes, and had warmed to pride.

Lifting to her toes, she hugged him. He held her close, nuzzling the place where the scarf met her neck, before breaking free and nudging her across the threshold. The door shut with a muffled thud behind her—a sound that echoed like a lonely sigh.

Yet she wasn't alone. The mice squeaked all around her, gray as the stones. Her eyes lit to amplify the soft light emanating from the spidery constellations. Shadows rose from the corners. She'd seen them following on the way here, but they'd kept to themselves, as if they'd known to wait for this moment when she'd need them most.

Empowered by their presence, she shuffled forward so as not to crush any night creatures, her bare feet cold upon the gritty stone. The moths drifted gracefully toward the nail bed, as if to lead the way.

The cheers grew louder down the corridor. They were almost outside the cell. A sense of urgency rushed Lyra the last few steps—close enough to lay her palm across the nails. Her heart quailed, anticipating punctures all over her body. Vesper had advised her about pressure points and positioning for the least damage. She rolled herself onto the spikes and tried to remain still. The points jutted against her, but nothing pierced through . . . yet.

She shut her eyes, but couldn't pull the lid down, couldn't seal herself within. Dread held her immobile, so she asked her shadows to do it instead. They obeyed, sandwiching her between the nails.

There was no time to panic, for the doors were already opening in the cells.

Vesper had chosen this room specifically. There were holes drilled in the walls to allow sound to filter through. It was a tactic for interrogation: locking up two or more criminals together, then guards hiding in the opposing cells on either side, waiting for the criminals to think they were alone and talk.

She heard the doors thud closed, then waited, keeping her breath shallow so she could listen for her cue.

Disgusted whimpers broke the silence. "Make yourself useful. Clean house for me," came the birdsong voice.

Lyra clenched her teeth against the urge to free herself from the confines of the coffin. She forced her muscles to relax and wait.

There was a shuffling, and the almost indiscernible scritchity-scratch of mice claws. A flutter of moths followed, then settled on the walls all around.

A pair of slippers pattered across the floor, stopping at the edge of the bed. "One of you get over here . . . I need a cushion."

Lyra tensed instinctively, enough to cause one nail to pierce her calf. Warmth oozed from the wound; still, she didn't move, even when the lid lifted.

Lying in place like a corpse, she waited for Lustacia's gasp then opened her eyes so their glint could be seen in the dimness.

Lustacia yelped. Backing up awkwardly, she fell to her rump.

Lyra rolled off the nails to the floor. She stood, looming in front of her cousin. She removed the scarf, freeing her hair, and raised her arms to call her moths and shadows into play. They formed a whirlwind, manipulating the waist-length waves to dance around her head like tendrils of silver flame.

My voice . . . my life . . . my kingdom.

The moths carried the mantra to Lustacia's ears, their wings fluttering the words around her. "Lyra!" She shrieked and sobbed, dropping to her belly in front of Lyra's bare feet. "Oh, please, shield me!" Several dark forms dove across her cousin as if to protect her.

Lyra's shadows peeled them away and flung them to the corners.

Lustacia cried out again as spiders dropped their webs from overhead, glistening, gauzy nets that circled around her. Taunting, yet not touching. "I never wanted to kill you!" She strangled on her sobs, batting at the spider silk then screeching when the substance caked between her fingers. "I never wanted to see you hurt . . . I didn't enjoy it like Wrath and Ava did." She gulped several breaths, rubbing her hands along her clothes. "This was mother's doing! She and Erwan and Bartley, they're responsible for all the dirty deeds. Just look what they did to the goblin smugglers." Lustacia pointed a shaky finger to the five black, sooty forms being pinned down by Lyra's shadow guards. "Mother went mad with power and magic. Look under her gloves, you'll find proof of her crimes. She did something abominable to me, too . . . worse than you can imagine!" Arms and hands trembling now, Lustacia parted the braids twisted around her head, giving Lyra a glimpse of pea-sized prongs beginning to sprout from two knots bulging from her scalp. "I'm growing antlers! All because I had to bathe in antler powder. All to look like you! I'm becoming a *beast*. The prince will hate me forever. Please, isn't that enough . . . isn't it?" A sob cut through her lyrical pleas.

Lyra's blood boiled at the confession. Griselda had slain Vesper's sickly stags and ripped them of their antlers, all to give Lustacia her moonlit coloring.

Lyra snarled. At her command, a mischief of mice crept into Lustacia's sleeves, neckline, and hem. Their forms tunneled beneath her dark gown like rain-swollen clouds rolling across a night sky. Lustacia screeched, leaping to her feet and slapping herself to shake out the infestation. Lyra's shadows jerked her cousin off the ground and levitated her, arms and legs held immobile to protect the rodents from being crushed. Her slippers fell from her feet. She begged to be set free, then howled for mercy again.

Yes. Scream . . . scream forever. The moths' wings repeated Lyra's demand: *Scream . . . scream . . . scream.*

And Lustacia did; she wailed and shrieked—a tormented and beautiful chorus of crystal-clear notes that echoed around the room. Lyra shut her eyes, gusts flapping her hair and clothes. The harrowing song encompassed her, and she welcomed it, craved it. Even without remembering, a hollowness gaped within her throat upon missing it.

When the final note rang out and Lustacia lay empty and panting on the floor, sticky with web and rodent scourge, Lyra knelt beside the nail bed. From underneath, she withdrew the enchanted seashell Madame Dyadia had planted there hours before. Lyra sealed it with its special willow cork and stood.

Using her sleeve, Lustacia wiped snot and tears from her face. "What have you done?" she mumbled, though her voice no longer rang with music. It was hoarse, unremarkable, and entirely her own.

The cell door flung open, revealing Nerezeth's and Eldoria's council members—Prime Minister Albous at the head—who had been gathered in the cell at the left of Lyra's, listening as everything unfolded.

Vesper and Queen Nova stepped forward with Selena—who had dressed as Lyra in a flowing gown and veil. She'd walked in the procession alongside Lustacia and took the cell on Lyra's right, so Lustacia would never suspect someone waited within her own.

All of them had witnessed Lustacia's confession. All had heard who was responsible for Lyra's long-winding, torturous journey back to her throne. Stray spectators wandered down the stairs into the corridor, filling the expanse. Word of what had taken place quickly spread to all floors of the castle in a ripple effect.

Lyra's cousin sat up, trembling as people peered in. "Vesper, please."

"Not a word from your deceitful lips," he growled. "Best make yourself at home. This is your room for the night. But take heart, your family will be joining you shortly. Though I'm not sure how receptive they'll be, considering you betrayed them all."

He offered a hand to Lyra. She cradled the seashell's silver stand to her chest, keeping its precious contents safe, and stepped over Lustacia's slippers.

Vesper's strong grasp enveloped her own, providing support against the exhausted tremors running through her limbs. The spiders vanished into cracks and crevices in the stones, and the mice and moths drifted through the open door, leaving Lustacia with her cursed goblins and Lyra's shadow guards to keep them in line.

The door slammed shut, and the sound of Lustacia's discordant, monotone wails trailed Lyra and her prince as they strode down the corridor hand in hand. The crowd parted and then followed them up the stairs, in silent shock and reverent wonder.

The Glitz and Glow of Bliss and Woe

he success of the princess test earned Luce both respect and fear within the courts, as the coup showcased his dark talents as well as his loyalty to Eldoria's true heir.

Before Luce had left with Vesper to the Rigamort, he had shifted to his ethereal form and siphoned into Griselda's chamber. Drawing on his ability to influence the desires of another, he put a thought in the regent's mind that there might be something in the shrine to give her the upper hand. When Sir Bartley found the box, she recognized it as the one Queen Nova had mentioned in her missive, and her confidence was bolstered. For who but Crony could be behind everything?

Griselda was too distracted by the witch's rivalry, and too sure of her own prowess with potions and poisons, to suspect Lyra might actually have lived. Thus, she allowed Lustacia to endure a test she could never win. Griselda's cry of foul play—however hypocritical—had opened up the opportunity to show both kingdoms what she herself had done, as opposed to Vesper having to convince them. It was a much more effective way to consolidate Nerezeth and Eldoria behind their one queen and win fealty, by letting them hear the confession unfold for themselves—on the very birdsong voice in which they had put all their faith.

Once Prince Vesper's royal guard rounded up the other four accomplices, the crowds buzzed with eagerness for the ceremonies that would bring the two lights of the sky together at last. However, Vesper proclaimed that their princess was exhausted after proving herself and should be allowed to retire to her tower chamber for the remainder of the cessation course, where she could have a hot bath—then rest her head on a pillow and her body on an eiderdown mattress for the first time in five years.

At that, a hush fell over the castle as serene as the snow falling outside the windows, and occupants found their ways to their own beds.

When the cessation course ended, the most important of diurnals began beneath Nerezeth's night sky. Three things of import were to take place: the joint coronation, the public sentencing of the prisoners responsible for Lady Lyra's attempted murder, and of course the wedding. Madame Dyadia had deigned the upcoming blink of dawn the ideal juncture at which to have the ceremony that everyone hoped would invoke a heavenly phenomenon. It stood to reason, being the precise moment when both Eldoria and Nerezeth shared a glimpse of one another's skies.

Within four hours of waking, and having dressed and eaten, the castle's occupants filled the halls and corridors, eager for the joint coronation to get underway. The ceremony took place in the throne room—a cavernous space defined by walls, ceiling, and floor of black marble flecked with silver. Sconces cast a soft, flickering glow, and crickets chirped. Moths puttered about the vaulted ceiling, some dipping down where partitioned balconies lined the walls from corner to corner, forming a second story for extra viewing spaces. Silver and sky-blue valances hung in entwined curves from the railings. Flush against the farthest wall sat a large dais. Gold and red ribbons hung around the edges, interlaced with a variety of flowers from Nerezeth's arboretum. The ribbons, in Eldoria's colors, were Griselda's contribution to honor the princess finally gaining her crown. Ironic, that the beautiful decor placed by the regent's own hands for her daughter would now pay tribute to the niece she despised instead. In the center of the platform, two silver thrones sat against the wall between opposing pillars carved of dark, sparkling crystal in the form of thorny vines. These provided a vertical perch for the royal salamanders which hung from their suctioned toes like brightly colored fruits. Their pearlescent and bejeweled stripes, blotches, and dots stood out against the black background, catching the eye.

True to Nerezethite tradition, the thrones doubled as coronation chairs for the incoming monarchs. Lyra and Vesper were seated beside one another, holding hands. On Lyra's left, Prime Minister Albous balanced Queen Arael's white-gold crown—encrusted with diamonds upon a frame as delicate as lace and ivy—atop her daughter's head. Following his lead, Queen Nova set King Orion's amethyst-studded crown—forged of black iron that resembled jagged spikes tipped in silver—upon her son's head.

Applause and shouts of joy resonated across the vastness and sent the moths and salamanders scrambling to new hiding places. The subjects of both kingdoms formed long, winding lines to pay homage to the new king and queen. Afterward, a luncheon feast was held in the great hall.

Some three hours later, the crowds disbursed into the corridors to seek naps in their chambers or guided tours of the arboretum where the wedding festivities would later be held.

Lyra and Vesper planned an appearance at the castle infirmary for those too ill to attend the coronation or nuptials. But first they took a detour to the Star Turret within the highest tower to retrieve her long-lost memories, the box containing them having released its lock the moment Lyra's head received its crown.

Luce accompanied their ascension up the wide, winding staircase.

Lyra vied for a glimpse around her chaperone. Vesper met her gaze and nodded.

Luce looked from one to the other and lowered a red feathery wing to cut off their visual. "Having a crown upon your noggins doesn't make your silent lovelorn declarations any less inappropriate and rude when in my company, Majesties."

No, we weren't mentally chatting . . . about anything. Lyra's wide orchid-lace cuffs rubbed against one another as she answered. The movement reminded her of the crickets in the throne room earlier, filling her with contentment. She belonged. She belonged here, and she belonged in Eldoria. Now, if only she could master looking regal while walking in a gown and royal robes.

She concentrated on taking the stairs in the sage-colored, velvet gown without stepping on the orchid ruffles of lace peering out from beneath the ankle-high hem.

Vesper tilted his head to get her attention once more, and she was the one who nodded this time.

The king and I . . . her signing to Luce stalled in midair as she shared a smile with Vesper, seeing him beam at the title. Her wild Pegasus, ruling a kingdom. She never would've thought it.

Luce rustled his illusory feathers behind him and sighed. "The king and you . . . what? Can't keep your eyes off one another? I've noticed. So long as it's not your hands or lips, I'll overlook it."

Lyra misjudged a step and her lacy hem caught beneath her toe. She ducked her head while retaining balance. Her crown slid askew, but Luce righted it atop her hair before it could crash to the floor.

There, that. Lyra gesticulated, using his swift reaction as her segue. *That's precisely what I was trying to say. The king and I have noticed how you're always there to salvage my crown.*

Luce smirked. "A necessary task, seeing as you've no horns to hold it on as the other princess did."

The jibe wasn't in the best taste, but both Lyra and Vesper smiled, mainly because it felt so good to have the violence and deceptions almost behind them. Vesper's stags would never be harmed in secret again, now that his mental communications with them had been restored.

Luce, I'm being serious. You've proven your loyalty to me a thousand times over. The fact that her fingers moved so stiffly was surprising. She never imagined feeling nervous in this moment. *Earlier, when Cyprian was organizing the subjects to greet Vesper and me on our thrones, I realized I should have a first knight of my own. And I would like it to be you.*

Luce stepped down from the stair they'd just taken, his backward retreat so swift it caused Lyra and Vesper to rise a step above before they noticed.

His orange gaze centered on Lyra alone. "I'm not sure someone of my . . . nature . . . is cut for such an honor."

Of course you are. You'd make a wonderful first knight. She looked to Vesper, begging his help with her eyes.

"I agree wholeheartedly. Can't think of anyone I'd trust more to guard my queen when I can't be there. Your part in the princess test alone earned you the position."

Even more, Lyra reclaimed the conversation, *my trust and faith in you demands that no other man could rival you for the position.*

Luce mussed his hair while rubbing the side of his head in thought. The gesture exposed one of his fuzzy, pointed ears and reminded Lyra of all the times he'd run alongside her as the fox, and how much she would miss that.

Taking a deep breath, he stepped up between them and they resumed climbing the stairs. A wreath of tension wrapped around them.

"If you need training with a sword"—Vesper broke the silence—"Cyprian and my guard would be glad to assist."

"A sylph's weapon is his tongue," Luce groused. "And I've more than proven my proficiency in wielding whispers." He turned to Lyra, an uncharacteristically repentant look upon his face. "I'm not the right man, little one."

Her eyes stung, but she refused to cry. Having been without tears for so long, she was stingy with them. To weep at each little disappointment in life was a waste. Thus, she had decided never to break down except in extreme moments of bliss or woe.

As it stood, Vesper had prepared her for this response. He himself understood how wind and weightlessness could bind a soul in a way few other things could.

It was selfish, she knew, to want the sylph to stay in her life. Too much to ask from an air elemental who'd only recently won his wings back, when all he wanted for the rest of his ageless years was to fly across endless skies.

Luce caught her elbow as they ascended. "It might serve you not to have a man as your protector at all. Have you considered asking Lady Selena?"

Vesper's attention perked. "She is an excellent swordsman."

Lyra shook her head. *But she's a princess. She's royalty. She shouldn't serve me.*

Vesper furrowed his eyebrows. "She would consider it an ennoblement, not a demotion. With her not being the crown heir, there's a lack of responsibilities that often bores her," he assured. "However, tradition dictates we devise a new title for any new position. And princess-knight isn't quite stately or unique enough."

"First Knightress has a nice ring," Luce offered. They all grinned at that, then fell into silent contemplation.

When they arrived at the Star Turret, the door stood ajar and the three seated themselves at a round table. A lone candle flickered in the center, warm wax scenting the air as it melted into a small dish.

The domed room had once been the solar. It was humble in size with a welcoming fireplace. Tapestries, hung upon half of the circular wall, depicted sun-swept fields in summer and snowy mountain peaks beneath starry skies. Shelves curved around the other half in rows of six, holding a variety of jars, vials, boxes, and crockeries with ingredients varying between the commonplace, the gruesome, and the mystical—reminding Lyra of the dirt room in Eldoria's castle.

At one time, the solar's many windows had allowed sun to shine in, aiding with tasks that required good lighting: reading, map-drawing, embroidery, or calligraphy. But the day Nerezeth fell into the earth and dragged the night sky with it, Madame Dyadia stepped up as the royal sorceress in the absence of her dead son and took the solar as her workspace.

Moonlight glimmered through the windows now, disrupted sporadically by thick swirls of snowflakes. Madame Dyadia riffled through a cabinet, only her backside visible behind the open door. She closed the door and carried over the box containing Lyra's memories, the enchanted seashell that held her voice, and a vial filled with a dark, oily liquid. The sorceress set the items on the table, her black-and-white-striped flesh blending into her gown.

Her catlike gaze settled on Luce, and Lyra tried not to stare at the empty socket puckering her forehead. "Well done, sylph. Revealing the 'princess - revolution' box to Eldoria's regent played out brilliantly. I apologize for doubting you when you first came to me."

Luce tipped his head in acknowledgement, absently tugging at the talisman around his neck. "It was in fact our Queen Lyra who gave me the idea, when she shamed Sir Erwan into confessing everyone's crimes in Eldoria. If only we'd had influential witnesses to overhear *him*, we could've forgone the princess test altogether."

Vesper shrugged. "I rather like the way it played out. Watching my wily thief become the queen she was meant to be while bringing her cousin to her knees. It was a thing of beauty." He grinned at Lyra and she smiled back, feeling a rush of pride. Vesper reached for the vial and held it up to a slant of moonlight. The contents illuminated, glittering like black diamonds. "So, this is what the regent used? For Lustacia's fraudulent shadows?"

Dyadia nodded. "Though this one is less potent. Fool woman had no business dabbling in such things. All it takes is a drop of the moonlit essence for the apparitional effect. By using an excess, she damned those miserable goblins to a half-light state forever—bound to her daughter. Though they still have some of their innate characteristics, they must do whatever she demands. They've no choice . . . no freedom to think on their own." She gestured toward the vial. "Whoever serves this will have the same power over their recipient. However, this diluted dose will last no more than two years, then the victim can return to their original form, while still remembering all they experienced as a half-light."

It didn't hurt the stags, did it? To make more? Lyra signed the question.

Dyadia, having lived as long as Crony, easily deciphered her gestures. "Not at all. Since such a small amount was required, I drained it from the edge of their antlers, still intact upon their head. No different than pricking a fingertip for a droplet of blood. And I awarded the donor stag with extra nutrients." She held up her own finger, revealing a miniscule hole. "It is a tradeoff. One must always give back what they take, or both parties suffer."

Lyra furrowed her brow. *What is the trade-off for me to receive my voice again?*

Vesper set the vial down, intent upon hearing Dyadia's answer himself.

"There's no trade-off for something that is rightfully yours. You shall have it back, but exactly as it was. You weren't able to talk with your voice before, and you shan't be able to now. It will be nothing more or less than it was in the beginning—a blessing for its beauty and the power to inspire peace and happiness in others. But also a curse, for it will never inure itself to words. Do you still desire it?"

Yes, Lyra answered. A part of her had hoped that since Lustacia had managed to mold her voice into speech, there might be some residual effect to help Lyra talk. But it didn't matter. Being able to emote through sound . . . to laugh aloud or yelp in surprise . . . to sing with a jubilation and joy that would make others happy upon hearing it—that was enough.

"Then you shall have it. First, I must make a trip to Eldoria for Crony's grimoire. It contains the transference recipe I'll need."

As if on cue, Luce lifted the talisman from around his neck. He pulled a few strands of hair free from the braided pendant. "So you can find her quickly."

Lyra now understood why the determinate elixir had carried Dregs to the Rigamort. Apparently, Dregs had used an icicle growth his cousin once lost in a game of cards for his elixir's personal ingredient. Since Slush had already become a half-light apparition when Dregs went looking for him, the magic carried him to the last place it remembered the icicle growth being.

As Luce handed over Crony's hair, a look passed between him and Dyadia—something indecipherable, but decidedly somber.

You'll be visiting Crony? Lyra asked. *Please convince her to come to the nuptials. Tell her she has an honored place in both kingdoms, protected by myself and the king. I want her to see us wed, to be with us when the skies unite. Tell her I still need her . . . she's the only mother I can remember.*

Madame Dyadia studied her palm where the strands of hair trembled on her every breath. "Do not worry, Highness. I will speak to her. And she will bear witness to everything; I vow it." She wrapped the hairs within a cloth, then pushed the memory box toward Lyra. "On the note of mothers, it is time you are reacquainted with Queen Arael and your place in Eldoria."

Lyra's heartbeat skipped as she reached up to touch her crown, the weight of it foreign upon a mane of lustrous hair to which she had yet to acclimate. As foreign as the mother she would never know.

She brought her fingers down and signed: *I don't expect any memories of Queen Arael in that box. She died giving birth to me.*

Luce, having had a pained expression on his face already, looked beyond miserable now. It was as if he wished to slip into his ethereal form and vanish altogether. Instead, he kept his lips clamped over pointed teeth and stared at the pendant between his fingers.

Vesper leaned around the sylph to catch Lyra's gaze, his crown's silver-tipped spikes warming to pinkish-orange in the candlelight, like black thorns dotted with morning dew. "There will be memories of your father telling you of your mother. I never met him, but I know how much he loved you. Enough to stop a war and sign a blood oath to win his daughter the nightsky she needed to be happy. Like my father, yours accepted you from the beginning as his own, even though you were different from him. A man like that would never let you forget where you came from. *Who* you came from."

Thank you, Lyra mimed. She'd learned many things about her kingdom's history from Prime Minister Albous at the luncheon feast, the most unsettling of which was that her father had a hand in King Orion's death through the panacea roses, however unintentional. She loved Vesper even more for forgiving her father and offering such kind sentiments.

Dyadia opened the box's lid and lifted out a stack of glass that jingled like chimes. Glowing magical threads bound the spine, forming a book of sorts. Lyra had watched Crony use the spinnerets in her horns to tie two or three memories together at a time. However, she'd never seen so *many* memories. And each one belonged to her . . . an entire past waiting dormant within these pages.

The sorceress turned her unnerving gaze to Lyra. "You said you wished me to animate it before the imprint, so our king can view the pages?"

Lyra nodded. She wanted to share her background with Vesper, just as he'd shared his in his notes. To intimately experience one another's pasts would perhaps awaken the magic that could bring the moon and sun together. As it stood, she felt nothing inside of her powerful enough to enact such a monumental, earth-shattering feat.

Luce started to rise but Lyra caught his wrist, asking him to stay without speaking.

He nodded and sat again.

The sorceress sipped from a cup. Steam curled over the brim's edge, smelling foul and putrid. When asked what it was, she replied, "Decomposing leaves gathered from a boneyard, a raven's skull ground to powder, and a mourner's tears." Having drank it all, she fogged the pages with her breath of death, one after another, animating a multitude of colorful shapes across the enchanted tableaus—stained-glass images coming alive.

Lyra flipped through, choosing which scenes to share . . .

Together, the three of them watched blissful moments. She cried upon her first memory, of her father's own tears upon her face as a newborn, giving her the taste of comfort. Then fury burned dark and deep upon remembering he'd died at the hand of his sister. While watching the scene when Lyra first met Crony in the dungeon, Luce's hands tensed around the talisman that he'd returned to his neck.

At last came the final memory . . . being dropped within a coffin at Bartley's and Erwan's hands. Vesper twitched like a predator waiting to pounce, his fingers clawing the table, knuckles bulging beneath his rich, lovely skin. He sat there long enough to witness the two knights dropping in the cadaver brambles and scorpions, making her writhe and scream until her voice was gone.

Choking back a growl, he shoved out of his chair, knocking it over. He knelt in front of Lyra. "My queen, your family belongs to you alone." His low rumbling voice, paired with flaring nostrils and embers in his eyes, was more unsettling than a roar. "But grant me one favor. Give me Bartley."

Lyra stroked his hand and nodded.

Kissing her forehead, he turned to Luce. "After the memory weave is done, see that she gets back to her chambers. She'll need to rest before we visit the infirmary."

"Of course," Luce answered.

Vesper left the chamber without another word.

Lyra's hands shook as she asked Luce if she'd made a mistake.

The barely contained fury on his face mirrored Vesper's. "No. He has been affected by this, too. And considering I got the pleasure of snapping Erwan's neck, it's only right your king has his turn. He grew up killing monsters. Let him put that talent to use."

Lyra looked back to the glass book. She was done viewing her memories like a distant bystander. She wanted to experience them, wanted them ingrained—fused to her mind and body with every emotion and sensory element that made them distinctly her own—no matter how painful.

She asked the sorceress to explain the procedure.

"Your part is simple." Madame Dyadia tugged at the glowing threads binding the book and drew them out into one long string that drifted in the air. Catching it, she spun and spun the strand until it frayed into pale, smoky mist. White sparks blinked within, like lightning trapped in a cloud. She guided the flashing mist to settle over Lyra's head and face. "These are the breaths of your resurrection. Close your eyes, and inhale."

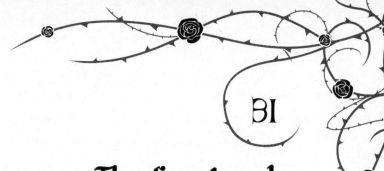

The Spectacular
Spectacle of
Merciful Doom

Queen Lyra was accompanied by Selena to the castle's infirmary, as her king had been detained by his appointment with Bartley and was to meet them there.

Inside the humid ballroom, the scent of panacea petals simmering in water overwhelmed, along with the sounds of coughing and choked gasps. This demonstration of Nerezeth's desperate need for sunlight weighed heavy on Lyra's crown. She walked alongside Selena between cots and looked at each face—whether sleeping or awake in their torment. Those who looked back she acknowledged with a dip of the head, an assuring smile, and a pat on the hand. Hearing the words "The stars bless you, Majesty" and seeing patients' eyes light up with awe and anticipation fed an all-consuming sense of duty—and the hope that she and Vesper could live up to such faith.

A few rows down, her king came into sight alongside Cyprian. The two men crouched next to a cot that held a small occupant. Selena caught Lyra's arm so they could watch and listen from a distance, unseen.

"Oh, please! Again, Sir Nocturne!" the boy on the cot pleaded with a groggy voice. "Start where his Majesty dragged the prisoner through the Grim. But more gore this time."

Vesper shook his head, the tips of his crown glinting gray in the lantern-light. "Now, Nyx, we must be gallant. There's a lady present."

The boy huffed, his feet wriggling beneath his sheet. "Where?"

"Me, you knob-head," a little girl in the adjacent cot answered.

The boy snorted. "Elsa's no lady! She's my sister."

The girl scowled at her brother then turned to Vesper. "Oh please, Majesty. I'm strong like our new queen. One day, I'll face the Grim and ride brumal stags, and wear scars prettier than diamond necklaces. I'm not wobbly kneed at all!"

Lyra and Selena exchanged smiles.

"All right," Vesper said with a laugh in his voice. "But after this, you both need to rest."

The girl tossed off her sheet and scrambled onto Nyx's cot, knees drawn to her chest.

"First," Cyprian began, "our brave king dragged Bartley outside the Grim to a snowy plot known to harbor a pack of cadaver brambles. A handful of groundsmen and guards followed to watch."

"I've been there!" Nyx nodded.

"You lie like a frog on a log," his sister scoffed.

"Shhh." Cyprian held a finger to his lips. "Next, His Majesty ordered everyone to stand back and not interfere, no matter the outcome. Then he loosened the prisoner's binds and gave the scoundrel the opportunity to fight for his freedom—hand-to-hand combat."

Vesper boxed the air and tottered about on his knees, demonstrating. His crown slid askew and he had to straighten it. The children giggled. Lyra's love kindled bright, to see how deeply he cared, how deftly he distracted the little ones from their drab surroundings and illness.

"They were well matched in their skills," Cyprian nudged Vesper with an elbow. "But our king had brute strength and fierce instincts driving him. Not to mention justice for his beloved betrothed."

Upon hearing this, Elsa cooed and stared moon-eyed at Vesper.

"After wrestling about in the snow, our king tricked Bartley into thinking he was tiring out, all to lure him to the tallest drift. He tackled him there, rolling them into a bramble. They were both captured by the spiny monster at one point, and it took all I had to hold the spectators back."

Vesper wrapped his royal robe around himself, as if he were tangled up.

"But they needn't have worried."

Vesper stretched his arms, the robe flapping open like giant wings.

"'Cause he broke free!" Nyx's sleepy eyes widened. "We know how to fight monsters here . . ."

Vesper and Cyprian exchanged somber glances.

"That we do. Our Majesty defeated his bramble and escaped. But Bartley didn't fare so well. By the time King Vesper freed him from the spikes, the prisoner was mangled and broken. So, his majesty drew the royal broadsword and put him out of his misery in one fell swoop."

"Then you dragged his bloody bag of bones and lopped-off head back here so Eldoria's regent could get a good long look!" Nyx added, before having to cover his mouth on a cough.

"We did," Cyprian assured. "She's well and duly primed for the sentencing now."

The story wound down as Vesper spotted Lyra. She waved, and he motioned her over to meet the children before they tucked them in again.

As they left for the throne room, Lyra held Vesper back so Cyprian and Selena moved a few steps ahead. Studying the fresh bruises, welts, and lacerations and cuts along her king's face, neck, hands, and wrists, she could only imagine the damage his royal robe, stockings, boots, and tunic were hiding. Though wildness shimmered hot in his eyes, there was a satisfaction that hadn't been there since this all began.

She squeezed his hand and he lifted hers to kiss her wrist. *You were wonderful with those children*, she said between them.

He looked into her eyes. *I want to be a good king.*

You already are. She smiled. To see the bounce in his step despite the bruised face and battered hands was like watching Scorch prance around in smoky circles with pointed shafts stuck in his hide after he'd blazed and trampled his way out of a rain of arrows. Just as Luce had said, Vesper had needed this victory, for his honor as much as hers. By meting out justice at the hand . . . or barbs . . . of the same beast Bartley had used to torment an innocent child, he had reinforced his reputation of a fair and assertive ruler capable of protecting and defending his people.

Also, I happen to know from my own experiences, Lyra told him, *that the best kings make the best fathers.*

His jaw dropped in remembrance of her monumental appointment with Dyadia. "Of course! Your memories." He brought her hand to his chest. "Tell me everything . . ."

Later, she promised as Luce came into view. They caught up to him, then to Selena and Cyprian.

Upon Luce's request, the first knight regaled him with the details of Bartley's demise. During the telling, Vesper slanted Luce a sly glance, waggling his brows. Luce rolled his eyes, though his lips twitched on what Lyra recognized as a rare smile of approval.

Once they arrived outside the throne room, Vesper sent Cyprian for something Lyra had specifically requested to aid in the sentencing.

Luce parted from the group and blended into the crowd as Selena, Vesper, and Lyra followed a fragrant trail of lavender panacea rose petals leading to the dais. Catching sight of their king and queen, the audience bowed their heads in welcome.

Lyra balked at the sheer number of people. Strangers' faces stretched wall to wall. Even the balconies were packed. The memories she'd absorbed only hours earlier had brought along with them old fears and insecurities. A distrust of crowds and accolades. But all it took was one look at the dais where her wicked relatives—Griselda, Lustacia, Wrathalyne, and Avaricette, hands tied behind their backs and guards stationed beside them—had been forced to kneel before the empty thrones, and the courage and fortitude she'd gained over the past five years while running with a witch, a sylph, and a Pegasus, came flooding back.

Lifting her chin high, Lyra led the way to the thrones. Prime Minister Albous joined the procession, walking alongside Queen Nova. Vesper held Lyra's hand as they climbed the stairs. He helped her sit, with Selena gathering her robe's train underneath and around the sides of the throne.

Selena, Prime Minister Albous, and Queen Nova took their respective places, standing next to the new queen or beside the king, their backs to the wall behind them. Lyra met Lustacia's gaze, and her cousin broke down into tears. Wrathalyne and Avaricette couldn't even look up, too overwhelmed by fear.

When Lyra met Griselda's belligerent glare, it didn't surprise her that her aunt had no remorse. During her memory transference in the Star Turret, Lyra recovered her aunt's confession: that she'd given away her conscience. As it stood, all of Griselda's final words were seared into Lyra's brain; she could still hear them ringing in her head, as clearly as she'd heard them through the closed lid of a coffin:

I suppose I should thank you. By freeing the witch while we still had her staff in custody, you made this entire setup possible. So, I'll return the favor and tell you how it all ends, since you won't be here to see for yourself. After you give up your voice, you'll become drowsy and your breath will slow. You won't be able to stay awake. And once you sleep, you will slip away. Give no thought to your faithful subjects. Any who become too curious or concerned will be cut down one by one. Mia will be first. Someone will attempt to poison our fare and she'll die a hero, proving her loyalty to Eldoria once and for all. As for the kingdom, Lustacia and I have it well in hand. You can slumber in eternal peace knowing this, little perfect princess. That is my gift to you.

Desolation had torn through Lyra when she'd relived those final moments. The realization that she had no family had brought her more anguish that fateful day than the horrors she suffered.

Spine pressed into her throne for support, Lyra looked into the audience where Luce's red hair stood out, then back to the dais from Selena to Cyprian. She caught Vesper's gaze last and a calm reassurance filled her heart: she had a family now, one that would never betray her; one that accepted her just as she was.

Riding that confidence, she gave Vesper the signal to begin.

He tipped his head, the jewels on his savage crown reflecting glints of candlelight, then raised his hand to get the audience's attention. The chatter died down as he stepped forward to address their four prisoners.

"To be clear, it was my personal intent to behead each of you, in the same manner I did your Sir Bartley. Due diligence for the heinous acts committed against a sweet, quiet twelve-year-old girl, whose only crime was being born of the same noble blood pumping through your own black hearts." He had everyone's attention. Silence reigned, the only sound the blubbering and sniffling of Lyra's cousins. Vesper's fierce expression fell on Griselda. "I have seen with my own eyes the horrors you inflicted upon my queen, in the name of hate and envy. I'm also aware of how far your barbarous acts spread, from Eldoria's honeysuckle- and death-infested castle to the Rigamort and the goblin camp, as well." He cast a glance at Lyra, then back to the stone-faced Griselda. "Consider yourself blessed your niece can gentle the beast in me. As she's the only reason you're still breathing." He took his throne then, his robe's hem swirling around his feet as he nodded to Lyra. "My Lady Queen, vengeance is yours. Bring on the spectacle."

That was the cue. Stunned ooohs and ahhhs rippled through the crowd as Cyprian led in two brumal stags. Behind them, Lyra's shadows herded in Lustacia's cursed goblin half-lights, forging their own path through the darkest parts of the room. Dregs came in, bringing up the end. Cyprian took his place among the other guards surrounding the dais at floor level. The stags had no reins or bits to guide them, no ropes upon their necks. All it took was Vesper's mental persuasions to bring them up the stairs and onto the platform, just as Lyra's thoughts beckoned to her faithful shadow attendants. Lyra stood upon their arrival, surrounding herself with Griselda's victims.

Lustacia screamed and shook her silver hair. "It hurts! My head!"

Griselda's stony mask slipped as agony showed on her face, too. She bit back a groan and struggled to free her blood-tinged fists, shoulders straining against the futility.

The stags bent their graceful necks, touching their antlers to the heads of the two who had maimed their own.

Griselda and Lustacia cried out as the seeds planted within their scalps burst and flourished into full-sized horns. Wrathalyne and Avaricette squeezed their teary eyes shut.

A wave of shocked astonishment stirred the crowd.

Lyra gestured for Griselda to be taken from the room, leaving her three daughters at Lyra's feet. The moment her aunt was gone, Lyra began signing and Prime Minister Albous stepped forward to translate:

"Are you not my cousins? You should've been my playmates, my sisters, my confidantes. Yet you laughed and teased, mocked my plight and my voice. You stood by as your mother fed me poison in a comforting glass of milk, doing nothing to aid me. Will you plead ignorance, being children yourselves when it all began? Will you seek to convince me you were victims, too? I might believe you. I have scars to prove my suffering. Perhaps yours are within . . . visible not by your skin, but by your calloused actions. I might have mercy, should you vow to change . . . to learn empathy and have kinder hearts."

Wrathalyne and Avaricette nodded and coughed on wet sobs. Avaricette spoke for them both. "Yes, we want to grow! To be kinder. We beg your mercy!"

"Then let it be so," came Lyra's answer on Prime Minister Albous's voice.

The two girls struggled to stand and put distance between themselves and their sister, believing they were pardoned.

"They are to kneel before their queen!" Vesper leaned forward and shouted through clenched teeth from his throne. The guards came forward and forced the girls back to their knees, holding their sword blades flat atop their heads.

The two froze, suppressing their cries.

"Lustacia, these creatures"—the prime minister paused as Lyra gestured to the goblin apparitions—"had families and lives. They made ill choices, serving your mother . . . but so did you. Is their penalty fair, taking this form forever? Being separated from all they know, being indentured to your will?"

Lustacia's neck bobbed forward, as if she couldn't bear the weight of the antlers. Her head drooped so low the pronged tips touched the floor. "I would rather be an apparition bound to another," she sobbed, "than bear this vile mutation. Their pain is nothing compared to mine."

"If you so believe, I can release you of the antler curse." The prime minister delayed interpreting as Lyra withdrew three vials from her robe's inner pocket and handed them to Dregs.

The little goblin shopkeeper stepped forward, face-to-face with Lustacia's kneeling form, and opened the first vial.

Lyra resumed her speech with Albous's aid.

"Since you're convinced the half-lights suffer less, you will share their lesser fate. Drink at Dregs's hand, and lose your horns. The trade-off, however, is you'll be bound to him as a half-life silhouette. You will serve the goblin, as your goblins serve you." She turned to her other two cousins, drawing them back into the sentencing. "Wearing another's skin is the most effective way to learn empathy. Share your sister's penalty. Drink, and prove yourself more human than you ever were in your present form. Demonstrate this desire to grow, and you will live. Refuse, and choose death."

As Albous delivered Lyra's ultimatum, the guards shifted their blades to the back of each girls' head, prepared to lop them off should they refuse.

Lyra's cousins cried out for their absent mother while gulping from the vials Dregs offered. Wrathalyne hiccupped, Avaricette coughed, and Lustacia gagged. Then, with nothing more dramatic than a poof, the three sisters disintegrated into black, smoky shapes that hovered around the goblin shopkeeper, awaiting his command.

Gasps and stunned cries erupted in the audience.

Lyra flashed a knowing smile to Vesper. She had shared her plan with him, not to tell her cousins that the potion's effect was only temporary. Her hope was that when each one awoke from their half-life in two years, they would be so grateful to be human once more, they would never take the responsibility of *humane*ness for granted again. Lyra wanted to allow them a chance to prove themselves above Griselda's wicked ways when no longer under her thumb, while keeping them out of kingdom business. This had been her solution.

Vesper inclined his head in a show of respect.

She returned her attention to her feet, where Dregs bowed prostrate before her. His three new half-light servants did the same, which forced those five apparitions chained to Lustacia to bow as well. "By avenging my family, you brought honor to our kind," Dregs said, his bulbous eyes filled with admiration. "From this day forward, fair queen, our loyalties are realigned. Come to us seeking any favor. Our fealty will never waver."

She touched his brow affectionately, and he kissed the slippers on her feet. He then stood and filed down the stairs with all eight apparitions in tow. He stopped and found a place in the front row where Lyra had asked him to wait within sight of Griselda. Once he and his band of silhouettes were settled, Lyra had her aunt dragged in again.

"What have you done with my daughters?" Griselda snapped as the guards shoved her to her knees.

"They are here," Lyra answered with her prime minister's assistance. "They're watching and waiting. Their fates rest upon you."

"You lie! I can't see them!" Griselda jabbed at Lyra's leg with her antlers but Lyra sidestepped the attack. From his throne, Vesper spoke a command to his stags. One leapt forward, tangling its prongs with Griselda's. The regent cried out for help. Lyra stroked the creature's coat, coaxing it to break free and settle at her side once more.

Lyra began signing again.

"It is time for you to answer for yourself, Lady Griselda." Prime Minister Albous's deep voice grew more somber with every word he passed on. "Are you not my aunt? You could've been a mother to me in the absence of my own. You might've been a comfort to your brother who lost his wife. Yet instead, you conspired to see us both dead. What have you to say?"

"I say I'm not to blame." Griselda spewed her rebuttal and glared at her niece, barely allowing the prime minister to finish. "It was my destiny to have a hand in the prophecy. Not yours. I was told thus and made it so."

"You were told by the shrouds."

Griselda's mouth puckered in disbelief at Lyra's insight. Lyra had remembered Griselda mentioning the shrouds to Lustacia those last moments in the coffin, as well. And when that memory returned, Lyra's own interaction with the collective made sense at last. Griselda was the Eldorian princess the shrouds had lost to a sylph—Luce, judging by the wings trapped within Eldoria's castle courtyard—so many years ago. It was Griselda they waited for, even now.

Lyra's hands and fingers—growing tired from strain—took up again, to give Griselda's cruel speech from that fateful day new life by making the sentiments her own.

"Take heart, Aunt, for you have indeed had a hand in the prophecy, as indicated by the blood tainting your skin. I abhor every crime you've committed, yet there is something for which I owe gratitude: Thank you for putting me in a box and sending my dying body to the ravine, for there I met a witch whose kindness showed me beauty beyond appearances, and a sylph whose persistence showed me that life could be found in ash and thorns. Because of you, I learned to look past the surface. Thus, when I met the prince in the form of a Pegasus, in a place between bias and kingdoms, outside of traditions and creed, I had no preset expectations of a prophecy or political pressures. We met on the common ground of anonymity, loneliness, and seeking hearts. At *your* hand, we forged a comradery that grew to unconditional trust and love. Now we're equals, capable of ruling side by side. Capable of uniting our kingdoms under one sky. So yes, you are responsible for who I am today, and for the queen I'll be from this day forward. To show my gratitude, I will tell you how it's going to end, since you won't be here to see for yourself. After you awaken from the sleeping draught you'll be given, you will find yourself exiled to the Ashen Ravine, just as you left me, in a box filled with every creeping, flying, and crawling creature you've ever crushed beneath your shoe, struck with a book, or fed to a bird. Should you escape your tomb, you will face the guilt of your crimes in the place it all began— among the shrouds. However, first I will allow you one chance to rescue your daughters, who moments ago received the same potion you thrust upon the goblin smugglers."

Dregs commanded his three half-light attendants to drift forward to the dais's edge. Griselda's eyes bulged upon realizing they were her children.

"No!" she screeched. She doubled over, her shoulders sinking as she wailed. Even without a conscience, she had claimed to love her girls. A shame that love was always secondary to her schemes.

"Declare me as your queen," Lyra continued, the volume of Prime Minister Albous's voice intensifying to regain the hysterical regent's attention. "Aloud, here before our Eldorian representatives and all of Nerezeth's witnesses. Pledge your fealty to me and give me the devotion my lineage warrants. Do this, and though it won't save you, it will free your daughters from their wretched fate. Perhaps this might make up for the experiences you robbed them of while isolating them from the world."

Lyra's chest tightened as Griselda lifted her head and snarled. She struggled against the binds holding her fisted hands at her back, bringing the guards to her side. This was the final part of Lyra's plan: to take the temporary quality of the half-light potion one step further. The effects would wear off eventually, yet only Luce, Dyadia, Lyra, and Vesper knew this. Griselda didn't have such knowledge, any more than her daughters did. If her aunt cooperated, Lyra would announce to everyone that her cousins would be freed after a short imprisonment in their cursed forms. Then Wrathalyne, Avaricette, and Lustacia would at last see their mother choose them over her pride. And they would see her accept Lyra as the rightful ruler. Should Griselda refuse, Lyra would send away her cousins with the goblin, ignorant of their short sentence, and they would have the next two years to contemplate their mother's selfishness and betrayal.

Either way, all three girls needed to witness this moment, to truly be free from Griselda's evil influence.

Lyra held her breath, hoping her aunt would do the right thing.

Griselda regained her composure. "I will see . . . that no one ever calls you queen!" Her refusal echoed in the great hall and she spun on her knees. Before the guards could gauge her intent, she opened her fisted hands, allowing a small orb—aglow with snaky turquoise light—to drop from her fingers.

Startled gasps broke through the audience. Luce's bellow from the back drowned them out: "She means to set the queen on fire!"

"Lyra!" Vesper leapt up from his throne and caught her around the waist, dragging her out of the rolling orb's trajectory and beside the thrones where prime minister, Serena, and Queen Nova already huddled along the wall.

"It must've been up her sleeve!" one of the guards shouted as he forced Griselda closer to the center. In the instant the sphere touched the ribbon draping the dais's edge—so meticulously arranged for the coronation by Griselda the prior day—the second guard slammed his boot down to stop it from falling into the audience. The orb burst on contact, enveloping him and his armor in flames of turquoise, rose-pink, and white. His sword dropped from his hands as blisters charred his exposed skin. The stench of broiled flesh tainted the air. He screamed and fell to the floor below. In his wake, the flowers and ribbons around the platform ignited. A blaze rose high and swift—cutting off the stairs and sealing everyone upon the dais in a line of enchanted, deadly flame. Heat singed Lyra's skin, and she coughed at the smoke surrounding her and her companions as they pressed their backs to the wall. Everyone lifted their robes and tucked them tightly around their bodies, putting distance between flames and fabric.

"Guards! Bring water!" Vesper commanded.

Dregs sent his apparitions—Lyra's half-light cousins and those five that belonged to Lustacia—to retrieve buckets from the kitchen, as they could move faster than any human feet.

"Water? Bring the ocean . . . it won't matter!" Griselda released a cackling laugh, as if she'd gone mad.

A chord of terror struck in Lyra's heart, seeing Vesper's dark eyes reflecting flames—outside of him instead of within—seeing his jaw clench in a vise, having no power over this element he once ruled. She beckoned her shadows. They dipped and swayed around her and the others, dispersing to helpless, sooty streaks and retreating to the corners of the room as the blaze overpowered them.

The audience backed toward the door while both Eldorian and Nerezethite guards joined forces and moved forward, dousing the holocaust with the water brought in by the apparitions. The searing crackle and roar only grew louder, brighter, hotter—muffling the panicked curses and shouts of the guards.

The stags brayed, hedging toward Lyra and her group where the fire hadn't yet sparked. Their safe spot was shrinking. Lyra held tight to her king, squinting against the brilliant glow. Griselda's hem was dangerously close to the dais's blazing ledge; a part of Lyra wanted her to erupt into flame, yet another part knew it would never be justice enough.

Luce appeared overhead in his ethereal form. "These flames are enchanted . . . made of sunlight. Only the purest strand of moonlight will squelch them!"

Upon that revelation, Queen Nova pressed close to Lyra and her son, her lilac eyes bright with fear. "Your stags, my son. You must bleed them of their moonlight magic. It's our only hope!"

Vesper's firelit face paled. He looked sick at the thought, twisted up with dread to consider the logic behind her words. If only Dyadia hadn't left for Eldoria, they could call upon her for help. But it was up to them alone.

Vesper looked at his family and Lyra. While withdrawing a knife from his belt, he called a stag to his side. It came willingly, lowering its prong tips. Lyra knew he'd do what he must as king, though it would kill him to do it.

Wait . . . she stopped him just as he caught the stag's antler and held his blade to the base that glimmered like silvery-blue diamonds. *Their blood isn't pure moonlight.* She blinked. *You once said my lashes are slivers of the moon. What could be purer than that?*

Vesper studied her blankly, as though shuffling through his memories as Scorch. Perception crossed his face and he sheathed his knife, cupping her chin with his hand. *Together?* His silent question passed to her.

She nodded. The flames were almost to their thrones now, close enough Lyra's toes burned within her slippers at the oncoming heat. Still, she looked nowhere but Vesper, reading the apology in his gaze as he plucked one long eyelash free. It surprised her, that the stinging pain lasted her only an instant this time, though it appeared to cut her king much deeper. Grimacing, he dropped the lash over the leg of fire creeping closest to them. The glistening hair caught an updraft and fluttered toward the ceiling. Within the space of a breath, it transformed to sheets of glowing liquid that sluiced across their heads and the dais in a cooling deluge. Lyra lifted her face, relishing the saturation of her clothes and hair as she stood beneath her first rainstorm. The flames snuffed out on contact, leaving the platform in a sooty, wet haze.

The first to arrive on the dais were Luce alongside Dregs' apparitions. Their half-light forms coalesced to a black, spongy cloud that absorbed all the wetness, leaving everything and everyone dry. Griselda's cursed daughters converged on her last. She shooed away their shadowy forms and slumped forward, soggy and defeated.

Once Lyra and Vesper saw that all—from his family to Prime Minister Albous and the brumal stags—were unharmed, they stepped forward to survey the losses as the audience trickled in again. The edges of the dais bore the brunt of damage, black and smudged. Griselda's ribbon decorations resembled curls of charcoal, crisp and crumbling to ash where the flowers once hung.

"Is he . . . ?" Vesper's voice cracked upon the question as he looked down at the guard who'd tried to stop the orb with his foot. Cyprian and several of the man's comrades knelt beside him. Cyprian nodded, and a deep sadness scalded Lyra's chest, as if the fire burned anew inside her.

Vesper turned on Griselda, whose face remained buried against the dais. "Lord Tyron had a wife in the infirmary," he growled. "And a baby on the way." Vesper picked up the guard's fallen sword and held it over Griselda's neck. "You should die by his blade." He tensed to take the fatal swing.

Lyra caught his shoulders to soothe the muscles coiled beneath his robes. *Together, we'll tell his wife of his heroism. But let me finish this. I'll see that she pays with what she holds most dear.*

Struggling for control, Vesper dropped the sword with a *clang*. He took a seat on his charred throne, his expression as hard and formidable as the points of his iron crown. The audience went so still, Lyra could hear the breaths of everyone who stood upon the platform. She exchanged a meaningful glance with her prime minister. He stepped forward, his intelligent green gaze bloodshot from smoke, and together they delivered Griselda's verdict.

"Aunt Griselda, you once said all the magic in my body was no match for your lifetime of wisdom. Yet I defeated you with naught but an eyelash. You are powerless against me and my king. The two kingdoms you murdered for, lied for, and plotted to steal are no longer your concern. Vesper and I have them well in hand. We will produce heirs to rule after us, forever keeping my father's bloodline on the throne. And for this final deadly act"—Lyra paused, redirecting her busy hands toward those who carried out the burned guard—"I will blot the word 'Griselda' from Eldoria's history, along with all record of your part in the prophecy's fruition. In its absence, only *Glistenda* will remain. The proper little princess, whose skin bruised at the touch of a feather. Voiceless—with no glory and no story. Forgotten and faded away. That is your just reward, and my gift to you."

Prime Minister Albous smiled upon the last few sentences of his interpretation.

Griselda looked up then, her face contorted in rage. Her answering screams vowed revenge as Lyra commanded the guards to carry her writhing form away. The audience sent the regent off with hisses and hoots which evolved to relieved hails and accolades in Lyra's direction as she stepped to her throne and took a seat.

Vesper caught her hand in his, the severity of his frown softening. "Thank you," he whispered.

Lacing their fingers, Lyra put the past and all its ugliness behind her and looked instead to the future, and the promise of a wedding that glimmered like stars behind her king's dark eyes.

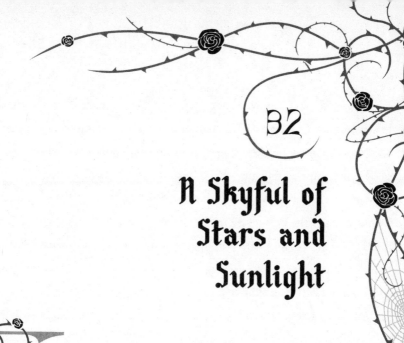

82

A Skyful of Stars and Sunlight

Some hours later, the courts of Eldoria and Nerezeth followed the wedding procession through the moonlit, snowy terrain and into Neverdark's warmth to witness the blink of dawn and the exchanging of vows that would heal the realms. In the selfsame moment, Griselda awoke in a pitch-black box to the revolting sensation of creeping legs and flapping wings befouling her half-naked flesh.

Not even a crack of light shone in, leaving her unable to view her attackers. The unknowing wrenched her stomach, dried her tongue, and tightened her throat. A hundred spindly legs clambered across her bald scalp, and she writhed to shake them off. The movement scraped her antlers across the panels surrounding—causing a sharp pain to shoot through her prongs. She gagged, having forgotten her mutation.

She howled behind closed lips, terrified to open her mouth for fear of swallowing a spider, a cricket, or a moth—whatever loathsome creatures shared her tomb.

Tomb. That's what her miserable niece had called it. That ghastly ghost-faced girl had somehow managed to win. Griselda had been so close to taking everyone down with her . . . lacing the ribbons with the incendiary before leaving Eldoria as a final recourse in case anything went wrong, hiding the fire orb inside her bodice while Vesper's guards searched her for weapons before imprisoning her. And then tucking it in her fisted hands before they returned to the cell to join her wrists at her back for the sentencing. It would've been the perfect plan, had she not been thwarted by . . . a hair.

Her blood brewed hot with rage, remembering the horrid fate of her daughters, imprisoned to a goblin's will and forced to aid in her downfall. She couldn't let this be the end.

She pounded on the lid. The creepers along her arms fell like patters of rain to the wood beneath her, then scrambled across her midriff and legs, biting and stinging through the scant chemise that clung to her body.

Pinpricks of heat bloomed beneath the needling sensations, making her bones ache and her joints catch.

Scraping bugs from her face, she cupped her mouth to scream, "Let me out! I want out!" Then she pounded the lid again.

There was a shuffle outside. She drew a tight breath. Footsteps . . . which meant a human, not a shroud. They were heavier, like a man's. It must be a thief or a murderer. The ravine was home to nothing but society's sewage. It was why she'd sent Lyra's dead body here.

The witch must've made a trade of some sort . . . gave up her immortality for the child—all to put a crimp in Griselda's plans.

Griselda fisted her hands.

The lid began to creak open, allowing a soft glow within. Griselda covered her chest in feigned modesty and practiced her most frightened expression. The man would see her vulnerable and either pity or desire her. She would use her wiles to break free then have her revenge on everyone: her niece, the arrogant prince, the meddling witch, and Elusion.

The stinging and scuttling infestation receded from her body as the lid fell away, washing her in greenish, hazy light. The scent of feathers and wind drifted to her nostrils, slamming her with nostalgia—almost as if the mention of his name had conjured him.

She sat up in the stale air and smiled smugly. "Of course. At the sentencing, you were playing a part, pretending to hate me. All so you could save me here, where no one could see."

Before Elusion could answer, she leapt into his arms.

Quietly, he forced her to stand, her bare feet still within the box. He removed his jacket. His orange eyes glinted in the dimness—not hungrily as they once had when he looked upon her in a nightdress. They glinted cold as ice, a foil to their fiery color.

Griselda shook off a bout of insecurity. "Now that you have your wings back, you must be grateful I took such good care of them." She raised her welted arms, expecting him to help her into his jacket. Instead, Luce folded it into a square and used it to dust the remaining few bugs from her body without crushing them or touching her.

"Such good care, indeed. I can't get the scent of smoke out, no matter how high I fly. But anything is better than being human, tied to an inescapable, aging form." He cocked his chin at her pointedly, then shrugged into his jacket, his crimson wings sinking through the fabric and reappearing to arch high behind him like feathery mist.

Griselda fumed, feeling exposed in her human body—every sag and wrinkle on full display. "I thought you preferred haggard and hideous, considering your attachment to the harrower witch."

The sylph bared his pointed teeth in a vicious, chest-deep growl. "Speak of her again and I will rip out your jugular and devour your bones."

Griselda withered at the threat, but refused to let him see her fear.

He straightened his lapel, regaining composure. "I didn't come to relive old times with you. I didn't come for you at all. Who would? You alienated or murdered everyone who once might've cared." He shook his red head in pity and helped her step out of the box, pointing to a tree with a thin layer of ash surrounding it. "Stand over there, would you? I need room to gather up these little darlings. My queen was concerned for their well-being. She feared her black widows and scorpions might suffer contamination should they be too long exposed to your toxicity."

Anger spiked anew in Griselda's blood, but she could only lean against the trunk—her limbs heavy, her stomach nauseous, and her head light. She'd been stung countless times and the venom was spreading. "So, you are her errand boy now?" She snarled, trying to stay focused. "Does your 'queen' know of your past? Does she know how you killed her mother?"

"We killed her, *Glistenda*."

The name made Griselda stiffen with fury. But even as her spine ate into the tree, the bark grew smoother, softer, as if it gave beneath her. *Hallucinations*. Her vision wavered, though she managed to stay standing.

"And no, Queen Lyra isn't aware of my hand in her fate. I'll not confess simply to soothe my guilty conscience. The gnawing ache within the pit of me will be my burden to bear. Something I'd never expect you to relate to."

"Of course. For you know who I am. Just as you know you're the reason I have no remorse."

He flapped his wings restlessly, as if bored by the conversation. "I once blamed myself, but no longer. I didn't influence your decision . . . used none of my sylphin gifts on you that day. Mistress Umbra looked within your heart and saw the truth of your desire. You chose to give up your conscience all on your own."

Griselda pressed deeper into the tree, her skin feverish and chilled. "As if your choices are so noble. Choosing to protect your scabby hide by lying to 'your queen.'"

"I'm protecting *her*. She's had too much loss in her life as it is. I refuse to take away another person—or place or thing—she needs or cares for." Elusion opened the bag at his feet. "But there's a penalty for my dishonesty—an obligation. Though I'll never be her errand boy, or a white knight, or any honored member of her court, I'll spend the rest of my ageless life tied to one portion of the sky, tethered to her." Elusion laid out several jars, then crouched to tenderly separate the bugs into each one before replacing their mesh lids. "Should she call, I'll always return. There are tasks she'll need done that only a sylph can provide." He tucked the jars into the bag. "Such as coaxing a corrupted regent into thinking she has the upper hand when all along she's been given the final nail for her coffin. A nail in the form of a boxful of memories. It's fitting, don't you think? Me tricking you the same as I once tricked Eldoria's queen *for* you."

Griselda howled and lunged, only to find herself stuck to the tree, unable to budge. The tree branches had hold of her antlers ... but they weren't branches at all. They were illusory arms and hands and fingers. She wrestled to get free, freezing when a cluster of formless silhouettes slipped from the trunk, their white eyes blinking.

Griselda's heart quailed. "No!"

Mistress Umbra skimmed into view and Griselda screeched louder.

Elusion lifted his bag, then took out a box. He looked from the mother shroud to the collective surrounding Griselda. "Crony's debt is paid. As is mine." He tossed the box to Griselda's feet, stirring a puff of dust. "Our business is ended, and I've a wedding to attend. See you on the other side of the moon, Mistress Umbra."

The creature released a hissing laugh. "Charming as ever, Elusion. Good to have you back to your old self. And may today be the beginning of Eldoria's night."

"Wait! Don't leave me!" Griselda screamed as the sylph drank a smoky mixture from a vial and vanished.

The box at Griselda's feet rattled. Even had her name not been scripted across it, she would've known those contents belonged to her, would've recognized the sounds within ... the clangor of wings and wails that called out on the voice of her many crimes.

"No, please! I don't want to *feel*!"

Mistress Umbra's beakish mouth turned on an appalling smile as she began to rip away Griselda's gown. "Didn't I tell you, little princesss? That you would come again to seek our company. Didn't I predict you'd need a place to hide those sins that twist and twine like the branches of a tree?" Her beady gaze shifted to Griselda's bald head.

Sobbing, Griselda slumped, held up only by her antlers now . . . by the prongs that jutted like twigs from her skull.

Mistress Umbra's scraggly, creaturely fingers opened the box and released the teal-feathered starlings. "And did I not vow to show you the same mercy you practiced throughout your life? No more . . . no lesss?"

Inky black lines crept into Griselda's flesh, taking the form of spiders and scorpions. They scuttled beneath the surface, engulfing her arms and spreading through the rest of her body until her hands were no longer the only things infested . . . until all of her was.

Griselda shivered beneath the intrusion. Her antlers came free and she fell to her knees. Her body grew weightless and her skin sheer, offering no barrier to the starlings slamming into her bones. Their claws and beaks scraped along her organs and innards, embedding the anguish and remorse within every piece and parcel of her being: poisonings, destructive potions, broken childhoods—her own daughters forced to pay the penalty for her wrongs with their lives: past, present, and future. The beasts she murdered, the niece she tortured, the brother she slayed after killing his wife. And Kiran's loyal first knight . . .

"Ah, and here we are," Mistress Umbra baited, viewing Griselda's thoughts and pain as she walked inside her mind. "At last we see him . . . Sir Nicolet, this knight you murdered who was the boy you once loved. You came here to make him return your love that day, so long ago. Well, it had been a needless trek, it would seem. Crony shared his final memory with us. Should you like to know it now?"

Griselda couldn't answer, for her bones were splintering. She coughed up blood, then watched it sink into her translucent skin to form black contusions.

"He loved you always. As the boy, as the man. He wanted to prove himself worthy of you, so he waited until he became a knight to court you. But then, you'd already married another. So he waited again. He intended to ask for your hand on the day you had him killed. That was his final memory, thinking of the life he'd wanted to live with you and your daughters, heartbroken over your betrayal. Your name upon his lips with his last breath."

Griselda wept then, the agony and regret too great to bear.

"Now, my children," Mistress Umbra murmured to her shrouds. "We feast upon her flesh. For our collective has no place for despair this deep."

As the shrouds swept in to devour her, Griselda cursed her wasted years. She begged for mercy to the stifling, ash-filled air, as there was no one else to hear. Then she turned to ash herself and lived no more.

❊ · I · ❊

Within Eldoria's gardens, Crony awoke to the excited flutter of Thana's feathers against her neck. She knew the identity of her visitor before her scent—snow, burning leaves, and sulfur—cut through the stench of singed hair and flesh. She knew before those soft hands dabbed salve atop her blisters to soothe the agonized pulses of Crony's shredded nerves. She only wished she could see her, for that would've becalmed her soul.

"Glad ye brought another dose," Crony croaked.

"I assumed what I sent with your sylph would be evaporated by now," Dyadia answered.

"Aye. Still can't believe he took time to go to ye for treatment, with the princess gone missing as she had."

"He kept quite busy in that interim. Tricked Eldoria's wretched regent, too."

Crony tried to smile, but without lips, the attempt was futile. It was enough to feel it in her heart. "Told ye I chose wisely. Ye have yer set of wings, and I have mine."

Thana cawed belligerently, offended by the comparison.

"The regent was exiled to the ravine," Dyadia said over her bird's antics. "I thought you would like to know. Queen Lyra sent her to the shroud's lair, half-naked and shaved in a coffin filled with bugs."

Crony cackled. "I would've giv'n me right horn to be a biting midge in that box." Her laughter halted abruptly as she coughed up a smoky lump.

Dyadia patted Crony's chest—a concerned gesture Crony hadn't expected. "Your sylph wanted me to tell you he's there now, taking care of things, tying up loose ends and settling old debts."

"Good. Will make it easier to leave, knowin' that. So, when the wedding be takin' place?"

"As we speak. And since it all must be timed properly, shall we watch together?"

"I be likin' that."

"Go then, Thana. Let us spy through your eye." Gusts of wind raked across Crony's numb skin as the giant crow took flight. Her flapping grew distant and an awkward hush followed.

Crony struggled for something to say, some way to keep the pleasantries going, not yet prepared for the airing of apologies and past mistakes.

"Well, you went and did it." Dyadia saved Crony the trouble. "Resurrected the girl and shirked the rules by stealing her memories. You took quite a chance."

"As did ye, splittin' the boy in twain."

"Ah, well, we both knew how important they were. It's been difficult, hiding the prophecy for all these centuries, waiting to share it with the humans until the right moment. Waiting for those two to be born and aged enough to jolt the kingdoms from their antipathy for one another. I'd almost given up hope. At last . . . our moment came. Then everything fell to rot—"

"Yet, fate assured they found one another, in spite of all the bumps and byroads."

"I'm so relieved. Elsewise, we wouldn't have this opportunity to fix our mistakes."

Crony's threaded pulse kicked an extra beat. "*Our* mistakes?"

"I've been blind for so long, as blind as you are today. Three eyes, yet none of them could see what my son had become, and the destruction he meant to unleash upon the world. You did what I couldn't do, even though you lied and broke my heart in doing it."

Crony's own heart shriveled at the hurt in Dyadia's voice. "That be me wrong to right. And I will. Can ye forgive me, when I be gone?"

Dyadia placed a hand over Crony's. "I forgive you now. We both know yours was the biggest sacrifice. I understand why you gave the princess what you refused my son. For she was worthy of it."

"More than that. There be two kingdoms dependin' on her livin', not her dyin'."

"Yes," Dyadia whispered.

Crony reached up blindly with her free hand and Dyadia bowed close so she could touch her cheek. "Me beloved one . . . I couldn't save yer Lachrymosa then, but I can bring him back to ye now—to cast his light upon yer windowsills in the eve." She sipped a painful breath. "It been a burden to bear, the waitin'. . . . I be glad it's almost here."

"It was wrong of me, to place the malediction on your head. All these years, unable to close your eyes because of my anger."

Crony's heart smiled again at the kind words. "Nay, I had to be lookin' anyways . . . so I mightn't miss the opportunity, so I mightn't o'erpass the recipient of me resurrective. I knew what I had to be given up to straighten what I turned askew. Keepin' me eyes open made me vigilant. I can rest now, soon enough."

"Yes. I suppose we both can." Dyadia forced a soft laugh, though sadness blunted the edges.

"Tell me, what ye think of me wee one for yer kingdom's boy?"

Dyadia tugged gently at the few strands of brittle hairs left dangling from Crony's scalp. "She's everything his queen should be. Clever, adventurous, indomitable. Bold in her passions, yet tender and kind. She balances his brutality, but only when necessary. She has a way with him . . . our king. He respects her, treasures her, defers to her as if she were an extension of himself. There is no question they will bring prosperity and peace to both kingdoms. There is no question they're the only ones who could." Upon saying that, Dyadia caught a breath. She sat up with a start and squeezed Crony's hand. "Thana has arrived in the arboretum. She's searching for a place to perch to offer a good view."

"The arboretum? What of the false sunlight? Lyra's skin be so tender."

"No longer. Taking Vesper's sunlit curse upon herself and defeating it made her stronger. She's no more sensitive-skinned now than any other Ner-ezethite. By curing him, she cured herself."

Crony chortled between gasps. "Just goes to show . . . the trade-off don't always have to be a bad thing." She didn't need to see to know that Dyadia nodded in agreement.

"Give me your hand, here." Dyadia guided Crony's singed fingers to the socket on her forehead. At the moment of contact, Crony could see every-thing Thana and her sorceress could—sharp and vivid within her mind.

Spaces in a latticework revealed a grand expanse of meadows, fields, ponds, and lakes outside, gilded with the soft glow of thousands of fireflies adrift on a breeze. A throng of wedding guests and witnesses stretched from the footbridge leading to the iron door's entrance, to a grove of wildflowers beneath an elm upon a hill in the distance. There waited a lone red fox, seated on his haunches. Crony laughed inside herself, unsurprised he'd worn that form. Luce couldn't get caught being sentimental, after all.

The portending crow had landed within the shrine upon a luminary, blocking the starry imprints of light from reaching the ceiling. No one seemed to notice or care. Everyone's attention stayed fixed upon their newly crowned king and queen as they entered through the latticework archway, holding hands, giving one another glances filled with desire and anticipation.

They were beautiful: light and dark, side by side, scarred yet lovely, representative of the two heavenly entities that once shared the skies but were torn apart.

They were both draped in long, elaborate fur-lined silver robes that gathered at the waist. The kings' fur cuffs stopped midway down his hands. A bejeweled belt peered out from his robe—binding a blue jacquard tunic embellished with braids and steel buttons. The tunic's shade complemented the sodalite-encrusted broadsword strapped at his waist, its tip nearly reaching the toes of his long black boots. It was a family piece, handed down from monarch to monarch in the House of Astraeus. Crony remembered seeing it at convocations, strapped to King Velimer's waist centuries earlier.

And then there was Stain in a beaded gown the blue of a spring sky, with billows of glistening web and sparkling white spiders cascading along the skirt and bell sleeves like diamond-studded lace. Living salamanders twined around her feet, their slick skin glimmering like precious gemstones. Her silver hair, thick and lustrous, swept across one shoulder and down to her waist in a long braid interwoven with amethysts and flowers. Her skin was aglow with moonlight and happiness. She looked like a princess at last. Princess Lyra.

But no, she was a queen, wearing her mother's diamond crown. That gentle, refined woman whom she never knew, that same mother Crony did her best to stand in for in her own rough, surly way. Her scorched innards clenched tight on the thought.

"We did it, wee one," she whispered, then strangled on a half sob. She pulled back from Dyadia's touch, jerking them both from the scene.

"Cronatia?" Her companion gripped her fingers. "The blink of dawn and dusk is at hand; why do you pause?"

"Be that indeed the best time, to make a moment legendary 'nough that no one be doubting its credence?"

"What did you have in mind?"

"The kiss. Aye, when they kiss."

"To make it belong to the king and queen alone," Dyadia said, her mind in synch with Crony's as it once was all those years ago. "Perfect." She leaned in again, about to press Crony's fingers back into place.

Crony hesitated. "Vow to me. The realms can ne'er know the truth of it. That no king and queen alive have the power to affect the sun and moon. That it lie in me alone, through yer son's moon-callin' spell. That the prophecy was ne'er about a marriage reuniting the skies, but about a pure and true love reuniting kingdoms."

Dyadia sighed. "Of all the things magic can mend, yet it can't break through narrow-mindedness."

"It be taken everyone's hands to knock down walls and rebuild foundations."

"Well, then these two will be the cornerstones. The example."

"Aye. So let's give 'em a fairy-tale endin' to stand upon. A pedestal, of sorts. One they know nothin' of. And the people will ne'er again doubt the strength behind solidarity. Be we in agreement?"

"Yes. I vow it." Dyadia caught Crony's hand once more. "I will see you in the heavens, Madame Cronatia Wisteria."

"Each and ev'ry night."

Dyadia turned Crony's palm and pressed soft lips to what was left of the charred flesh. She then guided Crony's fingers to revive the scene. The royal couple appeared again, standing in front of a dais covered in white silk and brimming with periwinkle flowers and ivy that cascaded down the sides. Deep lavender panacea petals, sprinkled atop turquoise moss, covered the floor and stretched all the way out the arched entrance, across a footbridge, and to the iron door.

On the other end of the dais, facing the bride and groom, stood two holy men—Eldorian and Nerezethite—each wearing vestments adorned by their kingdoms' prospective sigils.

The vows had already been spoken, for their left wrists were bound with ceremonial ribbons and thorns, to show the unification of their realms. The panacea rose ring—that Crony had seen within the bag in the dirt room—already sat upon the queen's hand. As for Lyra's part, she had her nose wrinkled while wrestling a metallic-black band into place upon her king's finger. They began laughing at the struggle, and the love and hope upon their faces gave Crony the strength to call upon the mage's dark spell, letting it fill her thoughts, letting it chill her blood.

Lachrymosa's voice and face were tied within it, for he'd become one with the moon, and when Crony had intercepted that bond, taking his breath and the spell, the moon had fallen, depleted and unable to stand on its own against the sun. Thus, it had stayed hidden beneath the earth where it would be safe. Now Crony would use the spell to bring the moon back to Eldoria where she waited. She would become one with it—release her spirit alongside Lachrymosa's within—to renew the moon's strength, yet contain its power. Together, they would help it find its place once more alongside the sun.

All she needed was the kiss . . .

As if on cue, the king cupped his queen's chin, mimed the words "Lady Wife," then joined their lips in a sweet, passionate embrace as everyone cheered around them.

Waiting one beat to admire the beauty of their bliss, Crony called up the moon and took her last breath.

❋ · I · ❋

The royal chroniclers would one day record it, filling scrolls with the miraculous event, pages upon pages of descriptions: How, when the raven-eyed king and his silver-haired queen shared their first kiss as husband and wife, the world began to shake and tremble. Nerezethites outside of the arboretum gave accounts of trees, once bowed from the blizzard's downfall, shaking off clumps of snow and ice and stretching upward as if reaching for the moon as it slid into the reopened seam of the earth—as it magically converted to smoke and clouds, then siphoned through the crack. And just as the moon pulled Nerezeth's province above ground—the populace, the forest, the castle, the arboretum, the Rigamort and its brumal stags, the hoarfrost goblins—the Ashen Ravine fell into the crack, sliding the opposite direction via its own bubble of magic, encapsulating and combining all the wicked and twisted residues of magic as it went: the thorns, the badlands of the Grim, the shrouds and cadaver brambles, the quag puddles and endless ash. These took form again within the belly of the earth in a new shape—dark and dangerous—before the rip in the earth closed with a magical seal, locking the evil far, far beneath the ground.

A reversal, the scrolls would say. For thereafter, Nerezeth's forestland was seated alongside Eldoria's mountains and hills and valleys, both surrounded by the oceans, as it had been from the very beginning.

When the dust settled, the sun, moon, and stars shared the sky for one day, with an enchanted rainbow barrier holding their light separate. The sun, warm and beaming over Nerezeth's forests, lured out the tender-skinned people from their homes and the infirmaries. Protected by the shade, they stood within the softened rays and felt true sunlight for the first time as snow and ice dripped and melted around them. Above Eldoria, the moon and stars held vigil, their glow too tender to feed the honeysuckle. White flakes fell from the sky. Within hours, the fragrant, vine-infested plague had disintegrated beneath blankets of snow that melted away to a nutrient-rich mud. The townspeople cheered, running to-and-fro with buckets, gathering it to use for compost in their neglected gardens and fields.

The next day, the sun broke at dawn over both kingdoms simultaneously, then set at dusk, and the moon ruled the night. Balance had returned to the skies at the hands of a star-boy and a songbird girl, just as the prophecy foretold. Both kingdoms came together to rejoice and rally around their rulers with pledges of honor and fealty.

That very first evening, Queen Lyra and King Vesper sat among advisors and council members within the great hall.

They hadn't had a moment to themselves since the event—Lyra making arrangements with Prime Minister Albous to send Eldoria's military and council back to the ivory palace to assure all was well and at peace, and to inform the people that their king and queen would take the two-week journey there to hold open court and meet all their subjects very soon; and Vesper, sending his own military forces to round up the thieves, murderers, and marauders running amuck through the forested province now that the ravine no longer housed them. However, Lyra had given him a list of those she thought worthy of pardon for their part in freeing Crony from Griselda's imprisonment, and upon consideration, the king found positions for them in his castle conducive to their peculiar and particular talents.

Lyra and her king had just issued a decree to bring down the walls of the arboretum and free all the wildlife when she saw Queen Nova, Luce, and Dyadia standing outside the hall's doorway. She nudged her king, who looked up from signing the parchment.

Perhaps they have news on Crony, she said silently between them. The last time she saw Luce and Dyadia together was only from a distance—when the sun, moon, and stars stretched across the heavens like a mystical trinity. The two had been deep in conversation, but had slipped away before Lyra could break free from her responsibilities to question them.

Now, with her king in tow, she wove through the crowded candlelit room, tipping her crowned head to people who knelt as they passed.

Together, they stepped out into the corridor where Queen Nova had already cleared the way for them to have privacy.

Both Luce and Dyadia bowed at their arrival. Vesper nodded and looked down at his mother.

Queen Nova rested her palms on her son's and new daughter-in-law's shoulders. "You both appear weary. I've heard rumors you've yet to retire to your chambers together."

Vesper grimaced and rubbed the stubble upon his jaw that had darkened considerably over the past few hours. "We've been taking turns resting. Every time we attempt to leave together, someone needs one of us to stay."

Queen Nova frowned. "You are the king." She turned to Lyra. "And you the queen. But you are also *human*. Two days hence from the marriage, and you've yet to share your wedding bed? It is time you let your prime ministers and advisors earn their titles. I'll make myself available for any questions or obstacles until you're well rested and well fed. Go now to your suite. I had a late supper sent up along with some honey mead. I don't want to see you again until the morrow . . . well after dawn." Brooking no argument, she ducked gracefully into the great hall and disappeared among the milling servants and council members.

Vesper met Lyra's gaze. She knew that glint within his dark eyes: challenging her to do something daring. Had he a tail, he'd be swishing it, defying her to walk away from such a grand adventure. Her entire body lit up with awareness as he wrapped an arm around her waist, low enough to brush her hip with his fingers.

"What say you, my lady wife? Shall we retire to our chambers for some well-deserved, long-awaited . . . *sleep*?"

He didn't seem the least bit nervous, but she was enough for both of them. She nodded in silent agreement, all the while wondering if the flush to her skin was apparent to Luce and Dyadia.

Luce cleared his throat and waved an arm toward the guarded staircase in the distance. "Let us escort you there. My last duty before I retire my position as Queen Lyra's proverbial chastity belt."

Lyra coughed a shocked laugh as they strode toward the stairs.

"Does this mean," Vesper asked, drawing Lyra closer so his lean muscles rippled against her side with every step, "that you'll no longer bark at us should we deem to have private lovelorn declarations when in your presence?"

Luce scoffed. "My time as chaperone has reached an end. Your mother is a formidable lady. She has royal grandchildren on the mind, and I'm not fool enough to stand in the way of crowned heirs."

"Nor am I," Vesper answered, his voice deep and gruff with conviction.

Lyra smiled, her nerves slowly melting into something sweet and hungry.

"Highness." Dyadia caught Lyra's attention, moving in beside her. "I have your voice's essence." She handed over a thick ceramic jar with a sealed waxed linen top tied in place with twine. "When you're ready, simply drink the contents." She turned her feline eyes toward Vesper. The third eye sat closed within its socket. "I thought perhaps you would like to share the restoration between you, privately, as you've been waiting for her song longer than any of us."

Vesper smiled down at Lyra. "Waiting to hear it from *her* lips, yes."

They'd reached the stairs that led to Vesper's turret chamber, now serving as the king and queen suite. The line of guards keeping vigil at the stairway stepped aside, prepared to return to formation upon their queen's and king's ascension.

"So we part ways then, for now." Luce took a step back.

Wait, Lyra signed. *I've seen the looks passing between you two. You've obviously seen Crony, to have received the transference potion's recipe for my voice. Why didn't she return with you? What aren't you telling me?* Vesper's hold on her tightened, as if he sensed ill news as much as her. Her eyes stung when Luce and Dyadia tried to maintain their stoic expressions but failed miserably.

I'm not weak, so stop treating me like I am. Her hands spelled out the words, though they trembled as if to disprove her claim. *I can stand strong. But you must tell me, or I'll forever wonder. I'll forever seek her in every shadow, in every turn of the moon, in every break of dawn.*

Dyadia spoke. "That is precisely where you should seek her."

Luce tossed her a stern frown, but she lifted a hand as if to assure him.

"Crony loved the moon. The night was a comfort to her. Night and all its creatures. You brought that back, gave her the crickets' songs and the night-flower's scent. But you see, she had waited so long for its return, that when the moon passed by, she dared not let it slip away again. It was too beautiful for her to resist. She wrapped herself within your magic that was piecing our world back into place, and let it carry her away. Immortals, we grow weary at times with the normalcy of life, and ache to find new challenges. So that's what she did, rose to the heavens to be among others of our kind, seeking new dreamscapes. But she wanted you to know how much she loves you, and that she's looking down on you always."

Lyra's heart pinched unbearably. Vesper pulled her against his chest, his chin knocking her crown slightly off-center. She closed her eyes and let the tears fall. Crony was worth every one of them.

Lyra wasn't sure how long they stood like that at the bottom of the stairs. She felt Luce's hand squeeze her shoulder, heard him promise to see her again on the morrow. She listened as Dyadia's footsteps followed his and grew distant until they faded to silence.

When her king at last pushed her to arm's length to wipe away her tears and straighten her crown, she met his concerned gaze. *There was more to Crony's departure . . . I feel like they're still keeping secrets.*

Vesper's expression changed upon her remark, his eyebrows crimping. "I sense it, too. But I also sense they're respecting her wishes. So we should do the same. We can honor her most by being good rulers. And by chronicling everything she did for you . . . for us . . . in our histories."

Lyra nodded. Behind him, she spotted the winding staircase and thought it looked rather like a mountain. All the weight of the past few days had settled in her feet and nailed her to the floor. Without a word, Vesper lifted her effortlessly, cradled her to his chest, and proceeded to carry her up the steps.

She wrapped one arm around his nape and leaned her head against his temple, the powerful thud of his heartbeat kicking close to her rib cage. She tightened her free hand around the jar that held her songbird voice. *I can walk . . . it just seemed daunting for a moment.*

Vesper scoffed. *This from the girl who used to beg me to carry her every day for five years straight.*

She laughed, her eyes burning with tears again—though these were bitter-sweet. *You're right. It slipped my mind that you have a payment to make. 'Only when the sun and moon share the sky.'*

Vesper laughed this time. He stopped and leaned his shoulder against the wall to balance them on the stairs so he could look into her eyes. "Just so you know . . . I'm much more receptive to such requests in this form. So never hesitate to ask."

He bowed his head to kiss her—his mouth coaxing hers to open slightly—engaging her in a gentle, slow dance of lips and tongue. When he pulled back with a tantalizing smile on his stubbled chin, she quivered in anticipation of more. His ascent started again, though this time much faster.

She admired how the moon streamed through the windows during their climb, how the light gilded Vesper's crown and strong profile with soft, silvery tremors. Tomorrow she would awaken within his arms, and she would see that precious face awash in yellow sunlight.

The world had indeed changed. She had reclaimed her kingdom and herself, and somehow, she and Vesper had won the skies. And along the way, she'd won the Pegasus's heart. Now at last they would fly, though not to escape as she had once dreamed. Instead, like Crony, they were to rise to grander schemes.

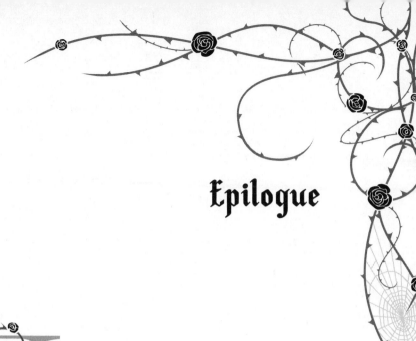

Epilogue

ost fairy tales, no matter how tragic the once-upon begin-ning, end with a happy ever after. However, Queen Lyra and King Vesper were far too pragmatic, due to their own experiences, to believe their future would always be roses and rainbows. Their world was filled with monsters, thorns, dark magic, and curses, however far beneath the earth those now dwelt. So, each stepped into their married life sharing only the hope of peace and unity for their two kingdoms, and the wisdom to work through challenges and dangers together, hand in hand. Most importantly, to never be too proud to take help when needed, however unexpected or humble the source: bugs or shadows, a dwarfish gardener with a penchant for bunny suits, a toothless cook, a greedy goblin, a capricious air elemental with the sneer and cunning of a fox, or a horned witch, old and withered, with quagmire eyes and a smile that could wilt the sturdiest weed. In time, the two kingdoms of Nerezeth and Eldoria came together as one, and adopted the name Nevaeh, for it was believed the reunited heavens had unified the people. Following the example of their young monarchs, the citizens of Nevaeh learned to accept one another again—content with their changing days, nights, and seasons once more. And for this they were rewarded with a more altruistic and attainable ending, in which they shared a *hopeful* ever after.

Acknowledgments

First and foremost, my gratitude goes out to my husband and children: Vince, Nicole, and Ryan. It takes great patience to live with an author. You're my true heroes and I love you more with each passing day. A special thank-you to my son, Ryan, for his incredible artistic contributions during the brainstorming phases of this story, and especially for the maps he helped design so every reader could see this fantasy world through my eyes. Thank you also to other family members who support my passion for writing and are always eager to read my next manuscript.

Heartfelt appreciation to my critique partners: Jennifer Archer, Linda Castillo, April Redmon, Marcy McKay, Jessica Nelson, and Bethany Crandell. I'd never have the courage to release my stories into the wild without knowing every word must first pass your careful and wise scrutiny. Also, sincerest thanks to my #goatposse for providing a safe place (aka, our cyber-pasture) where anyone in our herd is safe to vent or seek advice.

Thank you to my fantastic and devoted agent, Jenny Bent; also, to my discerning editor, Anne Heltzel, whose insights helped me get the most out of each scene. Much gratefulness to my savvy marketing team: Sam Brody,

Hallie Patterson, Jenny Choy, Nicole Schaefer, Patricia McNamara O'Neill, Jody Mosley, my publicist, Melanie Chang, and the publisher of the children's books division, Andrew Smith. Gratitude also to copy editors, proofreaders, and all the unsung heroes behind the making of every beautiful book at Abrams/Amulet. Thank you once again to Nathalia Suellen for crafting such imaginative and stunning designs for my covers that so perfectly capture the story within, and to our in-house designer, Hana Nakamura, for the fairy tale interior art. Also, gratitude to Tomislav Tomic for refining Eldoria and Nerezeth's maps.

Special hugs to online supporters and beta readers: Stacee (aka @book _junkee), Heather Love King, and Jaime Arnold of RockStar Book Tours. And to my Facebook Splintered Series Fan Page and RoseBlood fan-page moderators, whose help I value so much. Also, *waves* to all of the fan-page followers. And deepest appreciation to booktubers and bloggers and to all my Twitter, Tumblr, Pinterest, blog, Goodreads, Instagram, and Facebook followers—foreign and domestic—for keeping my books alive through interactions online. On that note, thank you to Natalia Godik for maintaining and contributing to the Pinterest Splintered fan art boards. I'm always excited and awed to see the newest renditions of my characters and world.

Also, a hat tip to the books and movies that inspired my own dark sensibilities. I cut my creative teeth on novels like *The Lord of the Rings*, *Howl's Moving Castle*, *The Princess Bride*, and *The Lion, the Witch, and the Wardrobe*. Violent and unsettling folk tales by the Brothers Grimm played their own distinct role, as did many movies from the '80s and '90s. *The Dark Crystal*, *Labyrinth*, *Edward Scissorhands*, *Ladyhawke*, *Legend*, *Willow*, *The Never-Ending Story*, and *The Crow* are but a few that fed my love for all things fantastical and unbalanced. Thanks to myriad talented writers, directors, and producers, I came to love Gothic fairy tales and dark fantasies and can only hope the stories I craft will help inspire a new generation of readers and authors to follow the same path.

And last but not least, I thank my God for the ability to weave worlds with words and for providing connections with people who champion reading in all its facets. Most of these kindred spirits I would never have met, had I not been give the opportunity to tell my stories in print.